6 May 2011
Wendy,
Don't k

Mike Delany

THE MOOSE JAW BOOK I

RINGS UPON THE WATER

A NOVEL
BY MIKE DELANY

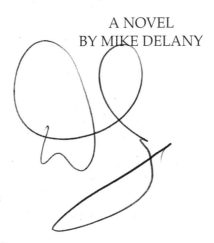

BOOK ONE IN THE FERGUS O'NEILL SERIES

Acknowledgements

I wish to thank my wife Cynthia, my daughter Shannon, son Sean, grandsons Nick and Nino Delany, as well as my many friends and neighbors who read and reread this manuscript and provided helpful criticism and valuable advice throughout its development. I'd also like to thank Jim Hagee, my best friend and longtime hunting companion. He lives in Alaska where he owns a small animal veterinary practice; he is a seasoned bush pilot as well. Those who know him may see a certain resemblance between him and Haywood Jennings, a character in this novel. I should like to make it clear that any resemblance between the two is purely coincidental. But I won't.

Further, many thanks to Jim's son, Justin Hagee, who agreed to let me use his gruesome trophy skull on the cover of this book. It is all that remains of a venerable old bull moose he shot while hunting with his father on Beaver Creek in the White Mountains north of Fairbanks, Alaska.

Finally, I wish to recognize Keith Brown whose photograph of Hagee's moose skull set against an Alaskan winterscape appears on the cover of this novel. Keith is a retired Air Force photographer who now does freelance work out of Eagle River, Alaska. Having captured three wars on film, he finds photographing moose skulls in the frozen wilderness infinitely more peaceful.

Michael Delany
Brookbend
March 2013

Author's note

This is a work of fiction. Like most works of fiction, the characters, settings, and events contained herein are fictitious. Moose Jaw Creek does not exist, nor does The Varmitage, the Snow Viper, or the Rainbow Lodge. The murders I have dubbed the Rainbow Lodge murders never happened.

That said, some of the things in this novel are real. Alaska is a real place. Skinny Dick's is a real roadhouse south of Fairbanks. Wolves and grizzlies are real too, as are yega. Hard Case Calis, fictitious character though he is, explained yega best when he described the spirit world of the far north in one of his journals:

Every tree, rock, river, drop of rain or breath of wind we find in the natural world has a supernatural essence also…a soul, if you will. A tree is a tree, but it is also a spirit or god or demigod. This duality in the nature of all things makes the supernatural a part of – rather than apart from – the natural world we live in. There is no impenetrable barrier that separates the "real world" from the "spirit world". The wall between the two worlds is one of gossamer, rather than stone…a fragile membrane, full of rents and tears, riddled with portals and passages.

Fergus O'Neill, Hard Case's friend, and also the main character in this novel, unknowingly discovered one of those passages.

Michael Delany
Brookbend
March 2013

Prologue

The Rainbow Lodge murders, brutal as any in Alaska's history, were relegated to page three of the Bush Telegraph. That was understandable, of course, considering the editor of that small Fairbanks weekly had more exciting stories to report. There had been a record number of trophy moose killed in the autumn of 1959. The entire front page had been dedicated to black-and-white photographs of proud hunters awkwardly holding their rifles. They stood, or knelt beside bloodied, fallen beasts whose enormous antlers pointed skyward while their tongues lolled in the dirt. Then too, Frances Howard had just become the first female admitted into the ranks of the Alaska State Troopers. As one might expect, this triggered a fusillade of outrage and consternation from the rugged males of America's last frontier. Nearly all the editorial page had been given over to the airing of their bitter protests. What little space remained was devoted to Alaska's recently granted statehood, and how federal oversight and regulation would sound the death knell for personal freedoms in the remote north.

With so much stimulating copy available, the killing of two men out in the bush was not likely to generate much interest among the hard-bitten denizens of the Interior. Violent death, in that untamed land, was commonplace. Just to survive men struggled with the elements, with wild beasts and with one another. Some lived – some died. It was expected. It was inevitable. It was not news. So the killings appeared in the "Police Blotter" column, listed among reports of bar brawls, wife beatings, claim jumping and poaching.

Moose Jaw Drainage - Two dead men were found in a burned fishing lodge on Rainbow Creek last Thursday. Trooper Tobias (Pokey) Brewster told this reporter it appeared the men had been murdered and the lodge burned afterward. The bodies were badly charred, but it was evident one of the men had died of multiple stab wounds. The other had been shot. Both victims were mutilated. Names cannot be released until family members have been located and notified.

With so little ink spared for a gruesome double homicide, it is not surprising that two people from Seattle, missing and presumed dead on Moose Jaw Creek, were not mentioned at all. It is also not surprising that the Rainbow Lodge murders were never solved. As to the missing persons – well, that's another story entirely.

Chapter 1

Moose Jaw Creek, Alaska
Summer Solstice – June 2000

It was a magic place – a place of clear water, cool breezes, snowcapped mountains and midnight sun. I stood on the gravel bar and listened to the rush of the creek as I watched Haywood's old airplane climb slowly into the blue sky, bank south, and head for Fairbanks. It grew smaller, became no more than a speck, then winked out. I was alone.

When I got back to camp I pulled a bottle of beer from the icy waters of the creek and popped off its cap. I sat on a log, sipped the beer, and contemplated the boxes and river bags stacked on the hard-packed earth around the crumbling stone chimney. It had taken two trips to bring all my gear in from Fairbanks. The plane's maximum payload was eight hundred and fifty pounds, including fuel and passengers. The boxes and bags contained all the material I would need to survive a summer of self-imposed exile. The intangibles – the courage, determination, and ingenuity I'd need – would have to come from within. But then, that was the whole idea.

The old monastic orders believed that men must retreat from the madness of the secular world and live a life of solitude, meditation and physical labor in order to find spiritual contentment. I agreed. I had come here to be alone. I wanted to work with my hands, sweat real sweat and seek that Holy Grail, inner peace. I was a builder; I had to build something. So, here I was on Moose Jaw Creek, deep in the Alaska bush. I had come to build a cabin, reflect on the past and decide what to do with the rest of my life.

When the beer was gone I lit my pipe and sat a while longer. There was no hurry. I settled in, puffed gently on the pipe, and let my eyes drink in the beauty around me as my ears took in the soft sounds of the water and the wind, and my soul basked in the silence. I was finally, truly and gladly – here. I was finally, truly and completely alone. I'd build my cabin on this very spot, and its solid structure, and this wild creek, and the Alaska bush would be my present and my future.

***

I had returned from England in early June, one of the first casualties of the dot.com crash. Losing both job and wife in the same day had taken its toll. ConSort, the British engineering firm for which I worked gave me the sack six months before the end of my contract, and Sylvia, my wife of twenty-five years, gave me notice of a different kind. She revealed that she had been having an affair with Gaspard, my trusted French friend, and she would not be returning to America with me. I needed some time alone to regroup, sort through the emotional wreckage, and see what could be salvaged. Outrage, anger and resentment simmered in me just below the surface. And, although I hated to admit it, wounded pride and self-pity pecked at my psyche like crows on a carcass.

I spent one week at Morning Rock, my home in the Colorado Rockies. It's an old stone-and-timber lodge situated on a few acres of evergreens along Bear Creek. I loved the peace and serenity of the place, but every room held reminders of Sylvia and the life we had shared. Then too, my Uncle Jack, a retired Bell Labs genius who had volunteered to house sit for us while we were in Europe had put down roots in our absence. He was writing a book on the best North American trout streams and Colorado was the perfect base camp for him. He had been both father and mother to me since my folks were killed in a car wreck when I was twelve years old. I needed time alone, but I didn't have the heart to ask him to leave. When he informed me that he'd given my son Casey permission to cohabit the guest cabin with two female "friends" from college, I knew I'd need a change of venue if I was to exorcize my demons.

I owned a small piece of property in Alaska. It was deep in the bush on Moose Jaw Creek, and accessible only by airplane or boat. I'd purchased it, sight-unseen, with last year's bonus money. It was time I had a look at it. At the end of the week I called Haywood and told him I was headed north.

***

Haywood Jennings is, and has been for many years, my best friend. He had moved to Alaska several years ago after a rather tempestuous divorce. He's a first-rate veterinary surgeon and has a small-animal practice in Fairbanks. Each September I would fly up, and we'd spend two weeks in the bush, hunting moose and caribou. We'd been very successful on our trips down the Moose Jaw, and it had been Haywood who alerted me to the property I'd purchased. He was clearly surprised to hear my voice but sounded pleased, nevertheless.

"Gustopher!" he shouted.

I laughed. Only Haywood could come up with a name like Gustopher. My name is Gus, Fergus actually, but only my estranged wife, Sylvia, insists on calling me that. To everyone else I'm just Gus.

"Hello, Haywood," I said. It had been six months since we'd talked. It made me feel better just to hear his voice.

"I'll be damned," he boomed. "Didn't expect to hear from you 'til moose season. You still in England?"

"No," I told him. "I'm at Morning Rock . Came back last week."

"They run you out of Europe?" he joked.

"Something like that. I'll tell you over a drink. It's a long story. It will take some telling. Can you put me up for while?"

"Sure," he said. Then, after a brief pause, he added, "If Sylvia's coming along you can have my room. Otherwise, you'll have to make do with the single bed in the guest room."

This, of course, was his oblique way of asking if there was trouble in the O'Neill household. He was not one to pry, but he didn't often need to. He picked up on subtleties and was insightful enough to understand their significance.

"Guest room will be fine," I told him.

There was another pause while he picked up on that particular subtlety. Sylvia and I never took separate vacations, so it didn't take Haywood long to grasp that all was not well in our marriage. His voice sobered a little.

"Right then," he said. "When do you get into Anchorage? I'll fly down and fetch you."

"Save your fuel. I get in Monday night, but I have to stop at the title company and pick up the papers for the Moose Jaw property Tuesday morning. I'll rent a car and drive up to Fairbanks that afternoon. I'll be at your place by late evening."

"Nonsense!" Haywood didn't just say things – he announced, pronounced, exclaimed, proclaimed, boomed, and bellowed. "No point you driving when I need to get in some flying time anyway. F.A.A. requires me to do one more take-off-and-landing to stay passenger legal, so I may as well collect you while I'm about it. You should be able to get all your business done Tuesday morning. Meet me at Calvin's Hangar at noon." It was no use arguing with Haywood, so I agreed and we rung off.

***

The sun still hung well above the western horizon when my flight arrived in Anchorage a little before ten o'clock on Monday night. I'd visited Alaska many times before, but the "midnight sun" always surprised me. I don't think it's something one ever gets accustomed to. It's a bit surreal, and there's this other-world quality to it that always gives me the illusion of having stepped into another dimension. But, of course Alaska is, in many ways, a parallel dimension to the rest of the world. It may exist upon the same planet, but it is a remote and distant place, seemingly suspended in another time.

I spent the night at the Susitna Lodge, one of the three best hotels in Anchorage. I often stayed there because it was clean, had a well-stocked bar and was close to the airport. My room, on the top floor, had a view of Cook Inlet, and beyond that, Mount Susitna, called The Sleeping Lady by the locals. I knew there was a Native American legend having to do with a young lady who went to sleep on the mountain while waiting for her lover to return from battle. I couldn't recall the details of the story, but looking across the water at the mountain, I could see how the ridgeline resembled the silhouette of a reclining woman. I suspected it was that feminine form that had inspired the legend. I said good night to the slumbering beauty, closed the curtains, and went to bed.

On Tuesday morning I ate a traditional Alaskan breakfast in the hotel restaurant: three eggs easy over, reindeer sausage, home fries, sourdough toast and lots of coffee. Sated, I left the dining room and crossed the lobby to The Sleeping Lady Gift Shop where I knew they carried my preferred pipe tobacco.

The clerk was busy with a customer and there was another waiting in line, so I browsed the gifts while I waited to pay for my purchase. A hand-carved chess set caught my eye, and I spent some time admiring it. It was beautifully done, with the white pieces carved of walrus tusk and the dark ones from polished moose antler. The pieces were not the typical renderings of human figures; they were of symbolic Alaskan creatures. Each king was represented as a giant Grizzly bear; the bishops were bald eagles; the knights were wolves; and the rooks were cleverly scribed moose heads, complete with antlers. The only human forms were the pawns, which appeared to be kneeling gold miners, and the queen, who was a tall, slender woman with subtle curves, long tresses and lovely features. I looked closely at her face and discovered that her eyes were closed. I assumed she represented The Sleeping Lady.

Haywood and I always took a miniature magnetic chess set along with us on our floats and hunts. We often enjoyed a game in the evening over our after dinner drinks. I thought that a fine chess set, like the one I was admiring, would be nice to keep at the cabin. I decided to buy it even though it was a bit pricey.

Tobacco and chess set in hand, I went back to my room, packed, took my luggage down to the lobby and checked out. The staff recognized me as a regular, and the bellman agreed to keep my bags in the storeroom while I did my business at the title company. I told him I'd be back to collect them about eleven o'clock, gave him a respectable tip, and he handed me a claim check. The doorman, another old acquaintance, flagged me a taxi and, after pocketing his gratuity, held the rear door open while I got in. As I gave the driver the address of Last Frontier Title Company it occurred to me that I was happy. It was the first time in a long time I'd felt relaxed and untroubled. I knew I had made the right decision. If I were to ever sort things out, Alaska was the place to do it.

The taxi ride into town took less than fifteen minutes. Downtown Anchorage, after all, just isn't that big. I paid the driver and, as he pulled away from the curb, checked my watch. I was ten minutes early but doubted that would present a problem, so I went right in.

The receptionist looked up and smiled as I entered. She was a plump woman with a round, happy face. Her nametag identified her as Alice.

"Good morning," she said. "Are you here to see Mr. Manning?"

I returned her smile. "Yes. Gus O'Neill. ·I have a ten o'clock appointment. Afraid I'm a bit early."

"No problem," she said. "Charlie will see you as soon as he's off the phone. Why don't you have a seat while you wait? Would you like some coffee?"

I told her I'd had a gallon with breakfast and couldn't face another drop.

"Just as well," she said. "Charlie makes awful coffee. I bring my own." She pointed to a thermos on her desk.

I selected one of the three metal folding chairs that lined the wall near the front door and sat down. While I waited for Mr. Manning I studied the inevitable prints of fishing grizzlies, prowling wolves and soaring eagles that decorated every office in Alaska. In the midst of them, I was surprised to see a work I recognized – a beautiful Celtic princess, seated in a boat at the water's edge. It was The Lady of Shalott, a classic Waterhouse; I'd always loved it. The original hung in the National Gallery in London. I had often stood before it, captivated by the loveliness of the woman and the serenity of the scene. It was a painting that had the power to draw one out of oneself and into the mystic landscape portrayed on the canvas. The lady's fragile beauty seemed completely out of place, surrounded as it was by the images of eagles, wolves and bears.

"Beautiful isn't she?"

As always, I had drifted off into some other time and place as I gazed at the Waterhouse. I hadn't heard anyone approach, so the voice startled me back to reality. I laughed a little to cover my embarrassment.

"Yes. She is. You must be Mr. Manning." I stood up and offered my hand.

He shook it. He was a small man, late fifties, and neatly dressed. His grip was firm.

"Everyone calls me Charlie," he said. "Come on back to my office, I have all the documents ready for your review."

As we passed the reception desk he said, "Can I get you a cup of coffee? Made it myself, fresh this morning."

I declined, shooting a quick glance at Alice. She made a face, and I smiled.

Charlie Manning's office was small but comfortable. He closed the door and offered me a chair. When I was seated he went around the desk, settled in his own chair and tapped a manila folder that lay in the middle of the desktop.

"Your Moose Jaw property," he said. "The title papers are originals; the plot plan and maps are copies, but they're clear enough to read. According to the terms of the contract, you have purchased the place as unimproved land since there is nothing left of the old cabin but a ruined chimney. There's a copy of the contract in here too. I think you'll find everything in order."

He slid the folder across the desk to me, and I opened it and scanned the documents. Charlie Manning seemed quite capable. I had no doubt that everything was, indeed, in order, so I didn't spend a lot of time scrutinizing details. When I'd finished, I closed the folder and stood up.

"Looks like it's all here," I told him. "I know you're a busy man, so I won't take up any more of your time."

As he had remained seated, a handshake would have been awkward, so I just thanked him, said good-bye and turned to leave. I was reaching for the door handle when his voice stopped me.

"Ah, Mr. O'Neill, there is one more matter regarding your property. If you could spare a few more minutes..." he trailed off. "It won't take long."

Something in his tone brought me up short. I returned to my seat, studied his face, and waited. He appeared very uncomfortable, as if trying to decide how best to begin.

"Another matter..." I prompted.

He remained quiet for a moment longer, then stood and looked out the window before he spoke. "Yes," he began. "It's probably nothing, really. Still, I thought you should know. And, of course, it's not something that would be mentioned in those documents."

"Go on," I urged.

"Well," he paused. "As the Deed of Trust indicates, you purchased the property from a Mr. Larkin, of Cleveland, Ohio."

I nodded. I'd seen the seller's name on the papers I'd signed.

Manning went on. "He inherited it two years ago upon the death of his uncle, Jake Larkin, who had homesteaded the place and built the original cabin in 1961. Jake was a trapper and worked his trap line along the Moose Jaw until sometime in the late seventies, when he pulled out. In 1985 The Nature Conservancy tried to buy the place from him. It was one of the last fee-simple properties along the river, and they were trying to work a three-stage sale that would transfer title to the Nature Conservancy – then to the State of Alaska – and, ultimately, back to a native corporation. They tracked Jake down to a nursing home in Seattle and, after a bit of haggling, he agreed to sell. They were in the process of getting the final approvals from the state when a group of Athabascan elders pulled the rug out from under the whole deal. They refused to accept the land."

"Refused? Why?" I still didn't know where all this was going, but I had to admit I was intrigued.

Charlie turned away from the window and faced me. "Yega," he said, as if the word should hold some meaning for me.

I waited for elucidation, but it wasn't forthcoming.

"Yega?"

He smiled, looked a little sheepish, and shrugged his shoulders. "Yes," he said. "It's an Athabascan word. It means spirit, or something like that...ghost, perhaps. It's hard to say, exactly. Athabascan is a complex language. Certain words have many connotations. It was never clear, specifically, what the elders meant by it. All that was certain was they wouldn't take the land. Keep in mind, I was just handling the title work. Never got involved with the negotiations, so everything I've told you is second-hand information."

"I see," I said. I didn't, of course. It was just something to say to fill the awkward silence that followed his eerie revelation.

"Are you a superstitious man, Mr. O'Neill?"

"No," I told him with more certainty than I felt. I was, after all, of Irish extraction. I knew there were some deep rooted superstitions lurking in my subconscious. I'd felt them stir on occasion.

"Good. Then all this yega business shouldn't trouble you," Manning said, with evident relief. "I'm sure there is no more to it than the stories of the Abominable Snowman, Big Foot, or the Snow Viper. I'm sorry to have taken your time with such nonsense. But, I thought you should know."

"Yes," I said, rising from my chair. "Thank you for telling me. It's good to know a little history of the place. Gives it a personality, so to speak."

Manning gave me a wry smile. "Considering some of the

meanings of yega, let's hope that's not the case."

"Right," I said. "Bad choice of words."

His phone rang as we were shaking hands, so I indicated I could find my way out, left his office, and quietly closed the door behind me. Alice was also on the phone when I passed her desk so I just gave her a wave and a smile, and she winked and blew me a kiss. It's a fine thing to meet a happy woman. It puts everything right. I went out into the sunshine, still wearing my smile. Ghosts and spirits, like vampires, don't fare well in daylight. The uneasiness I'd felt upon hearing Manning's story evaporated into the cloudless sky.

***

Calvin's Hangar is not, as the name implies, a hangar. It's a greasy spoon over near Merrill Field, a small airport that serves private aircraft such as Haywood's. The space is cramped, the food adequate, and the service good-humoredly hostile. But the location makes for a handy rendezvous among the flying fraternity so it always does a good business. Although the Lake Hood strip is much closer to the big airport, Haywood prefers Merrill Field because it isn't so busy. He was already there when I arrived. He wasn't hard to spot, even in the crush of the lunch hour mob, since he stands a head taller than anyone else in most crowds. He has a full head of bushy white hair and eyebrows to match. With his thin, wiry frame he somewhat resembles a large dandelion gone to seed. In physical appearance we're pretty much opposites. I'm medium height, solidly built, and have salt-and-pepper hair. Suffice it to say, I didn't have any trouble picking Haywood out, especially with him waving and flashing his big, toothy grin.

We ate a quick stand-up lunch, then walked over to the airstrip. I'd left my two river bags outside, against Calvin's wall, and we each shouldered one before crossing the street and the airport parking lot, en route to Haywood's airplane. Like its owner, the old blue-and-red Piper Clipper is a standout. Vintage 1949, it is a short-winged tail dragger. Since its frame is of tubular aircraft aluminum and its skin of fabric, rather than metal, it is referred to, in flying circles, as being of "tube and rag" construction. This feature, plus its somewhat oversized engine, makes it a bit noisy inside the cabin during flights. Nevertheless, the short winged Pipers had become favorites among Alaska's bush pilots. Aside from their light weight, compact wing structure, and exceptionally powerful engines, they adapted easily to tires, floats, or skis.

By one-thirty that afternoon we were airborne, bound for Fairbanks. The trip normally takes just under three hours, but since it was a clear day we circled Denali, or Mt. McKinley as it's known in the Lower Forty-eight. It was a rare treat, seeing the entire twenty thousand feet of it without the usual cloud cover. Haywood pointed out a small herd of Dall Sheep as we rounded the west slope. They are a close relative to the Bighorn Sheep we have in Colorado, but their horns are not as heavy and massive. Because of this, they are often called Thin-horn sheep. They were, more-or-less, at our altitude, but as Haywood was keeping plenty of distance between the airplane and the mountain, they were nothing more than a cluster of white dots against the darker backdrop of rocky escarpment. They were too far off for a photo, so I saved my film.

The rest of the flight was uneventful and, with the engine noise and wind rush, conversation was impossible without shouting, so we didn't try. We'd been friends long enough to be comfortable with extended periods of silence. There had been times, in duck blinds, or in hunting camps, when we'd gone hours on end without speaking a word to one another. If we had something to say, of course, we'd say it. If we didn't, we didn't.

Despite the little detour around Denali, we still managed to arrive in Fairbanks just after five o'clock. By six-thirty we were sitting in the living room of Haywood's split level, twenty minutes south of downtown, sharing a bottle of Tullamore Dew, The Legendary Irish Whiskey. Or so it said on the label. Haywood was comfortably seated in his rocker, savoring his drink. I was sharing an overstuffed chair with Bosworth, Haywood's overstuffed Maine Coon cat. Bosworth liked me and never failed to make me feel welcome by crushing my lap with his enormous bulk, and kneading my manhood into imaginary biscuits. I settled deeper in the chair, did my best to keep cat hairs out of my whiskey, and told Haywood the story. I just gave him the high points – the collapse of ConSort in Europe, Sylvia's announcement that she had a lover there with whom she intended to stay, and the awkward situation I'd found upon returning home to Morning Rock.

Chapter 2

Haywood never interrupted. He just rocked and listened and sipped his whiskey. When it was clear I had finished, he refilled our glasses and lit one of his noxious cigars. Then he leaned back in his rocker, puffed a bit and said, "So – what now?"

"So, now I'm going to spend a few months doing exactly what I damned well please. And, what I damned well please is to go into the Moose Jaw, camp, fish, and build that cabin we've been talking about for the past millennium. I'll stay there right through moose season. At least we'll have the luxury of a base camp this year."

He rocked and puffed and nodded. He'd suspected as much. "We'll have to get you outfitted. Better make a list."

Haywood loved lists. He went to his cluttered desk and brought back a legal pad and pen. By the time the bottle was gone we had filled three pages and were working on a fourth. He had two surgeries scheduled for the morning so we were saved from opening another bottle. After he'd gone to bed I sat at the table for a while, pondering the list through bleary eyes. When I realized I was trying to read through closed lids I gave it up, clicked off the upstairs lights, and made my way down the dimly lit stairway to the guest room.

Haywood was up at 5 a.m. He'd already had his breakfast, and was at the stove preparing mine when I came up to the kitchen an hour later. He handed me a cup of coffee and gave me a cheerful smile. It never mattered what time, or in what condition he went to bed, he was always up at five, fresh and chipper. When my son, Casey, was a little boy he had once observed that Haywood was a lot like Tigger, the bouncy tiger character in the "Winnie the Pooh" series. It was a good comparison; both were filled with a wonderful zest for life, a golden heart, and a cast iron stomach. Haywood had also been born with a world-class liver, and suffered no ill effects from excessive alcohol consumption. Unfortunately, I wasn't blessed with the same constitution. I always woke groggy and grumpy, and couldn't form a coherent thought until I'd had a cup of strong, black coffee. He knew this and didn't bother trying to communicate until I broke the ice asking for a refill.

He poured and said, "You'll need the truck today. Drop me at the clinic and come back and get me this evening. I'm doing my usual seven-to-seven. That should give you plenty of time to get started on the shopping."

I grunted something that sounded like concurrence and sipped my coffee. I could communicate this early, but I had to keep it simple. He dished my bacon and eggs out of the skillet, plopped them on a piece of toast, covered them with another piece, and handed me my breakfast.

He chattered on. "Took the liberty of reviewing the list this morning and made a few adds and drops. Gotta consider the weight. I don't want to be running a shuttle service into the Moose Jaw. Like to get you and all your gear in with two loads."

I gave him another of my affirmative grunts and took a tentative bite of my sandwich. Hot yolk and bacon grease oozed out between my fingers. I licked them off and continued eating. The sun was already well up in the sky, and its light came in through the kitchen window and gave everything a warm glow. Together with the coffee and hot breakfast it worked its magic, and I felt myself emerging to the next level of my morning consciousness. I wouldn't say my mood became suddenly rosy, but it was no longer black.

Haywood took his coffee into the den and booted up his computer. He always read the Fairbanks Daily News-Miner on-line in the morning, and caught up on his email. I dragged the legal pad across the table and scanned it. It was a daunting document, almost four pages long, listing everything I'd need in the way of camping, cooking, construction, and survival gear. My hangover headache had been bad enough before I started reading. Now my eyes were beginning to hurt. I pushed the pad aside and poured another cup of coffee. It would take a week to gather all that kit.

Haywood finished his e-business, buttoned up the computer, and came sailing back into the kitchen.

"Cheer up Pal," he said. "We've got a lot of that stuff already, and if we stick to plastic and keep the metal to a minimum, the loads won't be too heavy."

"Right," I said sourly. "Plastic saws and axes."

He smiled. He enjoyed my morning miseries. "Come on," he

said, "time we got rolling. You can suffer in solitude after you deliver me to the clinic."

***

The next week was spent in spurious bouts of shopping, packing and planning. I did the shopping during the day, while Haywood was at the clinic. The packing consumed a good portion of our evenings, as we had to vacuum seal all the food stuffs, and bag up everything else. When the packing was complete and all the new bags were labeled, we would pour a whiskey and devote ourselves to detailed planning. One evening our focus might be upon load and transport logistics; the next we'd concentrate on cabin construction. For the most part we'd discuss anything having to do with my upcoming adventure. Toward the end of the week, we brought out the plot plan for my property, and compared it with the topo maps and notes we'd made on our two previous float trips down the Moose Jaw. We remembered that particular stretch of river, but neither of us could recall a stone chimney.

Haywood conceded that I was the engineer, and cabin design was entirely in my hands. Nevertheless, he insisted my wilderness get-away had to have a name. All places of importance had names. He suggested The Hermitage. It sounded okay to me, Andrew Jackson notwithstanding, so we fell to calling it by that name.

We did get one break from our preperations during that week. Our good friend and legendary detective, Hard Case Calis, dropped by to put his blessing on our enterprise. When I say legendary, I do not exaggerate. His bulldog features and powerful frame have graced the pages and T.V. screens of the local news media for nearly three decades. Although officially retired, the Alaska State Troopers have kept him aboard as a consultant. He is the most famous Crime Scene Investigator in Alaska, and still gets calls from the FBI to assist them in cases in the Lower Forty-eight. Aside from Haywood, he was my closest friend, and I was delighted to see him.

He brought a bottle of good single malt Scotch, and the three of us nursed it while Haywood and I briefed him on "The Hermitage Project". He was as excited as we were, and volunteered to fly in and give my cabin a "test sleep" as soon as all the work was done.

Hard Case, of course, wasn't actually his name. It was a sobriquet bestowed on him, many years ago, by admiring subordinates in the State Troopers. He'd been born Kees Calis to a pair of Dutch immigrants. Kees had been the name of his maternal grandfather, and he'd been named in his honor. Kees, by the way, is actually pronounced Case, so he never objected to the nickname. In fact, we suspected he secretly liked it. Nevertheless, few, if any, called him Hard Case to his face. Even Haywood and I didn't cross that line. We all had the good sense to call him, simply, Case.

I'd first met him six years ago when Haywood had invited me up for a few days of waterfowl hunting at Case's place. They had met at a Ducks Unlimited meeting two years before. They were both avid duck and goose hunters, and had become fast friends. Hard Case had a hunting cabin back in a slough off the Yukon River with a heated three man blind and several hundred decoys. It was a good set up. We spent four days in there, just the three of us. We'd limited out on both ducks and geese by ten in the morning every day. We spent the rest of our time plucking feathers, playing poker, fishing off the dock, and getting acquainted. Hard Case and I had hit it off and, since, had become good friends.

Over the last of the whisky (there is no "e" in whisky produced in Scotland), he leaned forward and placed a big, meaty paw on my shoulder. "Gus," he growled, "you've got to remember a few things when you're by yourself in the bush. Strange shit happens out there sometimes, and you need to keep your head screwed on straight. The native Alaskans believe that white men, alone too long in the bush, go mad. Considering some of the things I ran across during my days with the Troopers, I'd have to agree with them."

"Okay, I told him. I'll try to keep my wits about me." Hard Case had spent a lot of years investigating crimes in remote Alaska. I respected any advice he was willing to share.

"I'm sure you will, Gus," he said. He finished his whisky and went on.

"Another thing to remember is to never be without your gun. You were in the Marine Corps so you know your weapon is your best friend. Things can go bad fast out in the bush, and you won't have anyone watching your back."

I nodded that I understood. That had been a long speech for Hard Case. I realized he was a good deal more concerned about me than he'd ever let on. He removed his hand from my shoulder to indicate he had finished, stood up, patted his impressive table muscle, and announced he had an early morning and it was time to go. We said our good nights. He wished me luck with the cabin, and made his way down the stairs to the entry hall. His voice boomed back up the stairwell.

"Don't let the bears eat you, and keep an eye out for the Snow Viper."

With that, he left and we heard the door slam behind him.

***

As daunting as the "outfitting" task seemed, the shopping was, actually, quite enjoyable. Haywood needed his own chainsaw during the summer, so I had to buy a new one. I settled on a big red Husqvarna with a sixteen-inch bar. I also bought six extra chains, including three for ripping lumber. Hard Case had an "Alaska Saw Mill" that attached to a chainsaw for ripping planks out of logs. He'd never used it, so he donated it to the cause.

I had a grand time at the shop that specialized in wood burning stoves. They had quite a selection. I'd intended to go with the simple barrel stove that seems to be the stove of choice for bush cabins, but a small, green cook stove caught my eye – The CozyGlow Cooker. It was almost the color of the Jag I'd left Sylvia. And, like the Jag, it was English made, and very expensive. But, it was perfect. It was only thirty-two inches wide, twenty-one inches deep, and stood twenty-nine inches high. It had the equivalent cooking surface of a four-burner range, a small oven, and was capable of heating six hundred square feet. It even had an optional boiler that attached to the side and would give you eight gallons of hot water!

It was extravagant, granted. And its shiny, dark green, enamel finish was a little fussy for a trapper's cabin, and it weighed about four hundred pounds. I didn't care. A barrel stove is really only good for heat. If you had one, you still had to do your cooking on a Coleman camp stove. I had nothing against my Coleman, but an oven for Pete's sake! And a boiler! I bought it. Haywood couldn't believe his eyes when it was delivered.

"You're mad," was all he said.

***

It seemed the preparations would never end but, mercifully, on the last day of spring, we were ready. My non-resident hunting and fishing licenses, which I had been eagerly awaiting, arrived in Wednesday's mail. Early on Thursday, the twenty-first day of June, we loaded all the gear aboard Haywood's pickup truck, and drove out to the airstrip where he kept his plane. The contents of each bag and container were clearly listed on its side. We'd sorted everything into two piles labeled "Load 1" and "Load 2". Load Two was noticeably larger, as I accounted for roughly two hundred pounds of Load One. Everything absolutely vital to survival was included in the smaller load, which would accompany me on the first run. This was Alaska, after all. Anything could happen and, if, for whatever reason, Haywood never returned after dropping me off, I had to be able to set up camp and eat for the duration. Therefore, tarp, water filter, sleeping bag, firearms, and foodstuffs were all included in the first load. The wall-tent, canoe, tools, hardware, and odds and ends for building the cabin were relegated to the second load. My little green cook stove would be coming in at a later date, after the cabin was complete.

With the weighing in and loading, and the regulatory and administrative details behind us, we took off from Fairbanks at ten o'clock in the morning. The flight into Moose Jaw Creek took a little over an hour. Haywood had, first, to get us to the right coordinates, and then find a suitable landing strip as close as possible to the property. The term "creek" was really a misnomer; the Moose Jaw was actually a river; Creek just happened to be part of its name. What one called it pretty much depended on one's relationship with it – if you were wading in it, it was a creek – if you were drowning in it, it was a river.

We knew the country pretty well by now. We'd hunted the Moose Jaw for the past two years, and the place I'd bought was on a stretch of the river we'd come to consider as particularly "moosey". We'd bagged four respectable bulls in the country just downstream over the course of those two years. The area also had its share of bears, caribou, Dall sheep, upland birds, and waterfowl. It was famous for its Arctic grayling and, in the past, had been renowned for its Rainbow trout and its salmon runs. But, its best feature, for us at least, was the fact that the Moose Jaw attracted very few visitors these days. Its popularity had faded. It had been over-hunted and over-fished during the fifties and sixties and the game population fell off and, eventually, the hunters and fishermen had stopped coming. It had seen very little pressure from man over the past forty years and we considered it our own secret, pristine Eden.

During the course of our two ten-day float trips we had encountered only three other parties. Fortunately, none of the hunters we'd met had seen any game and were clearly discouraged; they were not likely to come back the following year. Fishermen tended to avoid the Moose Jaw because the trout were gone and the salmon runs were better elsewhere. Casual floaters avoided it because there were too many nasty stretches of water you had to portage around. Rafters and kayakers don't like to get their feet dry. So, it was, to all intents and purposes, our own private preserve.

Haywood flew directly to the coordinates specified on the plot plan with no difficulty. He made a couple of low-level passes and we could see the remains of an old cache and what looked to be the original cabin site.

Haywood consulted his GPS and announced proudly, "That's the place! Looks like you might be able to salvage that cache." He had to shout over the noise of the engine.

I looked down at the small log structure seated atop five tall poles.

"Maybe. Looks like it could do with a new roof though."

Haywood agreed and added, "I'd say we're going to have to come up with a different name for this place. The Hermitage might be a bit grand, don't you think?"

I nodded. The only thing remaining of the old cabin was a crumbling stone chimney and the outline of the foundation logs.

As we made another pass over the property Haywood shouted, "How about The Varmitage? That would be more like it."

I laughed. It was, indeed, more like it.

"Yeah," I shouted back. "That fits. The Varmitage it is."

Our map had shown a long, relatively level gravel bar on the same side of the creek about a mile upstream, if you stayed to the river. It was less than a half-mile as the crow flies, and we were flying. As Haywood made his first run over it, he pointed out that downstream would have been better for bringing out heavy loads of moose meat, but upstream would do. We could always load up the canoe with bags of meat, then wade-and-tow it up to the landing strip from the cabin. Provided, of course, we enjoyed continued success on our moose hunts.

He made two low-level passes over the proposed landing strip, one from each direction. When he was satisfied there were no holes or boulders or logs his tundra tires couldn't handle, he banked into the wind and took us down. It wasn't my first bush landing with Haywood, but nonetheless, I closed my eyes, gritted my teeth and held on for dear life. His little Clipper dropped out of the sky like a rock, hit the bar and bounced, hit and bounced again, then Haywood jumped on the brakes. We swerved and skidded up the bar throwing sand and stones everywhere. We eventually came to a complete stop just off the gravel with both wheels hub deep in the water of Moose Jaw Creek. I wasn't sure if we'd landed or been shot down.

I looked at Haywood. He was positively beaming with self-satisfaction.

"Perfect," he pronounced. "However, you might want to extend this landing strip a bit while I go back for the second load."

I still couldn't talk so I didn't answer.

He revved the engine, swung the plane around in the shallows and taxied back up onto the bar. As the cabin site was beyond the far end, he taxied us all the way back. I looked at the ruts the tires had left in the gravel during our "landing" with some degree of dismay. Haywood seemed completely unconcerned that we'd just barely survived what should, rightly, have been termed a plane crash.

It took less than a half hour to unload and stack the cargo on the willow side of the bar. Then Haywood clapped me on the shoulder, said, "See you in about three hours," and jumped back into the cockpit. He'd already walked the entire length of the "landing strip" pacing it off for distance. I had accompanied him, moving the larger rocks and logs off to the side and kicking fill into the deeper holes. As he had to take off and land into the wind, his aircraft was already positioned at the proper end of the bar so, with a wave of his hand and a roar of his engine he shot bouncing up the bar, lifted into the air and soared off up the river channel until he had gained enough altitude to clear the tree tops. Then he rose rapidly in a sweeping arc that brought him back overhead and onto his course for Fairbanks.

***

I had three hours to kill before Haywood returned so I decided to have a look at my property. I had bought it, literally, sight unseen. Since it was right on the river, I was certain we must have passed it during our float trips, but I doubted we'd ever set foot on that particular piece of ground. I was sure we would have remembered the stone chimney if we had.

Haywood had seen it advertised on the bulletin board at the hardware store. It was a handwritten note that stated simply, "For Sale – Cabin site on the Moose Jaw…one acre…some improvements". He'd called the owner, determined that the property was in the middle of our favorite stretch of the river, and contacted me immediately. The price was right, so I bought it. Now it was time to inspect the "improvements".

I opened the gun bag and took out my .44 magnum pistol, loaded it, and strapped on the gun-belt before heading downstream. We hadn't seen any bears during the flyovers but that didn't mean they were not around. With that in mind, I decided to stick to the creek bank on my initial trip downstream. It was no more than a mile. Having had the advantage of recon-by-air, I knew it would be a short walk through the woods, but when you're traveling alone in bear country, it's best to keep to open ground if you can.

I took my time, studying the tracks in the mud and sand of the bank as I went. I found moose, lynx, black bear, grizzly bear, caribou, wolf, and three or four members of the weasel family – marten for sure, and perhaps mink and ermine. I'm not that good on weasel tracks. There were also duck, swan, and goose tracks, and several smaller birds and rodents, but I didn't take the time to try and identify them all. I had the whole summer to meet the neighbors.

It took, perhaps, thirty minutes to follow the creek down to my property. It was easy walking along the gravel bar, but I took my time and enjoyed the scenery. The Moose Jaw valley wound its way through a series of gently rolling hills. The river was a silver ribbon of water, flanked by open gravel bars, which gave way to thickets of small willows along the high banks. Beyond the willows, there were stands of tall, brooding spruce trees, and lush open meadows and marshes. When I got to the cabin site I pulled out the plot plan, and using the old stone chimney as my single point of reference, I staked out the boundaries of my parcel. I didn't have sophisticated surveying equipment, but a compass for direction and the time honored pacing method for distance was really all I needed. In less than an hour, four willow poles topped with scraps of red flannel marked my corners. Two were at the water's edge along the creek, and two were back near the tree line where the dusty-green spruce trees stood straight and tall on the high ground. The old cabin had been situated just about in the middle of the property. After I staked out the original outline of its foundation I went to inspect the cache.

The cache wasn't on the property. It was back in a small clearing, deep in the spruce stand, and somewhat downstream, perhaps two hundred yards from the cabin. This was typical. Most of the old trappers and prospectors kept their food cache downwind and well away from their camps and cabins. It was inevitable that a bear would catch the scent of food on the breeze and follow his nose upwind until he found it. The grizzly's sense of smell was well documented. According to an Indian legend, when a leaf fell in the forest, the eagle saw it fall, the wolf heard it fall, but the grizzly smelled it fall. If you located your cache downwind of your cabin, the bear could arrive at it without having to wander through your camp. Of course, the wind wasn't constant, and occasionally swung to blow out of another quarter, putting you and your camp in the bear's direct path to the cache. You just had to play the percentages and go with the prevailing wind. As the wind here usually blew out of the southwest, it tended to follow the streambed. Thus, the old trapper who had built the original cabin had put the cache downstream and back in the woods.

It was in better shape than it had appeared from the air. Basically, it was an eight-foot square log box, five feet high, atop five tall poles. The five upright logs were still sound and sturdy. They had been set in an X pattern, with four corner posts forming a square, and a center pole to support the mid span load from all directions. They were locked together at the top by the platform floor of the cache. The log walls of the cache still looked to be solid. It stood roughly fourteen feet above the ground so I couldn't inspect it closely, but I could see, through the door opening, that the poles supporting the old sod roof had simply rotted over the years, and buckled under the weight of the sod. I'd have to clear the remains of the roof out of the inside before any repair work could be done.

Underneath the structure itself I found some old leg traps, wire, chain and the remnants of the pole ladder that had once served as access to the cache. The traps could probably be salvaged with a little oil and a wire brush, but the ladder was rotted and broken. At best it would serve as a model from which to build a new one. I was excited to get started, and would have built a new one then and there, if I had the tools with me. But, they were coming in on Load Two. I glanced at my watch. It was past two o'clock, and I had just over an hour before Haywood returned, so I wandered back to the cabin site, lit my pipe and sat on a log near the old chimney and smoked and enjoyed the sunshine.

The sun was high in the clear sky now and the day was warm. The creek put forth a hatch of gnats and black flies, and the grayling began rolling on the surface as they fed on the insects. Their tall dorsal fins caught the sunlight and sent off flashes of red and purple as they rolled. I saw several fish that were in the twelve-to-fourteen inch range. They promised to provide many hours of fishing during the coming months, as well as some very fine dining.

A man couldn't ask for a better place to spend his summer. This was the perfect place for a cabin. Old Jake Larkin had chosen well. It was situated on a patch of high ground so as to take advantage of the breeze that came down the streambed, and it was far enough back from the water that the insects were not too thick. I'd learned, on previous trips, that the biting flies and mosquitoes could drive you crazy along the water's edge. They're also bad back in the woods or where the willows are thick. Haywood and I found the best camps to be in open, high ground, midway between the water and the tree line.

The cabin had stood on just such a spot. It also sat on the inside of a bend which afforded it a good view both upstream and down, and a field of fire of perhaps two hundred-seventy degrees. I decided to build my cabin on the same site. The old stone fireplace was in bad shape and would have to come down eventually, but I could use it for my campfires until I started construction on the cabin. The top half of the chimney had fallen over, but there was enough left to create a draft and pull the smoke up out of camp.

When I finished my pipe I checked the topo map of the area, picked out the cabin site, and then the landing strip. I marked them both with a yellow highlighter. I'd followed the creek bed coming downstream. Since I had seen no evidence of bears in the area, I wanted to scout the more direct overland route on the way back.

The land here had a few ups and downs, but nothing radical. The lines on the topo map were regular and widely spaced. Studying the map, it appeared that I could quarter the distance back to the landing strip by cutting directly through the woods on a southwesterly course. I folded the map, put it in my hip pocket, slung my jacket over my shoulder, and started up the rise toward the spruce stand.

Just inside the trees, I came upon a game trail that seemed to be headed in the right direction. I followed it across the high ground, through one dip, then up and over another rise. It was well-worn and wide open and the footing was good. In fifteen minutes I found myself in the willows at the edge of the landing strip. I could see the black, red and yellow river bags stacked out on the gravel bar. The overland route would clearly be the way to move them down to the cabin site.

Haywood was due to arrive shortly, so I stretched out on the gravel, my jacket for a pillow, put my hands behind my head, and closed my eyes. I felt the sun, warm on my face and the gentle breeze in my hair. I heard the creek burbling across its rock bottom, and an occasional splash as a grayling took a fly. I dozed for a while until the annoying drone of a flying insect insinuated itself into my consciousness. It came nearer and its drone grew louder. Eventually, I realized it was Haywood's airplane approaching.

I shifted up onto an elbow and squinted into the brilliant blue sky. My eyes had not yet adjusted to the light, so I couldn't make out the little Piper. I looked at my watch and was amazed to see it was nearly four-thirty. I had napped an hour and a half! I got to my feet, a little stiff and damp from the moist, rocky sand of the gravel bar. I brushed the sand from the back of my pants and shirt, and shook out my jacket. Haywood's plane came into view above the trees downstream. He made his low-level surveillance run over the bar, then banked into a turn that took him back downstream for his final approach.

Chapter 3

His landing this time seemed to be somewhat less hair-raising. Perhaps that was because I observed it from the safety of the gravel bar. He touched down a little closer to the downstream end of the bar, and only bounced once before settling into his rollout. He came to a stop with a good thirty feet of dry land to spare. I was duly impressed. I waited near the stacked bags and boxes of Load One while he brought the plane about and taxied back to me. When he cut the engine I walked out on the bar to meet him.

The door creaked open and he hopped down into the sand. He landed gingerly, bent at the waist. He put his hands on his lower back and slowly straightened up; he stretched and groaned.

"Jesus H. Christ!" he announced to the stream, and the sky, and the wilderness in general. "Had to shift the whole damned load from truck to plane all by myself! That goddamned tent has got to weigh a hundred pounds! And the cooler is a backbreaker! I can tell you it was a real joy getting that damned thing aboard – awkward bastard – if it wasn't full of beer I would have left it in the truck! I'm stiffer 'n a weddin' dick!" A colorful phrase he brought with him from his colorful Missouri childhood, and used whenever the opportunity presented itself.

As always, I laughed. You couldn't help but laugh with Haywood.

When he had completed his stretching exercises he added, "By-the-way, nice job on that runway extension. Had enough room to land a seven-forty-seven!"

"It was nothing," I said. "Nevertheless, nothing can sometimes be thirsty work. Since you won't be flying anymore today, why don't we lighten the load in that cooler a bit? A cold beer would taste pretty good after all our efforts. Besides, you need to give your back a little rest before we begin shifting all these bundles downstream."

"Excellent plan!" he responded "But the damned thing's buried. Never fear, however..." He produced his pewter hip flask with a flourish.

We had given it to him, Sylvia and I, several years before. We bought it at Purdey's of South Audley Street, London, during our first expatriate assignment in the U.K. Purdey and Sons were the premier gun makers in all of England and had their own line of upscale shooting accessories. Anything you bought at their shop bore their world recognized crest – and a very high price tag as well. Haywood loved the flask. He cherished it. It had accompanied us on several adventures, and had been the cause of more than a few misadventures. I'd considered buying one for myself, but I already had the one my father had left me.

I eyed it approvingly as he unscrewed the cap. "Dew?"

"None other!" he affirmed. "Nothing but The Legendary for this flask!"

He sniffed delicately at the bouquet, and offered me the first sip.

"After you." He said, with a deeply exaggerated bow.

I accepted, took a long pull from the flask, and handed it back to Haywood. While he tippled, I lit my pipe and savored the aromatic smoke as it coiled out of the bowl into the crisp, clear air. Haywood returned the flask to his pocket, then fired up one of his disreputable cigars. The ever-present flying insects retreated to a safer distance. I suppose even toxic fumes have their good points.

Before offloading the newly arrived cargo, we each shouldered a river bag from Load One, and I led Haywood up the overland trail to the cabin site. He was surprised it took so little time; fifteen minutes, even burdened with the weight of a river bag and debilitated by the poisonous smoke from his cigar.

We deposited the bags near the old chimney and I showed Haywood the layout.

"Nice little piece of land," he observed thoughtfully. "Solid, high ground, sand-and-gravel base for good drainage, excellent view of the creek in both directions, lots of firewood. Not bad."

I agreed. "Cache is back in the trees over there," I said, pointing off in its general direction. "Plenty of spruce back in there big enough for cabin logs, but I don't know how I'm going to get them all dragged out here. That'll take some doing."

Haywood thought for a moment.

"You know," he said speculatively, "I flew over an old burn

about a half-mile upstream of the landing strip, on the other side of the creek. Looked like there was a lot of timber still standing. It comes right down close to the creek. You might find enough seasoned logs up there to build the whole cabin. You could drag them to the creek and raft them right down to your doorstep."

I thought about this for a moment. It would certainly be easier than dragging fresh-cut green trunks out of the woods. The dry stuff would be a lot lighter and already cured. I could cut them to length up there and not have a lot of green brush to deal with. I'd also get a lot less shrinkage out of them once the cabin was up.

"Good idea." I said. "Let's walk up there and have a look tomorrow."

Then we went back for another load.

It took us the better part of four hours to transport all the cargo from the landing strip to the cabin site. First, we tried carrying the boxes and river bags one at a time, but after three round trips, we were getting a bit tired. It was shaping up to be a long, long day. We discussed putting the canoe to use. It was collapsible, and weighed only thirty-four pounds. The manufacturer claimed it was capable of handling a payload of six hundred and fifty pounds. We knew, from past experience, it could carry the two of us, all our gear, and the boned out meat of two fair sized deer. We decided to give it a go.

We unpacked and assembled it. That took only twenty minutes. Then we loaded it up with the heavy stuff in the bottom, and the lightest bags and boxes on top. Haywood insisted he wasn't carrying the cooler another step, so that went in first. I had the presence of mind to take out two bottles of beer before the lid got buried under the top layer. We slid the canoe into deeper water as the load became progressively heavier. We had learned this trick the hard way on our first float trip. We had loaded everything aboard the raft while it was beached and then tried to drag it into the water. It wouldn't budge. Since then, we always made sure to keep the canoe floating while taking on cargo.

We managed to get all but four river bags aboard. Haywood's back was giving him trouble from all the lifting and toting, so I suggested he attach a tag line to the bow and walk the canoe downstream in the shallows, while I took the last of the bags via the overland route. We took a short break and drank the beer I'd pulled out of the cooler, then went back to work.

"See you at the other end," Haywood said as he stepped into the stream and took up the canoe's tow line.

"I'll probably take a little nap while I await your arrival," I told him.

He muttered something unintelligible as he swung the bow of the canoe out into the current.

***

It took Haywood a little less than an hour to wade the canoe down the creek. During that time I managed to move only two of the bags. The second one contained the wall tent, and I regretted not having the foresight to have loaded it in the canoe. It was one of Cabela's Outfitter series, and was made of heavy cotton duck, and included a separate rain fly, as well as a stove jack. All in, the bag weighed ninety-two pounds. It took me a half hour of grunting, cursing, and sweating to get it to the cabin site. Those two little rises were a lot steeper than I'd thought. When Haywood came wading into view with the canoe I was sprawled on my back on the bank, trying to catch my wind. He looked fresh and relaxed.

"The tent?" He asked, clearly enjoying my suffering.

I didn't yet have enough wind to answer, so I just nodded. Haywood beached the canoe and began tossing boxes and bags up onto the shore.

"I thought about that when we were loading the canoe, but we already had too much in. Guess we could have taken out a couple of these lighter ones to make room, but I didn't want to deprive you of an opportunity to come up with one of your amazing engineering solutions."

I was scowling at him now, but still didn't want to waste precious breath cussing him.

He smiled sweetly and went on unloading the canoe. "Of course, you being a traditionalist and all, I can understand why you insisted on the old back-breaking-labor approach. Much more fitting…"

I finally had sufficient wind to respond. "Well, there're still two more bags up at the landing strip waiting to be moved. Perhaps you'd like to partake in tradition?"

He pursed his lips as if in deep thought. "I shouldn't," he observed, "having just freshened up and all. But, I suppose I could manage a light one. I could avoid getting all sweaty and disheveled if there were a light one."

By now I had, more-or-less, recovered. Haywood saw I was getting ready to launch a verbal broadside in his direction, so he quickly popped open the cooler, extracted two ice-cold bottles of beer, and held one out in my direction.

"No, no..." he said, magnanimously. "No need to express your gratitude. I see you struggling to find the words. Think nothing of it. Here, let's have a beer before we go get the last bags. That lazy wading in cool, shallow water wears a man down."

One hour and three rest breaks later, the canoe had been emptied and pulled up on shore, and the last two bags had been fetched down from the landing strip. There was no rain in the forecast so we decided to forego pitching the tent, and just cook dinner and sleep in the open. It was nearly ten o'clock when we finished eating our Chunky Beef Stew and bread. The sun was still surprisingly high in the sky and showed no intention of setting until after midnight. Tired as we were, we decided to have a nightcap and a last smoke before turning in.

I settled back against one of the river bags with my drink in hand.

"What time does the sun come up this far north of Fairbanks?" I asked idly.

Haywood sipped his whiskey. "Hardly goes down this time of year. You can figure on twenty-four hours of daylight for the next three weeks or so. The sun will drop below the horizon for a couple of hours, but it never really gets dark. Sunrise will probably be about three-thirty."

That didn't surprise me. I'd spent enough time in Fairbanks that the "midnight sun" was not new to me. Even down in Anchorage, I had always marveled at the length of their midsummer days. The Matanuska Valley, just outside of Anchorage, is famous for its enormous vegetables that grow in the long days of the short summer. Lots of water and sunlight – that's the secret. I wondered if it was too late for me to start some kind of crop. Then I thought of the permafrost, a foot or so below the surface, and wondered if you could even farm this land. Not that it mattered; the caribou and moose would get into anything I planted, and I'd end up eating canned stuff anyway.

Haywood puffed thoughtfully at his cigar. "You call Sylvia before we left?"

I shook my head. "No. No point really. I told her I'd be spending the summer up here. No need to go into detail. I did call Uncle Jack. Told him to contact you if anything important came up."

He nodded and puffed and sipped his drink. We were silent for a long spell.

Finally he said, "This is going to be one hell of an adventure, my friend. I envy you. Make sure you keep that journal up to date. Don't leave anything out. I'll want to read the full account."

I said that I would. I'd have plenty of time to think, and read, and write. I'd get it all down on paper.

We sat smoking a while after we finished our drinks and then, with the sun a little lower in the sky, we called it a night. However, because it really wasn't night, I found I couldn't sleep. Haywood, on the other hand, began snoring softly as soon as he'd zipped himself into his sleeping bag. Perhaps it was the midnight sun, or maybe just the excitement of being on the threshold of my great adventure, but whatever the reason, sleep came to me slowly. As I lay there, eyes closed, listening to the sounds of the creek and the rustle of the breeze in the willows, I felt the tension of the past few weeks slowly ebb from my being. The lost job seemed unimportant out here. I didn't need a job anymore, and I realized I didn't want one. The loss of my wife, were I honest with myself, troubled me no more than the job. I thought I wanted both while I had them. But, having lost them I was free. And here in the wilderness freedom seemed the sweetest thing a man could have.

Chapter 4

I woke up that first morning on the Moose Jaw a different man. I hadn't slept well or long, but I felt fresh and full of energy. Even the stiffness that comes with sleeping on the ground seemed a profound pleasure. Haywood was still snoring quietly in his sleeping bag when I crawled out of mine into the cool morning air. It occurred to me that perhaps our roles had reversed out here in the bush. I went back into the willows to attend my morning devotions and then down to the creek to wash my face in its cold water. It was a baptism, emerging from which, I felt renewed. I stood in the shallows for a long time listening to the rush of the water against my boots and the trilling of the birds that darted among the willows. I marveled that the sun could be so high so early in the day, and the sky so blue. And I wondered if anything truly existed beyond the rim of the hills that defined the valley that bounded the river in which I now stood. Was there really a Europe? Had there ever been a woman named Sylvia that had been my wife? They seemed part of a dream that I'd had in the night – a dream that was fading to feathery wisps of vapor in the cold, bright light of morning.

When I finished my ablutions I went back up to camp, put on a pot of coffee and began cooking breakfast. All the banging and clanking of pots and pans finally penetrated Haywood's blissful netherworld. His voice came muffled through the fabric and insulation of his sleeping bag.

"I have a gun, you know."

He sounded quite miserable. I was delighted.

"Sorry," I said, as I clanged the lid down on the skillet. "Most inconsiderate of me."

***

Haywood had taken Thursday and Friday off to give himself a four-day weekend so he could help me set up camp and squeeze in a little fishing while he was at it. We spent the better part of Friday morning clearing a pad for the wall tent and then cutting poles for the support frame. You can buy snap-together aluminum frames for any size wall tent, but six years ago, when we'd bought it, we had planned on setting it up just once a year and leaving it. Cutting poles once a year presented no problem, so we saved our pole money for more important supplies – alcohol, for example, and tobacco and ammunition. One might dismiss our tastes as somewhat "redneck". But the alcohol to which I refer is top shelf Irish or Scotch whiskies, not corn liquor – and we don't chew our tobacco or shoot our ammunition at road signs.

The spruce stand behind the cabin site offered a good selection of poles so we cut and dragged them, lashed them together with parachute cord, and set up the tent. I was always surprised at how much room there was inside. It was only ten feet wide and twelve feet long, and stood six feet at the walls and eight feet in the center. It was the smallest wall tent in the catalog. Nevertheless, there was plenty of room for two cots, a small table, a camp stove, and all the gear two hunters would ever need. There was more than enough space for one man alone. The tent would serve me well as my temporary digs until I got the cabin built.

After we pitched the tent and ate a quick lunch, we walked upstream to have a look at the old burn Haywood had spotted from the air. It was a little over two miles, following the creek, and we took our fly rods along in case a hatch brought the grayling to the surface. We studied the tracks in the bank along the way.

"Don't think I remember so many wolves around here." Haywood observed.

"Judging by all the other tracks, there's plenty of prey to keep them around," I ventured.

He nodded. "Yeah. There's plenty of carrion too. I imagine they enjoy a pretty fat diet."

I thought for a minute. "You know, I haven't seen many bear tracks up here – none, in fact. That's seems a bit odd."

"Oh, they're around. They just don't spend too much time along the creeks until the salmon start running. Then you'll see more of them than you can shake a stick at."

I supposed that was true. Still, there was something vaguely disturbing in the absence of the bears.

I didn't dwell on it. Instead, I asked, "When do the salmon runs start?"

"Already have out on the coast. It'll take them two or three weeks to get back in this far. They'll come up the Yukon and then up all the feeder creeks. My guess is you'll be seeing the Chinook – what we call King Salmon – around the second week in July. The Chum Salmon come up a month or so later. You'll want to have a smoker ready. And you'll need to have the roof on your cache. If the bears give you fishing rights, you'll be able to lay in a pretty good supply of smoked salmon."

I thought about that. Haywood was right. I had a busy two weeks ahead of me even if I didn't get right after building the cabin. There was a lot to do.

As we came around a bend we could see the bare, blackened tips of burned trees following a ridge line down from the distant hills to a meadow just off the creek. There were several burns along the river, the result of lightning strikes over the years. We struck inland and crossed a narrow marsh, and then came up against a beaver pond, which we skirted on the west. At the backside of the pond the terrain began to rise gently up through the burn. Haywood had been right. There was a lot of dead standing timber. This was a bit of luck I hadn't expected. Live trees were easier to cut and notch, especially in the early summer when they were full of sap. But live trees were also a lot heavier, and the bark had to be peeled off with a drawknife, and then they needed to dry. That was a time consuming process. Dead standing trees were already dry and free of bark and, with their much lighter weight, a lot easier to move.

Since this was just a scouting mission we hadn't brought the chainsaw; we had, however, brought the folding saw. I took it out, opened it, and cut down one of the taller trees. The trunk was straight as an arrow. It was no more than sixteen inches at the base, but the taper was gradual and regular so it didn't lose much girth over the first twenty feet. After I'd felled it, we inspected it for decay and insect damage. It was prime stock; I was certain it would make a perfect foundation log, perhaps a sill or a girder.

As an engineer, the construction of the cabin was to be the high point of my summer. I'd done a good bit of research, and had decided on the traditional trapper style cabin, which was, basically, a rectangular log box with one door, three small windows and a gabled roof. Originally I had wanted to keep it small, maybe nine by twelve feet, but I didn't want to build a stone fireplace, which would take time I didn't have. A freestanding stove was a better option, but it would take up a lot of space inside the cabin. It had been a tough call. I had, ultimately, decided to go with the stove which necessitated increasing the footprint to sixteen by eighteen. To accommodate that size interior plus a covered porch, I would require several logs over twenty feet, and they would be difficult for one man to handle. Nevertheless, I wanted the extra room inside, and I was eager for the challenge.

Before we'd flown in I had drawn up detailed plans for the construction, including a material take off list that specified the exact number of logs I'd need of each particular length. The longest were twenty-two footers. Fortunately, they would be roof supports, (ridgepole and purlins), and would be of smaller diameter than the foundation logs. I'd need five of that length. That was the good news – the bad news was that I would need three larger diameter logs, twenty feet long, for the sills and girder. Since they would be the heaviest ones of the lot, I wanted to get them cut and moved to the cabin site while Haywood was there to help.

I spent twenty minutes walking the slope above the beaver pond, counting the suitable standing spars. It looked like there were plenty. I hoped to be able to harvest all I needed from this slope so gravity would help me get the logs down to the beaver pond, and the slides and channels would provide a float path out through the marsh to the creek. The set up looked pretty good.

As we stood there, taking in the sun and inspecting our timber supply, we heard far off honking. Haywood pointed at the sky to the south. A huge flight of Canadian geese came into view, beating their way north to their breeding grounds. There must have been two thousand of them. What a magnificent sight. We watched them pass to the east of us and continue their journey north. We could still hear their honking, long after they had passed from sight.

Satisfied with the logs of the burn, we decided to make a test run with the tree I'd dropped earlier. I cut it to twenty-two feet. This would be the girder. Then I went the length of it and lopped off snags and limbs, rolled it over, trimmed the other side, and nodded to Haywood.

"Okay. Let's see if we can get this thing back to camp without killing ourselves."

We shifted it so it was pointed down the slope and then, using a couple of drag ropes, we sledded it down the grade and across the marsh grass and into the water of the beaver pond. It was hard work but, with two of us tugging and pulling, it didn't take long.

The pond was deeper than it looked, and Haywood found a hole halfway across. He filled one hip boot and almost lost the other in the mud bottom. I had been walking behind him and, being six inches shorter, had considerably less freeboard above my boots' water line. Laughing, I beat a quick retreat to the bank while paying out my towline, climbed ashore and walked the log around the pond to the downstream end where the beavers had built their earthen dam. I left Haywood to extricate himself from the mud. I waited at the spillway while he clambered out of the pond, sat on the bank, removed his right boot, and poured a couple gallons of black water back into the pond. He gave me his patented toothy grin.

"Good boot! Didn't leak!" he shouted proudly. "Didn't let out a drop."

I waited while he went through the same routine with the left boot. Reshod, he walked around the pond and joined me at the spillway.

"You might want to see about filling in that hole before I come back," he suggested. "Were I not so nimble, you might have lost me there."

"I'll see to it," I promised.

There was a pretty good channel from the spillway to the creek bank. It was about two feet deep and quite straight. Using the towlines we were able to slide the log along the slick mud bottom of the channel or float it where the water was deep enough. It took us less than thirty minutes from slope to creek, even with Haywood's boot dumping break. When we arrived back at the creek the grayling were jumping and rolling, and having a field day with a fresh hatch. We abandoned the log test there and then, and broke out the fly rods.

Ah! What a day on the stream. It appeared that the fish were feeding on a hatch of black gnats but, evidently, they weren't picky. I had a number fourteen Caddis on my line, and Haywood was sporting what looked to be a stuffed pheasant on the end of his.

"Tied it myself!" He'd stated proudly, upon noticing my silent and dubious scrutiny.

"And to think," I mused, "you do surgery on living beings with those very same hands."

Whatever my misgivings, and, whatever it was he'd tied, Haywood's haystack fly worked. So did my Caddis. And, when I lost the Caddis on my fourth or fifth grayling, they were equally happy with a number sixteen mosquito. It was just one of those wonderful days when anything you threw out on the water was just right.

As is always the case, it ended as suddenly as it had begun. One minute we were catching and releasing a fish every cast – the next, there wasn't a feeding ring to be seen, up or down stream, as far as we could see in either direction. Fortunately, we'd had the foresight to keep four of good eating size. We gutted and cleaned them there in the cold water of the creek. Grayling are, in most aspects, very much like a trout. Same bone structure, same flaky, white meat. The noticeable exceptions are the oversized dorsal fin, and the scales. One needn't scale a trout. Unzip the belly, crosscut the jaw, pull out the guts, a quick rinse, and Bob's your uncle. Not so with Arctic Grayling; you have to scale them first. Nevertheless, they're delicious and well worth the extra effort.

I cut a slender willow branch, stripped it of leaves and strung on the fish. When that was done, we dragged our test log out into the current, untied our towlines, and launched it downstream. We walked along the bank as it made its ponderous way down the creek. It got hung up in shallow water at several points along the way, and we had to wade out and push it free. When we finally did reach camp, we had a bit of bad luck. As the camp lies on the inside of a bend, the deep water follows the cut bank on the other side of the stream. We hadn't thought to reattach a guide rope to the log at any point along the way, so there was nothing we could do when it got caught up in the strong current. It swept around the outside of the bend, and shot past the cabin site like a rocket sled. We ran it to ground a few hundred yards downstream, tied on a towrope and hauled it back up to the gravel bar at camp. A good lesson learned. Glitches notwithstanding, it had been a very successful trial run. It appeared I'd be able to bring in most of the logs for the cabin using the same approach. Things were, indeed, looking up.

The following day, Saturday, Haywood suggested we get a

start on the repairs to the cache. We took a folding saw and a roll of polyethylene twine back into the clearing where it stood, and built a new ladder. We cut two slender spruce saplings for the side rails, and two more which we cut into rungs, then lashed them together with the twine. It was a sturdy ladder, but heavier than I would have liked, due to the green wood. Nevertheless, I expected I could manage it by myself when it dried a bit with age.

We propped it up against the platform in front of the door opening and I scrambled up to have a look. As it had appeared from the ground, all four walls were intact and looked to be in pretty good shape. The door was missing altogether, and there was no evidence of hinges or door hardware. I suspected the door had been nothing more than a hatch-cover held in place with a couple of pivot latches. I climbed inside. The platform appeared solid enough to support a sizable load. It was littered with the rotted logs and some of the sod that had once served as the roof.

The front wall, which contained the door opening, was roughly five feet high; the rear wall was a couple of feet shorter. You wouldn't have wanted to live in there, but it would serve nicely for a larder. Basically, it was an enclosed, lean-to type structure, which made the roof easy. All I needed to do was cut several poles long enough to span the distance from front to back and lay them in place as rafters. A layer of willow branches over these, and plastic tarp on top would serve as the roofing. The steep pitch would assure runoff. I made a quick estimate and determined I'd need about a dozen ten-footers. I climbed down and began cutting spruce poles while Haywood went up to clear away the litter.

When he came back down he volunteered to go back to camp and get a few more tools. We'd need an ax for splitting, and the adze for shaping planks for the door. We'd also need a hammer and some spikes. I agreed and pointed out that a couple of cold beers might come in handy also. He grinned wide as if the thought had never occurred to him, and set off for camp.

I cut and trimmed the poles for the roof and took them up the ladder two at a time. I was just setting the last one in place, across the walls, when I heard Haywood rustling around below.

"Hey," I said over my shoulder. "Toss up that roll of poly-twine, will you?"

The ball of string came sailing through the open doorway,

skittered across the floor and bumped against my foot.

"Lucky shot," I called down. "Thanks."

No answer came up from below, but Haywood, when preoccupied, couldn't be reached. I picked up the roll of cord and began lashing down the rafter poles. I had half of them secure when Haywood's voice boomed out from below.

"Hello in the compound," he shouted. "I'm coming in. Don't shoot!"

I looked out the door and saw him coming through the woods laden with tools, lunch, and beer.

"You had to make two runs?" I asked him, as he came into the cache clearing and deposited his load on the grass.

He gave me a puzzled look. "No. What are you talking about?"

"Didn't you come back about twenty minutes ago?"

He shook his head. "No. I just got back."

I experienced a slight tingling in the skin of my scalp.

"You didn't toss up the twine?"

He frowned at me. "Gus, maybe you've been out here too long already. I didn't toss up anything. I told you, I just got back. Now come on down and eat something. You appear to be getting light in the head."

I glowered at him for a second. He wasn't above playing practical jokes. But, he looked sincere. I shrugged and climbed down the ladder.

***

We sat under the cache, our backs against the support logs and ate our sandwiches, and drank our beer. Life was good. Haywood, among his other numerous achievements, was an accomplished maker of outrageous sandwiches. He was famous for his liverwurst, red onion and sardine on sourdough. That's what he'd made today. Both the liverwurst, and onion were cut into half-inch slabs and three sardines were squished in between the layers. Magnificent! We washed them down with the first beer and chased them with a second. While we were enjoying a leisurely post-lunch smoke, a ptarmigan wandered into the clearing to see what we were up to. We didn't take any great pains to remain still or silent, but the bird seemed perfectly comfortable with our presence and, after a thorough inspection of our project, it went on its way.

"They're pretty good eating," Haywood observed, "but it's considered bad form to shoot the local building inspectors when you're remodeling without permits."

I recognized the wisdom of this and made a mental note to learn more about local protocol. I was sure Haywood would be happy to fill me in if only I asked. I didn't ask. When we'd finished our second beer, we took up our tools and went back to work. I worked aloft, lashing down the remaining rafter poles, while Haywood cut logs and split planks for the door. As my hands worked with the poly-twine, my mind went back to my meeting with Charlie Manning and his mention of yega. I wondered what sort of spirit could chuck a ball of twine fourteen feet in the air and put it through a small crawl hole in a wall. In the end, I decided that Haywood was having a little fun with me. Yega, indeed.

After I had the basic frame for the roof built, I climbed down the ladder and went out to the creek bank where I cut several fresh willow branches and stripped them of their leaves. When I had enough slender rods to make up a good bundle, I took them back the cache. Haywood helped me get them all aloft, then returned to his door project. I laid the willows perpendicular on top of the rafters, then tied them down. The cache was shaping up nicely. The willows clearly defined the pitched roof, and their slender branches would provide a fine substructure to support the tarp. I didn't put the tarp on at this stage because I wanted to give the green wood a few days to dry out in the sun and wind – no sense encouraging mold. I puttered around up on top a bit more, adding a tie-down here or a new branch there and, finally satisfied, I went down to help Haywood with the door.

He'd made good progress and was just assembling all the cut parts into a recognizable door structure. He asked me to go back up and verify the measurements of the door opening. I did. And when, back on the ground, we compared them with his finished door, it looked like it just might fit.

"Pity we didn't bring an extra set of hinges." He lamented.

"Don't think we'll need them. Looks like this will snug into the gap nicely, and we can lock it in place with a couple of pivot latches."

"Well," he considered, "without hinges, that's what we'll have to do."

I went back to camp for a few more bottles of beer while he put the finishing touches on the door. When I got back to the cache, he was up at the top of the ladder fussing and cussing, and trying to make the door fit the opening.

"Trouble?" I enquired.

"It's a cunt hair too wide. We'll have to shave off a little."

We had a drawknife with us so, back on the ground, he held the door on edge and instructed me to take a little off the side. I made a few passes with the knife, going with the grain, the moist wood peeling off in a slick, white ribbon.

"Easy!" He admonished. "Only needs an RCH."

'Oh! A Red CH!' He hadn't specified the color earlier. We engineers take our measurements and calibrations quite seriously. I don't know how, or why, but every engineer alive – for that matter, every male alive – understands that an RCH is much finer than any other color CH. Another of life's little mysteries, but it's something we all know without ever being told.

"You didn't say red." I reminded him.

"I meant red." He affirmed, eyeballing my work. "Let's give it a try."

With that, he scrambled back up the ladder; door tucked under one arm, beer clamped firmly in the other hand. At the top he deposited the beer bottle on the skirt of the platform and maneuvered the door in place.

"Shit," he said. "Looks like red wasn't enough. Should'a gone with black."

Everyone also knew, without ever being told, black was the coarsest CH. Red was fine, black was coarse. I assumed blond fell somewhere in the middle.

"Bring it down," I told him. "We'll shave off a tad more."

Chapter 5

I pulled chef duty that evening. We were dining on grilled rib-eye steaks and potatoes baked in the open fire. Haywood had prepared the grayling the previous night, pan-fried and stuffed with herb butter, served on a bed of wild rice. There is simply nothing better than fine cuisine served on tin plates, al fresco.

I was busy tending the potatoes, wrapped in two layers of aluminum foil and placed directly in the coals of the campfire, when Haywood came up from the creek lugging a bucket of fresh water.

"You know," he observed, "the one trouble with this cabin location is its proximity to the creek. It's a long haul for water."

"Yeah," I agreed. "But I don't see any way around it. I could build a storage tank up here, but I'd still have to haul water from the creek by the bucketful to fill it."

"Well, shit," Haywood chided, "brilliant fuckin' engineer like yourself ought to be able to come up with something better than that!"

True, I thought, but, so far, that was the best I could do. I promised to put my mind to it while I was filling in the hole in the middle of the beaver pond.

When the potatoes had been in the fire about thirty minutes, I flopped the steaks on the folding grill we'd set up over the campfire. I'd marinated them in Madeira laced with Herbs de Provence all afternoon. When they hit the hot grill they hissed and released a delicious waft of smoke into the air. We both liked our meat closer to rare than medium, so I let them sear only a minute before flopping them over. Haywood pulled the cork on a bottle of Cabernet and filled two tin cups. We drank it while the steaks spit and sizzled on the grill.

When the rib-eyes looked just about ready, I rolled the potatoes out of the coals with a willow stick and unwrapped the two layers of foil. They steamed in the cool evening air and the smell of their butter and chives blended with the aroma of the hot, juicy meat. It was mouth watering. A baguette, split and drizzled with olive oil, and warmed on the grill, rounded out the meal, and the full, red wine added the finishing touch.

We had just settled down on a log by the fire and begun eating when Haywood suddenly froze, his fork halfway between the plate and his mouth.

"Uh-oh. Looks like we've got company."

He said it quietly and without any sense of urgency, but his voice conveyed danger. I looked up and saw the bear on the far bank. There was still plenty of daylight and I could see it clearly. It was an adult black bear. That can be good or bad. Black bears are smaller than grizzlies, but they're unpredictable. The ones that have been around humans can get very aggressive. Of course, I'd still prefer this one to a twelve hundred pound grizzly. Nevertheless, any bear showing up for dinner can present a problem.

It was clear that this fellow had picked up the aroma of our grilling meat and come upwind to see if he could mooch a meal. He stood on his hind legs and stretched full length and sniffed as he swung his head upstream and down. When he'd zeroed in on the source of the food smell, he dropped back down to all fours and ambled down the bank and into the water. He was coming across.

Until now, both Haywood and I had been cutting rib-eye and stuffing it in our mouths as fast as we could chew and swallow. That seemed the prudent thing to do if the bear was going to give us time. Now, with Bruno showing every indication that he intended to join us in camp, it was time for more direct action.

We were both wearing our side arms. I had my .44 magnum and Haywood was carrying a .357 magnum. But, unless things got out of hand, we preferred to rely on diplomacy. I set aside my plate and threw some more logs on the fire. I wanted to get it roaring and burn the meat residue off the grill as quickly as possible. There was also the chance that the fire itself would keep the bear at bay. Haywood went over to the kitchen tote and took out our largest aluminum soup kettle and started banging it with a wooden spoon. While he was doing this, I picked up a few rocks and began launching them skyward, in the general direction of the bear.

All the racket and activity brought the bear up short. He stopped before reaching midstream and backed off a few paces.

Then he stood up in the water to afford himself a better look at what was transpiring on the bank where all the inviting smells were coming from. A minute ticked slowly by. It looked like we were coming to a stand off, so I corrected my elevation and adjusted my windage a smidge, and let fly with a golf ball sized river rock. It hit him high-left – about where his shoulder would have been if bears had shoulders. The sheer surprise of the contact, rather than the impact of the rock itself, buckled his knees and he dropped back down on all fours with a splash, turned on his heels, and plowed back through the water to the far bank. He climbed out of the creek, took a moment to shake off the water and, without a backward glance, disappeared into the woods.

The incident had taken no more than five minutes but, already, our meat and potatoes had gone cold. We finished eating standing up while we kept an eye out for the return of our uninvited guest. Chances were good that he wouldn't bother us again but, with bears, you never know.

"That's the first bear we've seen." Haywood said.

"Yeah," I answered, "I saw some black bear tracks along the bank between here and the landing strip on the first day but nothing fresh. He was probably just passing through and caught the smell of the meat cooking and came to investigate."

"That's probably it. Let's hope he doesn't come back later for another try. We better clean up good tonight. Might be a good idea to get that bacon and some of the other food up in the cache before we turn in."

After dinner I took all the plates and pans down to the creek and gave them a good scrub while Haywood removed the beer from the cooler and put the bottles in the stream. We then filled the cooler and the red river bag with anything that a bear might find yummy and hauled it all back to the cache. When we had everything safely stored aloft, we moved the ladder and propped it against a tree at the edge of the clearing. Then we went back to camp, had a nightcap, and turned in. I hadn't slept with my pistol thus far, but I did that night. I didn't see Haywood's .357 laying around anywhere, so I assumed he was sleeping with his too.

I tossed and turned most of the night and woke at every small sound. But the bear never reappeared. I finally fell off into a sound sleep just as the sun was peaking over the eastern hills.

Considering sunup was sometime around four in the morning, it still left me plenty of time for half a night's sleep.

***

The next day, Sunday, we'd planned on bacon, eggs and coffee for breakfast. But, with the bear's visit still fresh in our memory, and most of our food stores up in the cache, we opted for instant oatmeal instead. After breakfast, Haywood brewed a second pot of coffee and filled a thermos before we headed upstream to do some logging. We'd decided, the night before, to go back up to the burn and bring out two more twenty footers. We figured I could manage the lighter stock alone, but it was best to tackle the long, heavy base logs while Haywood was there to help. Along the way we checked the bank carefully for fresh sign but didn't see any new bear tracks. There was plenty of other activity in evidence. The beavers had been busy along the bank, and it looked like wolves had been through recently. I noticed another track, which I didn't recognize. It resembled a very small bear track but there were only four claw marks on the forepaw. I pointed it out to Haywood. He said it was a porcupine. I studied it so I'd remember what it was the next time I saw one.

"Do they have any natural enemies around here?" I asked.

"Wolverine, maybe, but he'd have to be pretty desperate. As far as I know, the puma and the fisher are the only ones that will go after a porcupine on a regular basis. Certainly no pumas up here. For that matter, I don't think there are any fishers either. You'll find them farther south. They're basically oversized weasels, with a whole mouthful of very sharp teeth. They'll circle the porcupine until it gets tired, then go after its face. If they can get at it, they'll blind the poor bugger and bite and cut and slash at the face until the porky wears down. Then they go for the underbelly and the party's over."

"How big do they get? The fishers I mean."

"Not as big as a porcupine. They'll average about twelve pounds. Some get as big as twenty pounds but that's rare. They're not large animals, but they're quick and persistent and vicious. The porcupine always tries to keep its back to the danger. They'll even climb a tree to keep the fisher behind them. The fisher can climb too but if they go up the tree after the porky, they can't penetrate the quill defense from the rear. No way to get at the vulnerable face, unless, of course, there's another tree close enough so the fisher can go up and over and come down the porky's tree. Then it's curtains for the porcupine."

It didn't take us long to walk up to the burn and, by eleven o'clock, we had dropped two more long trunks and slid them down to the beaver pond. This time we guided them around the pond with guide ropes rather than trying to walk them across. We also left the tethers on them when, back out at the creek, we launched them downstream. As a result, we were able to fetch them ashore before they swept past our camp. After we had dragged them up on the bar and laid them alongside the other one to dry, we had a quick lunch. Haywood declined the bottle of beer I offered him to go with his sandwich. He'd be flying out in a few hours, and when it came to alcohol and airplanes he went strictly by the book. I knew he was anxious to get back to Fairbanks. He'd mentioned he wanted to get the plane into the hangar for some scheduled maintenance, and I suspected he was looking forward to an evening with Donna, his new lady friend, before returning to work tomorrow. I couldn't say that I blamed him. I'd like an evening with a lady friend too, if I had a lady friend. With Sylvia gone from my life I'd have to do something about that when I returned to civilization. For the present though, I was just going to enjoy my not-yet-divorced-but-nevertheless-single status.

***

After lunch Haywood packed a river bag with all the gear he'd be taking with him. I told him he could leave his sleeping bag and inflatable mattress if he wanted, but he said he liked to keep all his gear in the plane in case he had to put down in the bush sometime. You always had to be thinking survival out here. Then we made up a shopping list of items he'd bring in on his next visit. After that, we put in a little time on the creek, but the grayling weren't rising, and we, dry-fly snobs both, refused to resort to nymphs. It occurred to me as we stood there, casting and chatting, that I hadn't taken very good stock of my fly tying material before we flew in.

"Better add some dubbing wax and some more hooks to that list." I told him.

"What size?" he asked, fishing his notebook out of his shirt pocket.

"Oh, fourteens and sixteens, I guess. A hundred each ought to be enough. I think I have plenty of eighteens."

He wrote it down. "How you fixed for thread and head cement and all that sort of stuff?"

"Fine," I answered, "The hooks and the wax will do it."

At about two in the afternoon we gave up on the grayling and went back to camp to retrieve Haywood's river bag before heading up to the landing strip. I had mixed feelings about his departure. I enjoyed his company and wished he could stay a little longer. On the other hand, I was anxious to get started on my solo adventure and I couldn't really do that until I was, well, solo. I saw him aboard his Clipper and waited while he stowed and secured all his gear. Then I stood off a few paces and watched while he went through his pre-takeoff checks. Before he cranked up the engine he opened the door, propped a boot on the sill and leaned out.

"Okay. You've got enough beer and tobacco and whiskey to see you through a month. I'll be back in three weeks for the Chinook run so you should be all right until then. The tent's good enough to get you through anything the weather can throw at you in the summer months and you're well enough armed to fight off all the bears in Alaska plus half the Red Army. I'm not going to worry about you."

This, of course, was his way of telling me he was worried about me.

I patted the toe of his boot that was sticking out the door.

"I'll be fine, Mom. Stop worrying."

"Goddamnit. I'm not worrying! I'm just – well…" he laughed, "fretting. It's a mother's right, you know. Seriously though, you sure you'll be okay? This all-alone shit sounds exciting and all, but it can go wrong fast. I wish you weren't such an asshole about that radio. At least you could call out for help if you needed it."

I smiled. He was genuinely concerned. He was a good friend.

"That'd be cheating. Seriously, I'll be okay. It's only three weeks. I can make it alone that long."

"I know. I've just been thinking about what Hard Case said the other night, about strange things happening back in here, and about what can happen to a white man's mind."

"Haywood," I said with a bit of exasperation. "Three weeks, for Christ's sake! And I'll have plenty to keep my mind occupied.

Stop fretting!"

"Okay," he said with finality. "So, take care of yourself. Don't let the bears eat you."

With that, he swung his leg back into the cockpit and slammed the door. I watched the dog-ear handle rotate into place. Then I walked back to the edge of the bar and waited while he checked dials and flipped switches. Then I heard the winding of the motor and the propeller began its slow spin. When he had it revved up to speed he shot me a quick salute, swung the nose around and roared off up the gravel bar into the wind. His wheels lifted off, touched briefly down, and then leapt skyward and he was airborne. I watched as he made his slow turn with the river and then he was up over the trees and into the sky. I waited until his plane disappeared into the distance. As I walked slowly back to camp, I felt the solitude close in gently upon me.

Chapter 6

The next three weeks went by quickly. That happens when you're busy with projects you enjoy. I finished up the cache first. I got the roof tarp installed and added a knotted rope ladder as a safety device in case I got treed up there by a bear and had to jettison the log ladder. When that was finished I addressed my lack of furniture. I needed a bed and a table and two chairs. I would need them to furnish the cabin when it was built, so I decided to make them early and have the benefit of them while I was living in the tent. This was a good project to start with, as I wasn't ready to dive right into the cabin. I took the chainsaw up into the spruce stand and dropped one tall tree. Its trunk was roughly fourteen inches in diameter, and I cut it into five-foot sections. Then I put a rip chain on the chainsaw and rigged up the "Alaska Mill" and ripped all the sections into two-inch planks. Sounds easy, but it's a lot of work, bending over to keep the saw's bar parallel with the ground, while guiding it the length of each log, slow and steady, to make an even, straight cut. Difficult as it was, that one tree gave me enough lumber to build my table, and all the shelves and steps I would need for the cabin. Next, I dropped enough three, and five-inch stock to make the bed and chairs. After I skinned off their bark with the draw knife, I ripped a few of them into half logs for the seats and chair backs.

The first thing I built was a sturdy, half-log bench. It was nothing more than what it sounds like – a log, ripped down the middle, and fitted with four legs, flat side up. I figured it would serve me as a table until I could build a proper table, and, after that it would be perfect for lounging on the porch. The bench only took about an hour to make. It took me two full days to build the other four pieces of furniture, but when they were finished I was very pleased with my handiwork.

I used a foam mattress that had come in on Load 2 as a template to design the bed. It had once been a full sized mattress, but I'd cut it down to three quarter width so it would not occupy too much of the cabin's limited floor space. Consequently, the bed frame wasn't big, but when complete, it was still quite heavy. I built it in place, inside the tent, and made it so I could break it down and move it to the cabin when the time came.

The table was a rustic masterpiece. The plank top and log legs were rough hewn, but its form and solid structure were very satisfying. The chairs gave me the most trouble. I had a couple of false starts, and shaping the seats with the tip of the chainsaw took some doing, but in the end they turned out quite well.

I can't say which of these new appointments I enjoyed most. I had been sleeping on a thin ground pad directly on the gravel for a week, so my first night up off the ground, in a bed, with a foam mattress, was a pleasure beyond description. Nevertheless, the usefulness of a flat working surface, even one still sticky with sap, cannot be overemphasized. Sitting on logs and stumps, and trying to prepare and eat your meals on the lid of a cooler is fine when you're camping, but a real table, and a chair, quickly turns a tent into a comfortable home. When I had everything arranged inside, I was pleased see there would still be enough room for Haywood's collapsible camp bed, if he remembered to bring it in on his next visit.

The only thing I lacked was running water. As I worked on the furnishings, I gave this issue a good bit of thought. Jake Larkin, the old trapper who had chosen this site, knew exactly what he was doing. Would he have brought all his water up from the creek by the bucketful? I doubted it. I found it hard to believe he would have been so assiduous with regard to all other aspects of his cabin location, and overlook a primary consideration like water availability. So, the day after I finished building the bed, I decided to do a little snooping around, and within an hour, I discovered his spring. It came as no great surprise. My faith in old Jake proved to be well founded. I'd started by poking and probing around the perimeter of the old cabin, and unearthed a section of rusty pipe along the back wall. It appeared to be pointed upslope, toward the tree line. That made sense, as gravity was the only way to move water out here. So I followed the pipe to see where it led. It was covered with leaf mold and years of debris, and there were stretches where it was missing altogether, but there was enough exposed here and there to keep me on track. When I finally followed it out, it led me to a partially developed spring on a bit of high ground just inside the spruce stand. There was water seeping out of the ground there, but it quickly joined a small swale that drained into the creek, so it was almost impossible to see that it was, indeed, a spring. With a bit of work, it was clear that I could dig out a catch basin and shore up the walls with stone and have a gravity fed water supply down to the cabin. My faith in the old trapper had been justified.

I hung my hat on a bush next to the spring and paced off the distance back down to the chimney. It was a hundred and eight paces – just over a hundred yards. I didn't have a hand level but I judged, using my hat for a reference, the spring to be about twenty feet above the floor of the cabin. Not enough to develop much of a head of pressure, but definitely enough to deliver a steady flow. I'd have to ask Haywood to bring in three rolls of one-inch plastic pipe. By the time I had a cabin, the cabin would have running water. What else could a man want?

***

Once I had the tent well outfitted I began spending half of each day up at the burn, felling, dragging and floating logs out to the creek. I found I could manage about four each morning. Even with a few days off, at the end of three weeks, I had stockpiled over fifty logs, of varying lengths, on the bank awaiting their float trip down to the cabin site. At midday, when I'd break for lunch, I'd leave the chainsaw there at the burn and float a log down the creek on my way back to camp. In all that time, I never encountered one bear in the two-mile stretch of river between my camp and the burn. I never even saw a track. I found this to be very strange, but I was grateful, nonetheless; it made my logging a lot less stressful. And, by the time Haywood was due to return, I had moved eighteen logs down to the cabin site.

I spent my afternoons getting acquainted with my new surroundings. Sometimes I'd take the canoe and scout downstream a few miles, occasionally seeing a moose or bear along the banks. I never encountered a caribou or Thin-horn sheep, but I knew, from previous trips, they were indigenous to the area. They just kept to the high country during the warm summer months. Sometimes I'd walk back into the woods and meadows behind the cabin, or on the far side of the creek. I always wore the .44 when poking around on foot. I also tried to make plenty of noise, especially in the heavy cover. It must have worked, since I never ran into a bear.

I was already a fair hand at reading animal tracks, but I learned a good deal more about it while on these daily excursions. The abundance and variety of game to be found within a mile of the cabin offered a great opportunity for study. I'd brought along a field guide on the subject and carried it with me on my hikes. It came in handy when I ran across a track I didn't recognize. Whenever I saw the game itself I'd go check their tracks immediately after they had moved on. I'd make a point of going back to study the same tracks a few hours later, and then check them again the next day. This was a particularly good way of learning to read the age of a track. It worked best on the larger animals, but then, they were the ones I was most interested in anyway.

***

After a couple of weeks I'd become quite familiar with the country around my camp and had seen, or found sign of, most of the local wildlife. My new stomping grounds were, basically, divided into three distinct environments: the creek and its banks, the mixed spruce and birch woodlands, and the open marshes and meadows. From a purely dietary standpoint, I had the world at my doorstep. Big game notwithstanding, there were fish in the creek, spruce hens, ptarmigan and hares in the woods, and waterfowl in the wetlands. For living off the land, the property I'd purchased couldn't have been better situated.

There was also a very active beaver community nearby that provided me with a good bit of entertainment. They had built a series of three ponds in the meadow behind the spruce stand above my camp. Each pond had one lodge, and I often saw beavers, adults and their kits, working or feeding on the banks. I'd occasionally spend an hour or so just watching them. Whenever one spotted me there would be the inevitable KAPLOOSH of a beaver tail smacking down on the water – their danger signal. Then they'd all dive underwater. Even when I knew it was coming, the tail-slap never failed to startle me.

Haywood had noticed a red fox coming and going on the far bank when we'd first arrived. I now saw her often. She had a litter of at least five kits, maybe six, and I'd see them occasionally during the day. The vixen usually has her litter in mid May but the kits don't leave the den until late June, so I suspected they were no more than two months old. Whenever they would appear, I'd stop whatever I was doing and watch them. I was glad they weren't on my side of the creek. Foxes have the nasty habit of marking their territory with scat. If they claim an area as their own, they shit all over the place. Bears, at least, had the decency to mark their territory by clawing marks high up on a tree.

Every other day, more or less, I'd take along the shotgun and pot a ptarmigan or spruce hen for dinner. Twice I shot geese and cooked them up with rice and a packet of brown gravy mix. They were absolutely delicious, but much more than one person can eat. They were lesser Canadian geese, and they were fat and very rich. At least, nothing went to waste, as I ate the leftovers for breakfast and saved the rendered fat for treating my leather gear. When I wasn't dining on fowl, I'd have grayling, fresh out of the creek. I'd rub them with butter, stuff them with herbs, wrap them in tin foil, and roast them on the coals of the fire. I was using the old stone fireplace for my campfires. The hearth was built up about a foot above ground level and the chimney still worked well enough to draw the smoke up and keep it out of my eyes. It was a pretty good arrangement.

Eating fish or fowl every night can get a little tiresome. There were plenty of snowshoe hares around, so I tried my hand at setting snare traps to catch one. I know it's supposed to be easy, but I never had any luck. I had several opportunities to shoot them but, once I'd started my trapping experiment, I refused to resort to the shotgun. It was a point of honor, you see. When I couldn't face another meal of fish or bird, I'd get into the jerky. Thank God for jerky.

As I had with my days, I fell into a comfortable routine in the evenings. I suppose "evening" doesn't really apply in a country where the sun sets after midnight and rises again three hours later. I'll just call it my post-dinner routine. Most nights, when I had finished eating, I'd do a good clean up of the pots, pans and dishes, and dispose of food scraps and garbage in the fire. If I kept the camp clean there was less chance of having another bear visit. Then I'd spend some time tinkering with the cabin design or working on a project like cleaning out the catch basin for the spring. After that, I'd pour myself a whiskey, fire up my pipe, and update my journal as I had promised Haywood I would do..

I tried to remember all the things I'd seen and done during the day and record them as truly and accurately and objectively as I could. I know I tend to focus more on the activities and the positive aspects of a given trip or adventure and, I'm afraid, I did the same in my Moose Jaw Journal. In fact, to be perfectly honest, I left out things I didn't really want to share with anyone else. If I had been completely objective, I would have pointed out that it wasn't all peaches and cream that first three weeks. The splendid solitude of the first few days gradually gave way to a mild longing for some company and, ultimately, turned to aching loneliness. As much as I detested the hassle and hubbub of civilization, I had to admit, I was, at bottom, a social animal. I liked company. I missed companionship.

Perhaps it was this loneliness that accounted for my occasional feeling that someone else was near. Sometimes I'd feel them watching me from behind, and I'd snap my head around to catch them in the act; but there would be no one there. Other times, I'd hear what I thought was people talking, but I could never make out the words. I attributed this phenomenon to the wind, or the murmur of the waters of the creek. Twice I awoke in the night with the absolute certainty that someone was there, in the darkness of the tent with me. Both times, I got up and lit a candle, only to discover that I was alone. But, on both occasions, after blowing out the candle and returning to bed, the sense of the unseen presence remained. And, once I could smell just the slightest trace of a delicate perfume in the darkness.

Another subject I made light of in my journal was the element of danger. Aside from the bears, there were a number of ugly ways a man could meet his end alone in the Alaska wilderness. That point was driven home to me early in the second week. I was on a logging trip up at the burn and had, foolishly, gotten on the downhill side of a rather large tree I had just felled. I was shifting it with my peavey when the peavey, and my feet, slipped simultaneously and the tree rolled downhill. I found myself sitting in the mud with both legs pinned under it. I hadn't broken any bones, but I was well and truly stuck. It took me the better part of an hour to dig and twist and squirm my way out from under the weight of the trunk. When I had finally extricated myself from beneath the big timber, it occurred to me that such a simple accident could easily spell death to a man out here alone. Alaska didn't forgive stupid mistakes. I'd have to remember that and be more careful. Since this incident spoke volumes about my carelessness, I left it out of the journal.

Then of course, there were the bears. More of them began showing up along the creek below camp every few days. I don't think it was the smell of my cooking, as much as the approaching salmon runs, but by the end of the second week I had counted at least six new bears in the neighborhood. Eight if you counted the two cubs that traveled with their mother, an impressively large, cinnamon colored, grizzly sow. I, for one, counted them; one of the little bastards had nearly gotten me killed. I'd been doing my morning scouting up and down the bank, and was focused on the history lesson in the mud and not paying attention to the here-and-now and, all of a sudden, there was a bear cub in the water to my left. As soon as I registered the danger, the willows on my right exploded and a thousand pounds of hysterical motherhood came crashing out of the bush. I recorded in my journal, "It was one of those moments when you know you have to shoot or shit, or run and shit, or just stand there shitting and die. I ran. The shitting part is none of your business but, thank god, the cinnamon sow was more interested in the welfare of her cub than in catching me. So, for the time being, she let me live." I knew Haywood would enjoy reading that. He has a sick sense of humor.

***

It appeared that all the new bears I saw were grizzlies. There were a few males, properly called "boars", of various ages, and at least two sows with cubs. I didn't know if they ran off the black bears or tolerated them on their fishing grounds, but I never saw another black bear after the grizzlies moved in. I'd done a lot of reading on the habits of the Alaska Brown Bear, or grizzly as they are commonly called, and I had read and heard a good deal of advice regarding how to get along in bear country without being torn to ribbons or eaten outright. The basic rule of thumb was to never get caught between – as in between a sow and her cub, between a bear and his food, or between a bear and escape. That pretty much covered it. If you stayed out of the between situations, you could usually act calm and non-aggressive and sort of shmooze your way out of bear trouble. On the other hand, when you did find yourself in the between situations there was really nothing you could do or say that would keep the bear from tearing you limb-from-limb. It was prudent to carry a big gun.

Of course, as the number of bears increased in a given area, so did the likelihood that, eventually, you'd find yourself between. And, with my frequent trips up to the burn and back, and my evenings of fishing on the water, the odds were tipping, more and more, in favor of another close encounter. Having said that, I did have to live, and I had a cabin to build, and I couldn't very well just hole up in my tent and wait for the bears to go away. I'd just have to be careful and try to avoid them as much as possible. And, of course, I would tote a big gun. I decided to start carrying my .444 Marlin lever-action in addition to the .44 magnum. I didn't really want to shoot one of these guys, but if I had to, I would.

The Marlin itself was, I suppose, the symbol of one of my rights of passage. After proving that I could kill a moose with my tiny 6mm Remington, I realized that little ego trips like that would, one day, get me killed. The guide on that trip had brought it home to me as we sat around the campfire the night I'd shot the moose. He had told me, in no uncertain terms, that danger in the Alaska bush was real, and it wasn't to be taken lightly. I wouldn't always be able to shoot my way out of it with my little pea shooter. A bull moose, or a grizzly, charging through heavy cover, would be the last thing I saw in this life if I didn't grow up and get myself a sensible weapon.

He was right, of course. The Marlin was that sensible weapon. It was, to all intents and purposes, a cannon. It shot a three hundred grain ball and would stop a charging moose or grizzly in his tracks. It was, along with the .416 Rigby, the .375 Holland-and-Holland, and the .45-70 Government, one of the most devastating, close-range, big game rifles you could buy. I'd chosen it over the other three simply as a matter of practicality. The .444 would shoot any round that could be fired from a .44 magnum pistol, and, since my sidearm was a .44 magnum Ruger Blackhawk, I could use the pistol ammunition in both guns. This, of course, would never be necessary unless I ran out of proper rifle ammunition, which retained its hitting power well beyond a hundred yards. I considered that range much preferable to the "point blank" range of the Blackhawk. I hoped my targets would always endeavor to keep some distance between us.

Chapter 7

As the salmon run approached I began watching the creek more each day. One morning I took my coffee down to the water's edge. There were no bears in sight so I sat on a driftwood log next to the canoe and studied the stream. A grayling jumped and took an insect, and his feeding ring expanded across the glassy surface. A minute later another one rolled. I sipped my coffee and watched the rings spread across the water until they merged. I thought about the Chinook, coming up the stream. Their journey, in itself, was a wonder and a mystery. All of them, now making their way upstream would die after they spawned – every last one. It was predestined, yet on they came. What drove them? They sometimes traveled two thousand miles, braving sharks, and seals, and killer whales in the briny deep. Then, in the rivers, they'd run a gauntlet of waterfalls and bears on their mad dash to their spawning grounds. They would not eat along the way, and when they finally arrived, the bruised and battered males would fight one another to the death to win the "honor" of spawning with a female. A single female salmon could produce up to fourteen thousand eggs. Once she had deposited them in the gravel, and the male had fertilized them, they would both die, and the cycle would begin again the following spring.

That this beautiful tragedy would take place far back up in the headwaters of this very creek was a marvelous thing to ponder. From those headwaters, all the way down to the Yukon, the creek was one, continuous thing – like time itself. The salmon, now swimming upstream past Tanana, represented my future. And when they came up the Moose Jaw, to The Varmitage, they would be, simultaneously, my present and Tanana's past. And when they fought and bred and died, up in their spawning beds, for me, they would exist only as a memory.

As I sat, lost in the depths of this philosophical train of thought, it occurred to me that a willow leaf, now falling into the creek up at the headwaters, represented my future also. It would ride the current, down the stream, and pass me tomorrow, or the next day. So, the salmon coming upstream, and the leaf coming down, were both my future – and the creek was all one. The past, the present, and the future could all exist, at the same point in time, at any given point along its course. And the lives of men and bears were nothing more than rings upon its water.

I shook my head to clear my mind. What the hell was I thinking? Maybe I'd been out here too long. The salmon would come soon, and the bears and I would kill and eat as many of them as we could. That was the future. My coffee was gone so I went back up to the cabin for another cup.

***

I would have thought, with all the bear activity in the area, that I wouldn't see much other game. Quite the opposite was true. Moose, along with their calves, came down to the water on a daily basis and, although I knew grizzlies would take a caribou or a moose calf if the opportunity presented itself, the bears didn't seem interested in them at this particular time. Maybe they were fasting before the forthcoming fish fest. Who knows? Whatever the reason, the order of the day seemed to be peaceful coexistence among species. That was fine with me, as the lone representative of one of the species. I wasn't about to do anything to upset the status quo.

On the 10th of July, the first wave of Chinook came up the creek. The bears must have sensed it coming because they began appearing all along the bank on both sides of the creek. After a quick breakfast that morning, I went back into the cache and climbed up on top where I had a pretty good view of the creek for a mile in either direction. The trees obscured some of the view, but, with my binoculars, I was able to count eleven bears on the water.

I stayed back at the cache for the better part of the morning watching them stake out their individual fishing holes. They chased one another this way and that, but their rushes and charges seemed, for the most part, to be more in sport than in earnest. There was the occasional serious confrontation, but, all things considered, they seemed to be having a good time. Just before noon the main body of fish came through and all hell broke loose. The bears entered into a no-holds-barred splashing, lunging and plunging orgy. They came up with wiggling salmon in their giant maws, and impaled them on their hook-like claws, and smashed and kicked them with their paws. Any and every method of getting salmon from the water to the gravel bar was exploited. After watching the spectacle for a few hours I ventured down closer to the creek with my camera. A couple of the bears on my side gave me a passing glance, but didn't seem concerned or threatened by my presence. I took a few shots of them fishing and retreated back to camp.

The feeding frenzy continued for two days. Then there seemed to be a one-day lull, and then another wave of fish came up the creek and the rush was on again. I got so I could recognize a few of the bears by sight. They seemed to return to their same fishing hole each day and not stray too far up or down stream. Several of them had their own, unique, fishing technique. Some merely stood on all fours in midstream and bit at the fish as they came by. Others were more active, spending more time with their heads under water than above. One young adult male seemed to think he was an otter – he dove and swam after the salmon. I timed him as staying underwater for forty-six seconds on one dive, and he came up with a salmon in his mouth.

My old friend, the cinnamon sow with the two first year cubs, had claimed a narrow gravel spit in the middle of the creek a little below my camp, and I spent a good deal of time watching her show them the ropes. The cubs spent as much time chasing one another as they did fishing, and pilfered most of their meals from salmon their mother had dragged onto her bar. She tolerated their thefts, and stood by protectively while they ate, making sure neighboring bears didn't encroach on her domain. When the cubs did get in the water and try to fish, it was interesting to note that they copied their mom's technique exactly. I never actually saw either of them catch anything, but their enthusiasm made up for their lack of success.

The territorial lines between fishing holes were hard to distinguish, but the bears seemed to have spaced themselves roughly fifty yards apart, and they also seemed to alternate sides of the stream. There was really very little trouble during the two days of the first run. The fish were so plentiful everywhere in the creek it wasn't necessary for the bears to invade each other's territories. There was more than enough of the fat, oil rich salmon to go around. The bears didn't have to work very hard for dinner. One old silver tip male would just wade out a little into the current, dip in a thumb, and pull out a plum. Then he'd slowly retreat to the bank, place a forepaw on the still squirming salmon, and start tearing off strips of red meat with his sharp, white teeth. All the bears enjoyed similar success. They gained weight by the hour, and each day they appeared fatter and sleeker, and their coats took on a healthy sheen.

On the first day of the second run the bears began spreading out a little. Most appeared to be moving downstream, perhaps to get the jump on their upstream rivals. A gap opened in their ranks along the top end of my bar, and I decided to take my rod down to the water and have a go at the salmon. It occurred to me at the time that it would be safer to wander upstream, above the landing strip. There were never any bears along the creek up there, even now during the Chinook run, so I could fish without the prospect of getting mauled. But, truth be known, I never felt all that comfortable up there either. Perhaps it was that "yega" thing Manning had mentioned. I supposed the Athabascan elders could have been on to something. Maybe that stretch of water was home to some sort of spirit that even the bears avoided. Each time I made my way downstream from the burn I had the feeling I was not quite alone. It was as if I was in the presence of, well – a presence. I remember experiencing a similar feeling on the battlefield at Gettysburg, and another time in Ireland, atop the Hill of Tara. It was as if those who had died there never completely left the place. So, I opted to brave the real, tangible danger of a bear attack, rather than the unseen, unknown "something" that inhabited that part of the stream.

I took up my rod and wandered down to see if I could join the fun without getting run off. The sow with her two cubs was my biggest concern, as she had proved to be a little more territorial than some of the others, and she was my nearest downstream neighbor. She watched me carefully as I waded a few steps into the water but she showed no sign of aggression, so I tried to remain calm and go about my business. This was more difficult than it sounds under her steady, watchful stare.

I didn't begin fishing immediately upon taking up my position in the stream. I wanted to give my fellow fishermen a little time to get used to my presence. There were also two males upstream of me, one on each bank. Neither seemed to pay me much mind. They just kept to their rhythm of wading, dipping out fish, returning to the bank, and eating. I stood there perhaps five minutes before the sow lost interest in me and waded back out into the current for another snack. Just watching her power as she plowed, chest deep, through the water made me go a little weak in the knees. I recalled our first meeting, and realized how lucky I had been. I knew how quickly she could cover the distance between us if she chose. Grizzlies looked slow and cumbersome, but they weren't. They could come out of the gate with the best of them. They weren't long on endurance running, but they were hell on wheels in the sprint. One had been clocked at forty miles an hour over a short distance, while chasing a truck full of rangers.

After perhaps ten minutes I judged it safe to show a little more activity. I didn't actually let out any line but I made several false casts, waving my rod overhead to replicate a casting motion. One of the boars upstream and the ever-vigilant sow interrupted their fishing to watch me. Neither started in my direction, so I continued waving the rod, slowly, back and forth. After a few minutes they both went about their business, and I breathed a sigh of relief. So far – so good.

I considered quitting while I was ahead, and going back to camp. But, since I'd gone this far, I decided to get a line wet. I freed my fly from the hook-keeper on the butt section of my rod, stripped off thirty feet of line, and cast upstream. My red streamer settled in the current, slipped below the surface and drifted down past me. I paid out a little more line and, when nothing struck, flipped the fly back upstream with a roll cast. It had just submerged when – STRIKE! My line went taut and I lifted the rod tip and pulled down hard with my strip hand. The hook set, and the rod bent under a heavy weight. I didn't want any splashing and thrashing on the surface; that would attract the attention of the bears. I didn't want them getting excited and joining the fun. I preferred to land this one by myself. I lowered the rod tip a bit and relaxed my grip on the line. The salmon took up the slack and ran upstream, but, much to my relief it stayed underwater. I let it run half way to the boars, then applied gentle pressure and turned it into the fast water. The tension went out of the rod and I stripped in line as quickly as I could without too much frantic activity. As the salmon came down the current and passed me, I tightened my grip again and the line, once more, went taut. The rod took the fish's weight and bent under the strain. I gave him enough line to run halfway to the sow before turning him. I guided him across, then back up the stream. He was strong and I had to repeat this give-and-take for five runs before I could feel him tiring – all the time keeping mindful of the bears. On one upstream run, I let him go too far, and the boar on the opposite bank stopped his fishing and suddenly stood up in the current to look my way. I was ready to snap the line and make a dash for the camp, but he quickly lost interest when another salmon rolled at his feet and he plunged in after it.

When I judged the salmon to be tired enough, I eased him out of a downstream run and guided him into the shallows where I stood. He was still making swimming motions, but was listing a few degrees to starboard. Very good. Slowly now. As I took in line, a little at a time, he slid across the rocks of the bottom and rolled on his side - KERSPLASH!...KAPLOOSH!...KERPLASH! He started flipping and thrashing in the shallows.

I shot a quick glance both upstream and down. All three bears had gone still and were looking my way. I tried clamping a foot down on top of the frantic fish. It was no good, he was too slippery and he squirted out from under the tread of my boot, churning spray and clattering rocks as he did. I lost my balance and fell backward, sitting down hard in the shallow water at the stream's edge, making an even bigger splash than the salmon had.

The boar on my side of the stream couldn't contain his curiosity. All this splashing about was just too enticing. He began ambling downstream to see what all the excitement was about. I didn't wait. Without bothering to get up out of the water I grabbed a fist sized rock and, unceremoniously, smashed it down on the salmon's head. Then I took hold of the line a foot above the hook, snatched the quivering fish out of the water, scrambled to my feet and made a hasty retreat toward the camp. The sow didn't move, but watched me with interest as I squished and sloshed my way dripping out of the creek, and up the bar, the salmon dangling, stunned and helpless from my hand. If I didn't know better, I would have sworn I saw amusement in those cold, steely, little eyes. There was no salvaging my dignity; at least I escaped with my catch.

When I reached the tent I took a glance back over my shoulder. The inquisitive boar now stood in the creek, water dripping from his chest and paws. All three bears, in fact, were still looking up at me. One of the cubs had even broken off mauling his sibling, and now stood over his vanquished rival watching me in wonder. Maybe I should take a bow. Well, at least my first day among them hadn't gone unnoticed. My neighbors weren't likely to forget that remarkable performance. Maybe that was a good thing. Maybe they would accept my presence now and consider me a danger only to myself. I ducked into the tent, dropped the salmon on the dirt floor and stripped out of my wet things. The day was still young, and I'd have fresh salmon for dinner. All things considered, my little test-run with the bears had been a success.

Chapter 8

Haywood came back in on the fourteenth day of July, Bastille Day for that insufferable French bastard, Gaspard. The bears were still having their way with the salmon, but they seemed to have spread out even more and most of them appeared to be moving downstream. I counted only five adults and two cubs when I took that morning's survey. Haywood's landing caused a bit of a stir in the bear community, but by the time we'd unloaded the plane and shifted the cargo back to camp, they had settled down and were, once again, intent upon their fishing.

It was wonderful to see Haywood again. I had, literally, jogged up to the landing strip to meet his plane. I had so much to tell him, I began talking his leg off before we'd even started unloading the cargo.

He laughed good-naturedly and held up his hands. "Whoa, Gus! The prop hasn't even stopped spinning!"

I laughed too and gave him a bear hug. "You asshole. It's good to see you."

***

We took a break after carrying everything from the plane down to camp. Haywood had brought in several heavy items on this run: a collapsible camp bed, two roles of roofing felt, two rolls of tarpaper, roofing nails, five more gallons of gas for the chainsaw, a cooler full of beer and another, full of ham, bacon, eggs, butter and cheese. There was a twenty-pound sack of onions and another of potatoes and a third of carrots. As if this were not enough, he also presented me with four warm cases of beer, a case of wine and six bottles of Tullamore Dew. He even remembered the hooks and dubbing wax. You could count on Haywood to get it all right.

I opened the cooler and took out a couple bottles of the cold beer. It was a big cooler and he had two cases iced down in it. He'd surprised me with Heineken this time. I developed a taste for it while working in Europe. We toasted, and he sat on his favorite stump and I sat on the cooler.

"So," he said, firing up one of his huge stogies. "Now I'm ready. Tell me about your first stretch in solitary confinement. Looks like you must have been loafing – I don't see much progress on the cabin."

I pointed to the logs stacked below us on the bar and told him about the fifty I'd stockpiled up at the burn. He was impressed. Then I filled him in about getting the roof on the cache and fitting it out with a rope escape ladder. He puffed and nodded his approval. He asked if the bears had given me fishing rights, and I told him about yesterday's debacle. He laughed until he choked, and held up a hand for me to stop until he could recover.

"So," he gasped, "what you're saying is you only caught one fish?" This killed him and he had a relapse of gagging and choking. Tears ran down his cheeks. I hadn't thought it was that funny. I changed the subject.

"Wait 'til you hear this…" I paused for effect.

He took a deep, shuddering breath and dried his eyes with the back of a hand. When he was fully recovered, and I knew I had his attention, I told him about the spring.

"No shit!" He was as excited as I had been when I'd discovered it. He jumped to his feet.

"Show me!" He is, after all, from Missouri.

I led him up to the tree line and a few paces back into the trees. I had dug away all the loose sand and gravel from the bottom and sides of the spring, and lined the resulting catch basin with flat rocks. I'd left a little depression in the lip, so the water could run over and down the slope, into the swale. Haywood looked at it with undisguised enthusiasm. It was as if I'd discovered a gold vein.

"Ah, now, isn't that lovely. No more hauling water up from the creek."

"We'll need some pipe, of course," I told him. "I paced it off. It's just over a hundred yards. Three rolls of one inch black plastic should do the trick. How about adding that to your list for your next visit?"

He was clearly excited. "I've half a mind to jump back in the plane right now and head for the hardware store," he said. I believe he was serious.

"Too late." I reminded him he'd already been into the beer. "It will wait until next time; there's plenty to keep us busy. How long can you stay?"

He gave me a big grin. "Four days! Bastille Day, don't forget! Took a long weekend in honor of all things French – fine wine, shapely legs, stinky cheese, and work stoppages. Don't have to be back until Wednesday evening, or Thursday if worse comes to worst!"

I was delighted. With that much time, we would be able to move all the logs downstream. When we returned to camp from the spring, I showed him the furniture I had built, which all fit inside the tent with room to spare for his collapsible camp bed. He laughed and slapped me on the back.

"Hell, Gus," he said. "All you lack is a good woman and..." He stopped in mid-sentence and grimaced. "Ah, shit Gus, I'm sorry. Just take me out and shoot me."

"It's alright, Haywood," I told him truthfully. "I'm over it."

***

We accomplished a good deal during his visit. We rafted all the logs down from the burn, and cut a few more to boot. Considering the salmon run was well under way, Haywood was astonished to find there were still no bears along that section of the creek, except those near camp. I, of course, attributed their conspicuous absence to the bad juju up there, reasoning that the bears sensed it too, and avoided the place. I considered mentioning it to Haywood, but he seemed oblivious, so I didn't trouble him with my foolish superstitions. I did, however, suggest we scout further upstream to see how much of the creek was bear-free, but Haywood said we should just count our blessings, and get on with the logs before they decided to move back in. We'd been a little concerned how we'd get the logs downstream if we had to run a gauntlet of grizzlies on the way, so the bad vibes, or whatever it was, made our work a lot easier. I agreed to leave well enough alone.

With all our comings and goings, and dragging logs from the water up the bank, the bears near camp finally got disgusted and moved further downstream where they could pursue their fishing undisturbed. I'm sure they were reluctant to give up such a guaranteed source of entertainment, but our dashing and splashing about, and shouting and swearing was, no doubt, a distraction they decided they could live without. This was fine with us. Fortune was smiling on us. When they moved down, a wide stretch of fishing grounds opened up for us right there at camp. We set aside two hours each evening and dedicated them to the catching of salmon. Haywood, as an Alaska resident, could catch as many as he could use for his own personal consumption. He's a big eater. We averaged fifteen per man per evening so, when it came time for him to return home, his little Piper Clipper was bulging with fresh fish.

On the second evening of fishing the mosquitoes were particularly thick over the creek. I had some DEET in my fly vest so I broke it out and rubbed some into my forehead, neck and arms. I offered it to Haywood.

He shook his head. "Got something better," he said, and trotted off up the bank and disappeared inside the tent. I shrugged my shoulders and continued fishing. A few minutes later he came back down to the creek smelling – dare I say it? – lovely.

I cocked an eyebrow at him. "Chanel Number Five?"

He grinned conspiratorially. "Nice 'eh? Believe it or not, this sweet smelling tonic is the world's Numero Uno bug-keeper-awayer!"

This was hard to believe since the gnats and mosquitoes seemed to have completely abandoned me, and were all, now, swarming around Haywood.

"What is it?"

He winked and waved a hand in front of his eyes to clear the insect cloud that had gathered. "Avon's Skin-so-Soft! Donna put me on to it. Not only does it make your skin silky and fragrant, you mix it half-and-half with water and it serves as a great insect repellent." He slapped a mosquito that had landed on his cheek. "Smells good, doesn't it!" Slap…smack…slap.

"Certainly seems to," I observed. I was wondering how long Haywood would endure the feeding frenzy he had inspired. He was a proud man. Slap…Smack.

Finally he could stand it no longer. He dropped his rod and plunged his head into the creek. He came up sputtering and scrubbing furiously at his face and forearms, trying to wash away all traces of the magic tonic.

"Damn it!" he roared. "Must have got the mix wrong. I

could've sworn she said fifty-fifty! Fuckin' bugs are eating me alive! Quick! Throw me the DEET!"

***

That evening, as we sat having our whiskies by the fire, he entertained me with another of his astounding medical opinions.

"It all has to do with body chemistry you see," he began. "Donna says everybody she knows swears by the damned stuff."

I refilled my glass and settled my back against the rocks of the fireplace.

He puffed pensively on his cigar. "But, it only works when your body chemistry sets up a catalytic reaction with the chemicals in Skin-so-Soft to produce a compound that insects find repulsive. Obviously, there are exceptions to the rule. I represent such an exception."

I lit my pipe. Sometimes these dissertations covered a lot of ground.

He went on. "Now, clearly, my body chemistry is different from that of most humans. I've given this a lot of thought, and I think I have it figured out." He paused to sip his whiskey.

I sat quietly, puffing my pipe and enjoying the sound of his voice. He was full of shit, of course, but it was nice to have the company.

"Are you paying attention?"

I assured him I was, and asked him to please continue.

"It's the double dose of sweetness, you see, that causes the problem. You mix that sweet smelling Skin-so-Soft with my natural sweetness and the resulting compound attracts everything, even insects. Thank god there wasn't a bull moose in rut nearby."

I got a little whiskey down my windpipe and had a coughing fit. He shot me a look of disapproval.

"You laugh? You Doubting Thomas," he said, pointing his cigar at me. "You have the sour bitterness in you that would make you the perfect catalyst for Donna's toxic tonic. I think we should douse you with it, head-to-toe, tomorrow night and conduct an experiment! Stand you stark naked at the water's edge and watch 'em run!"

I explained that I too, had sweetened up a good bit since I'd come to Alaska, and respectfully declined.

He looked at me with sorrow in his eyes. "Oh, ye of little

faith."

He stuck out his glass and I refilled it.

***

We didn't always have a failed tonic experiment to dissect, but most evenings, after a couple hours of fishing and another of dining we'd sit outside and play a game of chess. Since the tent was large enough to accommodate both our beds and the plank table, we left the table inside for foul weather, and did our al fresco dining and drinking on the lid of the big cooler. We also used its broad, flat surface for our chess table. Haywood was impressed with the beautifully carved pieces of my new set. He said they had a nice heft to them. It was true; they were heavier than they looked, as each piece was mounted on a pewter base. At least they wouldn't blow over in the wind.

On the eve of Haywood's departure we had an early dinner and discussed the coming weeks and September's moose hunt. We put together a shopping list for his next visit to The Varmitage while we ate. We also decided the water system was so important he would make a quick run in the morning and bring back the pipe before he flew out for good. After that we played our customary game of chess, in which he check-mated my big grizzly king in less than a dozen moves. Then we retired to the fireside, where we put a good dent in a bottle of Dew and chatted about nothing in particular. I told him about my theory of the creek representing the complete span of time and about the salmon going upstream and the leaves floating down, and the rings upon the water. He told me I was full of shit and that Hard Case had warned me about going loony. He said he didn't think a man could go completely crazy in three weeks, but, somehow, I'd managed it. We both laughed. Maybe I hadn't explained it very well.

Chapter 9

In the morning, over breakfast, we reviewed our strategy for the day. We agreed he'd take off right after breakfast, go to Fairbanks, offload his salmon and get them on ice. Then he'd pick up the pipe and fittings I'd need and bring them straight back. Since this would be a relatively light load, we decided to have him include the cook stove as well. Because of its weight, we had planned on bringing it in after the cabin was complete, but we decided to take advantage of this extra trip and move it now. It was broken down into pieces, so Haywood was certain he could manage it himself. After he returned with that load, he would head out for good, and I wouldn't see him again until moose season. That was almost two months away. His mother was getting on in years and he'd promised to visit her in Missouri. He also had a conference to attend in mid-August. Then, too, most of his staff took their vacations during July and August and someone had to mind the store. There simply was no way he could get back before the second week in September. As moose season ended on the fifteenth, he said he'd come in on the morning of the eleventh. That would give us four full days of hunting.

After breakfast, we carried his gear and the empty chainsaw gas jugs up the path to the landing strip. He said he'd see me around noon, and hopped in his little airplane and roared off into the sky. I went back to camp to wash the breakfast dishes and tidy things up while he was gone. As I was putting away the chess set I discovered that one of the pawns was missing, so I spent a few minutes looking for it in the dirt around the big cooler. I didn't find it, but knew it would turn up sooner or later. I left the rest of the set laying on my bed until it did.

At one o'clock Haywood returned. We offloaded the stove parts and the rolls of black plastic pipe, for which he'd included a bucket full of plumbing fixtures, fittings, and glue. He'd also remembered three rectangular acrylic window panes he had in his garage and brought them along. In addition to the ten gallons of gas he presented me with two new rip chains for the chainsaw. Then he dragged out what looked like a carpet rolled up and wrapped in a blue tarp.

"No sense coming in with half a load," he explained.

"What's this?" I asked.

"House warming present for the cabin. Remember that bearskin rug I had in the Colorado house? Got it out of storage. It'll fit perfect right in front of the stove. Of course, you'll have to make yourself a rocker."

I was dumbfounded. I remembered it; it was a beauty.

"What a fine gift, Haywood. Thanks! I'll keep it wrapped up until the cabin's built."

"You do that! Oh! Almost forgot." He reached back inside the airplane and hauled out a small stainless steel sink. In it were two bottles of whiskey.

"Unlike you engineers, I hate clichés," he said. "I was afraid you'd say something like everything but the kitchen sink, so I brought it along. The Dew's to get you through the winter if I decide to leave you here."

I looked at the gifts and laughed. "Thanks."

We'd already said our goodbyes, and he was running late. He gave me a bear hug and jumped into the cockpit. Then he was off again. I hated to see him go. Eight weeks was a long time to be alone. But, that's the way I wanted it, and the first three weeks on my own in the bush had gone quite well. There was no reason to expect a longer stint to be any more difficult. I killed a couple hours moving the stove parts, gasoline, rolls of pipe and other stuff down to camp. Then I opened a Heineken and sipped it while I poked around looking for the missing pawn. When I didn't find it, I went into the tent and recounted the pieces on my blanket. They were all there. It was possible that I had miscounted them earlier; but, I was sure I hadn't.

***

July and early August were warm, sometimes hot. There were a lot of overcast days, and a little rain now and again, but for the most part it was like summer everywhere else, complete with bugs. Every insect known to man hatched in the river and swarmed to eat me. When it came to voracious insect life, the jungles of Southeast

Asia had nothing on the Interior of Alaska. I had learned a valuable lesson at Haywood's expense and resolved to avoid smelling sweet. That was no problem, when all I had to do was stop bathing. That, of course was a little drastic. I finally came up with a workable solution. Instead of bathing with water in the morning, I'd wipe myself down with 100% DEET. I'd brought in a good supply, and a little goes a long way. I started taking my showers in the evening, after dinner, and before cocktail hour. The water in the sun shower retained its heat nicely, and the smoke from the campfire kept most of the insects at bay. If they were particularly thick on a given evening, I'd reapply the DEET.

Each morning, liberally doused with bug repellent, I'd venture out into the day and go about my business confident I'd survive until dinnertime. I fell into a routine of putting the coffee on the Coleman, and leaving it to perk while I scouted the banks for fresh tracks, paid my morning visit to the woods, and returned to camp for my breakfast. Then I'd spend the day working on the cabin, and when the spirit moved me, taking my rod down to the creek for a little sport. The grayling were always cooperative and the Chinook were still moving up to their spawning grounds. They were decreasing in number every day, but I'd get one every now and then. I'd finally constructed a very small, stone smoker a couple hundred yards downstream of the cabin, back by the willows. It would accommodate four salmon at a time, split to the tail, and hung from the high crossbar.

I'd heard there were pike in the creek and also burbot. I tried a few streamers and a couple of big muddler minnows. I even resorted to a little red-and-white flasher. All to no avail; I caught no pike. They probably disappeared with the rainbow trout back in the sixties. As for the burbot, I decided to save them until the salmon run died down. They were more like a cod, and one had to resort to bait fishing to catch them. I think I mentioned I was a dry fly snob. But, of course, if the salmon petered out and the grayling didn't cooperate, I could, momentarily, set aside my snobbery.

***

The bears came and went with the salmon and I slowly felt myself merging into the landscape and becoming one with the creek and the salmon and the bears. The moon waxed and waned, and the wolves greeted her each night with their sad, mournful songs.

Each day I was treated to some new wonder of the wild. One day a Canadian Lynx came down to the creek for a drink. Another day, an eagle snatched a salmon out of the water as I sat having my morning coffee. And, every day, I'd see the family of red fox playing on the far bank. The vixen and her kits would come down to the water just as I started work on the cabin each morning. They seemed as interested in me as I was in them. I was glad they were on the other side of the creek; they can become pests.

***

What a wonder it was, watching the cabin go up a log at a time. As if by magic, it grew out of the ground and, by the middle of August, it stood, solid and strong on its gravel knoll above the bar. On the twenty-sixth day of the month, I moved from the tent into my new home and slept my first night inside its solid walls. I was very happy with my efforts.

The construction had gone a lot smoother than I had anticipated. Three things allowed me to complete the cabin, single-handed, in one month. First – I'd left the old stone chimney standing smack in the middle of my floor plan. I used it to support a fourteen-foot gin pole, from which I could lift logs with a block-and-tackle. Second – the chainsaw. I had, at one time, contemplated building the cabin with nothing but the old, traditional hand tools. Haywood had convinced me to reconsider, at least, the chainsaw. I was glad I had. Third – the come-along. The block-and-tackle was handy, I used it every day, but the come-along was indispensable. I used it, in conjunction with two skid logs, to slide the wall logs up and into place. As the wall grew higher, and the skid pitch steeper, the come-along proved my most valuable tool.

By using smaller diameter logs I had to use more of them to get the wall height, and I also had to do a lot more scribing and notching and fitting. But one man can only lift so much, even with a block-and-tackle. And, I liked the scribing and notching and fitting. There's a lot of engineering that goes into a good joint. There are four or five different ways you can fit logs together to make a corner. I'd opted for the simple "round notch". It's relatively straightforward, and is probably the best for keeping wind from blowing through, and water from rotting the logs. You only notch the bottom of each log. Water runs off the still round, uncut, top surface. The "saddle notch", like the ones in the toy Lincoln Logs, calls for a notch on both top and bottom. It makes for a nice lock, but it allows water to get into the top of the cut, and your logs rot eventually.

Once I found my rhythm, I managed to lay two courses per day – eight logs. As the walls were fourteen logs high, I was cutting and shaping the top sills after only two weeks of construction, the first week having been devoted to moving the big rocks into place for the foundation piers, getting them all level, and rigging up my gin pole. After I got the top sills beveled to accept the roof pitch, I hoisted the gable logs into place, left them extra long until I set the purlins and ridgepole, and then cut them to the appropriate length and pitch for the roof.

When the walls were all standing and the purlins and ridgepole were set, I dismantled my gin pole, and tore down the old stone chimney. This had to be done before I nailed on the roof decking. When I got the chimney demolished down to the hearth slab I discovered a curious thing. Clearly visible in the mortar of the slab were two footprints, side-by-side. One was the forepaw of an enormous grizzly. The odd thing about it was that it was missing two claws. The track looked malformed; the part of the paw where the missing claws had been was truncated, as if chopped off by an ax, or the steel jaws of a big trap. The other print was human. It was small and slender and delicate, and shallow. It appeared to be the track of a barefoot woman.

To get a better look at them, I swept them free of dirt and debris, and rubbed some goose grease into them to give them better definition. They seemed to come alive, as if they had a story to tell. Since the slab would be below the sills and girder, I decided to leave it intact. The prints made it special, and having it anchored in the earth beneath my cabin would, somehow, bond my new structure to the old – validate it by tying it to the past. Had I but known.

***

After the gin pole and chimney were gone I nailed on the roof decking and laid down the roofing felt and the tarpaper. That only took one day; it wasn't a big place, after all. I had a little trouble with the flashing for the stovepipe. The pitch wasn't quite right, and I hadn't brought along any tin snips. But, necessity is the mother of invention and, using a hammer and wood chisel, and proceeding very slowly, I was able to cut and reshape the flashing to fit the slope of the roof as if it had been special ordered. When that was done, I came down off the roof, dragged the ladder back to the cache, and called it a day. All I needed was one good rain to see if the roof had any leaks.

With the cabin shell complete, I decided it was time for a day off. I'd been going at it without a break since Haywood left. The next morning I lingered over my breakfast a little longer than usual and noted that the fox family, across the creek, seemed to disapprove of my laziness. I could almost see them checking their watches – why isn't that guy working on the cabin? It's nearly nine o'clock. After a bit they gave up on me and went about their business. The kits were ranging off on their own now and the vixen had her hands full keeping track of them. She didn't have time to worry about me.

By ten o'clock the day had warmed nicely, so I took all my laundry down to the creek and gave it a good wash, and left it to rinse in the current. I anchored each item with a rock in the shallows, and set about building a sturdy drying frame out of lodge poles and willows. This wasn't for the laundry; I already had strung a line between two poles for that. This new rack would be used for drying moose and caribou quarters. The season would begin soon, and I wanted to be ready. I built the rack down by the little stone smoker, far enough away from the cabin that it wouldn't bring bears to my doorstep, but close enough that I could keep an eye on it and fire a warning shot if something was bothering my meat.

When I finished the drying rack, I fetched my laundry out of the creek and hung it to dry on the clothesline. By then it was lunchtime so I made up a bag of crackers, cheese and salami, took a bottle of beer out of the creek, and spent the afternoon paddling the canoe up to the burn and then drifting back down again. I took my fly rod along and dragged a spinner behind me on the downstream run, hoping to catch a pike. Again, no luck. That night I spent a couple of hours updating the journal, drank two extra whiskies, and turned in early. I'd had my day of wicked idleness, so tomorrow it was time to get back to work.

The log work was finished; now it was time to mill some lumber. I needed enough two-inch planks to build the porch, outhouse and cabin floors, as well as the door and shutters for the windows. I set up the Alaska Mill, and after three straight days of ripping logs into lumber, I decided I had enough boards. Before I started laying the floor, I took time to dig out an Alaska cooler in the soil under the porch end of the cabin. This is nothing more than a hole in the ground, deep enough to take advantage of the perennial frost line that lies a foot-or-so beneath the surface in the arctic latitudes. I had used one in the tent all summer, to keep cheese and leftovers from spoiling. For the cabin's cooler, I fitted some short boards together to make a box; the floorboards would serve as a lid.

When I was finished building the cooler, I installed the floorboards and built the porch. What a remarkable difference a floor makes! There were a few gaps here and there, but I had been pretty consistent on the thickness of my planks so there weren't too many high or low spots. I hadn't walked on a hard, level surface all summer and I found it to be most pleasant, not to mention, it would give me something to stand on when I cut out the rough openings for the windows.

Next, I spent a couple of days building myself an outhouse. I had several long, slender lodge poles already cut and drying up at tree line. I dug a pit back there, downwind of the cabin, of course, and downstream and down slope from the spring. I dug down as far as I could until I hit permafrost, built a plank floor with a hole in it, and erected the lodge poles, tee pee fashion, around the pit. They could dry just as well standing up as lying down, and this structure would serve until I could build a proper outhouse. I covered the tee pee frame with a big, blue vinyl tarp and left one end loose so I could use it as a door flap. Not pretty, but very serviceable, and I was tired of looking for a new spot in the woods every day.

***

It was time to address the door and windows. I didn't have to cut out the rough opening for the door, as I had built a door frame on the right side of the creek-facing sill before constructing the wall. I had taken pains to keep that frame square and plumb while butting the wall logs against it. So, the door itself was not hard to make or install. In fact, contriving the lift latch and the locking bar was the most difficult part of the whole operation.

The windows were another story altogether. To begin with, I'd wanted them to be small – too small for even a very small bear to come through. This made keeping everything square a bit difficult. To make matters worse, I had forgotten to make the slots and install the splines after I cut out the rough openings in the walls. I had the first two window frames already nailed in when I realized my oversight and had to go back and tear them out. Then, I ran out of gas for the chainsaw half way through cutting the slots for the splines. I'd used a lot more than I had anticipated while ripping the planks for the door and floor. I thought I was out of business until I remembered that Coleman stove fuel is nothing but white gas. Fortunately I had three small cans of two-stroke oil left so I mixed up a gallon for the chainsaw and went back to work.

It took me two full days to set the three windows, and one more to build and hang the shutters. When the last shutter was hung, I stood back and admired my work. I had done it. I had built a cabin, complete with gabled roof, a porch, a solid door and three windows that opened and closed. All that remained was the chinking. I'd already laid a layer of moss between each course of logs as I was building the walls, but I still had to go back over the whole thing and stuff in more, then finish it off with mud. But, to all intents and purposes, The Varmitage was complete.

That night, as I lay in the tent I could feel the chill in the air that marked the end of summer. I'd sensed a subtle difference in the weather with each day of that past week. The animals sensed it too. Autumn was just around the corner and it spiced the air with a subtle urgency. The caribou had started moving down from the high country, and the Chum salmon had begun their run. The bears went at their fishing with more determination now and they seemed more intent than they had been during the Chinook run. There were fierce fights over territory and they appeared more aggressive and menacing than they had in midsummer. I began to see more moose in the meadows and along the creek – wolves too – probably following the caribou down from the high country.

The next morning, as I emerged from the tent, I was greeted with the first real frost of the year. As I stood at the Coleman waiting for the coffee to perk, I looked across the creek and saw the willows were showing their first hint of yellow. I thought back to my musings of the night before. Autumn wasn't coming – it had come. It was as if the summer had died in the night. In another week we'd have the full moon that heralded the new month and the colder weather. It would also mark the beginning of moose season. I looked forward to that. I'd seen enough good bulls in the vicinity that we wouldn't have to go too far afield for our meat. It promised to be a good year; perhaps our best ever.

Chapter 10

With the heavy construction behind me, I spent the final week of August putting the finishing touches on the cabin. The first thing I tackled was the stove. Fortunately, it came in pieces so one man could manage it. I'd kept all the parts wrapped in a tarp behind the tent throughout the summer and I'd forgotten how beautiful and green and shiny it was. I had stubbed in the stovepipe earlier, when I was finishing the roof, so installing the stove only took half a day. I assembled it in place, centered on the back wall, which, being the north wall, had no windows. After I had it all put together I was glad I had chosen it over a barrel stove. It was magnificent. With its cook-top and oven and boiler, it transformed my summer cabin into a home.

I spent the afternoon building a plank counter along the rear half of the east wall and cutting the rough opening for the sink Haywood had donated. He'd torn it out of the guest bathroom when he was remodeling and had never thrown it away; he never throws anything away. It was a small, round, stainless steel basin that had seen better days, but it was perfect for The Varmitage. However, once I started cutting out the hole in the counter top, I wished it were square. It took a little more profanity than usual, but by late afternoon, the counter was finished and the sink installed. I even bored a hole in the floorboards and fed a drainpipe down through it.

The following day, I ran the black plastic pipe from the spring down to the cabin. I left it dry until I had the garden spigot plumbed in above the sink and tied into the main. Then I went back up to the spring, filled the pipe with a dipper so I could get a siphon started, and submerged it in the water and anchored it in place with a big rock. That was that. Fifteen minutes later, I turned on the spigot over the sink, and I had a steady stream of running water. I had a kitchen! I spent the rest of the day moving the furniture out of the tent and into the cabin. I set the bed up back in the northwest corner, as far from the door as possible. I placed the table and chairs, more or less in the middle of the room, but closer to the front wall to allow enough floor space between the table and the stove for the bearskin rug. When everything was in place it looked pretty good, although devoid of anything resembling decoration. I solved this by setting up the chess board on the table as a centerpiece. It was perfect.

***

The days grew shorter as autumn settled on the Moose Jaw country. The sun rose around six in the morning and set about nine in the evening. With the darker nights, I knew I'd need more light than the candles could provide, so I hung two kerosene lamps from the roof beams. When they were in place, I lit a fire in the cook stove just to try it out. The directions warned me to keep my first few fires small to allow the metal and enamel time to "cure". I was glad I'd read them – the terrible metallic fumes coming off my curing stove were enough to drive me out of the cabin. I seriously considered spending one more night in the tent, but after an hour or so, with the windows and door open, it was bearable. That night, as I sat at the table, in a straight back chair, sipping my whiskey and admiring the clever details of my chess pieces, I realized the set was, once again, short a pawn. There was no need to count them; I had set them all up on their designated squares. The white pawn that had occupied the queen's pawn square was missing. Something cold brushed the back of my neck. I turned, but of course, there was nothing there. I looked under the table for the missing pawn, then expanded my search. I looked under the bed, under the stove, and in the boxes I had stacked along the back wall. No pawn.

I returned to the table, topped off my whiskey, and tossed it back in one gulp. Again, I considered spending another night in the tent. But, no, that would not do. I built this cabin, and I was damned well going to sleep in it. If someone, or something, was messing with my chess pieces – fine. I could play that game too. I removed one of the dark pawns from the board and set it off to the side of the table. Then I blew out the kerosene lamps and went to bed. I confess, I did not go to sleep immediately, but eventually the whiskey did its job and I drifted off. In the morning, the table, and the chess pieces were exactly as I'd left them before retiring.

***

After breakfast, I decided it was time to build the rocking chair Haywood had suggested. I poked around in the driftwood piles along the gravel bar and found a couple of slightly curved limb logs that I shaved into rockers. I worked on the chair itself, off and on over the course of two days. In the end, it turned out rather well. I made the seat a tad wider than the kitchen chairs, and I rounded the high parts a little to make it more comfortable on my back. After I carried it into the cabin and situated it near the stove, I sat in it and rocked. It creaked a bit, but it fit my form like it had been custom made with me in mind – which, of course, it had.

I was about to go to the counter and pour myself a celebratory drink when I noticed something had changed on the chess board. I walked over to the table and saw that the dark king – the bear carved of antler – now stood directly in front of the white queen, upon the square of the missing pawn. The dark pawn, which I had removed from the board, was right where I had placed it on the table. Beside it sat the white pawn which had gone missing my first night in the cabin. Like the prodigal son, it appeared he had returned.

"Okay, Yega," I said aloud. "Are we just having a little fun here, or am I to divine some cryptic message in all this?"

To my great relief, I received no answer to this query. I went to the counter, poured myself a double, gestured toward the table with my glass held high, and said, "Don't think you're driving me to drink. I do it happily, without provocation. Now, bugger off."

With that, I tossed back the whiskey, poured another, and took it out onto the porch. When I had imbibed that libation at a more leisurely pace, I went back inside the cabin, boxed up the chess set, and packed it away under the bed. Then I found an empty wine bottle, situated it in the middle of the table, and stuck a candle in it. I decided it would make a much better centerpiece than the ill behaved chess set. It also boasted the utilitarian function of providing me with a little more light.

Chapter 11

On the morning of the twenty-ninth of August, after my first few nights sleeping in the cabin, I was sitting on the front porch, sipping a cup of coffee, when a lone caribou cow wandered down the bar on my side of the creek. She had very thin, gnarled antlers; I had seen her a few times before. It occurred to me that I had never seen her with a calf…hmmm. I was just about fed up, literally, with ptarmigan, spruce hen and fish. So far, I'd only taken small game because I didn't have the time to properly cure or jerk anything bigger, and the days had been too warm to simply hang a quarter up in the cache. But this caribou's timing was, from my point of view, excellent. The days were getting cooler now, and with the cabin complete, I could devote my time to other pursuits. I considered this for a moment, picked up the Marlin, which I kept loaded and ready to hand, and shot the wayward cow in the head.

It was a little closer to camp than I liked, being right there on my door step as it were. I dragged it down to the creek and, with a great deal of heaving and grunting, wrestled it into the canoe. Then I went back up to the cabin, gathered my skinning and boning knives, a ground tarp and a few meat bags, and carried them down to the canoe. The bears had moved off the creek when the salmon runs had ended, but they were still around and would certainly smell fresh blood. I paddled my unfortunate cow a mile downstream, where I felt more comfortable leaving the carcass. Getting her out of the canoe was a lot easier than getting her in. After offloading my rifle and skinning equipment, I spread the ground tarp out on the gravel at the water's edge and hauled her over the gunwales and plopped her on it. The canoe helped out by tipping up on its side in the shallow water. I arranged her at the lower edge of the tarp so the blood would run off during the gutting process and I wouldn't be kneeling in it while I skinned and quartered her.

I quickly opened the stomach cavity and rolled out the guts, then busted into the chest cavity and took out the heart and lung sack. I dragged the steaming pile over to the side, took the heart and liver down to the creek and washed them off; I set them on a clean rock to dry. I'd fry up the liver with some onions for that evening's dinner. There is nothing better than liver, fresh that day, simmered slow with onions. The heart, boiled or pickled, made good sandwich meat when you sliced it thin, if you had bread, that is. I'd have to learn to use my new oven. Then I got out my skinning knife and touched up the edge on a steel. It's amazing how fast you can dull a knife while skinning out an animal. Caribou weren't too bad but a moose's hide was so thick and tough you often had to stop and sharpen your knife two or three times while skinning. I always carried a steel in my knife bag.

I took my time with the skinning. You can ruin the taste of meat if you get a lot of hair on it. It's important to keep it clean and get the carcass cooled down as soon as possible after the kill. Head shots made this a lot easier, since you didn't have a big, gaping hole full of bloodshot meat and bone fragments to deal with. I never shot at running game. I wasn't that good a shot from the off-hand position and, as a young man I had to follow too many wounded deer through miles of briars and thickets or poison oak because I, or one of my hunting companions, had taken a hasty shot. Now, I didn't shoot unless I could take a leaner or rest my rifle on a stump or something equally solid and stable. I also didn't shoot until the game was standing still. Then I'd go for the head. If I hit, the animal died instantly and dropped where it stood, and I didn't have to go chasing it into the next county. If I missed, I missed. No harm, no foul. Sometimes the animal took off for cover and that was that. Other times, it would simply lift its head and wonder if a high-speed hornet had just buzzed its ear, and I'd get another shot. But, as I said, the best thing about the head shot was you didn't ruin any meat.

When I had skinned half the carcass I took off the fore and hind quarter from that side and rinsed them in the shallows. I left them in the water to cool while I went back to my skinning and butchering. After taking the ham and shoulder off the other side, I put them in the creek with the first two and then touched up my knife again before boning out the back strap, neck and brisket. There was a little bloodshot running down the neck muscles from the shock of the three hundred grain ball slamming into the skull, but there was enough good meat for a couple big pots of stew. I rinsed all this and sacked it up in one of the smaller game bags with the heart and liver. Then I dragged my tarp into the creek and gave it a good wash before spreading it out in the sun on the bank. I wanted to let the quarters dry a little before I bagged them up, so I dragged them out of the creek and laid them on the tarp. The day was cool, but it was clear and it wouldn't take the sun and breeze long to dry them.

While they were drying, I washed my knives in the creek, touched up their edges on the steel, bagged up all my gear and stowed it in the canoe. Then I picked up my rifle and wandered downstream and around the bend to see what kind of tracks I could find. For the most part, it was the usual – wolves, moose, beaver and bear. But, for the first time that summer, I found the tracks of four or five Dall sheep. We had seen them in the high country on our two previous trips, but I'd never seen them along the creek. I'd heard they often came down out of the mountains in the autumn, and knew that sooner or later, I'd run across them. Twice, while scouting the banks, I'd noticed sheep hair in wolf scat I'd found, so I knew they were around. The wolves sometimes ran down and killed a weak or injured Thin-horn, but usually they just found a carcass and fed on the carrion. Grizzlies would do the same. Bears and wolves were opportunists and wouldn't pass up anything that offered a meal.

I scouted downstream another half mile after I found the sheep tracks, but didn't find much of interest other than some old tracks of a rather large bull moose. It looked like he'd been using the same crossing for a long time, but since there was nothing to indicate he'd been through there lately, I assumed he'd moved on, no doubt looking for a cow to woo. I didn't want to be away from the carcass too long. The longer you waited, the more chance there was that a bear would have claimed it when you returned. There weren't so many bears on the creek now as there had been during the height of the salmon runs, but as the salmon hadn't completely petered out, there were still bears patrolling the creek. I didn't want to have to fight a grizzly for my dinner so I turned around and started back.

Luck was with me. There was no bear guarding my kill when I returned, so I bagged up the quarters and loaded everything into the canoe. The carcass and guts were still on the gravel bar, and I had no doubt that a bear or a pack of wolves would find it by nightfall and clean everything up for me. I pushed off the bar and paddled my way back upstream. As I rounded the second bend I saw a grizzly sow, followed by one cub ambling down the bar. She stopped just long enough to stand upright, sniff the wind and then pick up the pace a little on her way downstream. Junior trotted along behind, trying to keep up. It was clear she'd detected the scent of the caribou carcass and was on her way to investigate. I imagine she was getting a little tired of salmon for breakfast, lunch and dinner.

Bon appétit, I thought as they disappeared around the bend.

It took me a little over an hour to make my way back upstream. The current was strongest in the channel, so I tried to keep to the calmer water off to the side. The trouble with that tactic is there's not always enough water to float the canoe, so one might have to do a bit of wading and dragging. Still, the day wasn't too cold and the canoe wasn't too heavy, and I had nothing better to do anyway. I beached a couple hundred yards downstream of the cabin, where I'd built the willow drying frame, and carried the quarters up and laid them out to dry. Then I went back down and waded the rest of the way upstream to the cabin, towing the canoe behind me.

After I put all the gear away, I washed up at my new sink and decided to have some lunch. I carried a box of crackers, a tin of sardines and a bottle of beer out to the porch and took up where I'd left off when the caribou had interrupted my morning coffee. I sat on the bench and leaned my back against the sun-warmed logs of the wall and stretched my legs out, resting my heels on the new boards of the porch. I was quite pleased with myself. The cabin still needed a little finish work, but to all intents and purposes, I was ready for guests. It would be another two weeks before Haywood came back, so I had plenty of time to tinker with the little refinements.

It clouded over in the afternoon and the cool breeze picked up strength. I couldn't have asked for a better day for drying and curing the meat. If I got a little frost in the night, so much the better. I could always hang the quarters up in the cache, but the air circulation wasn't so good inside, so I wanted to give them a couple of days on the drying frame before I moved them into storage. I'd have to keep an eye out for bears, but they hadn't been coming too close since I started running the chain saw almost daily. They knew I was here and gave me my space.

After I finished eating lunch, I lit a pipe and savored the rest of my beer. I had rationed myself to one a day since I discovered I was down to ten bottles. I still had plenty of The Legendary, but I wasn't much of a daytime whiskey drinker. I saved that for evenings by the fire. As I sat, I thought about what still needed doing. I had to have a project for the afternoon. Everything in the tent needed to be moved into the cabin, but that didn't appeal to me. I finally decided to make and set all the wall pegs I would need for hanging my gear and clothes. If there was time, I'd also build a couple of high shelves for storage.

When I had finished my beer, I took my folding saw and hatchet and wandered up into the spruce stand. There were plenty of ready-made pegs sticking out of the spruce trunks – hard, dead snags of broken branches, just waiting for me to come and harvest them. Within twenty minutes I had more peg stock than I needed. I didn't take anything less than three quarters of an inch thick. I intended to hang up everything from heavy coats to sacks of potatoes and carrots. I didn't want them snapping under the weight.

I set up shop on a stump near the cabin and cut about forty pegs, all eight inches long. I planned to anchor them three inches in the wall and I wanted five inches of peg sticking out. After I got them all cut to length, I used my pocketknife to taper the butts a little so they'd slip into the pilot holes before I pounded them home with a wooden mallet. This cutting and whittling took longer than I thought, and I began thinking how good another Heineken would taste. I was saved from myself by the arrival of two more caribou. I caught the movement out of the corner of my eye and looked up. Here they came, wandering slowly down the bar, following almost in the tracks of the unfortunate cow I'd shot that morning. I put down my tools and stood quietly in the shadow of the cabin and watched them mosey by. They stopped briefly and gave the cabin a quick sniff and visual inspection, deemed it of no interest, and continued their stroll. They never saw me. They must have smelled the blood when they neared the canoe and displayed a little anxiety by trotting a few yards up the bar, then looking back over their shoulders at the evil on the bank. They stared at it for a minute and then, tails twitching nervously, they trotted off into the cover of the willows. It reminded me I had to go wash out the inside of the canoe before it got any colder. If the caribou smelled the blood a bear would too. Bears were notorious for biting holes in rafts or breaking up canoes in the backcountry. There was a lot of debate as to why they did this. My theory was that hunters and fishermen usually left their boats smelling like fish or blood or rancid meat, and the bears came to the smell. They wrecked the boats because they thought they were food, or because they were enraged when they discovered they weren't food and just busted them up for spite.

It didn't take long to wash out the canoe. I simply walked it a little way out into the creek, tipped it up on edge until it took on a few inches of water and then scrubbed the bottom out with a pig bristle brush I had brought along for just that purpose. I repeated this a few times, giving it a good rinse in the end, and then dragged it back up onto the gravel and upended it to drip dry. When I'd finished, I went back up to the cabin and spent the rest of the afternoon inside, boring pilot holes in the logs for my wooden pegs. I used an old fashioned brace and bit. I only had to drill three inches into the logs, but it was all overhead work. After five holes I had to give my arms a rest, so I went out to the porch and dragged the bench in so I'd have something to stand on. This made things much easier, and by dinnertime I had set all the pegs and hung up my coats and jackets and anything else I wanted to keep from under foot. I drove several pegs into the wall above the counter and these provided a place to hang pots and pans and towels and such. I even put pegs over the door and windows, after all, I needed places to hang up my fly-rod and shotgun and rifle. What better place than over the door and windows – it added a decorative touch. After I'd hung up everything hangable, I stepped back to admire my work. I was very pleased with my efforts; the cabin was beginning to take on that "lived-in" look.

The evening was cool and clear, but the stars were so beautiful, I cooked dinner outside, on the Coleman. I fried up the fresh liver with the last of my onions, and sat on the porch steps to eat. After dinner I built a small fire inside, poured myself a generous glass of Dew, added a splash of water and got out my journal. I wrote about the caribou that came to breakfast and stayed for dinner. I knew Haywood would appreciate my, somewhat heavy-handed, humor. I wrote for nearly an hour before the long day caught up with me. Then I added another log to the fire and called it a night.

The nights were cold those last two days of August, and there was a frost on the ground each morning. The willows above the gravel bars showed a little more yellow each day and I noticed the beavers had begun coming down to the creek to cut and haul them back to their pond. The cool weather was perfect for the meat, so I left it on the drying rack an extra day before hanging the quarters from the roof poles of the cache. I took the back-strap and stew meat with me when I returned to the cabin, made a stew with some, and stored the rest in the Alaska cooler under the floorboards.

As I sat there, that first night in September, puffing on my pipe and rocking in my new rocking chair, I thought how lucky I was to have had this summer. It would all be over in two more weeks. Haywood would come and we'd spend a few days hunting and then I'd fly out with him. It saddened me that I'd be leaving this cabin behind until next summer. The time had gone by so quickly. I'd gotten over the initial loneliness and learned to enjoy my own company. I may have been talking to myself a little more than was considered normal, but that didn't make me crazy. I had to have someone to talk to. I didn't have a pet, and I had never been creative enough to conjure up an imaginary friend – even as a little boy.

"So," I said aloud, "I guess you're stuck with me, Gus."

"Could be worse," I answered myself. "I'm a good listener."

I chuckled at this nonsense, poured a whiskey and took it out on the porch to look at the sky, as I always did before turning in. There were a few clouds, and as they slid across the sky, the moon came out from behind them clear and bright. It would be full in just over a week. I could never remember if September's full moon was called the Harvest Moon, or the Hunter's Moon. But it wouldn't really matter this year; Haywood and I would be doing both with regards to our moose. I rapped my knuckles against the door frame.

"Knock on wood", I said aloud.

Chapter 12

The following night the moon was even brighter, and by its silvery light, I found the woman at the water's edge. I had taken the canoe downstream for a mile or so to get a few buckets of mud for chinking the cabin. There was no lack of the stuff near the cabin but the mud downstream had a bit more clay in it and it stuck and dried better. I'd noticed it when I'd been butchering the caribou down there a few days before. I also wanted to scout that bar again for fresh tracks. Haywood would be coming soon and I would need to know the best places to hunt. I'd deliberately chosen the close of day for my trip downstream. There was a better chance of seeing game on the banks at that time, but I didn't see any on the way down.

I beached the canoe on the same bar where I'd left the carcass. There wasn't much left. What the bears hadn't eaten the wolves had. I checked the area for other sign, didn't see anything interesting, so I gathered my mud and headed back upstream. I did see one good bull on my return trip. He was standing chest deep in a slough, a little way back in off the creek. It was only a few bends below the cabin. I thought he might have been the big guy that had made the tracks I'd seen while scouting the banks near my clay pit. I guessed he'd weigh close to twelve hundred pounds, and hoped he'd stick around 'til moose season.

It took no more than ten minutes to paddle the rest of the way home. The day had been quite pleasant, but now there were a few scattered clouds in the sky, and as the sun went down it started getting chilly. As I swung the bow of the canoe toward the shore in front of the cabin I was startled by the cry of a wolf, just upstream and around the bend, and very close. Then other wolves, farther off, joined the chorus, singing to the moon. I had gotten used to their presence, but their mournful keening, wailing voices never failed to send a little shiver down my spine. As I drifted in toward the bank I caught motion out of the corner of my eye and heard the faint clatter of rock on rock from the bar upstream. I squinted my eyes, trying to see what had moved in the dim light. It was too dark. I thought it was probably that first wolf. If so, he was coming in a bit too close. I'd have to run him off. I beached the canoe, toted the buckets of mud up to the cabin, grabbed my jacket and my rifle, and went to investigate.

By the time I walked up around the bend, the moon's light had grown stronger, and my eyes had made their slow adjustment to night vision. I could see pretty well now, and just as the moon slipped behind a cloud, I picked out the shape on the creek bank. Nothing more than a low, dark form really, but I knew the ground well here, and it wasn't part of the landscape. I levered a round into the chamber.

I moved cautiously across the gravel toward the mound, watching it all the way for any sign of movement. The clouds parted and I saw a hint of red in the moonlight. As I neared, I realized the red was crosshatched with yellow – a plaid shirt. Then I saw the Levis and I knew it was a body. I broke into a trot, thinking as I did, there was probably no reason to hurry. The body wasn't moving. But when I got close, I could see a wet drag trail coming a few feet out of the water, up across the rocks, ending at the booted feet. The body hadn't washed up, it had crawled up! And not long ago. I ran the last few steps of the way.

The tangle of red hair and the swell of breasts beneath the sodden plaid shirt left no doubt it was a woman. Her pulse was weak and her breathing shallow and a bit bubbly. The fact that she'd been able to crawl up on the bank coupled with the fact that she was still breathing, although weakly, told me she wasn't your classic drowning victim. Nevertheless, she'd probably swallowed a good bit of creek water and it sounded as if there was some in her lungs. I rolled her up on her side, checked to see if there was anything clogging her mouth, gave her a solid blow between the shoulder blades, then rolled her on her back and gave her about twelve puffs of mouth-to-mouth before I saw her abdomen heave and heard the warning gurgle. I quickly pulled back and rolled her up on her side again as she spewed out a burst of air and river water. We went through this twice more; up on side, clear mouth, flop on back, puff-puff-puke. But the volume of water was less with each discharge.

I continued until she was breathing well on her own and then took off my jacket and covered her with it. I sat back on my haunches and waited for her to recover. While I waited, I studied her. Early thirties; lean; quite tall; lightly freckled; red hair. She was probably pretty, but it was impossible to tell because of the bruising and the mud. Scalp wound, swollen and puckered but not bleeding; three long fingernails on the right hand, all the rest dirty and broken; minor scratches on face and backs of hands; left cheek bruised and puffy; hair tangled with twigs, grass and mud. No watch, no jewelry, no kit of any sort.

I wondered how she'd come to be in the river and assumed her raft or canoe must have capsized in the rapids up in the narrows. But the leather hiking boots didn't fit that theory. Float trippers favored rubber – hip boots, waders, ducks, even wellies. But, if she'd been hiking, how'd she get in the river? I'd been thinking this over for a while when it occurred to me that she should have come around by now. I checked her breathing and pulse. They seemed steady and strong, but she had not yet regained consciousness.

The sun had been down a good hour now and the earth was loosing its heat. I couldn't wait for her to come around. I had to get her back to the cabin before hypothermia set in, if it hadn't already. Before I moved her I felt her all over for broken bones. Everything seemed intact, and the shoulders, elbows and knees appeared to be in working order. So I sat her up, got one arm behind her back and the other under her legs, lifted and carried her back to the cabin. The moon lit my path.

She probably didn't weigh much stripped down, but with her wet clothes and boots, she was a load. I'd gotten in pretty good shape over the summer with all the chopping, dragging, cutting and lifting of logs. But it took me over ten minutes, with several rest stops en route, to get her back to the cabin. I kept hoping she'd come around and maybe help out a bit by walking, but she never stirred. When I finally reached the cabin, the wolves, now up on the ridge, took up their song again. They sounded disappointed. Perhaps they felt I'd cheated them.

I didn't want to lay her on the bed in her wet clothes, so I deposited her on the bearskin in front of the cold stove. It was still relatively warm in the cabin from the day's sun, but it was quite dark. I lit a candle. Since I'd worked up a pretty good sweat carrying her up from the river, I toweled off my face and took a couple of minutes to catch my breath and let my heart settle to a slower beat. Then I set about getting her out of her wet clothes.

I started with her sodden leather boots. No socks. Odd, but I didn't have time to ponder. I unbuckled her belt and skinned her out of the tight jeans; I thought I would have to cut them off her, but with a bit of shifting and tugging, they finally cooperated. No panties either – at the time I assumed they'd peeled off with the tight, wet jeans. I was more concerned with what I found, and didn't find, under the flannel shirt. She wore no thermal undergarment or bra. This was September in Alaska after all. Instead, I found three ugly, parallel groves running from her left shoulder blade to the small of her back. They were deep – not deep enough to expose bone, but deep enough to be very painful. The spread between them made it clear they had been made by the claws of a very large bear. A grizzly's claws are non-retractile; even when they walk each claw leaves a clear print. Something stirred in the back of my mind. I recalled the print of the three-toed bear in the hearth stone, beneath the floor I now knelt upon. And, I recalled the small, human footprint beside it. Coincidence, I thought, the hearth stone had been there before the original cabin was built. The bear that had made that track would be long since dead. There was no way that same bear could be responsible for the wounds I was studying. No, these wounds had been suffered recently. They were not fresh today, because they appeared partially healed, as if the bear had raked her some days earlier and the wounds had been cleaned and dressed. But, there were no bandages. Everything I discovered about this woman posed a new question. If I could keep her alive, it would be interesting to hear her tale.

When I'd stripped off the last of her clothes, I rubbed her down with a towel and hefted her up off the bearskin and settled her in the bed. I covered her with a polar fleece blanket and added a wool one over that. Then I set about laying a fire in the stove. I knew I should try to get some hot liquid into her, but it took longer to heat water on the camp stove than it did to warm up the cabin. Within twenty minutes the interior was toasty and the redhead felt warm to the touch. At least hypothermia wouldn't take her.

With the fire crackling in the stove, I turned my attention to dinner. I took the pot of leftover caribou stew out of the cooler. It wasn't the best stew in the world, due to lack of onions. I'd used the last of them with the liver the night I shot the cow. But, if the redhead came around, I had to have something warm to feed her. I put the pot on the cook top to simmer. I was still cooking most of my meals on the Coleman, which I had moved from the tent and set up outside, between a couple of stumps under the east window. But, since I already had a fire going in the cook stove, and I wanted to keep an eye on my guest, I decided to stay inside. When the broth had warmed a little, I gave it a stir and added a dollop of water to thin it. Then I sat at the table and smoked my pipe and thought about the girl in my bed.

Her breathing and pulse were strong, but she'd been unconscious now for at least three hours. I was no doctor, but I knew that was not good. She should be in a hospital. I had no radio because, as Haywood had pointed out, I'd been an asshole about it. The only way I could contact the outside world was to paddle two days downstream, portage over to Wolf Creek, and then paddle another half day upstream to the town of Chekov and call for help. As I'd have to leave her unattended for a good three days, that wasn't a viable option.

So, I had to keep her alive the best I could until Haywood flew in for our moose hunt. That was nine days away. If I could get her through until then, he could airlift her out to Fairbanks and then come back in. We wouldn't lose more than a day's hunting, and since I'd been keeping track of the bulls, that wouldn't be a hindrance. Keeping her alive was the problem, especially if she remained unconscious.

I knew enough to keep her warm, of course. That should prove easy enough. But, I'd have to do something about the wounds and get some nourishment into her. Water too. Food would be difficult if she didn't regain consciousness. An I.V. was out of the question, so I'd have to try to spoon some broth into her several times a day. Well, I wouldn't worry about that until the morning. If she woke up, the point was moot. If not, I'd have to deal with it.

With her in my bed, I was relegated to the floor. That wasn't truly an inconvenience, as I had the air mattress and sleeping bag I'd used in the tent before I built the bed. They were stored in the tent, so I ducked outside and fetched them. When I returned I gave the stew a stir, and opened the air mattress' valve so it would self-inflate, and spread it out on the bearskin. Then I pulled the sleeping bag out of its stuff-sack and laid it out to fluff. That done, I dipped myself a bowl of stew and sat down to a late dinner.

A few things had been troubling me since I'd undressed her, and as I ate, I thought about them – her lack of socks, the missing undergarments and the lumps and bruises. I finished my stew, set aside my spoon, went over to the sodden pile of her clothes and went through them. I checked the Levis first. They contained no panties. Nor was there any money, identification, matches, pocketknife, toilet paper, or anything one might carry in the woods. The pockets were all empty. Next, I inspected the plaid shirt. The two breast pockets were also empty. There was no evidence of rips or tears in the fabric, so it was clear she had not been wearing it when the bear raked her. I pondered this for a bit. She'd been attacked by a bear, someone had cleaned and dressed her wounds, and subsequently she'd wound up in the river wearing a different shirt and inappropriate gear for the country and season.

"So what do you deduce from all this, my dear Watson?" I asked myself.

"Curious," my inner Watson replied. "Further investigation is indicated."

I took up the candle and carried it to the bed, pulled back the blankets and examined her carefully from head to toe. I hadn't seen a woman for over two months, so I had to remind myself that the inspection was purely scientific. I was looking for clues to what had happened to her. Nevertheless, I started my inspections with her breasts. Okay, I'm a swine.

Swine or no, the breasts proved to have been a fortuitous starting point. Around her left nipple I could just make out what appeared to be a perfect circle of bruises – teeth? It looked like a bite mark, probably human. I looked closer. It was definitely a human bite, but there was a gap in the bruising pattern, perhaps a missing tooth. I could make out where the canines had been and, from their positioning, concluded that the biter was missing a lower incisor just left of center. I gave the rest of her equal scrutiny, front and back. There were two other issues that puzzled me. First, her feet showed no signs of trauma; no blisters or chaffing or hot spots. The toenails were still painted a startling red, and the color was a little worn, but no chipping. She hadn't walked far in those boots with no socks. Second, around her right ankle there appeared to be some chaffing. It could have been caused by the leather boot top, but if that were the case, I would have expected the same on the left ankle. I studied it closely. It looked more like a rope burn. I couldn't really read "foul play" into any of this. After all, the sex games some people played often included ropes and a little biting. I tried to keep an open mind. Maybe she was just kinky. Then again – maybe not. If not, the bear wasn't the only one who had savaged her.

I covered her with the blankets, poured myself a stiff whiskey, added a splash of water and pulled the rocker over next to the fire. When the whiskey was gone, I banked the fire and turned in. I didn't sleep well, thinking about the girl and all her mysteries. Then too, my sleeping bag was designed for sub-freezing nights in a tent, not a snug, fire-warmed cabin. I finally had to get out of it altogether and just throw it over me like a blanket. Eventually, I dropped off to sleep, but the redhead still wouldn't leave me alone. All the superficial restraints of civilized man are stripped away in his dreams. Just the smell of a woman, naked and close in the darkness, evoked the most erotic fantasies. I slept until the sun had cleared the treetops, perhaps because I was reluctant to emerge from those dreams.

I woke mildly puzzled as to why I was twisted up in my sleeping bag on the cabin floor. The strange events of the evening past came flooding to the surface of my brain. I threw off the sleeping bag and scrambled over to the bed. She was real enough. It hadn't been a dream. I checked her pulse, found it strong and tried to wake her. No luck. Still out cold. Nothing had changed in the night. I padded over to the counter, fixed a pot of coffee and went out into the morning to perk it on the Coleman. After a few pumps on the plunger to build up the gas pressure, I lit the right burner and set the pot on to perk. Then I walked down to the creek, as I did most mornings, to wash my face. This was no longer necessary, what with water plumbed to the sink in the cabin; it was just something I liked to do. I was wearing my hip boots over my trousers; I dropped my shirt on the gravel bar, hung the towel around my neck, and waded out into the stream a few steps. It was cold, so I made it quick. I had just finished washing and was still bent over, drying my face on the towel, when I noticed the bear's reflection in the water in front of me. I gasped and staggered back, looking quickly up at the far bank. It was an enormous grizzly. I had never seen one so large. He was standing fully erect on the far bank, not more than forty yards away. At the sight of him my mouth went dry. For the first time all summer, I experienced real fear. There was something evil about this one. He was staring directly at me. It was as if he were savoring me. 'Perfect,' I thought. I wasn't wearing my gun! I backed slowly toward my own shore. He never moved. When I got to the gravel bar I slowly picked up my shirt and kept walking, as fast as I dared, toward the cabin. When I was safe on the porch, I turned back to look at him. He was still there. He raised a huge paw, then turned and raked his claws down the trunk of a big spruce that stood on the bank. Its bark peeled away in ribbons. Even from that distance, I could see the three long, white stripes against the dark trunk. 'Three claws,' I thought. 'And why does this not surprise me?' As soon as this thought crossed my mind the bear dropped to all fours, wheeled, and disappeared into the dark woods.

I stood on the porch for a few heartbeats, looking at the white grooves on the spruce. When I felt it was safe, I would go over and look at them more closely, but for now, I was content to view them from afar. After my heart stopped pounding I went into the cabin and strapped on the .44 magnum. I also took the rifle when I went back outside to check on the coffee. The water was just beginning to perk, so I leaned the rifle against the wall, lit my pipe and sat down on one of the stumps. I smoked and waited for the coffee to perk and thought about the bear and the redhead.

What was there about the bear and the redhead? I recalled the hearthstone – a bear and a woman. A three-toed bear and a woman. I thought about the three claw marks on the tree, and how they resembled those in the flesh of the woman's back. The bear and the woman were players in the same game. The image of the chess pieces lurked in a corner of my mind – the dark bear king threatening the sleeping lady queen. And the queen's pawn hors de combat. Was I that white pawn? If so, I had no choice in the matter. I had to rejoin the fight. A pawn's role is to protect his queen. As things were, she certainly couldn't defend herself.

The water started bubbling in the little glass dome on top of the pot, so I turned the heat down and let it perk. There's a trick to making good camp coffee. It doesn't really matter how good a pot you have. It's the timing and the heat. You have to crank up the heat full bore until the water just begins to bubble up into the glass dome, then you back it off to simmer and let it plop away until it stops plopping. A good ten-cup pot takes about twenty minutes, start-to-finish. If you leave the heat high after it starts perking you boil it. Boiled coffee sucks. That's the trick – pay attention and turn down the heat after it starts bubbling. Don't think about redheads and bears. When the coffee gets thick enough so it can't perk anymore, it's ready to drink. It occurred to me this mental rambling about making coffee was just a defense mechanism to keep my mind off the girl and the bear. It wasn't working.

The coffee stopped perking, so I poured a cup and considered my predicament. Pretty redhead, naked in my bed, but I couldn't look at her that way because she was wounded, unconscious, and, as it were, under my protection. I'd have to behave myself. I focused on the physical evidence. She'd almost certainly been mauled by the big bear I had just encountered. She had also been sexually molested by a gap-toothed pervert, then dressed up to look "hikey", and dropped in the river. That's a lot to ponder over your first cup of coffee. .

Over my second cup, I wondered how I could keep her alive until she regained consciousness. Somehow, I needed to get some nourishment into her. I supposed the time honored chicken soup remedy was the best I could do. There were no chickens readily available, but there were plenty of ptarmigan and spruce hens. I hadn't done any bird hunting for a while, so I decided it might not be a bad idea to pot a few plump fowl for the benefit of my patient.

When I'd finished my third cup of coffee, I went in and checked on Big Red. That's right, Big Red – I had to call her something. Sleeping Lady would probably have been appropriate, but I recalled that the lady in the Susitna legend never woke up. I was hoping things would turn out better for my tall redhead. And, because she was a tall redhead, Big Red was a pretty good fit. Once I got to know her better I'd probably shorten it to Red.

She was just as I'd left her, sleeping peacefully and breathing well. Satisfied she'd live another couple hours, I grabbed my shotgun and headed back into the high meadow. If I was early enough, I could usually find some game birds in the thin spruce on the other side of the beaver pond. It was only about a quarter mile back in off the river, but the spongy muskeg and the thick slashings made the going slow. It took me about fifteen minutes to reach the beaver pond, and another ten to circle it on the east. In the mud dike that contained the pond, I noticed fresh bear tracks. It was him, alright – three toes on the right forepaw. I felt my scalp tingle a little just looking at his enormous tracks. I certainly didn't want to bump into him any time soon. He appeared to be heading roughly south, so I continued north.

I'd almost circled the pond when a ptarmigan trotted by. Their stupidity cannot be exaggerated. It came dashing out of a thicket on my right, paused, looked at me and then darted into the thicket on my left. Stealth is really lost on this particular species, so I just ran, headlong, into the ticket, flushed it and shot it as it took wing. One in the bag. One was probably not enough as they're barely the size of a small grouse. I tucked it in my pouch and headed back toward the cabin.

The moose surprised me. It must have been browsing in the willows on the other side of the pond when I shot the ptarmigan. They're not renowned for their eyesight but there's nothing wrong with their hearing. So, what with the shot and all, I'd have thought the damned thing would have just faded back into the woods. Maybe the wind or an echo disoriented him, but as I was half way back around the pond, he came sloshing and blowing out of the water, and damned near ran me down. It was a magnificent bull. A giant! Close to six feet across the rack and had to weigh in somewhere around fourteen hundred pounds. I knew there had once been huge moose in the area, but hadn't heard of anything this big in recent years. It was already moose season and I had my moose tag, but you don't tackle a big bull with bird loads. I graciously let him pass. Doubt that he even noticed me. My heart was racing, so I stood there in the mud of the beaver dike for a few minutes and listened to the fading sounds of the moose crashing his way to the river. This seemed to be a day for really big ones. I shook my head and laughed out loud. I loved this place.

The moose had taken an angle that, I assumed, would bring him out on the riverbank about halfway between the landing strip and the burn. I still needed another bird for the soup, so I decided to follow the big fellow's tracks. The heavy cover was full of spruce hens, and I wanted to know where the big bull crossed the creek for future reference. I had also been wondering if anyone else had washed up on the banks. It didn't make sense that Big Red had been traveling alone; it was just possible there might be another body or two lying around. I had a duty to check.

The woods were very thick with deadfall, saplings, devil's club and cranberries. I put up three birds in front of me, but I couldn't get a shot at them. Finally, I flushed a spruce hen and knocked it down with a lucky shot. After spending a few minutes poking around in the brush I located it and tucked it away in my game pouch. Then I continued following the moose's tracks toward the river. It took me another half hour, but eventually, I came out on the creek bank. My guess had been pretty accurate; the moose crossed the creek about a half-mile downstream of the burn.

Before I headed back to the cabin, I paused at the moose crossing long enough to dress the two birds. Best to do that sort of work away from camp. Didn't want to encourage uninvited guests. When I had finished with the birds, I took the time to mark the spot where the moose had come out of the woods so I would remember it. It would be a good place to set up a blind. Then I headed downstream.

I watched for animal tracks and human bodies along the bank. As always, while walking that stretch of river, I found sign of several wolves and weasels and various creatures of the night. There was no evidence of bears, of course, but I'd gotten used to that by now. I still didn't understand it, but it no longer surprised me. Halfway down to the landing strip, I discovered where the big bull moose had come across from the far bank in the night, and filed it in my memory. By ten o'clock I was back at the cabin.

I never return directly to camp without first hanging back a while to study it for danger. You never know what or who has arrived since you left, so I always come in slow. I stopped in the woods on the high bank a hundred yards upstream of The Varmitage. I hunkered down and loaded my pipe and looked the place over. It didn't look like anything had changed since I left. The door was still closed and smoke was curling lazily out of the chimney. I waited a few more minutes, then lit my pipe and set off down the hill. The two birds in my jacket's game pouch bumped against my back with each step as I ambled down the slope to the gravel bar and across the ground to the cabin.

She was still out cold. Hadn't stirred since I left. Man, this was going to be a long nine days. I lay my palm on her forehead and she felt a little hot. Maybe it was my imagination. I had, after all, been exercising, so maybe the heat was my own. I threw off the top cover and pulled the fleece blanket down to her waist. Then I checked her over. I couldn't say what I hoped to learn from this activity but, let's face it, I liked to look at her. As fate would have it, I did notice something. She was drying out. I don't mean she was finally drying out from the drowning. I mean her skin didn't have the sheen to it you see in healthy animals. She appeared to be dehydrating. 'Great,' I thought. 'What next?'

I filled a tin cup with spring water from the tap and sat on the edge of the bed. I lifted her head with one hand while trying to get her to sip the water. I managed only to dribble it down her chin. It obviously wasn't going to work with her flat on her back. Even if I succeeded in getting the water into her mouth, I'd probably drown her. I sat her up a bit so gravity would help keep her mouth open. I had to get an arm around behind her back and snug her up against me to keep her upright. A bit awkward, but effective – also, not unpleasant. After holding her that way and pouring small sips of water into her mouth for about ten minutes, I managed to get nearly a cup into her. She could swallow; that was a plus. And, after a few mouthfuls, it seemed her mouth was cooperating by opening and closing at the appropriate times. Reflex, I supposed.

When she'd finished the cup, I was satisfied that I'd be able to get broth into her using the same approach. I toweled off her chin and chest and belly, then lay her head gently back on the pillow and covered her with a blanket. Since there was nothing more I could do for her, I went outside to set a pot to boil on the Coleman. Holding her close and nursing her had left in me a warmth and contentment I had not felt for a long time. Solitude is wonderful, but it quickly becomes loneliness. It was nice to have another human in the cabin. It was especially nice that the human was female and young and slender. Her vulnerability and mystique only enhanced her charm for me. I found myself whistling softly as I went out into the sunlight.

After I had the water heating, I went back in to rummage

through my kit for anything that might moisturize her skin. The only thing I had was some rendered goose grease I used to waterproof the leather uppers of my boots and soften the leather of my rifle sling and knife sheath. I kept it in a two pound coffee can. It seemed to work well on my skin, as I always rubbed it into the leather with my bare hands, and my hands seemed to benefit from it. I had plenty; the can was three quarters full. Why not?

I fetched the tin off the shelf and, by way of a test, went to my patient and rubbed a little goose grease into the skin of her arm that lay exposed above the blanket. I thought I detected some improvement. The grease would work, but I decided it would have to wait. The first thing she needed was a good washing. I put the can back on the shelf and went outside to see if the water was boiling yet.

It was close, but not quite ready. I hadn't yet tried out the boiler on the side of the cook stove, but since I had a few minutes to kill, I took the time to go in and fill it. When I went back outside, the water on the camp stove was boiling, so I poured a little into the wash basin and set it aside for Red's bath. Then I cut up a few carrots and potatoes and plopped them, with the two birds, into the pot and clapped on the lid. I left it to simmer on the Coleman, then took the basin into the cabin and added enough water out of the tap to cool it. When I judged the temperature to be just right, I snatched a clean washcloth and towel off their pegs and took everything over to the bed.

I worked quickly, trying to wash all of her while the water was warm. I reminded myself to behave and didn't wash any part or parts of her more thoroughly than the rest of her. When I'd washed her top to bottom, front and back, I rubbed her down with the towel and covered her with both blankets. I didn't want her to catch a chill while she was still damp. Then I went about my normal daily chores. Since installing the running water, the only thing I really had to do was lay in a day's supply of firewood. I had planned to do a bit of chinking, but that could wait. I had a little laundry to do, but I usually did it on a day when the sky was clear and there was a breeze to help with the drying. Today was overcast, so once the wood was organized, there really wasn't anything left to do. I decided to resume the aborted goose grease test. I was beginning to suspect my efforts on Big Red's behalf weren't entirely altruistic.

Behave, I reminded myself. I had a brief inner struggle and won. Take that to mean anything you like.

I went back into the cabin, took the can off the shelf, gave it a sniff and decided its scent could do with some improvement. I sat it on the stove lid to warm and soften while I went back to the odds and ends shelf and found Haywood's Skin-so-Soft. There wasn't enough of it to do her much good, but there was enough to lend fragrance to the goose grease. I took it over to the stove, poured it into the coffee can, and stirred it into the grease. After it cooled enough to use, I gave it another sniff, approved, and decided it was time for Red's rub down. I dragged the table and candle closer to the bed and stripped back the blankets. Scratches, broken nails and tangled hair notwithstanding, Big Red was magnificent. I tossed the blankets to the floor at the foot of the bed and began applying the grease. I worked it into the claw marks on her back and then her bottom, and on down the backs of her legs. It appeared to be doing some good, so I rolled her over and concentrated on her front side. I started with her feet, one toe at a time. After a half hour or so I'd done her, quite literally, head to toe, but in reverse order. It goes without saying that I spent a disproportionate amount of time greasing her buttocks and breasts. I'm not a lecher; they just seemed drier than the rest of her.

When I was satisfied that she was well oiled, I collected the blankets from the floor and, reluctantly, covered her. I had a comb, so I broke it out and began combing the snarls and twigs out of her hair. I talked quietly to her as I worked, telling her she would recover soon, and gently chiding her for letting herself fall into such disrepair. It was a pleasant chore, and I was surprised to find her hair was a good bit longer than I had imagined. I combed and groomed her for nearly an hour. When I had finished, I was pleased with the results. I sat back and admired her; she was, indeed, quite lovely.

I went out into the afternoon and satisfied myself that the birds were simmering properly and the Coleman had enough gas. Since my hands were still greasy, I worked on my rifle sling and gun belt and even oiled the leather case of my father's old hip flask. I was amazed to see it was still half full; Haywood must not have noticed it. When I'd finished tending to all my leather gear, I settled down on a stump, enjoyed a few sips from the flask, and basked in the afterglow of the goose greasing. It had been too long since I'd enjoyed a woman and my "nursing" had been as close to sex as I'd come in a very long time. I experienced a few moments of guilt over taking advantage of a helpless female, but they passed quickly in light of the fact that it was all for her own good.

"Right," I said aloud and smiled. "Pervert!"

Chapter 13

My musings were rudely interrupted by the arrival of two strangers in an old aluminum canoe that had seen better days. I could tell it had once been a deep green, but now showed more bare metal than paint, and was badly battered and dented. It had come downstream and now, as its bow swung toward my landing, I studied the two men paddling it. They appeared as battered and shopworn as their canoe. Both were bearded and looked like refugees from a lumber camp. Since moose season had opened yesterday, I assumed they were hunters. But something was wrong; neither was wearing camouflage, and they had nothing in the canoe but their rifles. That was odd, but it was possible that they were camped upstream and had left all their gear at camp while they hunted. Maybe. But I couldn't shake the feeling that something about them was half a bubble off plumb. I recapped the flask and slipped it in my hip pocket. Then, recalling Hard Case's warning, I stood and strapped on the .44 magnum. It would have been rude to carry a rifle or shotgun when greeting visitors. A holstered revolver, on the other hand, was pretty much uniform of the day. You even wore one when chopping wood or fetching water – or washing your face in the stream if you had any sense.

I went down to the landing. The prow of their canoe grated on the shallow bottom just as I reached the gravel bar. The big man in the bow stepped over the side, into the water. He then gripped a gunwale in a massive paw and effortlessly dragged the boat, and its remaining passenger, well up onto the shore.

He was truly enormous, perhaps six foot-seven or eight, and had to weigh well over three hundred pounds. His right eye had a droopy lid and his mouth hung agape in a way that suggested an open circuit somewhere in his wiring. He was dressed in a wool hunting shirt and black rubber waders. They barely fit him. He accessorized this ensemble with a striking leather gun belt and enormous revolver worn on the outside of the waders. The fur flaps of his hat dangled loosely each side of his head, like the ears of a hound. There was a bloody bandage peeking out from under one of the flaps. 'Fashion plate, Alaska style,' I thought.

When the canoe was securely grounded, the smaller man, still seated in the stern, greeted me.

"Howdy," he said flatly. At least he wasn't long winded.

I nodded to him, "Hello."

Since they had come calling, it was incumbent upon them to explain their presence. I waited.

Formal greetings behind us, he surprised me with, "We're neighbors from upstream. I'm Roy McCaslin. That's Larry. He's my brother."

He had a hillbilly accent and drawled each word out slow and easy, but there was an undertone of menace in his voice. There was no way these two were neighbors; I'd been up and down the creek all summer, and had never seen so much as a single man track.

Roy was still talking. "You'll have to excuse Larry, he don't talk much. He's a little slow, and shy around strangers. You understand."

I studied Larry briefly. He was standing ankle deep in water, gazing across the creek, mouth agape, with one forefinger two knuckles deep in his left nostril. I had to admit he didn't exactly radiate intelligence. Roy didn't strike me as brilliant either, but I could tell he was quick and crafty. They both looked mean.

"I understand," I said sincerely. "Didn't know there was anyone else living back in here. How far upstream is your place?"

Roy mulled that over. "About three miles, I reckon. We got a lodge a little way up the first creek beyond the burn. Been in here off-and-on a lotta years now."

Judging from the condition of their canoe, that much, at least, was probably true. I'd never ventured up Deadman Creek, so there could have been a dozen cabins back in there I didn't know about.

"What brings you this far downstream? Hunting?"

I didn't really believe they were hunting moose this far down. They looked like experienced woodsmen. Seasoned veterans knew enough to kill their moose upstream of camp, if possible. It was hard enough paddling an empty canoe against the current. If you had to kill a moose downstream, you did it as close to home as possible. Three miles would be out of range.

"Just doin' our civic duty," Roy said solemnly. "Found a grounded raft couple miles above us. Nobody around. Looked like maybe a bear attack. Lookin' for survivors to see if we could maybe help. Ain't had no visitors, or seen any strange man tracks or woman tracks around lately have ya?"

Nothing about these two inspired trust. I decided to keep Big Red to myself until I got a better read on the McCaslin boys.

"Fraid not," I told them.

Then, to change the course of the conversation, "Haven't heard of any bear attacks lately. You been having trouble up at your place?"

"Nuthin' but," Larry grumbled, studying something on the tip of his finger. Roy ignored him.

"Sure have. Big three toed griz what's got a hard-on for mankind. Damn near tore Larry a new asshole couple weeks back. Caught him comin' down the ladder outa our cache. He was lucky to get back up top and throw down the ladder fore he got him. Kept him treed up there over a hour. If I hadn't come alookin' for him he'd still be up there. Ran the big fucker off with the shotgun – gave him a load 'n the ass. He'll remember me alright."

Larry nodded miserably as Roy talked.

I looked across the creek and thought, 'Three toed griz. How about that?' I decided to keep quiet regarding my encounter with the bear too. I didn't want to give them any reason to hang around. I wanted them to get back in their canoe and go away.

"Only trouble I've had around here was with a cinnamon sow," I said. "Got between her and one of her cubs."

While Roy and I discussed the bears and the weather, and the past salmon run and the opening of moose season, Larry wandered off upstream, scouting along the water's edge. Before he got around the bend, he turned and came back to join us. It was just as well he hadn't gone any further. I didn't know their business, but I didn't want them seeing the deep tracks I'd left while carrying Red from the bank to the cabin. I didn't know why, but I knew I didn't trust these guys, and I didn't want them privy to my business.

When Larry had rejoined us Roy said, "Larry, why don't you just scout around downstream a ways? See if that ole' griz been botherin' our neighbor here."

Larry grunted something unintelligible and headed off downstream.

Roy was stirring the gravel with the toe of one of his hip boots.

His hands were in the pockets of his canvas pants. He looked up suddenly.

"Don't happen to have any coffee on do ya?"

It was clear they were making some kind of re-con run, and he wanted to get a look inside the cabin. I tried to make it just as clear that I wasn't going to invite him in.

"Sorry," I said. "Just threw out the dregs of a pot. I'd brew up another but I'm runnin' kinda low."

"No problem," he said, "just thought it would be neighborly to share a cup of coffee."

He closed one eye and squinted the other at me. He figured he had come up with a clever ploy and was waiting for me to cave in. "Neighborly" is a big deal in the bush. Protocol demanded that you offer visitors the comfort of your campfire and something to eat or drink. Fortunately, I still had my hip flask in my pocket. I produced it.

"Well, this ain't coffee, but if you don't object, I guess we could share a neighborly drop of dew." 'Good lord!' I thought, 'I'm beginning to sound just like them!'

Roy was momentarily taken aback. He knew I'd played a trump card. There was nothing else he could say to work his way into the cabin. I hadn't invited him in, but I'd offered hospitality. That it was offered at the water's edge didn't diminish the gesture one bit.

"Well," he said, recognizing defeat, "mighty neighborly of ya. Don't mind if I do".

He took the offered flask and gave me a silent salute, then put it to his lips and took a delicate sip. He smacked his lips, nodded, took a bigger sip and passed it back to me with an appreciative smile. His teeth were yellow and tobacco stained, and there was a gap in the bottom row. The hair on the nape of my neck bristled.

"Fine whiskey," he pronounced thoughtfully. "Mighty fine indeed."

I don't think he saw my hesitation before taking the flask from his hand. Nor did he notice that I didn't take a drink myself before screwing the cap back on and returning it to my pocket. He was still trying to figure an angle that would get him a look inside the cabin. He didn't lack for persistence.

"Nice place you built here," he offered. "Looks cozy. You got it all fixed up nice inside?"

He cocked his head and grinned at me.

"Not yet." I countered, "Pretty raw still. It'll be a while before I can entertain company."

Larry came trudging back up the bar. When he got to us, he looked pointedly at Roy and shook his head. Clearly, he hadn't found what he'd been looking for. I was beginning to get the uncomfortable feeling that I knew what that was. He began absently picking at a scab on the back of his hand.

"You check the cabin, Roy?" It was as if I weren't even there.

Roy shook his head. "Nope – didn't get no invite."

Larry shifted his pig eyes to me. He tilted his head back a little and cocked it to one side so his right eye could peek out at me from under the droopy lid. When he had me in focus, he studied me as he continued, slowly, picking at the scab. Sizing me up.

He must have decided I was of no consequence because, at length, he announced, "I'll go see."

It stood to reason that Larry wasn't often invited places. So, like a bear, he just went where he pleased; if you wanted to try and stop him, have at it.

A small, speculative smile crossed Roy's lips as he waited for my reaction. I didn't make him wait long. I was still positioned between them and the cabin. They stood with their backs to the creek and they weren't close enough to their canoe to reach their rifles. Larry, of course, was wearing a sidearm, so the winner of this little battle of wills was going to be the guy that got his pistol out first.

I don't know what Larry had in mind, but he took a step in my direction. I pulled out my .44, aimed directly over his shoulder, and squeezed the trigger. KABOOM! Larry let out a startled yelp, clapped a massive paw over his bandaged ear, and dropped to his knees in the mud.

The muzzle blast of a .44 magnum is deafening. It even sounded loud to me, and I was standing behind it. Its effect on the McCaslin boys was most satisfactory. Roy had lost his nasty little smirk, and had thrown both hands up over his head. He was looking at me in terrified astonishment.

I let a few moments pass before I spoke. "Sorry," I said calmly. "Wolf on the far bank. Pushy bastards have been coming in too close lately. I don't like them crowding me. Know what I mean?"

I still had the .44 in my hand. I don't know if either of them could hear yet, but they understood.

Roy studied me for a moment, looked at his brother still kneeling in the mud, and slowly lowered his hands. The fear that had been in his eyes was gone. Now, there was only hatred.

"Sure," he said, his voice flat. "Thanks for the whiskey. We gotta shove off. Lotta river to cover fore dark. Let's go Larry."

With that, he climbed back aboard the canoe and took up his perch in the stern.

At the word whiskey Larry's face took on a look of total bewilderment. It was clear he had no idea what had just happened, but he knew he hadn't been offered a drink. He rose slowly from the mud, glowered at me, and then, as Roy had instructed, walked to the canoe. He took hold of the bow, lifted it effortlessly free of the mud, and waded it out into the current. Then he swung it downstream and stepped in.

I hadn't moved, and I still held the .44 in my right hand. I watched both of them very carefully, making sure they picked up their paddles and not their rifles. It looked like Larry thought about it, but Roy uttered something low and menacing. Larry spit in my direction, then took up his paddle and plunged its blade into the water.

***

I watched them until they were out of pistol range and then I ran back up to the cabin and got my rifle off the porch. I quickly checked to make sure the magazine was full, and levered a cartridge into the chamber. Then I replaced the spent round in the revolver. My hand was steady as I thumbed the fresh cartridge into the cylinder, but my mind was racing. This had been quite a day, I thought. First that damned bear, then I nearly get run over by a moose, and now these guys show up. I ducked inside, checked on Red, and grabbed a box of ammunition for each weapon.

Back outside, I quickly scanned the creek and its banks, then jogged down to what remained of my log pile and crouched in its cover on the upstream side. It was a good position from which to watch the creek below the cabin, and the gravel bar and willows all the way back to my drying rack. I didn't know if the McCaslins would come back soon, but if they did, I'd be ready.

As I waited there in my makeshift bunker, I thought about the implications of their visit. They were looking for Big Red. I was pretty certain of that. I took out my flask, wiped the neck with my shirtsleeve and took a generous sip. I thought about my redhead in their hands, and what they might have done to her. Then I tipped up the flask again and drained it. It made me sick to think about it, but I couldn't get Roy's gap toothed smile out of my mind.

I waited there an hour. When my visitors failed to materialize, I trotted upstream to the place where I'd found Red, cut a willow and rubbed out my tracks all the way back to the porch steps. So far, the McCaslins had no reason to believe the girl was in my cabin; they had just been snooping around. But the deep tracks I had left while carrying her would have told them everything they wanted to know. They weren't very smart, in the conventional sense, but they were woodsmen. If they came back to do some more scouting, they would, no doubt, find my erasures. They'd wonder about them, but still, they wouldn't know for sure.

After my cover-up exercise I went back down to the landing and studied both their boot prints. Larry's wouldn't be hard to recognize; you didn't see many that big, so I focused on Roy's. His showed a faint saw-tooth tread pattern, and they were distinctly smaller than my own. I judged them to be about a size nine. I stored that in my memory for future reference and hoped I'd never cross their tracks again. Somehow, I didn't think I'd be that lucky.

I kept myself busy outside the cabin while the ptarmigan and spruce hen bubbled away with the carrots and potatoes. I also kept a wary eye on the river for the McCaslins' return upstream. It was nearly dark when they finally paddled into sight. I was chopping wood and paused long enough to raise a hand. I wanted them to know I was watching. The silhouette in the stern lifted a hand in acknowledgment, and they continued silently upstream. When they had rounded the bend, I tossed aside my ax and trotted up the path into the spruce. I took up position on the ridge overlooking the landing strip and the next two upstream bends. I'd just ducked into some cover when their canoe came into view. I watched them until they had rounded both bends. There was some cloud cover, but the moon was still quite bright, and it lit the landscape well enough that I could follow their progress until they passed from sight. I breathed a sigh of relief, and then made my way back to the cabin.

The soup smelled rich and good in the cold night air. I went directly to the camp stove, lifted the lid off the pot and decided the birds were thoroughly cooked. I dipped them out of the liquid, boned them out, and returned the tender chunks of meat to the bubbling broth. I left the pot to simmer while I disposed of the carcass bones. I had a pretty good system for that now. I simply took my scraps down to the creek and tossed them across for the fox family. That served two purposes; it kept my camp clean, and it encouraged the foxes to remain on their own bank. When I came back up from the creek, I turned off the stove, carried the steaming pot into the cabin, and left it on the table while I checked on Big Red. She was still out, but she'd obviously stirred. The blanket lay half on the floor and both her arms and one breast were completely exposed. I couldn't help admiring her; she was lovely. Before I covered her I took another close look at the bruising around the exposed nipple. I wanted to see if it matched my memory of Roy's dreadful dental work. Unfortunately, the bruises had faded to a pale yellow, and I couldn't read the pattern for certain. Nevertheless, I brought over the candle and examined her closely for as long as I considered decent. I'm nothing if not diligent.

Having satisfied my scientific curiosity, I thought I'd best get the windows covered so no one could see in. Due to the grade, the east side of the cabin was a few feet higher off the ground than the west, and there was no high ground downstream, so I could leave the window over the sink uncovered. But the windows in the front and west walls needed to be addressed. Anyone standing on the porch could look directly in the front window, and anyone up on the rise, at the top of the path could see in the west window. I dug out a couple of my shirts and hung them on the pegs over those two windows. That did the trick. I also decided to make do with candles, because the kerosene lamps put out quite a bit of light and I didn't want to throw definitive shadows. Once satisfied of our privacy, I set about getting some nourishment into my beautiful patient.

I'd already ladled out a bowl of broth and left it to cool on the table. I carried it to the bedside, propped her up in my arm and spoon fed her until half the bowl was gone. Then her mouth stopped cooperating and I gave it up. A little was better than nothing. I dabbed the misses off her chin and breasts, lay her back on the pillow and covered her with the fleece blanket. The green stove was throwing out plenty of heat so I folded the wool blanket and draped it over the post at the foot of the bed.

Ordinarily, I turned in pretty early. In the long days, of course, that was difficult because it never really got dark. But September had a reasonably normal day/night pattern, even in these latitudes. Lately, I'd been going to bed shortly after sundown and rising at first light. Tonight, however, I thought it might be prudent to stay up late and keep an ear cocked for prowlers. I doubted the McCaslin boys would do anything rash, but I had humiliated the big one, and maybe even ruptured one of his eardrums. Somehow, they didn't look the forgiving kind. On the other hand, they may have decided I was crazy and a little too trigger-happy, and it was best to leave me alone.

I nudged my mind away from the McCaslins and tried to focus on the problem lying in my bed. I went back over everything I could remember since finding her on the bank. Fact: She'd come out of the water, under her own power, sometime around sundown. Fact: She'd nearly drowned, as evidenced by the bilge water I'd pumped out of her. Fact: She wore leather hiking boots with no socks, yet her feet were in pristine condition. Fact: She bore signs of a bear attack, but they were beginning to heal and so, must have been inflicted at least two or three days prior to my finding her. Fact: She was lovely. Fact: I was lonely. Fact: She was helpless and we were alone – bad train of thought. I forced myself back to the issues at hand.

One significant issue was Roy's missing tooth. That troubled me. The bite mark on the breast was faded now, but I remembered it clearly. Ten-to-one Roy had been the biter. Yet, it was hard to imagine Red as a willing recipient of the bite. I thought about the McCaslins' visit. Roy had mentioned a raft. Had they really found a raft upstream? And, if so, was it hers? Had she been alone? Roy had used the word survivors. Did he know there was more than one person missing from the raft, or was he just using the plural form in a general sense? He also asked about any strange "man tracks or woman tracks". He didn't seem a likely candidate for Mr. Political Correctness, and he hadn't cluttered up his sentences with the "he-or-she" bullshit required in every official document. He was a redneck. The only reason he'd even mention "woman track" was if he was hunting a woman. Were they hunting for a woman or just looking for a woman's corpse? They wouldn't be looking in my cabin for a corpse. I thought about this for while.

Finally I decided they'd probably raped her, then knocked her in the head and tossed her into the Moose Jaw. Now, they were just following up, doing their due diligence, checking to see if her body washed up anywhere. It was obvious, since they were still searching, they hadn't found anything yet. They were probably beginning to get worried that, maybe, she had survived. They couldn't let that happen, so they were ranging farther afield. Then again, I could be completely wrong. There might have been two or three people in the raft. It didn't make sense that Red would have been out here alone. There must have been others with her. The McCaslins could be looking for any or all of them. In the end, it really didn't matter. If they came back looking for anything at all, I was going to have to stop them. Larry worried me. The only way to stop him would be to kill him. I didn't want to do that but, like the bears, if I had to, I would.

I stayed awake until midnight. I updated my journal by candlelight and kept the fire low in the stove. Everything about the night seemed normal; even the wolves sang their sad song to the moon. I decided we were safe, at least for the night. Before I crawled into my sleeping bag, I took the candle over and had one last look at her. She looked a lot better than when I'd found her yesterday evening. And, in her vulnerability, she was simply young and beautiful and angelic. It was hard to imagine the mentality that would rape and kill such a delicate creature.

I said, "Red, I think I know what they did to you. But you're safe here. I won't let them hurt you again."

It didn't matter that she couldn't hear or respond. I meant it. Then I snuffed the candle and called it a night.

Chapter 14

I dropped off to sleep as soon as my head hit the pillow. The ordeals of the day had taken their toll. My exhaustion combined with the intoxicating smell of a woman in the cabin produced the most remarkable dreams. Images of giant bears and moose and men, twisted and evil beyond recognition, cavorted across a surreal landscape of ice fields and broken tundra and mist filled woods, foam dripping from their fangs as they howled and bayed like a pack of hounds on the scent. A lone female, tall and sleek and naked, led them on a chase like a fox before the pack, her long white legs flashing through the high grasses and the dark woods, her red hair streaming out behind her in the savage winds of her wake. She plunged through thicket and briar, stream and bog, leaving her small, delicate tracks stark and luminous in the black mud and the soft earth and the wet sands she crossed. The pack pursued her relentlessly, ever closing the gap, slathering and steaming and stamping their monstrous footprints in the landscape she had, only moments before, traversed. They were closing on her, slashing at her willowy, retreating form with glistening fangs and claws.

I started awake, panting and sweating, shaking with fear and dread. The monsters had been so real, I could feel them there in the darkness of the cabin.

I lay there, listening to the pounding of my heart in the silence until my trembling subsided and my mind convinced my ancient, atavistic soul that it had been, indeed, only a dream. I was still very hot and my mouth dry as tinder. I rolled out of the sleeping bag, went to the sink, and gulped a few handfuls of water. Then I went to the bed, satisfied myself that Red was alright, and returned to my bedroll. My mind now at ease, I fell to sleep quickly and didn't wake until first light.

***

The next day passed quietly. I gave Red a sponge bath in the morning, and then spooned a little broth into her. At noon, I gave her more broth, and held her and talked to her quietly afterward. I doubted she could hear me but it was pleasant holding her, and it was nice to have someone to talk to.

All day, while I tended Big Red, I kept a sharp lookout for the McCaslins. They never showed. I was grateful for that, but when I'd done my morning scouting up and down the bar I found the big three toed grizzly's tracks near the drying rack. He probably smelled where the caribou meat had been laying; it had only been a week since I moved it. I was surprised he hadn't damaged the rack. Apparently he was just checking it out. I wished he would move on. Roy had said he'd been up at their place three weeks ago. Now he was hanging around here. Maybe he was making his way downstream, one mile per week. If that were the case, I'd just have to get through the next few days.

That evening I gave Red a good working over with the goose grease. I know, I know. But it seemed to be doing her some good too. Her scratches and cuts were healing nicely, and her skin had taken on the luster of wet ivory in the candlelight. I found myself talking to her again, as I kneaded the oils into her flesh. I told her she was not hurt badly, and that she was safe, and that if she'd just wake up, everything would be okay. I also told her she had beautiful hair and silky skin, and I wished I could keep her. I guess I just liked the sound of my own voice. After the grease rub, I managed to get a full bowl of broth into her. That was definitely doing her some good. Her color looked much better than it had in the morning.

That night, as I sat smoking my pipe by the fireside, I began to worry about her bodily functions. She hadn't eaten much since I'd found her. Hadn't had much water either – but still. I wasn't equipped with diapers or rubber sheets, or any of that. It was just that, well, sooner or later, if she lived, I couldn't keep stuffing food into her without it coming out. While I was thinking of it, I took a bucket over and set it next to the bed.

"Oh, please, Red," I said to her earnestly, "wake up soon."

***

The next morning I broke routine. As soon as I had the coffee perking and the bacon frying on the cook stove, I got out my razor and shaved. My hair had gotten pretty shaggy over the summer also, but there wasn't anything I could do about that. I hadn't thought about how scruffy I looked until I had a look at the

McCaslins. That prompted me to take a close look at my reflection in the creek. It was pretty scary. If she woke up and saw me like that it would probably shock her back into a coma. I decided to pay a bit more attention to my appearance, just in case she came around.

When I'd finished my own primping and preening, I took the comb over and went after her hair again. I must have combed and picked snarls and twigs for over an hour, talking quietly to her all the time. By the time I'd done it was gleaming. Such a lovely color. I've often wondered why we call them redheads. It's really not red at all. Strawberry blond is nearer the mark, but it still doesn't capture the true color. Copper is close, but too harsh. To me, her hair was more like the autumn pelt of a red fox vixen – rich and lustrous and, well, red. Images of the nightmare flashed across my mind, but I shook my head and continued combing. I got so engrossed with the grooming that I burned the coffee and the bacon. That didn't trouble me, I had plenty of both, and the smoke left a pleasant, if somewhat acrid, smell about the cabin.

When I'd finished her hair I broke out the goose grease. Getting low. I'd have to pot a couple more geese to replenish the supply. I sat on the edge of the bed and pulled away the blanket. I admired her for a moment, and then set about the usual anointing ritual. First, I worked on her toes, one little piggy at a time, then her feet, then up each leg to quite high on the inside of the thigh. It was tempting, but I never went that high. Then I'd stop and go over her hips for a while, rolling her slightly so I could get plenty of grease worked into each cheek. Wouldn't want them to dry out now would we. Then I'd lay her flat again, and begin on her belly, working slowly up from there. I was somewhat startled when, in mid breast greasing, I realized her eyes were open, and they were looking into mine. My hands froze on her breasts. Our eyes locked. Hers were a startling shade of green. Time stopped. I felt like the proverbial boy, caught with his hand in the cookie jar.

I quickly removed my hands from her jars. It's hard to imagine, but I'm sure I blushed.

She smiled gently at me. "I really don't mind," she said languidly. "I like it. But I'm very hungry. Do you have any more of that soup?"

Her voice was soft and cultured, but her speech was a little slurred.

I hurried to the stove, dipped out a bowl of broth, took it back to the bedside and offered it to her. My hands were shaking, and the spoon rattled in the bowl. She didn't notice. She was trying to sit up but couldn't.

"Can you help?" she asked. "I know you've been holding me and feeding me for…" she paused and looked mildly puzzled, "for some time. You've been so kind, I hate to impose. But I can't quite manage…." She trailed off again.

I was mortified. Although unconscious she had, obviously, been aware of what was happening to her. I was, to say the least, shamefaced. Nevertheless, I quickly got an arm behind her shoulders, and helped her sit up. Then I spooned broth into her mouth slowly and rejoiced that she was back among the living. The soup was hot so I had to let each spoonful cool a bit before putting it into her mouth. She took each mouthful greedily and her eyes never left the spoon as it dipped, cooled, and then approached her lips. She was so intent upon her eating that she didn't talk at all. The silent activity gave me a bit of time to regain my composure.

When the bowl was empty she asked if she could have more. I advised that she'd better not take too much too fast. She said she understood, and I lay her head back on the pillow.

"Thank you," she said.

I started to cover her with the blanket, but she shook her head.

"Too warm. Besides," she gave me a knowing smile, "since we've been so intimate, I don't see much point in being shy."

Seeing her lying there, naked to the waist, had been quite pleasant before. Now, with her eyes open, it was somewhat discomfiting. I hurriedly took the bowl to the table in an effort to cover my embarrassment.

She said, from the bed, "Now, if you'd be so kind, would you tell me where I am and what day it is and who you are?"

I told her it was Wednesday, Sept. 5th, and I was Gus O'Neill, and she was in my cabin on the Moose Jaw, three miles below Deadman Creek. She looked around the inside of the cabin as she took all this in. Then her eyes came back to me.

"Deadman Creek?"

"That's right," I told her. "The Deadman is the next creek upstream. We're on the Moose Jaw. I found you on the bank just up around the bend on Sunday night. You were half drowned and very nearly frozen. I pumped a little water out of you and carried you here, and have been trying to keep you alive ever since. Looks like I'm a better nurse than I thought."

"Yes. You are. Thank you," she said absently. Her mind seemed to be somewhere else.

I went to the bed and sat down on the edge. She didn't object, but pulled the blanket up to cover her breasts. Not a defensive gesture, just reflex.

"Now," I said, "you know who I am, what is your name?"

"Morgan." She seemed to search her memory for a minute, then smiled. "But you can keep calling me Red if you like."

So, she knew that too. At least she didn't seem upset.

"Is Morgan your first name or last?"

She looked puzzled for a moment, then shrugged her shoulders. "I guess it will have to be both for the time being."

Partial amnesia, I thought. But then, perhaps that was just as well. Maybe she couldn't remember the details of her ordeal. That would account for her relaxed acceptance of our "intimacy". Recently raped women tend to be a little skittish around strange men, especially when they wake up naked and find a strange man fondling their breasts.

"Well, Morgan," I said, "it appears that you've been through a rough time. Do you remember what happened?"

"Rough time?" she said. "Well, yes, I guess I must have if you found me on the river bank. But, I'm a little confused. I've never heard of the Moose Jaw, or Deadman Creek for that matter. Where, exactly, am I?"

It was clear she had either lost, or blocked out, the memory of her session with the McCaslins. 'Just as well,' I thought. 'At least for now.'

So, I told her she was about a hundred and fifty miles northwest of Fairbanks, on Moose Jaw Creek, which ran north and east from here, and dumped into the Yukon, two hundred miles further downstream.

"Fairbanks..." she gasped and stared into my eyes, "Alaska?"

"Yes," I said, "Alaska."

She fainted. At least, I hoped that was all it was. Perhaps the mention of Alaska had been the key that unlocked her memory. If so, remembering had been too much for her. If not, just the fact of her being in Alaska had pushed her over the edge. Either way, I guess I'd have to wait for her to regain consciousness before I'd know.

***

Morgan didn't come around again until evening. I was beginning to get concerned that she may never recover, but apparently the smell of dinner cooking brought her back to the surface. I held her and fed her two bowls of broth. When it was gone she thanked me and then pushed her face into my shoulder and began to cry softly. I set aside the empty bowl and held her in my arms, rocking her gently and stroking the top of her head.

"There, there," I kept saying over and over. "There, there."

What an inane thing to say. Nonetheless, it seemed to help. After a few minutes she stopped sobbing. I kept holding her anyway.

I don't know how long we sat like that, but when a long time had passed she said, "It seems like I've been in a black hole forever. I can't remember anything except your voice and your hands. I've lost so many days. I live in Seattle. I know that. I work for a law firm. I shouldn't be in Alaska."

And then she began to cry again. So I just kept holding her close and saying "There, there". Nurse Gus.

Eventually I realized she'd dropped off to sleep. I eased her head down on the pillow and covered her with the blankets. It was getting a little chilly, so I went to the stove and added more wood to the fire. I hoped tomorrow Morgan would wake and remember what had happened to her. We'd just have to wait and see. I poured myself two fingers of whiskey, and slumped into the rocking chair. I remembered the first words she'd spoken. She had said she didn't mind my rubbing goose grease into her breasts. She'd said she liked it. I knew I was a cad for locking in on this particular part of our conversation. Nevertheless, first thing tomorrow I was going goose hunting. I snuffed out the candle and turned in, as happy and contented as I'd been in a long, long time.

***

I awoke well before first light. There'd been a noise outside the cabin. Something was moving out there. I came awake instantly and reached a hand out of the sleeping bag and found my shotgun. I always kept it handy and loaded with double-aught buckshot.

You never know what's going to happen while you sleep, and if trouble comes in on you, it comes in fast. You don't have time to think about it and select the appropriate gun and load. For in close, in the dark, there's nothing more effective than a twelve bore loaded with double-aught buck.

With my hand gripping the shotgun, I lay quietly in the dark and listened. It wasn't a bear. Bears aren't subtle. They don't worry about being sneaky. Everything was quiet, but I knew someone, or something was out there. I looked at my watch. The luminous dial said it was quarter past one. All was quiet for a good five minutes, then I heard the sound again. Metallic, and close. It sounded like the wind was rattling one of the side flaps on my Coleman stove. I rolled out of the sleeping bag, eased across the floor, and found my flashlight hanging from its lanyard next to the door. With the shotgun in my right hand and the torch in my left, I eased up the locking bar on the door with my knee. The door opens in, so there was an awkward moment as I tried to keep the bar balanced on my knee while hooking the edge of the door with my toe. I was also trying to maintain my balance exclusively on my right foot. A tough combination of tricks, especially in the dark. It didn't work. The bar slipped off my knee and dropped into its cradle with a resounding clunk. I heard something beat an undignified retreat through the willows as I wrestled the bar back up and pulled open the door. I switched on the torch and its beam lanced into the treetops across the creek. I swung it quickly toward the rapidly fading sounds of crashing brush. The light hit the yellow wall of willow leaves and couldn't penetrate. I switched it off and stood listening in the darkness. I thought I heard gravel crunch on the bank upstream, followed by the knee-buckling roar of a bear, a scream, two shots – then silence.

I stood paralyzed for a moment, then switched the torch back on and played its beam over the packed earth surrounding the cabin. I couldn't see anything definitive. I considered going out to investigate, but quite frankly, I was scared. There was someone out there with a gun, not to mention a very angry bear. I could go poking blindly around in the darkness or I could just close and lock the door and go back to bed. Whatever had happened had happened. I could investigate in the morning. I switched off the flashlight and went back into the cabin and lay it with the shotgun next to my sleeping bag before crawling in and zipping up.

Some time before dawn another noise outside brought me immediately out of a restless sleep. Same metallic sound I'd heard earlier. I slid out of the sleeping bag, took up gun and torch and went to the door. This time I hung the torch around my neck by its lanyard so as to have a hand free to deal with the door. I quietly lifted the bar, snatched the door open and stepped into the cold morning air. My left hand instantly found the torch, and I switched it on as I brought it around toward the Coleman. The muzzle of the shotgun followed the beam of light.

Three red foxes stood frozen in the torch light, their eyes shining red in its glare. They'd found their way across the creek.

"Ah, shit," I said, relief flooding through me like a breaking wave.

They hesitated only a moment and then made their way off down toward the water. My heart was thumping. I clicked off the torch and sat down on the floor in the doorway in the moonlight. 'Bloody foxes,' I thought. Now there would be crap all over the place. If I had another night like this one some of it would be mine.

I crawled back into my sleeping bag, but it was no good: I tossed and turned for another hour and finally gave it up. Adrenaline wouldn't let me get back to sleep. I was wired. I'd thought it was the McCaslins coming back around looking for Morgan. It was a good bet they would, and I'd subconsciously known it and been waiting for it, but hadn't really taken any precautions against it. As I lay awake in the predawn I resolved to see to that problem first thing in the morning. The geese would have to wait.

***

When a muted glow lit the east window I noiselessly slid out of the sleeping bag and dressed. Morgan never stirred. I eased the door open and went out into the cold morning. All was quiet; small birds flitted in the willows, but they weren't yet singing. I put together a pot of coffee and set it on the stove to perk. Then I walked down to the creek, washed, visited the privy, and went to have a look around for whatever sign my night callers had left.

I circled the cabin three times, farther out each time. I saw where the foxes had come up from the creek and knew without looking where their exit path had been as I had watched their departure. But I wasn't really interested in fox tracks. I was looking for man tracks and bear tracks, and they were there. Size nine, sawtooth tread – Roy McCaslin. Of course, it would have had to be Roy; he wouldn't send Larry on a covert night recon. He had come out of the woods near the outhouse and gone directly to my west window. Across this stretch, his footprints were close spaced and the heel hardly left any impression at all. It looked as if he spent some time under the window because the ground there was well compacted and several prints and partial prints were in evidence. I was puzzled for a moment by the spruce bough leaned up against the cabin wall. Then I realized he'd brought it along to erase his tracks on his way out. He'd planned to take the same route back to the privy and wipe out both sets of prints as he went. He was good. I'd have to be very careful with our boy Roy. The noise I'd made trying to get the door open had, no doubt, caused him to abandon that plan. He had bolted for the willows, leaving the spruce bough behind.

His exit tracks were wider spaced and appreciably deeper than those of his approach, especially the heels. They led straight into the willows on the upstream side of the cabin. I followed them in. I could only pick up a footprint now and again, but I didn't need them. He'd crashed and broken enough brush as he ran that his path was clearly marked. I tracked him a hundred yards through the willows and came out on the creek bank. That's where he'd run into the bear. Judging by the tracks it had been a very close call. He'd come within forty feet of a very unpleasant demise! His tracks took a radical jag to the left and became much deeper and farther apart all the way down the bar to water. I studied them as I descended the slope to the creek. I didn't walk in his tracks, but kept off to the side six feet or so. The bear had been right behind him, his three toed track superimposed over Roy's until they were fifty feet from the water. At that point the bear had wheeled and bolted into the willows, due to the shots no doubt. When I neared the waterline I could see where Larry had waited. The sand was well torn up where he'd paced up and down the shoreline by the canoe. I found two spent .45-70 brass cases in the gravel. Larry must have fired the shots that drove off the bear; I doubted Roy would have carried a rifle to creep the cabin. I noticed Roy's tracks ended eight feet from the water. This made me smile; he must have vaulted into the canoe without ever breaking stride. The sand bore the impression of the canoe bow with Larry's right boot print stamped clearly in the middle of it. The toe print was, at least, six inches deep. He'd pushed off hard. I guess they were in a hurry to get home. I didn't blame them. They'd had quite a night. I had spooked Roy; he had made a break for the canoe and run into the bear; the bear had chased him down the bar; Larry had fired a couple of shots and the bear retreated. Then Roy had jumped in the canoe and Larry had pushed off as fast as he could. Damn, I wish I had been there to see that. Clever old Roy had hit the nail on the head. The big griz had remembered him alright! Too bad he didn't catch him.

I followed the giant bear's tracks through the willows and up into the spruce stand. Once again I thought of the prints I'd found in the mortar of the old hearth – a woman and a bear. The same bear? Charlie Manning had said Jake Larkin built the old cabin in 1961. That was forty years ago. I knew Grizzlies rarely lived over thirty years, so I couldn't see how this could be the bear that left his print in the mortar. But the track sure looked identical. As I was looking for blood, I kept my focus on the tracks leading me through the willows. I'd think about the mysterious footprints in the hearth later.

After twenty minutes of concentrated search, I turned up no sign of blood, so I assumed Larry had just loosed off a couple of shots to spook the bear. Either that or he was a terrible shot. In any event, he hadn't hit the bear. I let out a little sigh of relief. The last thing I needed was a wounded grizzly prowling around the place.

As I walked back to the cabin, I thought about how to deal with the Roy and Larry problem. They were looking for Morgan, and for whatever reason, suspected I might be harboring her. Now, since the botched recon run and all the sign they'd left behind, they knew I knew they'd been snooping around. If they came again, it wouldn't be sneaky. It would be full-scale frontal assault. I had to prepare for that eventuality.

There's a booby trap you can make with a short piece of three-quarter inch plastic pipe, a pipe cap, a shotgun shell and a nail. It's sort of a mini-claymore. It's not a very effective weapon. Invariably, the plastic pipe blows up when the shell goes off, but it makes a lot of noise. Rigged to a trip wire, it makes a particularly good alarm system. It also scares the shit out of the wire tripper. After their ordeal with the bear, it might be just the thing to keep Roy and Larry busy with their laundry.

I rummaged through Haywood's bucket, found the necessary components and set about constructing three of the little devices. There were even a couple of six inch steel pipe nipples and caps with which I could have made two very nasty ones if I'd wanted. But I wasn't trying to build mini shotguns, so I stuck with the PVC. No urgency in deploying them, that could wait for tonight, but I wanted to have them ready and I didn't want Morgan asking any questions. I put them together while having my morning coffee and tucked them into the spare parts box. Then I made oatmeal for two.

What did mankind ever do before the advent of instant oatmeal? It's one of the greatest inventions of the modern era. Rip open a packet, mix in a little water, heat for a bit and, presto, you have a hot, hearty breakfast, ideal for woodsmen and campers. It also has the added benefit of not smelling like bacon, and therefore, doesn't entice your neighboring bears to join you for the meal.

When the oatmeal was ready I added a little brown sugar, stirred it in and took the two bowls into the cabin. She was still asleep so I sat at the table and ate mine while hers cooled. When I was finished I went to the bed and knelt at the edge. I took her by the shoulder and gave it a gentle squeeze. She opened her eyes. The light in the cabin was not yet good so it took her a moment to focus. Then she gave me a radiant smile.

"Time for my bath?"

I was tempted. "Breakfast." I said, producing the bowl of oatmeal for her inspection. "Think you can handle something a little more solid than broth?"

"What is it?"

"Quaker's finest instant oatmeal, with brown sugar."

I dipped a spoon into the porridge and offered it. She sat up a little, shifted to settle her weight on one elbow and opened her mouth. I inserted the spoon.

"Good?"

"Mmmm." She nodded.

So, I gave her another. She took it and then sagged back on the pillow. She'd spent what little energy she had just sitting up for a few minutes.

"Need a bit of help?" I asked and sat on the edge of the bed so I could prop her up and hold her like usual.

She smiled softly and nodded. I got her up into position, held her close against me and fed her the rest of the oatmeal. When it was gone I set the empty bowl on the chair, but remained where I was for a long time, just holding her. It was nice. Romantic even. Then I felt her tense.

"Oh, God," she said, "I have to…"

Having been a father, I knew the signs. I quickly leaned her head over the bucket so the mess would end up there, rather than on the bedding. I should have let her finish the sentence. I had the wrong end over the bucket. The blanket was not spared. Then her body locked in another spasm and she, once again, suffered the same indignity. So did the bed.

She was crying now and sobbing. "Oh, God, I'm sorry. I'm sorry."

"It's okay, it's okay," I kept saying. 'There, there' didn't seem to fit the occasion. All the time, I was wondering how I was ever going to get this mess cleaned up. Then, as if she could read my mind, she sounded even more miserable.

"I'll clean it up. Please let me clean it up. Oh, god, you shouldn't have to clean it up."

'Damn,' I thought. 'And I had been worried about the foxes!'

***

Twenty minutes later the trauma was over and I, at least, had regained a semblance of composure. Somehow, I'd managed to make the cabin habitable again. I'd had to leave her lying in her own mess until I could bring some hot water and rags over to the bed. Then I cleaned her bottom like one does a baby's. I'd admired that same bottom at length during my scientific inspections. Today I just cleaned it as best I could and tried not to gag. Then I shifted her over to my sleeping bag. Before I zipped her in I stroked her head and gave her a warm smile.

I said, "You don't have any more rounds in that magazine, do you?"

She managed a weak smile in return and shook her head, but the tears of embarrassment leaked out of her eyes and ran down her cheeks. I wiped them away with my thumbs.

Then I stripped the bed and was relieved to see the wool

blanket had been spared. Wool takes forever to dry. But, the cotton sheet and the fleece blanket needed washing, and the foam mattress would need a serious wash and dry. I bundled up the bedding, and with head and nose averted, marched them straight down to the river where I gave them a preliminary rinse before leaving them to soak in the current. I placed a heavy rock on each to keep them from washing away, then went back in and delicately retrieved the mattress. It too went into the creek, but since the foam was of the closed cell variety, it tended to float. I had to give it a complete wash there and then. I wrung out as much water as I could and lay it on the porch to dry.

Back inside, I was happy to see that very little had gotten on the floor. I cleaned that up with a strong solution of Pine Sol, and then opened the windows so the place could air out. It was better already, since I'd left the door open while down at the creek with the laundry.

I went to her side and knelt down and stroked her forehead. "No damage done. The breeze will have all that stuff dry by late afternoon. You okay?"

She'd stopped crying but was clearly weak. Nevertheless her lips curled slightly in a gentle smile.

"Yes." She said. "I am truly sorry. I just couldn't help it."

"I know you couldn't. No harm, no foul." I said. "But, we need to work out a better alarm system for next time. I've set a bucket by the bed. If you think that's going to happen again, cry out 'Oh, shit!' I'll get the idea."

She reached a hand out of the sleeping bag and held it on mine as I stroked her head. She gave it a little squeeze and then closed her eyes and drifted off to sleep.

'Poor thing.' I thought. 'What a thing to have happen. Must have been awful for her.' I remained kneeling beside her, stroking her head with my hand for a while. Then I left her to rest while I set about cleaning up the breakfast dishes. When that was done, I brought in more firewood and topped off the water in the green stove's boiler. It looked as though I might be needing a lot of hot water.

The cloud cover lifted at midday and the sun broke through, so, with the light breeze out of the west, the bedding dried quickly. The foam would have taken another day to dry completely so I rigged a couple of leftover logs into a makeshift mangle and pressed out most of the water. That helped, but there was no way it was going to be ready for action that night.

Just before sundown I scouted up and downstream to mark all the tracks that were there at the time. This would give me a ready reference in the morning. When I got back to the cabin I strung a perimeter trip wire about twenty paces out from the cabin and deployed my mini-claymores. If anyone, or anything came prowling in the night I'd be alerted by the blast of a twelve gauge shot shell detonating. As I said before, the chances of actually wounding or killing an intruder with these things was slim, but the shock factor is superb. And, since they were number four shot loads, there was always the off chance a few of the pellets would find their mark. Hit or miss, the intruder, man or beast, doesn't waste any time making tracks. Better yet, they're so rattled, they never take time to cover those tracks so you get a good read on who came calling. Of course, I already knew who my visitors would be. I just hoped the foxes didn't come back for a while and alarm us all unnecessarily. I'd cleaned up enough shit for one day.

When I came in from setting up my perimeter defenses, I was surprised to find Morgan up and around. She'd commandeered one of my flannel shirts and was padding barefoot around the cabin looking very much at home. She was setting the table with plates and bowls and flatware for two when I came through the door. She looked up as I entered.

"Hello." She said it as if she said the same thing to me every day of our lives when I returned home from work.

"Hello." I replied dubiously. "Should you be out of bed? I mean, are you sure you're not overdoing it?"

"I'm alright, I think. I feel stronger. The oatmeal and the sleep did me good. I wanted to do something to help." She smiled apologetically. "I couldn't fix dinner. I don't know where everything is, but I thought I could lay the table."

I returned her smile. "Not much to fix," I said. "Soup and crackers."

I'd added a few more potatoes and some potherbs to the bird soup during the day, and had left it simmering on the stove while I went about my business.

"I can open a can of something else if you're tired of the soup."

She indicated the soup would be fine, so I took the lid off the pot and gave it a stir. Then I clanged the lid back in place and added a few logs to the fire.

"Be ready in about twenty minutes." I announced professionally. "Isn't much, but we'll cook up a hearty breakfast in the morning."

The fire started popping and snapping as the new wood began to burn. It was getting comfortable in the cabin but it still wasn't what you'd call toasty.

"Are you warm enough in just that shirt?" I asked, thinking how beautiful her hair looked cascading over the green and black checks of the buffalo plaid.

Her feet and legs were bare to well above her knees. She looked down at the shirt and gave it a tug.

"Do you mind?" she asked.

"Not at all," I said. "It never looked better."

I had lit the kerosene lamp that stood in the middle of the table, and in its light I could see she'd brushed out her hair and washed her hands and face. The sleeves of the shirt were still rolled up to her elbows and the skin of her forearms and legs glowed like white marble. It occurred to me that I'd never seen her standing up before. She was taller than I'd imagined. Close to six feet I guessed. The legs below the hem of the shirt were sleek and long and beautifully formed.

"You clean up nice." I said, acknowledging her efforts.

She snorted in derision, but smiled at the compliment nevertheless.

The soup began bubbling, so I brought it to the table and we sat down to eat. She ate one bowl hungrily without speaking and I offered another. She held out her bowl. I filled it and she ate half of it before setting her spoon aside.

"I think I know how I got in the river." Calm, matter-of-fact, but I could tell she was restraining a lot of emotion as she spoke.

"I haven't got it all yet, but it's coming back, a little at a time. I know most of it but there are still some black places. I will tell you about it, but I want to have it all right in my mind first. You understand?"

I had a mouthful of hot soup so I just nodded.

She went on. "I looked around the cabin while you were gone.

I couldn't find a bathroom so I went outside and found your, ah, your facilities – out back. A little primitive, but it has all the comforts of home. Except running water, of course."

I was glad I'd thought to add a few refinements to my privy since the original design. It really was quite nice now. I'd built a box seat with a lid on top of the planks covering the pit. And there was toilet paper in a two pound coffee can on the floor, and stove ashes in a five gallon plastic bucket. Rustic, but still, a pretty good privy. I even provided handy wipes and a spray can of insect repellent.

"Sorry," I said, "I should have told you about the outhouse before I left. We can make it a little more user-friendly if you like."

She smiled. "It's fine as it is."

I remembered to add, "If you have to use the, ah, facilities in the night, wake me. We get the occasional bear so I've rigged an alarm system around the cabin. Don't want you setting it off. I'll go out with you and light your way. She said she wouldn't trouble me, that she would be careful. But I insisted, so she agreed to wake me if the need arose. To move off the subject of booby-traps, I said how happy I was to see her fully recovered.

"Now that you're up and about, I'll show you around tomorrow. It'll be another week before my friend Haywood comes in with his plane, so I'm afraid we'll have to make do until then. Best you know where everything is."

It occurred to me as I said this, how odd it was that, thus far, she hadn't even mentioned getting back to civilization.

She put that one to rest. "I'm in no hurry. I feel safe here with you. I'm very much at home in this cabin. It's almost as if this is where I belong." She laid her hand on mine.

"Now, I hope you don't think I'm awful, but I've eaten, and I'm getting drowsy and wish to go to bed. But there is no mattress on the bed. Am I to share your sleeping bag tonight?"

I thought that would be a very nice arrangement indeed. But I resisted the temptation.

"That would be cozy, but I'm afraid there's room for only one. We'll share the bearskin, though. You get the sleeping bag tonight, and I'll curl up next to you with a blanket. I'll bank the fire so it will be warm enough."

She came over to my side of the table, bent down and kissed me on the forehead and said, "Thank you. I'd argue, but I'm too tuckered."

With that, she crawled into my sleeping bag, and in a matter of minutes, was fast asleep.

I had a small nightcap, banked the fire, and turned in myself. The floor was a bit harder than the cushy air mattress under the sleeping bag, but the bearskin offered some padding. I dropped off to sleep almost as soon as I'd settled under the blanket.

***

I can't imagine that I didn't hear her unzip the sleeping bag, but I woke up instantly when she joined me under the blanket. She put her arms around me and pressed her face into my neck and said, "Please. Just hold me."

I thought she was crying but I couldn't be sure. So I held her. She was still wearing my shirt, but it had come unbuttoned and now covered nothing but her arms and back. I was acutely aware of the pleasant sensation of her naked breasts and belly pressed up against me. Once again, she fell into deep sleep shortly after I wrapped my arms around her. I didn't. How could I? It had been so long, and she smelled so good. But, be that as it may, I must have dozed off sometime during the night because the false light before dawn was soft in the east window when, at last, I awoke. She was still in my arms and breathing in a slow, rhythmic pattern of untroubled sleep. I didn't want to move and wake her so I just lay there holding her and watched the light grow brighter in the window. It was a beautiful way to greet the new day.

Pleasant as it was, my bladder was bursting. Reluctantly, I disentangled our arms and legs. She stirred only slightly as I lay her head gently on the pillow and backed out from under the blanket. Then I went out into the cold morning. In my haste for the tree line I nearly forgot the trip wire. That would have been a nice little surprise on a full bladder! Fortunately, I remembered and stepped over it without breaking stride.

On my way back, I stopped long enough to remove the claymores from their triggers. I pocketed them, but left the trip wires in place. Then I got the coffee brewing and took my morning stroll up and down the water's edge. Not much of interest. It looked like a few caribou had crossed downstream in the night, but no bears, and even better, no McCaslins. I went back and sat outside by the Coleman and smoked a pipe while I waited for the coffee to perk. It was getting colder every morning and this morning there was a frost on the ground. The air was nippy but there was no wind. Still, my fingers were a little stiff as I laid out all the fixings for breakfast. I wouldn't start cooking anything until Morgan was up, but I wanted to have it all ready. The coffee had just started perking when she appeared in the doorway wearing my heavy down jacket; she was also wearing my ducks on her feet. Her hair was a soft, red tangle and her eyes were still swollen with sleep. I thought she was the most beautiful creature I'd ever seen.

"I keep borrowing your clothes," she said apologetically as she passed, headed for the outhouse.

I caught her just before she reached the perimeter wire. I pointed it out and told her to step over it. She looked at me curiously, but did as I said.

"Alarm system," I explained, and pulled one of the claymores out of my pocket so she could see the shotgun shell inside the pipe.

She nodded her understanding and continued up the path to the privy.

While she was gone, I went into the cabin, added some wood to the fire and filled a washbasin with hot water from the boiler. I set it next to the sink with a bar of soap and a towel. Then I went back outside and started breakfast.

**

The bacon had just begun sizzling in the pan when she returned. I watched her step over the trip wire gingerly, taking care to keep my rubber shoes from dropping off her feet. She didn't stop when she got to the cabin. One hand clutched at the front of the baggy coat, holding it closed; she kept her head turned away from me and extended her other hand in a straight-arm gesture as she passed.

"Don't look at me," she pleaded. "I'm a mess."

Then she was through the door and into the cabin.

I turned the flame under the bacon to the lowest setting. She obviously needed a little time to perform her toilet. I didn't want to rush her. It took fifteen minutes or so before the bacon got transparent. I judged she'd be ready in another five so I shifted the strips over to the side of the big pan and cracked four eggs into the sizzling grease. There's nothing like that sound. I covered the pan and poured a cup of coffee for myself. I didn't even know if she drank coffee. I didn't really know much about her at all. I resolved to address that today. She was strong enough now, and it appeared she was handling the mental trauma pretty well. Remarkably well, I thought. I hadn't much experience with rape victims, but I thought it had to be unusual for a recently raped woman to crawl naked into the bed of a strange man. Granted, she came just seeking comfort, but still…

Chapter 15

The eggs had just reached the "easy-over" stage when she reemerged from the cabin. She had combed out her hair and washed, and was wearing her own Levis and shirt under the down jacket, but she was still sporting the ducks. Her lips shone with a transparent luster, which I credited to Chap-stick, since I didn't have much lipstick in my kit. All in all, she looked good. Better than good – lovely.

I raised the coffee pot toward her.

"Please." She said.

I poured her a cup. "Sorry I don't have any cream. There's condensed milk if you like."

"No," she said, taking the offered cup in both hands. "I've learned to drink it black. Thanks."

"How do you like your eggs?" I asked.

"Scrambled, but any way is fine as long as they're not too runny."

I lifted the lid and let her have a look. The steam and the aroma of the bacon rolled up into the frosty air.

"Mmmm," she said, "they look just right."

I killed the flame under the pan and filled our tin plates. To each I added half a muffin I'd toasted directly over the burner, then carried the plates, steaming, into the cabin. She followed, bringing her mug in one hand and the coffee pot in the other. I indicated the green cook stove, its pipe now glowing a soft rose in the dim interior.

"You can set the coffee on there to keep warm."

She did, then removed the jacket, hung it on one of the wall pegs and came to join me at the table. I watched her as she moved. It was the first time I'd seen her in her own clothes since that first night. Then they'd been sodden rags, covered with mud. I'd laundered them during the first few days, wondering as I did, if she'd ever recover to wear them again. Watching her approach the table, it occurred to me how very happy I was she had. I looked at her with open admiration. She noticed and a blush touched her cheeks, visible even in the dim light. Once again, I marveled at the complexity of women. She knew full well she'd been naked for the better part of her time with me and that I'd bathed and oiled every inch of her many times. Just last night she'd slept naked in my arms and yet, now, catching my eyes on her, fully clothed, she blushed!

The hint of a smile touched her lips and her eyes fell coyly to the floor, then quickly back up to meet mine. She covered her moment of awkwardness with a radiant smile, and echoed the words I had spoken last night.

"I know – I clean up nice."

I returned her smile and admitted, "That you do."

As we ate our breakfast I noted that she had excellent table manners. She sat primly and quite erect, one hand in her lap while she chewed. She also held the fork in her left hand and knife in her right when cutting, European style. I had always been embarrassed by the dining habits of my fellow countrymen when visiting Europe. They tended to lunge forward, mouth agape, to meet each forkful. They took it like a trout hitting a fly. She, on the other hand, simply inclined her head slightly forward as the fork came up. When it neared her lips, her mouth opened, the fork went in, her lips closed, and the fork came out clean. Then she would place it quietly on the edge of her plate and, keeping her mouth closed, chew. She'd either been to a good finishing school or she'd spent some time abroad.

Again, she caught me watching her. She was delicately dabbing the corner of her mouth with a paper towel; I didn't have napkins. This time she didn't blush, but met my gaze fully and with the confidence of a beautiful woman, secure and on her own ground.

"You've been watching me a lot this morning."

There was no hint of annoyance in her voice. She was simply stating a fact and offering it as a topic for discussion.

"I'm sorry..." I began, but she cut me off with a smile and a shake of the head.

"No need," she said. "It's nice."

She paused to sip her coffee, but she kept her eyes on me as she did. Then she set the tin cup back on the table, and once again, patted her lips.

"Last night was nice too. I needed holding. I think you knew that was all it was, and I want to thank you for being – well, for being a gentleman. There were times, during the night, I could tell that it was hard for you."

At the double entendre we both blushed. She laughed and buried her face in her hands. We both laughed. The ice was broken. We had been being quite formal all morning. Now we relaxed.

She went to the stove and lifted the coffee pot and shot me an inquiring glance. I nodded and she brought it to the table. I held out my cup. She rested her left hand on my shoulder as she poured with her right. Then she refilled her own cup and put the pot back on the stove. When she was settled back in her chair she sipped at her coffee for a bit, then, looking me straight in the eye, she took a deep breath.

"You've been very patient, in many ways. And I appreciate it. Last night I had dreams, but they were more than just dreams. I was remembering. It was frightening and awful. That's when I joined you under the blanket and asked you to hold me. I know what happened now, and I'm going to tell you. But first, there's something I need to do. After, I'll tell you everything."

I didn't know where all this was going, but I've learned that the best thing to say in these situations is nothing. So, I said nothing.

She must have taken my silence for acceptance.

"Good," she said. "Have you finished your breakfast?"

I nodded and pushed my plate a few inches away to indicate I was, indeed, done eating.

She went to the shelf, took down the can of goose grease, and brought it to me. I accepted it. Then she walked over to the bearskin and began undressing. I watched in disbelief as she slowly, deliberately, unbuttoned her shirt, took it off, and dropped it to the floor in a heap. She kicked off my shoes, then slipped out of her jeans and dropped them on the pile.

As she stripped, she said, "When I was "sleeping" those first days after you found me, I wasn't truly unconscious. There were times I was conscious of everything. It was as though I was suspended in darkness on the other side of a curtain. I couldn't move or talk or open my eyes, but I could smell and hear and feel. I was so hungry the smell of the soup cooking nearly made me cry. When you fed me I wanted so badly just to say "Thank you, thank you", but I couldn't. When you'd wash me you were very gentle, and your voice was soothing, and your words told me what I needed to hear. I knew you were a kind man. And, when you'd pull back the blanket and start rubbing my toes with the oil I wanted to cry out with pleasure. I could feel your hands, working slowly up my legs, and then on my belly and my breasts, and I wanted you to do more, to go farther. I could feel it in the pressure of your hands that you wanted it too. But, you always stopped, and I thought I might go crazy. This isn't my way of thanking you. I need this for myself. Please."

What could I do? After all, I am a gentleman; and she did say please. I began, as always with her toes. I won't bore you with the details of the next hour or so. At any rate, it's none of your business. You have an imagination; use it. I will tell you that I used the last of the goose grease. And, at her request, I promised to murder a flock of geese before the sun set. It was nearing ten o'clock when, spent but happy, I emerged from the cabin and went through the motions of my daily routine.

My feet found their way up and down the creek bank, and my eyes looked at the yellow of the willows and the blue of the sky and last night's caribou tracks in the mud. My mind, however, was still back in the cabin, on the bearskin rug, where I had left her dozing. I didn't notice the cub until it bawled. Instantly, I snapped out of my reverie. Then I saw the sow, perhaps fifty yards downstream, wading and fishing with her other cub. I froze. Her nose came up and she sloshed a little way upstream, swinging her big head, sniffing the wind and looking my way. The wind was in my face and there was a willow bush between us that provided a good enough screen that she hadn't yet seen me. Her crybaby brat darted across the gravel and plunged into the water, apparently unconcerned at my presence. The sow stood watching it for what seemed an eternity and then, apparently satisfied all was well, she turned and resumed the fishing lesson with the one nearest her. I faded into the willows and quietly made my way back to the cabin. My heart was pounding. That was too close. I had to keep my wits about me. You don't often get a second chance in Alaska. I was now working on my third with this old girl.

After taking the first load of firewood to the cabin, I hauled the foam mattress off the porch and lay it on the willow drying frame.

The wooden rack had worked well with the caribou quarters. It had good exposure to sun, when it shone, and wind, when it blew, which was nearly every day. Its open grillwork provided excellent circulation beneath. The day had warmed and the clouds had broken up and blown away. Now the sun was high in the clear blue sky. Barring rain, the mattress would be dry by nightfall. I gave a fleeting thought to tonight's sleeping arrangements, but recalling my recent encounter with the sow, kept focused on the here-and-now. Still, as I went about my chores, I whistled.

When I went back inside with another load of firewood, Morgan was up and dressed, and busy clearing the table of our breakfast dishes. She looked up and smiled softly as I entered. I took the wood to the box near the stove and dumped it in.

As I filled my pipe bowl with tobacco, I asked her if she minded my smoking inside.

"Not at all," she said. "It has a pleasant aroma. But, you're very kind to ask."

I settled into my rocker, lit the pipe and rocked and puffed, and watched her move about the cabin. I was content.

"Mattress should be dry enough to sleep on tonight," I told her. She said that was nice.

I told her about the bear and the cubs, and warned her to be careful when she went outside. She said she would, she knew about bears. By now it was clear she wasn't really listening. She was thinking of something else. I shut up and just puffed and rocked for another five minutes while she kept puttering and moving things from place to place, and dusting dusty surfaces.

Finally, she put down the kerosene lamp she had been slowly polishing with a rag and said, "That lotion you call goose grease... What is it really?"

I was pleased to know where her mind had been. I wasn't the only one basking in the afterglow.

"Goose grease," I told her.

"Goose grease?" She looked doubtful, like she suspected I was pulling her leg but she wasn't quite sure. "As in the grease of a goose? A real goose?"

I nodded and continued to rock. My pipe had gone out so I knocked out the dottle in the open door of the stove. We had let the fire die down to gray coals.

"I thought you were joking when you said you'd have to kill more geese." She paused, musing for a moment.

Then, still dubious, "Well, whatever it is, it certainly worked wonders on my skin. I can't remember when it's felt so soft and silky. You should bottle it and sell it. You'd make millions."

I smiled. "Can't," I told her. "Special stuff. Sacred even. Not for the masses, they'd abuse it. Probably use it in kinky sexual foreplay. Simply wouldn't do."

"Unthinkable," she agreed. "We should probably keep a little on hand though, for emergency situations."

We both knew it was time to have our serious chat, but we were reluctant to break the spell. We made more small talk for a while, and finally we just fell silent. She came over and sat on my lap and put her arms around me and snuggled her face into my neck.

"Just for a little while longer," she said. "Hold me. Then I'll tell you all of it."

So I held her and rocked her for… I don't know how long. At length, I thought she'd fallen asleep, but then she raised her head and kissed me on the lips and slipped off my lap. She went to the table and sat in one of the chairs. She folded her hands in front of her, took a deep breath, and began.

Chapter 16

"We came up here for the trout and the salmon. We were floating the river in a raft and fly-fishing our way downstream. Jason and I. He's a friend from work. We flew up from Seattle the last week in August. Spent a day in Anchorage, drove up to Fairbanks and flew in here. A bush taxi put us in somewhere called Panner's Bar."

I knew the place; it was thirty miles upstream and popular with the bush pilots because of the long flat gravel bar and relatively small rocks.

She went on. "On the second afternoon a bear attacked us. We'd run aground in the shallows trying to avoid the sweepers on the cut bank. We got out of the raft and were both standing in the water trying to pull it back into the deep channel when this enormous bear came out of nowhere. It hit the raft first, and lunged across as we both dove away into the middle of the river. It raked my back with its claws just as I went under. Jason had been quicker, and the bear didn't get him.

We let the current take us downstream around two or three bends, and then Jason helped me ashore and saw I'd been hurt. All our gear was in the raft so he made me as comfortable as he could and then went back upstream. He found the raft still grounded with two of its bladder tanks punctured, but almost everything was still aboard. He waited until he was sure the bear had gone, then waded across and got our river bags and came back to where he left me. He had to leave the raft where it was. There was no way to move it with two flat bladder tanks.

We had a first-aid kit in one of the bags, and he cleaned my wounds and dressed them with bandages. He was wonderful. He made us a camp there, and tended me all the rest of that day and through the night. But, in the morning, I was running a fever and the pain was quite bad. We didn't have any painkiller so he gave me aspirin, four at a time. It helped a little. Then he went and tried to repair the raft, but it was torn and punctured in more places than he had patches. We knew we'd have to get help.

Two days after the bear had attacked us, two hunters came upstream in a canoe. Jason hailed them and said we were in trouble. They came ashore and looked at my wounds and said they better get me back to their lodge where they had medicine and more bandages. Jason asked if they had a radio and they said they didn't, but they had a bush plane bring in supplies once a week and it was due in a couple of days. We could wait at their lodge until the plane came.

They looked pretty rough – scary really. Both had beards and bad teeth and Okie accents. The smaller of the two looked at my back and did all the talking. The other one was a giant. He seemed a little slow, but did everything the small one told him to do."

'The McCaslins, without question,' I thought. At this point I had a good idea what happened when they got back to the lodge, but I let her go on.

"They asked Jason about the bear that attacked us. They also wanted to know where it had happened, and where we'd left the raft and what was still aboard. He answered all their questions but, I could tell, they made him very nervous.

Their canoe wasn't big enough to carry the four of us and all our gear, so we had to leave our river bags and all their gear behind. They said they'd come back up and get it after they took us to their lodge. It was downstream and it took us about two hours to get there. They just kept the canoe in the fast, deep water and drifted. They didn't talk at all on the way. We got there about noon, I think. It was a pretty big lodge. Not on the Moose Jaw proper, but a little way back up a feeder stream."

She thought it was Rainbow Creek. I'd never heard of it, but resolved to see if I could locate it on the map when I had a moment. She took another deep breath and continued.

"The little one sent the big one back upstream for our gear. He told him not to bother with the raft this time; they would go find it later."

***

She talked for an hour. She seemed to be remembering bits and pieces as she went along; hesitating now and then to see it all clearly before she told it to me. She was remarkably calm through most of it, but she began silently crying toward the end, and I held her in my arms while she got it all out. It was pretty bad; much worse than I'd imagined.

Roy had, apparently, been trying to keep things on the up and up at first, providing the wilderness version of roadside assistance to stranded travelers. He'd had a big row with Larry outside the cabin after Larry had returned with the gear. She couldn't hear all they had said, but it was clear that Roy was telling Larry to keep off the booze and behave himself, and that they had enough trouble with the Indian and didn't need anymore. Larry had come in sulking, gathered up his sleeping bag off a bunk in one corner of the main room, and went into an adjoining room and kicked the door closed.

Roy came back in and gave Jason the lodge's medicine kit. Then he went about cooking dinner, while Jason changed her dressings and gave her Codeine for the pain. After he'd fed them dinner, Roy retired to yet another room and let Morgan and Jason sleep in the main room near the fire. She assumed she'd been given Roy's bed and Jason took the one Larry had vacated. She'd slept deeply that night and didn't remember anything until late the next day.

When she awoke, the three men were sitting at the table eating lunch and it was raining. Jason had given her more painkiller and tended her wounds again. She slept fitfully the rest of the day. When she finally came fully awake it was dark. She woke to angry voices. Roy and Larry were shouting at one another, and it was obvious they had both been drinking heavily. There was a bottle sitting on the table, and the smell of whiskey was overpowering in the close quarters. Jason was not in the room. She had wondered where he was. Then she'd heard weeping in the next room and understood it was Jason.

It was at this point in the story where she began to cry. She finished as I held her. She'd already set the scene pretty well, and I thought I knew what was coming. Nevertheless, I was unprepared for what she told me next.

It had rained all day, and the men had stayed inside. She thought maybe they had just sat around drinking. She didn't know how Larry had gotten Jason alone in the other room. Maybe Jason got drunk, maybe Roy fell asleep – she didn't know. But she heard what Roy had been shouting at Larry and she knew Larry had raped Jason, and had beaten him badly in the process. She remembered that Roy had made Larry leave the cabin and go out into the rain until he could figure out what they had to do. After Larry left, Roy had sat alone at the table quietly drinking for a long time. She had tried to keep awake, but the drug finally got her and she slipped off. When she woke up again she was naked, and her wrists were bound together over her head and tied off to something in the wall. One of her ankles was also tied to a bedpost. She heard the noises from behind the closed door to the other room. She could hear Jason crying and the sickening sound of heavy slaps and punches, and Larry's voice calling Jason a punk bitch and that he'd better learn to like it.

Then Roy had come over to the bed. He was very drunk and he told her he was sorry. He'd tried, but it was no good, and he may as well have his fun too. He'd dropped his pants and tried to mount her, but she had bit him hard on the shoulder and he'd flown into a rage calling her a skinny fucking cunt, and if she liked it rough, he'd give it to her rough. He hit her hard in the face with an open hand and she'd momentarily lost consciousness. When she came around, he'd calmed down but was still drunk – mean drunk – and he'd taken off the rest of his clothes. He said he'd waited for her to wake up so she could enjoy every minute of what he was about to give her. He said he liked to do a little biting himself, and he wanted to see how she liked it. He'd bit her breast hard. The pain was almost unbearable. He had started to climb on top of her again when there was a crash from the other room, and Larry came out screaming and holding his ear. She remembered there was blood running down his cheek and dripping on the floor. Roy jumped up, and he and Larry started yelling at one another. Then Jason bolted out of the other room and was through the door and outside into the rainy night before they could stop him. They both ran after him, shouting and swearing.

That was it. She had no memory of anything after that until she woke up here in my cabin. She had no idea of what had happened to Jason, or how she'd gotten in the river. No memory, but she thought she knew.

***

I held her until the sobbing subsided. Then I built up the fire and put a pot of water on for tea. It was past noon and we hadn't had lunch, so I cut some cheese and got out a bag of jerky. We sat at the table while we waited for the water to boil. I reached across and took her hand.

I said, "I might know the two men you described but I need to be sure. Can you remember anything else? Anything at all?"

She shook her head miserably, "No, I told you all I remember. We were there two nights. They tied me up and hurt me, but it was nothing like what they did to Jason. I can't believe that monster actually raped him. Beat him up and raped him, and probably killed him in the end."

"Do you think Jason's dead?"

Again, she shook her head, not in negation, but just to indicate it was too painful to think about.

"Probably. I saw his eyes when he ran out the door. He looked straight at me. There was so much pain there. Still..."

She shook her head again. "I don't know. He might have been able to get away from them in the dark. They were both drunk. But, if they caught him, they would have killed him. I'm sure of that."

"You saw him when he ran out of the other room. What was he wearing? Did he have on shoes?"

She thought for a moment. "I didn't see his feet, but he clunked as he ran. He must have been wearing boots. He was naked, but he was carrying a bundle, tucked like a football under his arm. It must have been his clothes."

"I'll need to know what he looks like. Can you describe him for me?"

She looked at me across the table. There was a look of hopelessness in the green eyes.

"You're going to look for him?"

"I have to. First I want you to tell me about him. You know, age, height, weight, physical description. I also need to know about his footwear. Were they hiking boots or water boots? Better yet, what kind of track did they leave, if you ever noticed? When I do go looking for him, I'll need to know what I'm looking for."

She nodded. She understood. "He was a lot shorter than me. Maybe five foot eight. He was a champion wrestler in college, and he kept in good physical condition. I'd guess he weighed one sixty, perhaps a little more. He just turned thirty-three; I went to his birthday party. Everyone from the office was there. He was an up-and-comer in the firm, on track to be a partner in a couple of years."

I was a little worried that she was using the past tense almost exclusively. It was as if she had already written him off as dead.

Tears welled in her eyes. "He was smart and ambitious, and very good looking – almost pretty. All the girls chased him. He kept most of them at arm's length, I think. He had two passions: The Law, and fly-fishing. My father had taught me fly-fishing when I was a teenager. I guess it's my passion too. That's how Jason and I became friends. Fly-fishing. That's why we came to Alaska, to the Moose Jaw."

"You were just, ah, fishing buddies?" I asked hopefully.

She smiled and laid a hand on my cheek. "You're sweet," she said. "We slept together a few times. I think that's what you're really asking. But, there was nothing serious between us. Fishing buddies pretty much described our relationship."

I had to admire Jason's taste in fishing buddies. I had Haywood, Jason had Morgan. Nothing against Haywood, but Jason, clearly, won that one hands down. I went over to the counter, made two cups of tea and brought them back to the table with the jerky and cheese. She took a piece of cheese and nibbled it delicately.

"Okay," I said, "The boots. What kind of track does he leave?" I wasn't yet ready to relegate him to the past tense.

"I know you have to look for him," she said. Then, after a long pause she looked sadly into my eyes and said, "You won't find him. He's dead. I can't tell you how I know. But I know."

"No," I told her. "You think you know, but you can't know for certain. What if he's still out there, injured maybe. We've a duty to try and find him."

She looked at me as if I were a child, but she didn't argue. "Look for him if you must. We all have our code, and our destiny."

Her words sounded almost prophetic. They sent a little shiver up my spine, but I shook it off and pressed on.

"Please, I insisted. "Tell me about the boots."

She sighed and ran her hand through her hair.

"He was wearing hip boots when the bear attacked us, but I think he changed into his hiking boots while we were camped. I'm pretty sure that's what he was wearing when those brutal pigs took us to their lodge."

"What kind of hiking boots?"

"I'm not sure. Regular hiking boots," she said.

"What kind of sole?" I persisted.

"I don't know!" She was getting exasperated now.

I went to the corner and brought back one of my hiking boots that had a waffle-stomper tread.

"Was it like this?" I showed it to her.

She studied it for a minute, and said, "Yes, something like that."

"Good," I said. "What size did he wear? Do you know?"

She shook her head. "I'm not sure. Not as big as yours. Almost, but a little smaller."

I wore size eleven, so Jason probably wore a ten. That was close enough.

"Okay," I told her. "Now, was he a good woodsman? Could he have survived out here if he got away from the McCaslins?"

"McCaslins?" She looked at me pointedly.

"The two men you described. They came here the day after I found you. They said their name was McCaslin. Roy and Larry. I didn't want to tell you. I had already guessed most of what you just told me. I didn't want you to worry about them finding you."

"They were here?" She seemed incredulous but not troubled.

"Yes. They came that first day. And they came in the night, just after you had regained consciousness. I didn't see them that time, but I scared them off. A bear nearly got them. They left a lot of clear sign."

The wisp of a smile touched her lips. "A three toed bear?"

I'm sure my mouth dropped open in astonishment. How would she know that? I studied her for a moment. There was something I hadn't seen before, far back, deep behind those green eyes.

"Yes," I said, troubled. "A big grizzly with two toes missing on his right front paw. He's probably the one that attacked you. How did you know?"

She gazed into the candle flame as if it were a crystal ball. Her voice came from far away.

"Sometimes it's as if I'm floating above it all, looking down, seeing what has happened – or what will happen. It's very strange, but I know, because I see. And, yes, he is the one that marked me. Now, he ..." her voice trailed off.

This was eerie. There was something about that bear, I had felt it the moment I'd seen his reflection on the water. The fear I had experienced then had not been the fear of man facing beast. It had been that of a child facing all the forces of nature – the storms, and the seas, and the dark of night, and the unknown gods and demons that ruled them. I had felt his supernatural power, and I had seen the message in his cold, cold eyes, even before he scratched it into the living bark of the tree. I couldn't yet fathom its meaning, but I knew it had meaning. It was as if I had been told the first two parts of an ancient trilogy, but part three had not yet been revealed to me. I sensed, rather than knew, the bear had a role for me in his final episode. I resolved that I would be the one to write that closing chapter. It might be his trilogy, but I intended to be the master of my own destiny.

***

It occurred to me that I, too, had been lost in the depths of the candle's dancing flame. I shook my head, got up and poured us each another cup of tea. I set hers in front of her but she sat quietly, still far off in some mystic place.

After a few minutes, I leaned across the table and blew out the candle. There was a little light coming through the east window, but I stood and lit the kerosene lamps and turned them up high. The spell was broken.

She noticed her tea and sipped it. "They're looking for me. That's why you hang your shirts over the windows."

"Yes," I said. "They present a problem. I've got to go look for Jason, just in case he's still alive, but I don't dare leave you here alone with the McCaslins still prowling around. Have you ever shot a gun?"

She nodded. "A shotgun."

"Good. Tomorrow I'll scout around a little upstream. I'll set up a few booby-traps outside before I leave."

She looked puzzled. "Booby-traps?"

"Like the little gadget I showed you this morning. I hook them up to the trip wire you stepped over. I'll rig a few to go off if someone comes sneaking around in the willows. I'll also leave you with Haywood's twelve bore. It holds five shells and makes a lot of noise. It's a semi-automatic. You don't need to do any pumping to reload; all you have to do is keep pulling the trigger. If you poke it out the window and squeeze off a couple of shots, no one will stick around to see who's doing the shooting."

It wasn't the best of arrangements, but it was as good as I could hope for. I spent the rest of that day setting up mini-claymores with individual trip wires in the cover surrounding the cabin. Since it was possible that they might come back at any time, day or night, I did my best to conceal the trip wires in the undergrowth. I set one across the path where the overland route came out of the trees, and two more in the willows up and downstream of the cabin. These would be the most likely avenues of approach if the McCaslins decided to rush us. They'd want to keep to cover as long as possible before crossing open ground in a frontal assault.

When I had all three of them in place, I went back to the cabin and stowed my tools and extra material in their appropriate boxes. Morgan sat on the edge of the bed brushing her hair. She was humming softly and seemed to be off in her own world, so I didn't bother her with idle talk. Then I noticed the empty tin of goose grease setting prominently in the center of the table. I got the message. I smiled and took my field jacket off the peg and filled the pockets with goose loads from a box of shells on a shelf near the door. I picked up my shotgun, went over and kissed her on the forehead and said, "I may be a couple of hours."

"Pick big, fat ones." She said. Her beautiful lips turned up at the corners and there was a mischievous glint in her green eyes.

Chapter 17

There were still a couple of hours of daylight left when I closed the cabin door behind me. I took my time walking back into the beaver meadow. On the way in, I crossed the tracks of the giant grizzly again. Enough was enough. If I saw him, I'd kill him. End of story. No more trilogy. No more Trilogy! There, now he had a name. I paused long enough to take the .44 out of its holster, check the loads, and work the action. I spun the cylinder, enjoying the well-oiled, metallic click-click-clicking sound. Then I thumbed down the hammer, slid it back into its holster, and continued on my way.

There were no geese on the pond when I arrived, so I moved around to the southwest side where the wind would be at my back, and settled into some cover. They usually flew back to water an hour or so before the sunset, so I just hunkered down and waited. While I sat there a pair of beavers came out of their lodge, swam across the pond and out the spillway. They were probably going out to the river to cut willows to haul back in for their winter food stores. I'd watched them many times before. They cut four or five good leafy branches and swam them up or down the creek, and brought them up their channel to the pond. They'd drag them over their dike and then, one by one, dive down and anchor them in the mud at the bottom of the pond. When winter came, they'd have a good supply of food under the ice, just outside their lodge door. Pretty good system if you weren't hung up on variety and could be content with mere survival.

I'd been sitting there in the cover by the pond for a little less than an hour when I heard the far off sound of honking on my right. A flight of geese appeared in the sky to the south. They were losing altitude the closer they came, so I knew they were coming in. There were about a dozen of them. They made a recon pass over the pond, swung around to the east, and then came dropping toward the water, faces into the wind, wings set. I let them get close before I moved.

When they were ten feet above the surface of the pond I snapped the shotgun up to my shoulder and dropped the leader. He folded and plunged into the water with a thunderous splash. As always, the two behind him peeled off in opposite directions and began flapping hard and rising, trying to get some altitude while swinging around to get the wind behind them. I had jacked a fresh shell into the chamber as the first goose hit the water. I swung my barrel and blasted the one on the right. I pumped in another round as he fell, and shot the third one just as he cleared the dike. He folded and fell into the marsh just beyond the spillway. Three for three. Not bad shooting. By now the others were all scattered and well out of range. They honked their protests as they gained altitude and swung into the western sky to regroup.

I stood up from my improvised blind, pumped the spent hull out of the chamber, and reloaded the gun with three fresh rounds before wading out to collect the first two I'd downed. I was wearing my hip boots, but I'd had them folded down for easy walking; I now pulled them up and slipped the garter straps through my belt and snapped the snaps. Then I waded out into the pond. The first goose was floating along the edge, quite close to where I'd been concealed. The other was half way out to the middle. It took only a few minutes to get them both and bring them back to shore.

With my shotgun in one hand and a pair of warm, wet, slender necks clamped in the other, I walked around the pond, stepped over the dike, and went down into the rushes of the marsh below the spillway. It took me a few minutes of poking around, but following the down and feathers, I located the third. All three were prime and plump. They'd roast up beautifully, and provide enough fat to keep us in skin oil for another month. A pleasant thought, but first things first. I stopped there in the marsh long enough to gut and rinse the three geese. Then I looped a leather thong around their necks, slung them over my shoulder, picked up my shotgun in the other hand and made for the cabin. The hunter home from the hill…

***

It was nearly dark when I topped the last rise and came out of the spruce stand. The evening was clear and cold and there was no wind. The temperature had dropped quickly when the sun had gone down behind the distant hills; steam puffed out of me with every breath. I paused for a moment at the top of the trail to look down at my little cabin by the creek. A straight column of smoke rose from the chimney into the still evening air. Golden shafts of light spilled out of the windows onto the hard packed earth at each side of the cabin. The stars were coming out above the dark spruce trees across the creek, and the creek itself looked like hammered silver in their weak light. It was a lovely picture. Even more lovely because I knew Morgan waited for me inside.

She was standing by the table pulling the cork from a bottle of red wine when I came through the door. She was wearing my favorite outfit – my green and black plaid shirt, and nothing else. She was even barefoot. I had dropped the geese outside before entering. I closed the door behind me, set the shotgun in the corner and began unbuttoning my field jacket. She set the wine bottle on the table and came over; she helped me out of the sleeves.

"I heard three shots," she said, and hung my coat on its peg beside the door.

"I left them outside. I'll tend to them after we eat."

"Are they fat?" She asked, smoothing the collar of my wool shirt with one hand, while twisting a finger of the other in my hair.

"Very," I assured her. "We'll get a quart of grease out of each of them. Your skin will positively glow."

She laughed a throaty laugh and kissed me on the lips. "It's glowing right now."

Indeed it was. She'd obviously been grooming herself all the time I'd been away. Her red hair glistened in the candlelight, and her skin shone like alabaster. I don't believe there has ever been a woman more lovely than she was at that moment. I felt my throat tightening. She noticed my admiration, and a mischievous smile touched her lips. She looked at me meaningfully and unbuttoned the top two buttons of the shirt.

"That little green stove puts out a lot of heat. It's a bit warm in here, don't you think?"

It certainly was. I was getting uncomfortably hot. She walked to the table and poured wine into two tin cups. She brought them over and handed one to me and then, with her free hand, she unbuttoned another button. She was definitely toying with me. She was obviously in a mood to play. That was fine by me. I was ready to play. Shooting and killing and the letting of blood does that to you. No, really! It does! There's still a lot of the cave in us.

She went over and sat on the edge of the bed. She kept one foot on the floor and stretched out a long, bare, ivory leg on top of the dark wool blanket. She ran a hand through her long, red hair; it gleamed in the candlelight.

"Too bad we've run out of your goose grease. It was always so cool and slippery against my skin."

She was looking directly into my eyes now. She undid another button.

"Maybe we should just lie down for a while before dinner."

She unbuttoned the bottom button and the shirtfront fell open. It wasn't enough to expose her completely, but it was enough. I took a gulp of my wine.

"Maybe we should at that," I heard myself say.

My voice sounded strange, even to my own ears. She gave another throaty laugh and sipped her wine. The shirt fell open a little more. She stretched out full length on the bed.

"I really haven't had a proper bath today. Maybe that would help cool me down a little."

She didn't have to ask twice. I stepped quickly to the boiler and put an inch of hot water in the basin, cooled it with a splash from the spigot, snatched up a washcloth, and hurried to the bedside. She had put me in a playful mood.

"Don't worry lady," I said, affecting a rescuer's tone. "Everything's under control. The first thing we have to do is get you out of those wet clothes."

She walked into it. "My clothes aren't wet," she said.

I threw half the basin on her. She gasped. Her mouth and eyes flew open in surprise. I maintained my official posture.

"As I was saying, we must get you out of those wet clothes – AT ONCE!"

With that I took a grip on the lapels of my, now wet, plaid shirt and, with a single downward jerk, peeled it from her shoulders and down the length of her back. She was giggling uncontrollably, and couldn't very well resist.

I said, "You're obviously hysterical madam. I hope I won't have to slap you silly."

Her giggling became helpless laughter; she was, literally, in tears. I undertook to comfort her.

***

I awoke at first light. Morgan's warm, naked form curled contentedly around mine. The wine bottle stood, still open and unfinished, on the table. We'd burned the stew, and the geese were still outside the door, waiting to be dressed. We'd never left the bed. Somehow, I felt no sense of guilt at the wasted food, or the dereliction of duty. We had accomplished something. We'd managed a night of delightful and inventive sex without a drop of goose grease. She certainly was a wildcat; she'd clawed me with her three long fingernails while in the throes of an orgasm. I was sure she'd drawn blood; I could feel the scratches, hot and stinging down my back. I guess I'd been initiated into the club.

She sensed I was awake and turned to snuggle inside my arms. Her lips settled against my chest. She was purring, or murmuring something. I couldn't tell. I didn't care. Slowly, I realized she was kissing, or licking, one of my nipples. My God! After last night, I doubted I could rise to the occasion. Her tongue was hot and wet. Yes, perhaps I could. I was already a quart low on seminal fluid, but I resolved to begin eating more eggs and oysters.

***

It was more than an hour after sunrise when I finally rolled out from under the blankets and ventured outside into the cold morning air to perform my ablutions in the icy waters of the creek. It had been one hell of a night. It had been one hell of a morning. I had never felt so drained, yet so alive. I was happy. That's the only word for it. Happy. Before I had gotten out of bed Morgan had taken my face between both her hands and looked very deeply, and seriously, into my eyes.

"I'm not a slut. I want you to know that. You must think I'm sex crazed or something, the way I've been acting. But I'm not that way. I've needed you to hold me and love me, not just screw me. After what happened at that awful place, I needed physical proof that people still feel for one another – that they're kind and gentle to one another, and that sex isn't some brutal and ugly thing; it's beautiful when people do it to become closer, or because they are in love."

I think she was trying to tell me that she loved me. No wonder I was happy.

Happiness notwithstanding, I had some serious work to do this morning. The first thing on the agenda was to dress the geese. Thank heaven I'd taken the time to gut them before I came down from the beaver pond. That was the only blessing. The morning was cold, and there was the usual September frost, heavy and thick on the ground; the geese were stiff as boards. There was no point in trying to pluck them, so I just skinned them. I took my time, in order to save as much fat as I could. After all, that was the primary reason they had died. It would be a pity to loose any.

It took me three quarters of an hour to skin and rinse all three. I hung them from a willow to let them cure a little in the cool air and the breeze. Then I gathered up all their left over parts, and took them down and tossed them in the creek. Again, it was all natural and biodegradable, so I felt no guilt. After I'd dealt with that, I went around and checked the trips on the claymores. By ten o'clock I was done.

I went back into the cabin and found Morgan sitting quietly in the rocker, reading one of my fly-tying books. The fire was hissing gently in the stove, and the smell of fresh brewed coffee filled the interior. I poured a cup and stood by the fire to thaw out.

She looked up from the book. "Do you tie your own?"

"Uh-huh."

"Where do you keep your material?"

I gestured toward one of the wooden boxes stacked against the back wall.

"In the top box. Vice, scissors, hair and feathers are all there. Just about anything you need to tie trout or salmon flies."

"I tie too. Would you mind if I get into your stuff today while you're gone? I'll make you a few of my Specials."

"Have at it. I am getting a little low on Elk Hair Caddis and I'm completely out of streamers; the salmon wiped me out."

"I'll make you some of each. What size do you prefer?"

"Number sixteen Caddis, and ten or twelve for the streamers."

"Good!" She sounded excited to have something to keep her occupied during my absence. "My Specials are actually based on the Caddis. You'll love them. They never fail!"

"What makes them special?" I asked, sipping my coffee.

I didn't really care. Everyone that ties flies has their own secret ingredient for their special flies.

"If I told you that they wouldn't be so special." She pursed her lips for a minute and cocked her head at a coquettish angle. "Well, that may not be necessarily the case with you. I think you'd find them particularly special."

She had my interest now. I took another sip of coffee. I really did want to know but I was damned if I was going show it. I waited.

"I'll just make them and you can inspect them when you get back. Maybe you'll be able to spot the secret ingredient."

I nodded. "Okay, but I have to warn you, I have a pretty keen eye. Don't bet your shirt that I won't be able to tell."

She reached a hand up, took a fistful of my shirtfront, pulled me down and kissed me on the lips. Then she gave me a dismissive little shove.

"Now, go attend to your business and leave me alone to enjoy this book."

My business that day was to try and find some sign of Jason. I had given it a good deal of thought and decided that I would do best to leave the canoe and do all my snooping on foot. Any sign I might find of Jason would be in the woods. A man hiding out doesn't spend a lot of time wandering around on the open creek bank. Further, as my search would take me up into the McCaslins neck of the woods, I couldn't risk them seeing me on the river. I didn't know how pissed they were at this point, but I wasn't going to underestimate them. They were well aware that I knew, by now, they were the enemy, and I'd humiliated them twice. I didn't think they'd hesitate at putting a bullet between my shoulder blades if they got a chance. I wasn't about to give them the chance.

I got out the map and spread it on the plank bench. I studied the grids upstream of my cabin site. Roy had said their lodge was on the first creek upstream of the burn. I verified that tributary was, indeed, the Deadman. Morgan had said she thought it was called Rainbow Creek, but I scanned all the feeder streams and there was no Rainbow Creek. She must have been mistaken. I could see where Deadman Creek joined the Moose Jaw, and I did a little mental arithmetic to try and determine, roughly, where Morgan and Jason had abandoned their raft. She'd said they had escaped downstream around a few bends after the bear attack. From there, it had taken them a couple hours, more or less, to drift downstream. I seemed to recall she said the McCaslins had just stayed to the deep water and hadn't paddled much.

So, I reasoned, the current moves about three miles an hour in the straight stretches of the creek, a little faster where there are lots of switchbacks. The section of the Moose Jaw upstream of Deadman Creek was full of twists and turns. Even if that meant the current was probably moving four or five miles an hour along there, it also meant my as-the-crow-flies miles would be significantly reduced in relationship to the river miles they had traveled.

As I worked it out, Trilogy had attacked them roughly eight river miles above Deadman Creek. I put a green dot on the map to mark the approximate location. Then I plotted an overland route that would take me past the McCaslins place and bring me out in the general vicinity of my green dot. Once I got upstream that far, I'd probably be safe walking the banks until I found the raft. I figured that would be the best place to start my search for Jason. It stood to reason that he would have struck for the raft immediately upon escaping from the McCaslins. He'd need to put distance between him and their lodge and he'd need to outfit himself to survive. I didn't know if Larry had gone all the way back up to the raft or not. If he hadn't, there would still have been some gear aboard and Jason would have gone back up to get it. It was all speculation, of course, but I had to start somewhere.

Satisfied that I had a plan, I folded the map and put it in my hip pocket, then went back inside for a last cup of coffee. Morgan was still reading in the rocker when I entered. I asked her if she wanted more coffee. She nodded that she would and held out her cup without lifting her eyes from the page. She was a remarkable woman. I'd never known any female to become so engrossed in a fly-tying book. In my mind, she was approaching perfection.

I chuckled and shook my head. She looked up.

"What?" she asked.

"Nothing," I said. "Just marveling at your broad range of interests. Any others I should know about?"

She smiled, "I play a fair game of chess," she said.

I looked beyond her smile, into her eyes. Was there something...? No. I took the pot over and poured coffee into her proffered cup.

"Pardon the interruption, but I need to get a couple more things straight before I go up looking for Jason."

She marked her page with a finger and closed the book. I went on.

"How much of your gear do you think was left on the raft or at your camp?"

She thought for a moment. "I can't really say. Jason had brought two river bags down from the raft. One was the tent and our sleeping bags; the other held a lot of things he'd stuffed into it from other bags on the raft – a backpacker's cook set and food and some of our clothes and toilet kits. I think our rain gear was in it also."

"So, everything else was still on the raft?"

She nodded. "Yes, I assume so."

"Can you remember what was still aboard?"

She took a moment to consider. "Well, our fishing gear, I suppose – rods and vests and waders – you know. And a cooler full of food and beer. He didn't bring the big frying pan or Coleman stove or any of the fuel down to the camp so all of that must still have been on the raft. Our tarps and ground cloths and the camp kitchen were still aboard. And my shotgun."

"Shotgun?"

She looked at me as if I were a idiot. "Well, of course, a shotgun. You didn't think we'd come into the bush without any protection did you? We each had a shotgun. Jason brought his down to the camp with the other stuff I mentioned. He left mine in the raft."

"What loads were you carrying? You know – what kind of shells?"

"We had slugs, of course, in case of bears but we had birdshot too. We hadn't intended to live on a fish-only diet."

"Both guns the same gauge?"

She sipped her coffee. "Yes. They were both twelve-gauge." She hesitated for a little, staring off into the distance. "You're thinking Jason would have tried to get back to the raft if he got away. He knew the gun was there, and enough supplies to keep him alive."

"That's what I would have done."

She nodded. Then a look of sadness clouded her eyes.

"Gus, don't get your hopes up."

"I won't," I said. "Still, I have to look for him."

She squeezed my hand. "I know. You won't find him, but you have to try. Please be careful; those two men are evil."

I finished my coffee and put the cup on the sideboard of the sink. I'd been wearing my fleece vest and rubber ducks while doing my morning chores. Now I changed into my hip boots and took my field jacket off the peg. The pockets were still full of goose loads from the night before. I had plenty of ammunition, in case I ran into man trouble. Nevertheless, I grabbed a handful of slugs out of the box on the shelf and put them in a breast pocket of my coat, where they would be kept separate from the goose loads and would be ready to hand if I needed them. I thought about packing the .44 also but the overland route I'd laid out had a good bit of up and downhill in it, and the round trip to the raft and back would cover about ten miles if I didn't have to take too many detours. I'd calculated that eight river miles, along that part of the Moose Jaw, worked out to roughly five miles as-the-crow-flies. I didn't need the extra weight.

Morgan was watching me as I buttoned up my coat and put my hat, gloves, scarf and water bottle in my daypack. I gestured to the gun belt hanging from a peg.

"Ever shoot one of those?"

She shook her head. "They scare me. I don't even like shooting the shotgun but I'm comfortable with it."

I pointed to the corner where Haywood's Remington stood.

"I'll leave you that one. I told you how it works. You want me to load it for you before I go?"

She said that would be nice, her gun was a pump. She'd never loaded a semi-automatic before. I took it out of the corner and made her watch while I loaded it. I showed her the release button for the bolt and told her to keep her fingers out of the loading window when she pushed it. Then I showed her the safety and asked her if she thought she could handle it if she had to. She said she could. There was nothing left to do so I kissed her good-bye and went out the door.

She didn't say, "Good luck" or "good hunting" or "be careful". She simply said, "I'll be waiting." She had said it in such a way it gave me a chill. I don't know why. It was a common enough thing to have said. It was just the way she had said it. As if there were a "forever" in there somewhere that was unspoken, but absolute.

Chapter 18

It had been clear, but a few clouds were forming far off in the southwest and a breeze was beginning to stir. It looked like I might get some weather before I got back. I hoped against snow. Snow would obscure any tracks Jason may have left and would leave my coming and going clearly charted on the ground. Should the McCaslins be out and about, they just might run across them and understand what they meant. They weren't very bright, but they were woods savvy and wouldn't miss the significance of man tracks in the snow. They'd be certain to come looking for me.

When I got to the landing strip I continued upstream, around another bend. The river widened at that point and became shallow, and Haywood and I had always crossed there when going up to the burn. I had planned my route to take me to the burn where I would strike up and over the ridge, and then cross a big, wide open meadow that contained several more beaver ponds. The creek, at that point, had to make a long sweeping bend, along and around the ridge before cutting back up the other side and along the meadow. By crossing over the ridge and cutting across the beaver meadow I could save myself about two miles of walking. This route also had the added advantage of bringing me back to meet the Moose Jaw a little upstream of where Deadman Creek came in from the other side. I hoped that once I was upstream of the Deadman I wouldn't have to worry about the McCaslins. Again, that was pure speculation, but I had to take the chance. If Jason had, indeed, made for the raft following his escape, my best chance of picking up his trail was upstream from the lodge. Odds were he'd probably stayed on the other bank of the Moose Jaw but there were a few runs of shallows where he could have crossed if he'd noted them on the trip downstream in the McCaslins' canoe. It also stood to reason that he would have tried to get into the water as soon as he could after running out of the lodge so he wouldn't leave any tracks to follow.

As I started uphill through the blackened spars of the old fire I tried to put myself in Jason's mind. I considered what I might have done in his place. I didn't know how badly he was hurt. From Morgan's brief account of what she'd heard, it sounded as if Larry had given him a pretty sound beating. He'd also sodomized him, which must have resulted in significant physical trauma. Running, for that matter, walking would certainly have been painful. That train of thought made me very uncomfortable. I put it out of my mind and focused on his probable first actions upon fleeing the cabin.

Morgan had said it was raining, or it had been raining. She'd said Jason had been naked, carrying his clothes under his arm when he ran out of the lodge. It had sounded to her as if he were wearing boots. With the McCaslins hot on his heels he wouldn't have been able to stop to dress until he'd put some distance between them, or until he was able to, somehow, shake them. It was possible he'd simply ducked into the brush and lost them right off the bat. I thought about this for a little and concluded it could have happened that way. Morgan had said she didn't remember anything after Roy and Larry went running out but she'd also said Roy, at that point, was very drunk, and that he'd been naked too. Larry had been drinking heavily also. If that were the case, Jason might have been able to give them the slip early in the chase.

By the time I reached the top of the ridge I was breathing hard and sweating. I sat down on a blackened log and removed the daypack and shucked out of my field jacket. I dug my water bottle out of the pack and drank a few swallows. It was midday and the sun stood high in the sky. A few clouds were moving in from the southwest and the breeze felt cool and good against my damp shirt.

From where I sat, atop the ridge, I could see a great distance in all directions. I looked down behind me at the burn where I'd harvested all the logs for the cabin. I hadn't been back there since late July, but I could still see the stumps I'd left and the drag marks leading down the hill to the beaver pond. I'd spent a lot of time down there; it seemed so long ago. I let my eyes follow the Moose Jaw upstream. It hugged the bottom of the ridge off into the distance and disappeared around the tip. It came back into view on the other side, a mile downstream from the beaver meadow I'd be crossing in a little while. I could also see, a bit further up, across the stream, the valley of the Deadman, winding down out of the mountains toward its confluence with the Moose Jaw. It looked so far away. It was like looking across a vast and impenetrable distance – across time itself. I shrugged and started my descent. I'd studied the map. I knew I had a long walk ahead of me but I'd pick up the Moose Jaw in another hour or so. Distances were always deceiving from the top of a hill.

It took me only twenty minutes to make my way down the backside of the ridge. There were several game trails, and I simply followed one that took me down. At the bottom, I came upon Trilogy's tracks in the mud bank of the highest beaver pond. It occurred to me that his were the only bear tracks I'd ever discovered upstream of my cabin. Apparently the bad juju didn't scare him. Maybe he was the bad juju. It was just possible that this was his territory, and all the other bears feared him and didn't trespass. I scanned the open meadow for any sign of him, but saw nothing. He certainly got around. I'd run across his tracks just the night before, when I'd been goose hunting back behind the cabin. Those tracks had been very fresh. So were these. He must have crossed the creek and come upstream sometime in the night. It seemed everywhere I went lately, I found his sign. It was unnerving. I remembered the specter of him standing full height, across the creek from the cabin the morning after I'd found Morgan. He was a monster, or perhaps something else entirely.

Before I set out across the flat, marshy meadow, I jacked the shell out of my chamber and, leaving the bolt open, fished in my breast pocket for a slug. When I'd found one I dropped it in the loading port and pumped the slide forward. A slug was now in the chamber. The four shells in the tube were still goose loads. If I ran into him back here I'd probably have time for only one shot anyway. I wanted it to count. I considered replacing all the goose loads with slugs, but if I didn't drop him with the first shot, he'd be charging. The number two pellets would serve just as well at point blank range. I reminded myself to keep a sharp eye out and not spend more time than I needed in the heavy cover. I didn't want to surprise him. As long as I stayed to open country, I'd have a chance of seeing him before he got too close. And it would give him a chance to see me coming also. That would give us both a chance to avoid a fight. I hoped he wanted to avoid one. Roy had said the old bear had a "hard-on for mankind". From what I'd seen so far, he was not far off the mark.

A large flight of geese went over, honking and shifting position, maintaining their ragged V. They were headed south. It was September after all, and the cold was moving in; it was time they started migrating down to their winter nesting grounds. I watched them disappear into the distance, and then I started across the meadow.

It took me over two hours to work my way back to the Moose Jaw. The meadow was wet and the mud sucked at my feet. When I'd finally slogged my way across it, I ran into muskeg and then thick, tangled cover. I broke through to the willows along the creek bank about a mile upstream of the confluence with the Deadman. It took me another hour to find where the raft had been.

I'd located the campsite first. There was nothing left there but the fire pit; Larry had come back upstream and taken away all the gear. I poked around a while, trying to find one of Jason's old tracks. I assumed he would have changed into his hiking boots at some point during the two days they had camped here. There were some tracks but they were too faint to be of much use, so I gave it up and went to look for the raft.

Morgan had said they let the current carry them downstream a few bends from where the bear had hit them. They'd crawled out of the water then and made camp close by. I worked my way upstream a quarter mile or so, until I came to a bend where there were a lot of sweepers extending far out into the streambed. It was a spot where a raft coming downstream would have to move way over toward the shallows to avoid them. That fit Morgan's description of the place where they had run aground. There was no raft to be seen, but I really hadn't expected to find it. Either Jason or the McCaslins would have come to fetch it by now. I was on the cut bank side where the water was deep, so I had to walk another half mile upstream before I could find a shallow crossing. Then I came back down the other side. The gravel bar there was long and flat with a lot of sand along the water's edge. I found the man tracks just below the sharp bend, where several big sweepers extended from the opposite bank. Their withered tips seemed to point across the creek at the tracks, like the accusing fingers of a skeleton.

The tracks were Larry's; his oversized waders left an unmistakable print. It was difficult to say how old they were. I quartered the bar searching for any indication that Jason had also been there. There was no sign of him. The only tracks in evidence were Larry's. He'd stayed close to the water from what I could determine. This was ominous. He hadn't scouted the bar for sign of Jason. This suggested he knew there was nothing to find. It looked like he'd beached his canoe ten yards downstream of the raft. He'd made several trips back and forth between them, transferring the load, no doubt. Then, somehow he must have patched the raft up enough to float or he deflated it altogether and loaded it aboard his canoe. Probably the latter. He would have been in a hurry, and patching and pumping would have taken half a day, at the very least.

The clouds had moved in from the southwest while I'd been making my way up the creek. Now the sky was darkening to that flat gray color that promises snow. All the heat had gone out of the day, and I knew it was time to start making my way back downstream. I broke out my hat, gloves and scarf, put them on, and struck for home. I set a good pace, knowing it would be dark by the time I reached the cabin as it was.

I had decided to keep to that side of the creek and walk along the bank all the way down to the Deadman. I doubted that I'd bump into the McCaslins on the way. Now that the raft was gone, they had no reason to be prowling around upstream unless they were looking for Jason. When I got to the Deadman I would snoop around the woods near their lodge to see what I could learn and then head home. I didn't know on which side of the Deadman their lodge would be, but I'd worry about that when I got there.

As I made my way down, I thought about what I'd learned so far. Nothing, really. I hadn't found Jason's footprints, but that did not mean he hadn't made it back to the raft. With the McCaslins after him, he would have taken care to wipe out his tracks. If he had returned to the raft, he would have taken some survival equipment and Morgan's shotgun, and headed straight back to the lodge to help Morgan. He'd seen her bound and naked on the bed when he fled the lodge. Once he was armed, her rescue would have been his first priority. I didn't know much about him, but he and Morgan were friends, sometimes lovers. He would have gone back for her. Assuming, of course, he'd got away in the first place. I had to proceed on that assumption. There was no point in looking for him otherwise.

I tried to imagine what had happened after Jason ran out of the lodge. Roy and Larry chased after him, but probably lost him in the rain and the darkness. If so, they would have searched for him a while, and then gone back to their lodge. Roy, at least, needed to get some clothes on; perhaps Larry did too. What would have happened next was hard to say, but sometime that night or early the next day, Roy would have sent Larry up to check the raft. Roy probably would have stayed at the lodge in case Jason showed up back there. I didn't like to think of what might have happened at the lodge if Roy had, indeed, stayed behind with Morgan, naked and tied to the bed. She'd said she had no memory of anything after Jason went out the door. Maybe that was a good thing.

I considered Larry's mission from two angles. When he got to the raft he either discovered that Jason had been there ahead of him – or that he had not. If he found all the gear still aboard he probably would have hidden his canoe, and settled down in some cover and waited for Jason to show. On the other hand, if he found Jason's tracks at the raft, he would have gone straight home. One way or the other, I still had to look for Jason, or any sign of him, back at the lodge. I'd come up empty at both the camp and the raft. The McCaslins' place was my last chance.

***

It was dusk by the time I found my way to Deadman Creek. It came in from the northwest and was almost as wide as the Moose Jaw. It was moving slow, and its waters merged with those of the larger stream with little turmoil. The Deadman appeared to be smoother and calmer than the Moose Jaw, but I knew its current and character could be radically different further upstream. Eventually, I was going to have to find a place to cross so I could continue down the Moose Jaw to my cabin. But I didn't yet know upon which side of Deadman Creek the lodge was to be found. I decided to scout up the side I was on for a half mile. If I found nothing, I'd cross over and scout back down the other bank. I had to be careful and quiet now; I didn't want to blunder into a clearing and find myself standing on their front porch. As it was cold and getting dark, it stood to reason that they'd have a lamp lit, and a fire in the fireplace. As I made my way up the Deadman, I kept an eye on both banks for the first sign of light, and I kept my nose alert for the smell of smoke.

I hadn't progressed more than a hundred yards from the fork when I was startled by a splash in the creek just to my right. I spun and saw a ring spreading on the glassy surface. I relaxed a bit. It had been a big splash, not as loud as a beaver's tail slap, but loud enough. I realized it had only been a fish taking an insect off the surface. Nevertheless, it had given me a good start. I realized I had brought up the barrel of the shotgun and snicked off the safety as I'd spun to see what had made the noise. I was getting jumpy. I stopped for a minute to let my heart slow down and my nerves settle. While I waited, two more fish jumped. One actually cleared the water before splashing back down. It wasn't a grayling. It was too big to have been a grayling. It looked like a Rainbow, but that was highly unlikely. I'd fished the Moose Jaw up and downstream from the cabin, all summer. The two previous years I'd floated its entire length, fishing every day. I had never caught, for that matter seen, anything but salmon and grayling. SPLASH! Another one rolled right in front of me. It was a Rainbow! He must have been twenty inches long! And fat! Four or five pounds, at least!

The wind picked up. It had ice in it, and ripples began showing on the surface of the water. It reminded me that I had to hurry if I wanted to beat the snow. I turned up my collar and moved on. Finding Rainbows in this creek had come as a surprise. It was more than a little odd. I knew this area had once been famous for trout as well as salmon, but it was common knowledge the trout had been fished out forty years ago. Maybe they'd staged a comeback. No one ever came in here for trout these days, so nobody knew. One thing was for certain; I wasn't going to be the one to spread the word. I'd tell Haywood, but I'd swear him to silence.

Just as the dusk slipped into darkness, the first snowflakes began to fall. I halted to pull down my earflaps. As I turned my head to tie their laces under my chin I caught a flicker of light off through the trees across the creek. I moved a little farther upstream, placing my feet very carefully as I went. After a few steps I could see a solid stream of light coming through the tree trunks. I'd found the lodge. And it looked as if at least one of the brothers was at home.

The water here was too deep to cross, so I kept going in the direction I had been traveling. As I came abreast of the lodge, I saw there was a dilapidated dock running parallel with the far bank. The battered old canoe was tied up alongside. Chances were good that both the brothers were inside. I needed to get across the creek and have a quick look around their place before the snow started sticking to the ground. If I hurried, I wouldn't need to cover my tracks, the snow would do that for me. I didn't want to miss this opportunity. I lengthened my stride and hurried upstream. It took me fifteen minutes to find a wide spot in the creek where it looked shallow enough to cross. The night was overcast and there was no moon. It was difficult to judge the depth of the water, but as the streambed had almost doubled in width and the current was moving faster, I decided to chance it. I didn't have much time. I pulled up my hip boots as high as they'd go and snapped their garter straps to my belt. Then I stepped into the water. It was only ankle deep next to the bank. I moved as quietly as I could, sliding my feet forward a step at a time, making sure I had good purchase on the slippery rocks of the streambed before moving the other foot forward. Normally I used a walking stick when crossing creeks. It served as a third foot and had saved me from falling more than once. I didn't have time to search for one tonight. By the time I reached midstream, I wished I had. The water came above my knees here and the current proved stronger than I had thought. It was sucking at my legs, and each step became more perilous.

I didn't see the channel coming. I took a step, didn't find the bottom, lost my balance, and before I knew it I was in waist deep water. I would have gone down if I hadn't sacrificed the shotgun. Gripping the barrel, I thrust the butt into the water. It struck and held on the bottom. I regained my balance, silently cursed my luck, and continued the crossing. The damage was already done. I was soaked to the belly and both boots were full. Not to mention the dunking my shotgun had taken. Fortunately, it was a Remington 870 Ducks Unlimited Special, which had been specifically designed for wetland hunting. It had a waterproof, black matte coating on the metal of the barrel and receiver and pump tube. Of course, that didn't do the internal mechanisms any good, but I'd dropped it in duck ponds a time or two before, and a thorough wipe down and oiling kept it from rusting.

When I finally clambered out of the water and up onto the far bank, I immediately sat down and pulled off my boots. I made as little noise as possible when dumping out the water. My pants and underwear were soaked, so I took the time to strip them off and wring them out. I was shivering with cold by the time I got back into them. Then I pulled on the boots and addressed the shotgun. I knelt under the cover of an overhanging spruce branch and jacked all five shells out onto the ground. Then I gave the gun a quick wipe down with my scarf, and reloaded with dry rounds. It was a miracle I had any. The bottom of my field jacket was also wet, but the shell loops, sewed above the pockets, had stayed clear of the water. The shells were all goose loads, but a slug wouldn't have served me any better at this point. If I ran into a bear in the darkness, it would be at close range.

Stopping had consumed fifteen precious minutes. The snow was beginning to collect on the ground, so I had to move fast. I dropped the wet shells in my empty breast pocket, put on my gloves and scarf, and went back downstream directly to the lodge. I hoped they didn't have a dog. Morgan hadn't mentioned one, but the way my luck was running, they'd probably have two or three on patrol.

I got there sooner than I had expected. There were no dogs to set up an alarm and no one was moving around outside. I offered up a silent prayer of thanks as I studied the log structure before me. It was a big building, not just a cabin, but a genuine fishing lodge. Of course, it had seen better days. Some of the windows were boarded up, but light was spilling out a few of them on the wall facing the creek. It lit up the boards of the covered porch and the ground beyond.

I was squishing with each step so I didn't dare go too close. I circled back around to the left. All the windows were boarded up on that side so I continued around behind. I found the same thing back there, although I could see light peeking out narrow gaps in the back door frame. When I got around to the downstream side, the four rear windows were dark but the front two showed light. As I approached I heard voices, muffled and unintelligible, through the wall. I moved a little further back into the woods and angled toward the stream so I could see inside.

A body passed between the light and the window, and a shadow was cast out on the ground. It moved past the window, and the light came bright and full again. I crept a few steps closer, and I could see Roy just sitting down at the table. He was having dinner. I shifted a little for a better view. Larry was already at the table eating. He was slumped over his food like a bear over a carcass. His huge arms encircled his plate and he kept his face just inches over his food. I couldn't tell what they were eating, but they seemed intent and weren't talking much.

By now, my teeth were chattering, and I was shivering uncontrollably. I didn't have much time. I took a deep breath, moved across the open space between the trees and the lodge like a shadow, and didn't stop until I was up against the wall beside the window. The sill was just about at chin level and I could see half the big room from where I stood. I could see the bed in the corner where Morgan must have been tied. It was empty. I ducked under the sill and slid across to the other side of the window and peered in. Both men were still at the table. I could see deeper into the room from my new position. There was a second bed, but there was nothing on it except a rumpled sleeping bag. They were alone. I don't know if I was disappointed or not. If Jason had been in there, what would I have been able to do?

If I didn't start back home immediately, I was going to freeze to death. I was also beginning to leave tracks, as the snow was starting to cover the ground. The flakes were coming down faster and bigger now. It was a wet, heavy snow. I couldn't wait any longer. I took an angle off the corner of the lodge and hurried straight for the creek. I didn't think there was any way either Roy or Larry could see me from where they sat. Nevertheless, I held my breath as I crossed the open ground. There was always the chance one of them would stand up just as I was backlit by the light coming out the window. I had to take the chance. I didn't exhale until I had made it to the creek bank and turned the corner of the tree line. I didn't relax completely until, a hundred yards downstream, I lost sight of the light from their windows. Then I made for home.

It only took ten minutes to walk from their lodge to the junction of the two creeks. From there, I held to the Moose Jaw all the way. I could have saved myself a lot of walking if I went overland and cut off some of the bends, but I hadn't been this far upstream from the cabin before and didn't know the country. The last thing I needed was to get lost. That would mean certain death. I kept moving, staying close to the water's edge. It was easy, open walking along the gravel bars on the inside of the bends, but the outside of each bend, above the cut bank, was choked with slashings and thickets and devil's club. It was not only slow going, it wore me down. While trying to fight my way through the second such section I got my feet caught in tanglefoot and fell heavily, gashing my left hand on a sharp spear of dead branch wood sticking out of a downed tree. It tore through my glove and bit deep into the heel of my palm. It bled heavily until the snow and the cold stemmed the flow. By the time I fought my way back to the next gravel bar I knew I'd never make it home if I didn't change tactics. As I was considering my options I came across deep, widely spaced tracks in the snow. I looked carefully at them; old Trilogy had been through here no more than five minutes ago. He appeared to be going back downstream. I followed them the length of the bar, and when it came to an end at the next bend, his tracks disappeared into the water. I looked across the stream. I could see no tracks on the other side, but I could see where the new bar began. It occurred to me that I'd been trying to avoid getting wet when I was already soaked. Bears didn't keep to one side of the creek. They went where the walking was easy. If the bar ended on one side of the creek, they just waded across and picked up the next one. The big grizzly was showing me how it was done. I hoped I didn't catch up to him, but if I didn't hurry, I was going to die anyway. I didn't hesitate. I simply stepped off the bar, and waded across the creek. In the channel, the water was over the tops of my boots, but at this point, it didn't matter; I was already as wet as I could get. Or so I thought.

I followed the bear tracks for an hour. The wind had dropped off, and the snow was coming straight down now – big, wet, heavy flakes. I realized I was not moving as fast as the bear. More snow was accumulating in his tracks than when I'd first begun following him. That may have been because it was coming down harder, or because I was running out of gas. I knew it was both. I was tiring quickly, and the repeated soakings in the river kept me wet, and my legs and feet were now completely numb. If I stopped to rest, I'd never be able to start again. I had to keep moving.

I don't know how long the wolves had been following me before I noticed the shadows moving stealthily through the willows at the top of the bar. They must have picked up the scent of my blood. I'd lost a good bit back where I had fallen, and the wound had been bleeding steadily as I moved downstream. I didn't have a torch. Not that it would have mattered, as my hands were stiff and numb from the cold, I probably couldn't have switched it on, even if I had one. But I knew they were wolves, I didn't have to see them. I could tell by the way they were stalking me, keeping back in the cover and moving along parallel with me all the way down the creek. I didn't know how many of them there were, however, and that troubled me.

They would be reluctant to attack a man; at least a living, breathing, walking man. They were just following along to see if I was going to make it. I didn't think they'd bother me as long as I kept moving. I kept moving. I'd already fallen two or three times, and my falls were becoming more frequent as I tired. Each time, the effort to rise required more and more of my flagging strength. When, at last, I fell again, I wondered if I would ever find the will to continue. I had stumbled in a deep rut just as I came up out of the water onto a gravel bar. As I lay there, utterly exhausted, the muzzle of a wolf appeared out of the falling snow, very close to my face. They were getting bold. I put every ounce of my remaining strength into rising to my knees. I still had the shotgun with me, and placing the butt on the gravel, I literally pulled myself up to my feet using the barrel for support. That was about all the good the gun would do me. I doubted I could fire it; I only had one serviceable hand, and its fingers were stiff and numb with cold. Still, if the wolves came in close again, I'd have to give them something to think about; I'd have to find a way to get off a shot. I started moving again. I had staggered just a few steps when I stumbled in another rut and nearly went down. Somehow I kept my feet. I looked at the rut. It was almost impossible to see under the blanket of snow, but the surface of the snow showed a clear depression in the gravel bar beneath. It extended off up the bar in a straight line. Hope suddenly galvanized me. I lurched a few steps to the left. There was a second one, running parallel to the first. I was standing on the landing strip! I could have wept with relief. Knowing there was no time to lose, I struck inland, and within a few minutes, found the overland path. I couldn't go fast, but I kept one foot moving in front of the other. I experienced a moment of panic because I couldn't recall the uphill grades being so long or steep, but then I realized it was my own fatigue that made them seem so. I hadn't taken the wrong trail. I kept moving. Every now and then I'd catch a glimpse of a wolf slipping silently through the trees alongside the path. My deadly escorts, waiting to see if I could make it to the cabin. I was determined that they should be disappointed. I was, indeed, going to make it home. Then, suddenly, I broke out of the trees at the top of the ridge, and there below me was my cabin. A sob barked from my throat. It sounded horrible, even to my own ears, and must have startled the wolf that was guarding my left flank. He gave a surprised yip and darted a few paces back into the woods.

He had just regained his composure and was closing in again when my next step tripped the claymore. I had forgotten about them. The wolf must have been right next to it when it detonated. He cried out in pain and went yelping off into the woods. His mates followed. I didn't care. All I could think of was the warmth of the cabin.

Chapter 19

As I shuffled my way down the path it struck me that I had never seen any sight so beautiful as the light in the cabin window and the smoke curling out of the chimney. The door opened as I staggered up the steps to the porch. The golden light spilled out into the night, and Morgan stood just inside. She held a shotgun pointed at my midsection. I never broke stride; I just kept my feet moving into the room and made straight for the stove, dropping my shotgun as I crossed the bearskin rug.

"Thank God," she said. "I heard the booby-trap go off and didn't know what to think."

Then, when she got a good look at me, "Oh, Gus!"

She quickly closed the door, leaned Haywood's shotgun against the wall, and hurried over to where I stood dripping water and snow on the floor by the stove. I was trying to get the buttons of my coat open. She knocked away my hands and quickly undid the buttons and got me out of the snow-covered coat. She flung it on the floor, eased me into the rocker and pulled off my boots; water and ice sloshed out of them onto the floor. She stripped off my sodden socks and then hauled me to my feet again and began working at my belt buckle. I stood like a statue of the Frankenstein monster. I was too cold and stiff to help her. She talked frantically while she worked.

"When you weren't back by dark I began to worry. Then the snow started. I've been out of my mind for the last three hours. What happened to you?"

My teeth were chattering so badly there was no way I could talk. I didn't bother trying to answer. I just stood there shivering and shaking with cold and dripping ice and water on the floor. When she got the belt unbuckled she pulled my pants and underwear down to my knees, stripped me out of my shirt and undershirt, resettled me in the rocker and then pulled my pants the rest of the way off in one tug. I now sat, naked and freezing in the chair. She added the wet pants to the pile of clothes already on the floor, dashed to the bed and snatched off the wool blanket. She quickly wrapped me in it and began rubbing me all over, trying to stimulate the blood flow with the friction of her hands. It hurt. It burned. It felt wonderful.

After five minutes or so, my hands began stinging with pinpricks as the blood began warming them from within and the heat of the fire from without. No pain had ever seemed so welcome. My toes were also beginning to have feeling. I knew I was going to live. Up on the ridge the wolves began their mournful wailing – cheated again.

Morgan stopped rubbing my back. She said, "They sound so close."

I still didn't want to try talking so I nodded and offered her a weak smile.

She stood up, patted my knee, kissed the top of my head and said, "Now let's get something warm inside you."

As I huddled there, leaning as close as I dare to the fire, she filled a tin cup with stew that had been simmering on the stove, poured a dollop of whiskey into it, and brought it to me. She held it to my lips so I could use both shaking hands to clutch the blanket closed over my chest. The thick broth burned going down but I could feel the warmth spreading from my stomach through the rest of my body; I gulped it down greedily. She filled another cup and let me down half of it before she took it away from my lips.

"Not too much. Wait a little. Are you getting warmer?"

My shivering had subsided somewhat and my hands were shaking less. I nodded.

She relaxed a little and smiled. "Good. I'll give you more stew in a few minutes. Just sit there and let the fire warm you."

I nodded.

It took me close to a half hour before I had warmed enough that the shivering stopped. By then I'd eaten four cups of the hot stew and followed the last with three fingers of whiskey. While I ate with my good hand Morgan cleaned the gash in my other palm and put a bandage on it. When that was done she gathered my wet things, wrung them out over the bucket, and hung them on the wall pegs behind the fire. I didn't have a mop, but she sopped up the water and ice off the floor with a towel and spread it to dry also. Then she upended my boots and suspended them from the rawhide loops I'd hung from the roof beams near the back wall. I'd dropped the shotgun on the bearskin when I'd first come in, and she picked it up and went to stand it in the corner. I told her to wait.

"I dropped it in the creek; it needs to be wiped down and oiled."

She looked at me with mild wonder.

I tried to smile. "Sorry, old habits die hard – take care of your weapon and it will take care of you, and all that."

"Army?" She asked.

"Marines," I told her.

"Did you fight in the Pacific?"

"You could say that," I told her. "South-east Asia."

She nodded and took the shotgun to the bed. She expertly fingered the slide release and pumped out three shells."

"Two more," I cautioned.

She looked puzzled. "I thought they only held three."

"The law only allows three. They hold five. Yours probably has a plug in it."

She worked the pump twice more, and two more shells plopped out onto the fleece blanket. It was clear she didn't know what to do next so I asked her to bring it over to me. When she had, I unscrewed the spring retention cap and removed it, then I slipped the barrel's locking ring off the pump tube.

"There," I said. "You'll find some oil and rags in the box on the shelf next to the shells."

She found them and brought them to me. By now I was feeling much better. There is something about a simple chore that confirms a man's grip on life. I took the oil from her and dripped a few drops inside the receiver and along the pump tube. I did the same with the barrel. She handed me a rag and I used it to rub the oil into the metal. I spent about three minutes pampering all the gun parts, and then asked her to get the cleaning rod off the shelf. She did, and I threaded a patch through the loop on its tip, soaked it with oil, and made several passes through the barrel. Then I replaced the dirty, oily patch with a clean, dry one and ran that through a few times as well.

Morgan sat quietly on the bed while I cared for my shotgun. When I was satisfied that it was thoroughly cleaned and oiled, I reassembled it and worked the action a few times, reloaded it with fresh shells from the box, and clicked on the safety. Then I held it out to her. She took it to the corner and stood it against the wall. Then she came back and kissed me gently on the forehead.

"Now," she said, "tell me what happened."

I filled her in. There really wasn't much to tell. I hadn't found any sign of Jason, nor had I found the raft or any of their gear. I had found where the raft had been, and I'd located the lodge, where I'd watched Roy and Larry eat their dinner. I got caught in a snow storm; I got in water higher than my boots; I'd fallen down a lot; I'd hurt my hand, and I'd almost been eaten by wolves. A lot of excitement, but the day, to all intents and purposes, had been a bust.

"So what now?" She asked.

"I'm not sure," I told her. "I didn't get a good look at the inside of the lodge. I could only see the main room. It's still possible they have Jason in one of the rooms in back."

As I said this I recalled seeing light around one of the doors out back. There must have been some reason they had lit a back room.

Morgan waited for me to go on. She knew what I was going to do. She was just giving me time to figure it out for myself.

"When the weather clears, I'll go back up there. I've got to make sure they don't have him locked up in one of the back rooms."

She reached out a hand and rested it on my knee. I looked up. Her eyes held a great sadness.

"Jason is dead." She said it with absolute certainty.

"You can't know." I protested.

"Yes." She said it simply, quietly. "I do know." She put her other hand over her heart. "Here."

We both sat quietly for a few minutes and then she went on, as if we hadn't paused.

"I was thinking about that night all the time you were gone. It all came back. I had thought, before, that I couldn't remember anything after Jason ran out the door, but I was still awake then. Today I remembered the rest. I remember hearing two shots outside, and I remember hearing a cry of pain. I remember my heart breaking, and then there was only the blackness."

There was really nothing to say. She had already let him go. I realized that, even though she hadn't remembered the details until today, she had given him up for dead before I'd found her on the bank. Perhaps that helped explain her conduct since waking in my bed – her easy acceptance of a new man in her life, her need for the comfort of physical contact, and her insistence on the futility of my searching for him. For her, Jason was dead. She needed her own life reaffirmed.

I knew two things: I would never understand what went on inside a woman's head – and I had to continue looking for Jason until I found conclusive evidence that he was dead or alive. When Roy McCaslin had asked if I'd seen any strangers around lately he had mentioned both man and woman tracks. Would he have bothered asking about man tracks if he knew Jason was dead? I doubted it. That meant it was still possible that Jason was alive. The bush has its code, as do most societies of men. It dictated that I keep trying until I knew. I looked at Morgan, sitting there quietly on the bed. I realized the sadness in her eyes was not for Jason alone. Some of it was for me. She knew I would go back when the weather cleared. I didn't have to tell her.

There was no lovemaking that night. I was exhausted from my ordeal and the whiskey knocked me out. When my head slumped forward on my chest Morgan had come and helped me from the rocker to the bed. She tucked me in, undressed and climbed in beside me, and wrapped me in her arms. I remember nothing but the sweet sadness of lying there with her arms around me and the delicious smell of her skin in my nostrils as I slipped off into sleep.

Chapter 20

I slept the sleep of the dead and did not wake up until the evening of the following day. It was cold, and I ached all over. The wind was howling in the stovepipe, and the candle on the table guttered and danced in the drafts coming through the poorly chinked walls. I tried to sit up, but a spear of pain lanced through my left hand. I looked at it and saw that Morgan had changed the dressing while I slept. She brought me a cup of tea and sat on the edge of the bed. She held it to my lips and I sipped.

"Stay in bed, you still need more rest. In any event, there's nothing you can do until morning with this weather. The snow didn't stop until midday; now the wind has picked up and it's bitter cold out."

"We'll need more firewood," I protested.

"I brought in enough to see us through to morning. Now, go back to sleep. I'll join you as soon as I bank the fire." She took my empty cup away.

I nestled my head back into the pillow. I doubted that I could sleep again, but it was pleasant and warm under the covers, listening to the sounds of Morgan moving about the cabin. I thought I'd just doze a little while I waited for her to slide in beside me. When I next awoke there was light streaming in through the east window.

The storm had passed in the night and a warm front had moved in behind it. The new day was clear and bright. Morgan was already up and busy at the stove when I, reluctantly, opened my eyes. There were the wonderful smells of coffee and bacon in the cabin, and I realized I was famished. I was also sore and stiff all over. Sore from all the falls I had taken, and stiff from lying abed for almost thirty hours. I threw back the covers and gingerly sat up. My arms and legs had some lovely patches of blue and purple, and my left hand throbbed with pain.

She saw me sit up and said, "Good morning. I wondered if you were going to sleep today away as well."

I looked out the window over the sink. The sun was well above the treetops. It was close to ten o'clock. She brought me a cup of coffee, and I took it with my good hand.

"Thank you. Smells good."

She sat next to me on the bed and rubbed my back with one hand.

"You're pretty banged up. I haven't had a look at you since I put you to bed two nights ago. You're a study in black and blue. You still haven't told me any details of your ordeal."

I sipped the coffee and shrugged my shoulders. "Stepped in a few holes and fell down a lot in the dark. If it hadn't been for that damned Trilogy I don't think I would have made it."

"Trilogy?

"Your pet grizzly. The one with the two missing toes."

She studied me for a moment. "So you've named him too. I know him as "Trident", the spear of Neptune, because he got me in the water and left me with three marks. But Trilogy is more fitting. It suggests he is a story in himself, one of many parts."

She was lost in thought for a few moments. I sat quietly and sipped the hot coffee. At length, she began rubbing my back again.

"Trilogy saved you?" This seemed to intrigue her.

I took another sip of coffee and thought about that.

"Well, I wouldn't go that far. But, he helped. I'd been trying to follow the left bank without crossing the creek; I was already wet enough. I was having a lot of trouble. Then I saw his tracks in the snow, going downstream. I followed them. He stayed on the gravel bars all the way, no matter which side of the stream they were on. We must have crossed the creek a dozen times. I don't know for sure. I lost count.

She looked at me with compassion. "You didn't have many crossings left in you."

I agreed. "Don't think I had any left. I fell the last time just as I reached the landing strip. I didn't think I could ever get up. The wolves had been following me since I cut my hand and they came in real close while I was down. That was enough to get me back on my feet, and when I recognized tire tracks in the gravel bar I realized where I was. Just knowing the cabin was near kept me going. I forgot about the claymores and tripped the one at the top of the path. It may have blasted one of the wolves."

I paused for a little, thinking how close I had come to dying. Then I put my arm around her and said, "If you hadn't been here, with the fire going and the stew bubbling, and if you hadn't been here to get me out of those frozen clothes, I would have died anyway – right there on the floor in front of a cold stove."

She mussed my hair. "You would have pulled through somehow; it's not your time yet."

***

At noon the sun stood high in the clear blue sky and the day was pleasantly warm. I didn't have a thermometer – I made a mental note to add that to the list – but I judged it to be in the sixties. We took our lunch out on the porch to eat in the sunlight. Morgan had spent the better part of yesterday experimenting with the cook stove while I slept. She had roasted two of the geese in the oven; their rendered fat was already in the can on the shelf. She had boned them out and saved the meat for today's lunch. We ate them cold, with a can of green beans and a loaf of bread she had baked this morning. It was delicious, and I told her so. She promised to roast the last goose that afternoon so we could have it hot, for dinner. I teased her about being in a rush to get more goose grease in the can. A blush colored her cheeks, but she smiled.

Most of the snow had melted by two in the afternoon. There were still patches where drifts had formed in low places, and a few inches remained under the trees, but the gravel bar was clear. I walked up the path to the tree line and found the spent claymore. The PVC pipe had, indeed, blown up when the shell went off. While I replaced it with a new one I said a silent prayer of thanks that I had decided against the steel pipe models. I might have been the architect of my own demise. I looked around for fur or blood near the claymore. I didn't find anything, but I hadn't expected to; the snow had continued to fall after I got back to The Varmitage, and it would have covered any sign the wolf left. Then I went back down and sat on the porch in the sun.

There was no putting it off. I had to get back up to the lodge and find out, one way or the other, about Jason. Haywood would be back in tomorrow, and Morgan would be going out with him. I assumed the first thing she'd have to do was notify the police of what had happened out here, and file charges against the McCaslins. It would help if we knew what happened to Jason. But, aside from that, if he were still their prisoner – a thought that made me shudder – I had to get him out of there. If they hadn't already killed him, sooner or later, they would. They couldn't afford to let him live to tell his story.

I procrastinated as long as I could. It was such luxury to just stretch out on the porch in the sun. I spent the better part of the afternoon there; my head back against the warm logs, the sun healing my bruised body and spirit. Morgan came out and sat on the top step. She'd borrowed one of my Levi shirts and the sleeves were rolled up above her elbows. Her legs and feet were bare. She had lovely feet – very slender and delicate. Her legs were lustrous white. Like most redheads her skin, all over, was very fair. I'm sure she had to be careful in the sun.

She saw me admiring her legs and gave me a knowing smile. "You seem to be recovering quickly."

She was right. I was. She held out her hand in my direction, fist closed and upside down.

"A present."

I leaned forward and held out my right hand. She dropped a tiny, clear plastic box into my palm. I recognized it; I had several like it in my fly tying kit.

There were two small flies inside, Deer Hair Caddis, quite expertly tied.

"You're good!" I meant it.

She clamped her arms around her bare legs and pulled them up to her chest.

"I promised to make you some special ones. Take them out of the box. See if you can tell what makes them special." Her eyes held mischief.

I popped open the lid, took out one of the flies and held it up in the sunlight. It looked much the same as the ones I tied – number sixteen hook; black thread; the body was built up of gray dubbing and wrapped with grizzly hackle; and the wings and head were of brown deer hair. As I studied it I detected a flash of color in the wings – a reddish copper glint. I took my glasses out of my shirt pocket, put them on, and again held the fly up in the light. Morgan was rocking slowly back-and-forth on the floorboards, watching me intently, an impish smile curling her lips.

My glasses were nothing more than two power magnifiers I

used for reading and tying flies. Through the lenses I could see clearly every detail of the fly. It truly was beautifully made. The head was wrapped and whip-finished expertly, the wings fanned out fully, and the ends of all the hairs were perfectly aligned, all except one – the red one. 'A red deer hair?' I examined it more closely. It was curly.

"Hmmmm." I kept the fly held aloft and gave Morgan a sidelong glance.

"What do you see?" she asked, still with that impish smile.

I resumed my examination. There was no doubt about it; I recognized that hair. It wasn't from a deer. It was one of Morgan's, and it hadn't come from her head. It was, indeed, a very special fly.

She was becoming impatient. She slapped my knee. "I know you see it," she said. "Tell me what you think it is."

"I see it," I said slowly. "And I believe I recognize it, but I'm trying to figure out how it got there. Did you tie these flies in your lap?"

She pushed at my leg and said, "Oh, you knew all along."

"No. Honestly, I didn't. But, I must say, I like the idea. I tie a lot of flies, you know. Will you let me harvest some for my own personal use?"

She gave me her shy, sidelong look and batted her eyelashes. "Maybe, if you're good."

I promised to be good.

***

It was time I went back up to the lodge and had one last go at looking for Jason. She must have read my thoughts, and indicated the flies she'd made.

"You should try one, just to see how they work. The fish have been rolling all afternoon."

I knew I should be going if I were to make it up to the lodge and back before dark. But I was also reluctant to leave, and I didn't want to disappoint her.

"Okay," I said. "If you'll fetch my rod and tie on one of your Specials, I'll see what the grayling think about them."

She smiled and jumped to her feet and disappeared inside the cabin. Almost immediately she came back out. My rod was already rigged.

"All set!" Her smile was radiant. "I tied three; the third one's already on your tippet!"

I laughed and took the rod from her hand. Her excitement and happiness were contagious. I felt good all over as I walked down to the creek, despite my bumps and bruises and bandaged hand. Morgan sat back down on the porch step and watched me. I turned to look up at her when I reached the water's edge. She waved – God, what a lovely sight.

I stripped off some line and tugged at the fly to test her knot; it was strong and tight. Then I waded a few steps into the water and flipped the fly upstream. It settled on the surface and started down the current - WHAM. I jerked my rod tip skyward - SNAP. My fly line floated back through the air and coiled at my feet.

"Damn it!" I said, retreating up the bank to the cabin. "Got a strike on the first cast and set the hook too hard. I snapped off your Special."

She was laughing and clapping her hands in delight. "Try again!"

When I plunked down on the step next to her she took the end of my fly-line, popped open the box, picked out another fly, and expertly tied it on.

"There," she said.

I strode purposefully back down to the creek and waded in. I cast upstream, the fly lit, then twisted in the current before starting its downstream run – WHAM! Another strike! I hooked this one. It was a fair sized grayling. I played it for a minute, then guided it into the shallow water, took hold of the line just above its mouth and lifted it clear of the water so Morgan could see it.

She clapped her hands. "Bravo!"

I lowered the fish back into the water, took a grip on the fly, and gave it a shake. The grayling rolled off the hook, hesitated momentarily, and then darted out into deeper water. I secured my fly to the hook keeper on the butt of the rod, and went back up to join Morgan.

She came down to meet me halfway. When I reached her she put an arm through mine and walked me back to the porch.

"You see," she said. "They really work."

I had to admit – they really did.

***

I looked at the sun. It would be setting in a little over an hour.

It was time to go. I told her so. She nodded sadly and said she knew. She insisted I take the canoe this time. If I got in trouble up there I wouldn't have to get back under my own power; the current would bring me home. I agreed.

She took my rod into the cabin while I got the paddles and a seat cushion out of the tent. I always carried two paddles, even when I was alone. There was always the chance of breaking one or losing one over the side. I had just stowed them in the stern when Morgan came out of the cabin carrying my field jacket and shotgun. She'd thought to bring the flashlight also. She brought them down to the canoe and stood in the soft mud along the water's edge; it squished up black between her white toes. I took them from her arms and thanked her. The jacket had dried well on its peg behind the stove, and the pockets were still full of shells. The afternoon was warm so I laid it on the forward seat. Then I checked the shotgun to make sure it held five shells. Satisfied, I secured it in the canoe, its barrel resting against my jacket. Before I pushed off I hugged her tight against me.

"I know," I said into her hair. "You think this is stupid. You think I shouldn't go."

She shook her head sadly; her red hair swayed and glistened in the lowering sun.

"No," she said softly. "Sometimes we just don't have any choice. Some things are preordained."

Then she kissed me on the lips and said, "Hurry back. It's our last night."

Chapter 21

Morgan stood on the shore as I pushed off and swung the bow upstream. The paddle handle bit into the palm of my wounded left hand, but the dressing padded and protected it enough that I knew I'd be able to make it three miles. I glanced back as I swung into the first bend. Morgan stood there, watching me go. She saw me looking back and raised a hand into the air. A wind came up suddenly, and her hair and shirt stirred and billowed around her. She reminded me of a painting I had once seen of a Celtic goddess, standing at the water's edge with the wind and the sun playing in her flaming red hair. My eyes remained fixed on her pagan, mystic and lovely form until my canoe slipped around the point, and she disappeared.

It was then I realized I hadn't been paddling. The wind had shifted and was pushing me upstream against the current. A shiver ran down my spine. It was an odd day. I couldn't recall the wind having ever come out of that quarter. All summer long it had come down the streambed. Destiny, I wondered, or just the shifting of the wind?

The sun was just above the treetops when I swung my bow into Deadman Creek. The wind dropped off as soon as I left the Moose Jaw and the waters of the Deadman were glassy and serene. I dipped my paddle slowly and carefully, making as little noise as I could. I glided into shore downstream of the lodge, where the bank was soft and muddy. I didn't want to grate across a gravel bottom and announce my arrival.

The canoe's bow nudged gently against the bank and its stern caught in the current and swung silently under a stout willow that overhung the water. I quietly stowed my paddle and took hold of the willow to keep me in place while I waited and listened. When I was certain my arrival had gone unnoticed, I tied off the bow to the willow, knowing the current would keep the stern pressed against the bank.

I had made good time coming upstream with the wind behind

me. The sun was not yet down behind the hills so there was still too much light for me to approach the lodge. I decided to just sit quietly in the canoe and wait for sunset. I wasn't sure what I was going to do, but whatever plan I worked out, I wanted the cover of darkness. As I sat there I got the sudden urge for a smoke. That, of course, was out of the question but I slipped my pipe out of my pocket, and clamped the stem between my teeth. Even not lit, its familiar, solid weight in my jaws was comforting.

A big trout broke the calm surface of the water out in midstream. Then another, further up the creek. I watched the ripples spread out from the feeding rings until their outer circles merged. The sun was slipping behind the distant hills now, and I could see it through the trunks of the trees. Its fading light lent a rosy glow to the sky. The air began cooling quickly, and a mist began rising from the surface of the creek, as the water gave up its warmth to the coming night. I laid my shotgun on the bank and slipped into my jacket. Then I sat and watched with wonder as the sky grew darker and the mist thickened and twisted and metamorphosed into a graveyard fog. It was damp and heavy on the water, and it crawled up the banks from the surface of the Deadman and silently spread its tendrils through the trunks of the trees, until it lay, like a shroud, upon the forest floor.

***

The screams came from the direction of the lodge. They sliced through the fog and transfixed my soul like a spear of ice. My blood froze in my veins and the hairs bristled on my scalp. My pipe dropped out of my mouth and clattered in the bottom of the canoe. The shrieks grew wilder and more terrible and then abruptly stopped. The fog and the night now vibrated with terror and agony and silence.

I tried to jump out of the canoe but slipped on the mud of the bank and came down hard on top of my shotgun. One foot splashed into the water and my leg became, momentarily, wedged between the canoe and the bank. I pulled it free and scrambled to my feet. My shotgun lie pressed flat in the mud.

"Shit!" I hissed, as I snatched it up and quickly checked the barrel to make sure it was clear.

There was a little mud around the lip, but it didn't appear plugged. I made sure the safety was on, then plunged my little finger into the muzzle and wiped it clean. It was a dangerous thing to do but there was no time for the usual precautions.

I jumped to my feet and sprinted through the fog toward the lodge. I thought I was on the path but I couldn't tell; the trees were merely dark shapes that loomed suddenly out of the mist and then faded to nothingness. The screams had stopped, but their silent echoes reverberated through the foggy woods. I had no idea what the hell was going on in there or, for that matter, who had been screaming. I couldn't tell if it had been a man or a woman or a banshee. It could have been Jason. I hoped I hadn't waited too long.

As I broke into the clearing the fog took on an amber glow. There was movement, dark and fleeting, in the trees across the open ground. I tucked and rolled and came up in a kneeling position, staring down my shotgun's barrel into the glowing fog, but whatever I'd seen move was now gone. Out of the corner of my eye I could see that the door to the lodge stood open, and the surreal light that illuminated the fogscape spilled out from the great hall, across the porch, and onto the black dirt of the clearing.

I hesitated for a moment. I wasn't certain the screams had come from inside the lodge. They may have come from the trees. I could check the lodge quickly; the woods would take longer – the lodge then. I rose to my feet and started through the fog toward the rectangle of light, all the time watching the trees out of the corner of my eye.

I was ten feet from the porch when Roy McCaslin came flying out the door, a specter borne upon an ephemeral tide of light. He was naked and covered with blood; his eyes glowed like the fires of hell! Light glinted red on the steel blade of his knife as he launched himself at me.

I'd been carrying the shotgun low as I crossed the clearing, so I fired from the hip. The blast blew him back against one of the posts that supported the porch roof. He was still on his feet. His eyes locked with mine as he clutched at his shredded testicles, blood dripped from between his fingers. He sagged to his knees, his hate-filled eyes still burning into me. He opened his mouth in a silent scream. I could see the gap in the bottom row of his wolfish, yellow teeth. The vision of a pink nipple encircled with blue bruises flashed across my mind. Beautiful, helpless, Morgan.

I worked the pump on my shotgun and stepped closer. His eyes never left mine as I brought up the barrel, its muzzle now inches from his open mouth. I slowly squeezed the trigger. His offensive teeth disappeared in an explosion of blood and brains and bone fragments. I ejected the spent shell into my hand and put it in my pocket. Then I looked around until I found the first one I'd fired. I pocketed that one also. Evidence. Mustn't leave evidence.

I went back to Roy's mutilated body and looked down at him. He was, indeed, a horror to behold. My first shot had hit him in the genitals. I hadn't aimed there. I hadn't aimed anywhere – I'd just pulled the trigger. While studying the damage, I noticed an odd thing. There was a string, or wire, or something, tied around what once had been his scrotum. It trailed off into the dirt beside him. It looked to be about four feet long. His left hand still gripped it. I nudged it with the tip of my shotgun barrel; it made a metallic sound. It was a wire. There was another lump of bloody meat attached to the other end. I would never have recognized it as a sack of male organs taken out of the context of this horrible scene, but all the parts were there. I swallowed my gorge, and knew I'd have to go in and look for the organ donor.

I stepped over Roy's corpse and moved quietly across the porch. Silly really, considering I'd just let off two shotgun blasts. Did I think I was going to sneak up on someone? I let the muzzle of my shotgun precede me through the door and into the lodge's main hall, which was big and well lit. It was also empty. That is, there was no one in there. Another door stood ajar across the room, in the back wall. I crossed the room, opened it the rest of the way with my foot, and poked my head through the doorway.

The inhuman shape was grotesquely large and naked and covered, literally, covered with blood. There was blood everywhere. I didn't go inside the room. I didn't want to leave my footprints in the blood on the floor. Roy had left plenty of his own. A candle burned on a table near the bed and I could see all I needed to see from where I stood. Thank god it was Larry. He was spread-eagled on the floor near the far wall, and there was a ragged, gaping hole where his crotch had been. He had bloody holes all over his chest. He looked like he'd been run over by a lawn aerator. Roy had savagely butchered his brother.

Once again, I had to struggle to keep from vomiting. I'd seen carnage before, but never anything like this. I tore my eyes away from Larry's hacked up body and went to check the other rooms. I had come to look for Jason, and that's what I was going to do.

I looked in every room. It had been a fair sized lodge; great room, kitchen, dining hall and five sleeping rooms. There was also a bathroom complete with toilet and shower, apparently gravity fed from a water tank I had not yet seen.

After I'd satisfied myself that there was no one else, living or dead, inside the lodge, I went back out the front door. I'd been careful not to touch anything or leave any footprints inside. I thought about what I should do next. If I left Roy's body laying out here, the wolves or a bear would find it. I wasn't troubled with the thought of Roy being eaten by wild animals; it would have served the bastard right. But I didn't want my local bears or wolves developing a taste for human flesh. I wanted to come back next summer and I didn't want to be on anyone's menu.

I leaned my shotgun against the porch railing and grabbed Roy by the ankles. Thank God it wasn't Larry; I never could have budged him. Roy, on the other hand, didn't weigh much over one-sixty. Dragging him up the steps was the most difficult part. I pulled him inside the lodge far enough to allow clearance for the door to swing shut. Then I pulled it closed and wiped the handle with my coat sleeve. Before returning to the canoe I took the time to check the woods where I had seen movement earlier. Morgan had remembered to give me the torch, so I spent about ten minutes playing its beam over the ground back in the trees.

This time my efforts were rewarded. I found two footprints. I couldn't tell if they were Jason's or not. There didn't appear to be any noticeable tread. I could tell for certain that they were neither Larry's nor Roy's. One was too big, the other too small. Someone else had been here. I studied the tracks in detail before switching off the light. If I didn't know better, I would have thought they were moccasin prints. I'd have to ask Morgan if Jason had brought along a pair of moccasins. Then I had a thought. What the hell – there was nothing to lose.

"JASON!" I shouted as loud as I could into the fog. "JASON! MORGAN SENT ME. COME OUT IF YOU'RE HERE!"

There was a rustle in the treetops and I felt, rather than heard, something large and silent pass overhead. The fog above me stirred and shifted with its passing. I'd probably startled a night bird with my shouts. I waited five minutes. When no one answered or appeared, I broke off a spruce bough and wiped my tracks out of the dirt of the clearing. I tossed it under a tree as I backed into the woods, and then made my way slowly through the dense fog to the canoe.

When I came out of the Deadman and swung my bow into the current of the Moose Jaw the fog lifted and the night was clear. The wind that had been blowing upstream was now blowing, gently, out of its usual quarter. Luck, or something else was with me. With the wind and the current both working for me, my trip home was swift. I glanced at my watch as I came around the last bend, and saw the light in the cabin windows. I couldn't believe I had been gone only two hours. It seemed a lifetime.

I beached the canoe and pulled it up on the gravel bar. I decided to leave the paddles and cushion in it; I was in a hurry to get inside. It was to be our last night. I know killing Roy should have troubled me. It didn't. He was a pig, a rapist and probably a murderer as well. There was no judge or jury out here, nor jails or executioners either. But justice had been served. Rather than being upset, I was, quite frankly, at peace. Elated even. I still didn't know what had happened to Jason, but Morgan was probably right. It stood to reason that the McCaslins had killed him that night, and then dumped his body in the river. They did the same thing to Morgan, but I'd found her and brought her back to life.

I had just taken my shotgun out of the canoe and started up the bank toward the cabin when I noticed the huge, deep tracks, just visible in the moonlight. I took out my torch and shone it on the mud of the bank.

'I'll be damned,' I thought. 'The bear has been through here again'.

There was no mistaking the track; the three toes were quite distinct in the mud. He looked to be headed downstream this time. I followed his progress with the torchlight until it neared my launch pad. Something tugged at my psyche, so I went closer to the water, keeping my light focused on whatever it was that had beckoned me.

When I came to the water's edge I saw what it was. There, stamped clearly in the bank of the creek, was an image I had seen before; the paw of a three-toed bear beside the footprint of a woman. The woman track was Morgan's, of course. She'd left it when seeing me off that afternoon. And the bear was Trilogy. In my mind I could see the tracks in the slab of the old hearth, now buried beneath the cabin – a woman's track, slender and delicate, and that of a three toed bear. They had been together a long time, it seemed. They were part of this valley, part of my cabin, and now – part of me. Hard Case's words came back to me. "Strange shit happens out there sometimes," he had said.

'Indeed it does,' I thought. 'Indeed it does.'

I peered up at the moon. It cast an eerie glow tonight. I looked at it until a cloud moved between us and a shadow fell over the land. Then I turned and went slowly up the gravel bar to the cabin.

Chapter 22

Morgan was standing at the stove when I came into the cabin. She looked up and smiled as she closed the door on the oven.

"We'll have fresh bread with our goose again tonight," she said proudly.

She came over to me and took my shotgun from me as I hung up my coat. I didn't know how to tell her what I'd done. Maybe it was best I didn't. As I turned to take her in my arms I saw she was still holding the shotgun, looking at it pensively. The hint of a smile curled her lips. She looked up into my eyes.

"You killed him." She said it simply.

"How..." I began, but didn't finish.

I didn't really want to know. I took the gun from her and leaned it against the wall. Then I put my arms around her and held her close for a moment.

"Let me pour a drink, then I'll tell you about it."

"Maybe you should pour me one too."

She followed me to the counter. I took two tin cups off the shelf and poured three fingers of Dew into them both. I added a splash of water to mine and looked at her to see if she wanted water also.

She shook her head. I handed her the neat one and raised my cup.

"Cheers."

She raised hers. "Salute."

I went over and pulled the rocker away from the hot stove. I settled in it, and Morgan sat at the table.

"Tell me," she said.

"Well," I said, "we can take the shirts down from the windows."

She waited, delicately sipping at her drink.

I went on. "I didn't find Jason, of course. You didn't expect I would. I did, however, find the McCaslins." I was considering how to tell her what happened.

"And they are dead."

Again, I was unsettled by the simplicity – the certainty – of her words. I took a large slug of my whiskey.

"Yes. They're dead. They are very, very dead."

I expected her to ask me what had happened. She didn't. She merely shrugged her shoulders and raised her cup to salute me.

"Good," she said. "That's done. Now we can have our farewell dinner."

I was a little disappointed. I had wanted to tell her I'd blown out Roy's yellow teeth, the teeth that had violated her perfect breast. I wanted to tell her that they died as eunuchs, their manhood hacked and bloody in the dirt. I wanted her to know that both she and Jason had been avenged – that their violators had paid a terrible price for their crimes. But she didn't ask. Perhaps she already knew.

After we finished our drinks we ate our last dinner by candlelight. It was superb. She'd stuffed the goose with rice and wild mushrooms and cooked it slowly all day. Her bread had baked perfectly and we ate it hot with the meal. I still had two bottles of white wine left over from Haywood's last visit, so I opened one that had been chilling outside the door. If the Varmitage had crystal, tonight we would have used it. But, there was no crystal so we drank our wine from tin cups as always.

We were very quiet throughout dinner. The prospect of her leaving tomorrow cast a pall of sweet sadness over the cabin. When she had finished eating she studied me over her wine. Her green eyes were deep and inviting in the soft light of the candle. I lay aside my fork and lifted my wine cup to her. She smiled and raised hers to me. A silent toast. A good-bye?

Once again I suggested that Haywood's plane was big enough to carry three, and I could fly back to Fairbanks with them in the morning if she liked.

She shook her head sadly. "No." She said, "When he comes, I'll depart alone."

Then she stood up and took my hand and led me to the bed. She undressed slowly for me and said, "I think my skin is getting a little dry. Maybe we should try out that new batch of goose grease."

I brought the candle over near the bed so I could see her clearly while I worked. I believe it was my finest greasing ever. I don't know when we finally fell asleep. It must have been near dawn.

***

I didn't wake until I heard the drone of an airplane passing low overhead. I opened my eyes to a stream of full sunlight coming in through the east window. I looked at my watch. It was nine o'clock. Haywood was right on schedule.

Morgan stirred in my arms and, as I sat up to get out of bed, she pulled me back down and kissed me long and sweet on the lips.

"Haywood's here," I told her.

"I know," she said. "I'm ready. I don't have much to pack do I?"

I swung my feet to the floor and stood up. She still held my hand. She squeezed it.

"You're a kind and gentle man."

She paused as if to say something else, then released my hand.

"You'd better go meet your friend."

Chapter 23

I dressed quickly and took the path up through the spruce, over the high ground and down to the gravel bar to welcome Haywood. He had already landed and was taxiing his old Clipper back downstream. He brought the craft to a halt and cut the engine. The propeller slowed and gradually wound to a stop. Haywood always fiddled around in the cockpit for a few minutes before getting out of the plane, checking dials and gauges and switches. It gave me time to cover the last hundred yards. He was just opening the door as I reached the plane.

He hopped down and his boots crunched into the gravel. He gave me a bear hug.

"Hah! Fergus, my boy! Looking fit and well fed. What happened to your hand, ruin it pounding your forehead every time you made a mistake on the cabin?"

I laughed. It was always good to see him. He was full of life and it made you feel more alive just being around him.

"Poked it with a stick," I said. "The bandage makes it look worse than it is. But, forget my hand, we need to unload quick and leave the gear here on the bar. I've got a passenger for you."

He sobered quickly. "Passenger?"

He studied me carefully for a moment. "Female, if I don't miss my mark."

I was astonished. "How did you know?"

"Elementary my dear Watson," he chuckled. "You've knocked off your beard and smell like you may have showered recently. And you're grinning like a fool. So, where'd you come up with a woman?"

I filled him in about Morgan as we unloaded. Not everything, but about finding her on the bank and her recovery, and the story about Jason, the McCaslins and the trouble at their lodge. I didn't mention killing Roy. That could wait.

He looked puzzled as I gave him the highlights. But he kept silent until I'd finished. Then, as he hauled out the last of the cargo and carried it to the pile, he said, "Who are the McCaslins? I never ran across them. Never even heard of them. Far as I know, you're the only one that's been in here this summer."

I told him they had turned up the day after I found Morgan and said they had been living in a cabin up where Deadman Creek comes into the Moose Jaw.

"Said they'd been there on-and-off for several years."

"Huh," he said finally. "Don't ever remember a cabin up there. In fact, I'm sure there's not one up there. I've flown over that creek several times now and I would have noticed the roof of a cabin."

He studied me closely for a long time. He looked concerned.

Finally he said, "Maybe we better go have a look at my passenger."

And, with that, we started back to the cabin. I asked him about the news as we walked. When he didn't answer I turned to look at him. He was deep in thought and, clearly, hadn't heard a word I'd said. I smiled to myself. When Haywood was pondering a problem he was in a world of his own. You couldn't reach him. I gave it up. We'd have plenty of time to chat after he delivered Morgan to Fairbanks.

***

When we got back to the cabin Morgan was not inside. I told Haywood to go ahead and make his initial inspection of The Varmitage, while I checked out back; she was probably using the "facilities". He raised an eyebrow at the use of the word. I grinned, went out and fired up the Coleman, and put on a pot of coffee. All the while, I kept an eye out for Morgan to come down the path from the outhouse. After a few minutes, Haywood came out of the cabin, sat on a stump and lit one of his Churchills. He pointed the glowing tip in the direction of the privy and said, "The facilities?"

I nodded and he said, "Saw it when I was doing my flyover. Looked like a blue tee-pee from the air. Thought it might be the shitter you were threatening to build. And, by the way, nice job on the cabin; it's perfect."

I grunted something to show I was listening when, in fact, I really wasn't. I was getting concerned that Morgan had not yet returned. I filled and lit my pipe to kill a little more time. After a few minutes, she still hadn't shown, so I walked up the path to the tree line and called her name. No answer. I went closer to the flap that served as the door to the privy.

"Morgan?" I said softly, "You in there?"

Still no answer. I pulled back the flap. It was empty.

I hurried back down the path and ignored Haywood's worried expression as I swept past him and went through the door into the cabin. She was, indeed, gone. There was no trace of her. No Levis, no shirt, no boots. I turned quickly and almost ran into Haywood who was standing in the open doorway. I tried to get past him so I could go down and check the creek bank. His pitchfork hands clamped around my upper arms. His grip was like a vice. I tried to pull away but couldn't.

"God damn it Haywood! I've got to..." I began, but he cut me off.

"What you've got to do, Gus," he said quietly, "is you've got to get a grip on yourself."

He said it gently but he meant it. Concern showed in his eyes.

"Remember what Hard Case told you. Funny things happen to a guy's head when he's out here alone for a long time."

I laughed, relieved. "No, no. You don't understand," I told him. "She's real. She was here. Look at the table."

He still had a death grip on my arms, so I couldn't look back into the cabin myself, but he could. I knew the remains of last night's dinner would convince him I wasn't crazy. He looked over my head.

"What about it?" He asked, still holding me immobile.

"We ate dinner together there last night!" I cried out in exasperation. "Use your goddamned eyes – two plates, two cups..."

I never finished. Haywood had released me and I turned as I spoke. I was lifting my arm to point, but I stopped. A single lit candle stood on the table. Nothing more. I stared, speechless. As if in a trance, I walked to the table, ran my hand over its clean, wood surface, and sagged into a chair.

Haywood pulled up the chair across the table and sat. He didn't say anything.

"This isn't right," I said. "This isn't right at all. We had a good-bye dinner last night – goose stuffed with rice and mushrooms. We had a bottle of white wine. She must have cleaned it up while I was meeting you. But where would she...why would she..." I trailed off.

Haywood was a good friend. We had been close friends for many years and had come to know each other well. He puffed on his cigar slowly, pensively.

"Okay," he said, appealing to my reason, which he respected. "If – I say if – she was here, and mind you, I'm not saying she was or wasn't. If she was here and she walked away, she had to have left sign. Agreed?"

I nodded.

"Right," he continued. "So, if she left sign, a seasoned old sign reader like myself ought to be able to cut her trail, don't you think?"

I nodded again. He nodded too.

"Good. So, you sit here and smoke your pipe and wait for the coffee to perk. I'll go out and scout around a bit. What was she wearing on her feet?"

"Hiking boots," I answered. "Old style, high-top lace ups. L.L. Bean I think."

"Vibran soles?" he asked. "Waffle stompers?"

I thought for a minute. "No, just smooth leather soles. You know, old style."

"Right then!" He slapped a big hand down on the tabletop and stood up. "Save me a cup of coffee."

With that he went out the door.

***

I sat there, lost in thought until the hiss of coffee boiling over on the stove brought me back to the present. I went outside, removed the pot from the burner and turned off the flame. The acrid smell of burned coffee hung in the cold morning air. The simple task of cleaning up the stove and making a fresh pot took my mind, for the moment, off Morgan. But, while I sat there on the stump waiting for the new batch to perk, I kept asking myself why she had left. Where had she gone? I remembered our conversation over dinner the night before. I remembered her looking at me with those beautiful green eyes and raising her wine cup to me. And I remembered her words.

"When he comes, I'll depart alone."

Could she have meant precisely that? She would leave, literally, alone? But that made no sense at all. She had nowhere to go. She had no food, no equipment, no jacket. She didn't even have socks or underwear. As I went over all this in my mind, it occurred to me that, perhaps, she had just decided to go off alone for a little while before flying back to civilization. Soak up a little store of wilderness before she left. I could understand that. I'd probably do the same thing myself. I felt a little better with this line of reasoning. When the coffee stopped bubbling up in the perk dome, I went over to the stove and turned the flame to low. As I did so, I scanned the tree line and the creek bank, hoping to see her striding back toward me.

I kept watch while the coffee settled, and through my first two cups. She didn't appear. When I was pouring my third cup, Haywood came into view from upstream. He was working his way slowly along the creek, eyes to the ground, stopping now and then to study something he saw in the mud or the sand. I had a cup poured and waiting when he finally walked up the bank to the cabin. He took it and sat on his stump.

"Anything?" I asked.

"Plenty," he said, sipping his coffee. "Moose, bear, wolf, beaver, ducks, geese and martens. No boot prints other than your own. He looked at me pointedly.

"She was here," I insisted. "She was real and she was here! She ate, drank, slept, walked and talked. She even shit my bed for Christ's sake!" I was getting angry.

"Shit your bed?" he asked, incredulous. I explained.

He sat thinking that over. He lit the stub of his cigar and puffed it until it glowed to his satisfaction.

"Well," he said, "I can't see you making up a dream girl for company and then having her shit your bed. Unless there's a dark side to you I don't know about, you're just not that sick. Besides, I've read all your journals and you haven't got that much imagination."

He held up a hand in anticipation of my objection. "Don't take that wrong. You're a good writer but you write about stuff that really happened. You report. You write facts. Sure, you embellish it some but, at the end of the day, you write honest-to-god, it-really-happened stuff. Unless you've undergone a hell of a sea change while you've been out here, I don't think you could make up something like this. Be that as it may, I've been all over and around this place and your mystery woman didn't leave any tracks."

"That's impossible," I said. "She left tracks in the mud down at the landing yesterday. She was barefoot. You didn't see them?"

He shook his head. "I checked the landing very carefully. The only tracks down there are yours."

I stood up. "Come on, I'll show you."

I marched down the bar to the landing. Haywood didn't follow; he stood by the cabin and watched me. He knew, of course, I wouldn't find what I was looking for. I didn't. Her tracks were gone and so were the bear's. This was too much. I walked downstream a few paces and looked at the tree on the far bank. I'd been confronted daily by the sight of those three white scars on its trunk since Trilogy had clawed them into the bark. Now, they too were gone. So was the tree.

I walked slowly back up to the cabin. Haywood didn't say anything when I returned. He just handed me my cup as I sat down on the stump. There had to be an explanation. We sat silently sipping our coffee for a while.

Finally, I said. "Okay. No tracks. That's possible. She usually wore my ducks when she went outside and I didn't actually see her put on her boots this morning. She may have left barefoot. If so, and she stuck to the gravel, you wouldn't have been able to pick up her trail."

"True enough," he agreed. "But, you'd figure, sooner or later, she'd have to cut up into the woods or down to the water. Either way, she would have left a print in the sand or mud, barefoot or not. I would have found that track."

I thought about that, but I could still see where she might have walked away without leaving any sign. Then too, good as Haywood was, he could have missed something.

"Yeah," I answered, "you'd think so. But, for now, let's just say she left no sign. As I see it, the first thing I've got to do is convince you she was real, and I haven't gone round the bend. Let's look over the inside of the cabin. She spent nine days in there. There's got to be a red hair on the pillow or something that will prove she was there."

He nodded and stood up. "A redhead, no less," he said, and followed me into the cabin.

We went over every inch with a fine-toothed comb. After a half hour of searching we had found nothing. No hair, no nail clipping, nothing. I slumped into one of the chairs. Haywood tossed the mattress back on the bed, folded the blankets and laid them on top of it. Then he went to the shelf and brought over the bottle of Dew. He poured us each a generous dollop.

"It's close enough to noon," he said. He lifted his tin cup in my direction and then sipped the whiskey. I took a mouthful and swallowed. We finished that drink and he poured us each another. It was helping.

"How much of this stuff you been drinking?" he asked me.

"Not much," I answered truthfully. "Couple of shots at night before I turn in. Certainly not that much. You left me with six full bottles when you went out in mid July. Still got this one."

He looked at the half full bottle on the table and nodded.

"Been eating any strange mushrooms?" He was smiling a little to take the sting out of the question.

"No stranger than usual." I told him. "Boletes and Scaly Tooth mainly. I scrambled up a couple of Shaggy Manes with some eggs last week. No exotics, if that's what you mean."

He considered this in silence. After a little while he leaned back in his chair and his face took on a look of mild amusement.

"Haven't been scooping a handful of that goose grease and having a go at yourself, have you?"

"Haywood..."

He went on as if I hadn't interrupted. "Man can wank himself to death, you know. It's a proven medical fact."

"Haywood!" I wasn't in the mood for good-natured ribbing.

"Injure yourself at the very least."

"Goddamnit, Haywood!" I started out of my chair.

He held up a hand. "Alright." He was serious now. "That was out of line. Sorry."

Then, after a slight pause, "You do look like a wanker, though."

In spite of myself, a laugh snorted out me.

Humor had always been Haywood's weapon of choice. The hurt and rage I had experienced at Morgan's departure drained out of me as we sat quietly and sipped our whiskies. Over our third, Haywood said, "Well, can't hunt the day you fly. May as well get drunk. Let's finish these, fetch all the gear I brought, and then we can settle down to some serious drinking. There's more whiskey in one of the big totes. And, while we're getting shit faced, you can tell me the whole story. I know you well enough to know you kept a good bit back. I want to hear it all. Fair enough?"

I saluted him with my cup. "Fair enough. You didn't happen to bring in some proper whiskey glasses did you? I'm getting tired of drinking everything out of a goddamned tin cup."

"As a matter of fact, I did."

"Good." I downed the rest of my drink in one gulp. "Let's go get 'em."

***

It took us four trips to haul everything up from the landing strip to the cabin. He'd brought his sleeping bag, all his hunting gear and several game bags. There was also enough food and whiskey to restock the cabin and leave it well enough supplied to see a stranded traveler through the winter. This was a common courtesy in the bush. He'd included a real set of dishes and glasses and a teakettle. House warming gifts he said; they weren't for me, they were for The Varmitage. There was also a fold-up camp bed, complete with mattress, not for me either. It was for himself. My present was two cases of Rolling Rock beer. I was delighted because I had run out two weeks ago. We opened a couple of bottles and sat on the cooler by the airstrip and drank them. I'd forgotten how good a cold beer tasted.

The real surprise, however, was rolled up in a canvas sack. He said he'd show me when we got back to the cabin. So we gathered up the final load and headed back. After we had everything stowed in its proper place, and he'd unfolded the camp bed and laid out his sleeping bag on it, we opened two more beers and went back outside. He indicated the canvas bag with the tip of his boot, and told me to open it.

I undid the tie straps and shook the contents onto the ground. There were two, seven-foot long one-by-three pine boards and three short one-by-sixes. There was also a roll of fiberglass screen and door hardware; all the makings of a screen door. I was very pleased. It was a great gift. Now I could air out the cabin during the day without the black flies and mosquitoes taking over the place. That had been a problem in the tent all summer. I laughed and thanked him.

"There's enough mesh in that roll to make screens for all three windows too. You'll have to make the frames out of limb wood, of course. But you've got everything you need for the door. Now you've got your first project for next summer."

I clapped him on the back and we opened two more beers and drank a toast to a bug free summer. He settled down on the top step of the porch, and I sat on the bench so I could lean my head back against the warm logs, close my eyes and feel the sun and the breeze on my face. It was a comfortable afternoon.

Haywood lit a fresh cigar and inspected the glowing tip.

"Start from the beginning," he said. The truth, the whole truth and nothing but the truth."

So I started from the beginning. I didn't dwell on the goose grease sessions, but I told him everything else. He only interrupted once, when I mentioned shooting Roy. He held up his hand for me to stop.

"Are you telling me you skulked up to these guys' lodge and just shot one of them? Dead?" He had been listening with interest until this juncture; now he was riveted.

"Dead."

He shook his head in wonder.

I continued, telling him about what I'd found inside the lodge, and how I'd left things. I could see he was incredulous, but he kept silent until I wrapped up the story with his arrival this morning.

He motioned for me to open another beer for him and then, as I was digging one out of the cooler, he thought better of it.

"Never mind, I need a whiskey."

He went into the cabin, and I opened the beer for myself. It was good to have gotten all this off my chest. It was good to have Haywood to tell it to.

He came back out with one of the new whiskey glasses full to the brim and spread himself out on the steps again. He took a gulp and shot me an exasperated look.

"Okay, let's see if I got it right." He puffed his cigar furiously for a moment, took another gulp of his Dew, and began.

"You found this redhead by the water. You carried her here, to the cabin. On the third day she rose again from the dead. She marked your bed as her territory, fox style. You nursed her back to health. You got, ah – chummy. She told you she and the guy she was rafting with got attacked by a bear. Then two Okies show up that promise to help them, but fuck 'em instead. Her corn-holed companion goes screaming, naked, into the night. Then she winds up in the creek with a knot on her head, and can't remember how she got there."

He sipped at his drink. "How we doin' so far?"

"So far, so good." I had my eyes closed and my head still resting against the logs of the cabin wall.

"So, you go looking for her fellow traveler. You don't find the raft or any of their gear, or any sign of the friend. You go back downstream to the woods near the bad guys' cabin. It gets dark and a storm moves in, so you call it a day and head home in a snow storm. You damned near freeze to death before you reach the cabin, but your girlfriend thaws you out and everything's hunky-dory. Two days later the snow's gone, and toward evening you take the canoe and paddle back up to visit the McCaslin brothers. You hear screaming. You run to the lodge. When you get there one of the assholes comes charging out the door, naked and bloody, and rushes you with a knife. You shoot him in the face with your shotgun. Then you find the other one inside, already dead, also naked. He's full of knife holes, and his cock and balls have been hacked off. You drag the mortal remains of your victim, gonads still intact, back inside, wipe the place down, and scrub out your tracks as you back out of there."

He paused to take a sip of whiskey and a few puffs on his cigar. I waited. He went on.

"Then you drift back down here in the canoe. You've just killed a man but you come in here, pretty as you please, and share a candlelight dinner with your girlfriend, spend the night putting her to the pork sword, and then, in the morning, when I arrive – she disappears." He downed the remains of his whiskey to signal he'd finished. "Is that about it?"

"That's about it," I said. "One minor correction – my victim's gonads were not still intact. My first shot shredded them."

I opened one eye to see how Haywood had received this last bit of news. His mouth was agape, and he was staring at me in undisguised disbelief. I couldn't blame him; I was finding it hard to believe myself. Was it possible I had dreamed it all up? I didn't know. The alcohol was getting to me and my mind was fuzzing up. I really didn't want to think about it any more.

"Your first shot," Haywood repeated softly. "So, after blowing his balls off, you pump in another round, and, for good measure, blow his face off too. Nice touch."

He took a few more puffs on his cigar. The smoke rolled lazily off into the afternoon air.

"And you still believe she was real; all this really happened."

It wasn't put as a question. It was more a hopeless observation. Nevertheless, I forced myself to consider it for a minute.

Finally I said, "Yeah. I guess I do."

"Well," he said, looking up at the sun, "we still got maybe three hours of light. How far is it up to this place where you blew off this guy's head and nuts?"

"Couple of miles above the landing strip," I answered listlessly. "You aren't suggesting we go back up there are you?"

"Yes. More than suggesting. I'm going up to have a look, with or without you. If you have any sense you'll come along. It's the only way you'll ever know if any of this shit really happened."

He puffed furiously at his cigar. "Besides," he said, "if you really did kill this guy we have to get rid of the body, and make damned sure there's no way to tie you to the killing." He was, truly, a good friend.

I thought about what he'd said for a minute and, reluctantly, agreed. While Haywood paid a visit to the outhouse, I retrieved our jackets from the cabin. Then I fetched the other seat cushion out of the tent and walked down to the water's edge. The paddles were still in the canoe; I had left them there overnight.

I was seated in the stern, ready to launch when Haywood came down the bank. He had stopped by the cabin to get our shotguns. He handed them to me and I tossed him his jacket. He slipped into it, then climbed aboard as he shoved us off.

"I doubt we'll need the guns," I observed.

"I hope you're right." He replied, digging the blade of his paddle deep into the water and swinging the bow upstream.

The wind wasn't with us as it had been with me yesterday. It took us nearly an hour of hard paddling to reach Deadman Creek, and another ten minutes to reach the spot where I'd beached on the previous day. We swung into shore and our bow slid aground on the muddy bottom. Haywood stepped over the side into the shallows, pulled the bow up against the bank and tied us off to the willows. I handed him the shotguns and climbed ashore. I pointed at the game trail running along the bank, and he followed as I led the way. When we had walked for a few minutes Haywood laid a hand on my shoulder. I stopped to see what he wanted.

"How much farther?" he asked.

"Just around that next bend." I said.

He nodded. "Okay. Now listen to me. I want you to stay put right here until I get back. I want to have a look around that bend before we go charging in there."

The whiskey and beer and paddling had left me too tired to protest. I nodded.

He turned and went up the path. I had just settled down on a fallen log when he reappeared. His face was grim.

"Oh, shit," I said. "What is it?"

"Describe the cabin," he said flatly. "Give me every detail you can remember. How did it look when you were here yesterday?"

"What...?" I began, but he cut me off with a quick gesture of his hand.

"God damn it, what did it look like yesterday?" He was clearly agitated.

"Ramshackle old fishing lodge," I shrugged. "Log construction, roof and porch sagging pretty bad. Some of the windows boarded up. Inside there was a big stone fireplace at one end of a large room; half log flooring; six or seven other rooms off the main room. That's where I found the second body – in one of the smaller rooms."

Haywood thought for a minute. "You sure this is the right place? Did we come far enough up the Deadman?"

His line of questioning was beginning to wear on me. This was the right place. It looked a little different last night in the fog, but there was no doubt in my mind.

"This is the place Haywood. Now, what's the problem?"

He took a deep breath and sighed. "Better come have a look."

I followed him up the path. When we rounded the last bend what I saw made me want to cry. In the center of the clearing stood a blackened, crumbling stone chimney. Around it lie a few charred timbers of a long forgotten fire. The lodge that had stood on this spot had burned many, many years ago. There wasn't even any smoky smell to the charcoal pieces scattered across the ground.

As the realization came to me that I'd imagined it all, it also occurred to me that I hadn't actually killed Roy McCaslin. I suppose I took some comfort in that; at the same time, I was a bit disappointed. I looked up at the sky and watched the clouds passing overhead. As I did, I became momentarily disoriented and was overcome with dizziness. I took a knee until it passed.

"You alright?" Haywood asked, real concern in his voice.

"Yeah," I finally said, "I'm okay. Just a little crazy I guess." I didn't try to stand up.

"It was all in my mind, wasn't it?"

He laid a hand on my shoulder. "Fraid so," he said, miserably. "It happens. You were out here too long, too alone. Come on. Let's go home."

***

The return trip took no time at all. I sat in the bow and dipped a paddle occasionally just to show I hadn't gone catatonic. Haywood did most of the piloting from his stern position. We didn't talk. I guess each of us was lost in our own thoughts. The current and the wind carried us along quickly and we were back at the cabin well before sundown. When we pulled the canoe up on the landing Haywood suggested I go and start dinner, and he'd do a little scouting for moose back in the high meadow. We both knew he didn't need to do any scouting. I had spent enough time scouting over the past month that I knew every bull in the area and his habits. He just wanted to get off by himself for a while and think. And he wanted to give me time to come to grips with what I'd just seen. He was, truly, a good and sensitive friend.

I said I'd have something ready when he got back. He nodded, shouldered his shotgun and took the trail up into the spruce. I went up to the cabin, opened the door, and stood there in the doorway for a long time just looking into the gloom of the interior with the dying light of day behind me. She'd been there, in that bed, just this morning. She'd pulled me down and kissed me and told me I was a kind and gentle man. I could still smell her scent hanging in the air. Was it possible she wasn't real? That she never existed? That I had dreamed her? I didn't believe so, but there was no other reasonable explanation.

I leaned my shotgun in the corner and went through the motions of putting on a pot of rice to cook, and got out two caribou steaks to pan fry later. I poured myself a stiff whiskey and took it outside to drink while the rice water boiled. I lit my pipe and sat on the bench and smoked and savored the whiskey. I wondered if Haywood was concentrating on moose sign or thinking about the burned out lodge we'd found that day, and worrying about me going crazy. I didn't feel crazy. I felt bewildered. I felt empty. I felt sad. Not crazy. But then, they say crazy people never think they're crazy. So, I probably was.

***

I had the steaks and rice ready when he finally came back out of the woods. It was well after sunset, and I had been getting concerned since I didn't think he had a torch with him. When he did get back, we had a drink and ate our dinner. He told me about the tracks he'd found back by the beaver pond. He had seen some big bear tracks and also those of the giant moose. He seemed excited, but I was too wrung out to muster much enthusiasm. We ate our dinners, had another drink and turned in. It was a day I was glad to see come to an end.

Chapter 24

The next day dawned clear and cold. A heavy frost covered the lid of the Coleman when I went out to make the coffee. Haywood was still snoring softly in his sleeping bag on the camp bed when I woke. I'd slept well, considering the ordeal of the previous day. I felt refreshed and clear headed. In truth, I had the sense of having awakened from a much deeper sleep. Everything this morning looked sharper, crisper and brighter than usual.

Haywood didn't stir as I went about my morning rituals. When he finally appeared, mussed and bleary eyed in the doorway, I had breakfast ready and waiting.

"Drank too much," he announced, on his way up the path to the facilities.

I smiled to myself. It was a rare day that I had breakfast waiting for Haywood. It had bothered him too. I could tell.

He paid his devotions, and went directly to the creek to wash his face and rinse away the last remnants of sleep. Then he joined me at the Coleman and took the proffered cup of coffee.

He sipped it, sipped again, and said, "You were up early."

"Yeah," I answered. "Habit. I've been getting up at first light all summer."

He finished the coffee and held out his cup. I refilled it. He eyed me over its steaming brim as he took a tentative sip.

"You okay?" he asked.

Yeah," I told him. "I'm okay. Some very weird things happened yesterday and it's going to take me a while to sort it all out. Don't know if I ever will. But, you came in here to hunt moose. That's what we're going to do. If I begin raving and foaming at the mouth, just shoot me. I'll understand."

He smiled and looked relieved.

"Well, at least you sound more like yourself. Maybe you haven't gone completely over the edge. Nevertheless, I'll honor your wishes and shoot you dead at the first sign of dementia."

"Good," I told him. "That's settled. Let's eat breakfast, then go see about filling these moose tags. That big fellow you were talking about last night spends a lot of time back there by the beaver pond. If we spook him, he'll head straight for the river. I know where he crosses."

"Have you seen him?"

"I saw him," I said. "Up close. Damned near ran over me last week."

Haywood took the tin plate of bacon and eggs I handed him, and sat on his usual stump.

"He as big as his tracks suggest?"

"Bigger," I said around a mouthful of hot eggs. "Rack's gotta be nearly six feet across. He's the biggest one I've ever seen anywhere. Could go sixteen hundred pounds. His head would add a touch of desperately needed class to your den."

In truth, neither of us had ever been "trophy hunters". We hunted for the meat, and because we liked to hunt. I subscribed to my father's oft-stated belief that "antlers make thin soup". Dad wasn't a trophy hunter either. Nor did he limit his meat harvest strictly to the male of the species. But it wasn't idealism, solely, that prevented Haywood from decorating his walls with trophy heads; his den was nothing more than a converted ten-by-twelve bedroom with the low ceilings favored in Alaska. He'd be hard pressed to mount a fox head in that room, let alone a moose.

He wiped his plate with a bit of toast and shook off the suggestion.

"No. Now that Sylvia is no longer in residence, I think you ought to start putting the man stamp on Morning Rock. Always seemed a little too feminine for a house built of stone. A moose head over the fireplace in the main room would be just the thing."

The banter felt good. Morgan and the McCaslins were still in the back of my mind, but that's where I left them. Haywood had put in a lot of his own time, money, and effort to give me this summer in the bush. He deserved my full attention and companionship for the next few days, and I resolved that he should have them.

He finished the last of his bacon and stood up. "You cooked, I'll wash up."

"Fair enough." I went up the path to the privy leaving the dishes to him.

**

By seven-thirty that morning we had walked up to the crossing and built Haywood a suitable blind. We'd situated it in a clump of young willows midway up the bar from the water's edge. Its position allowed for a good view back up the bank and into the woods, while providing a three-sixty field of fire. If the bull followed his normal route he'd pass within forty yards of the blind and offer an excellent broadside shot. If he smelled trouble and bolted up or downstream Haywood would still have a good chance of dropping him. Of course, there was the off chance that the big fellow would double back into the cover, but since he'd be on his way to cross the river we doubted he'd do that.

It was a good blind. We rigged a small horizontal frame of dead branches to some of the standing willow trunks and then draped it with cut branches. Haywood had thought to bring along a folding campstool and a thermos of coffee. When he was comfortably settled in, I added a few more branches to the screen, then walked up to where the moose's path left the trees and looked back at the blind. It was just about perfect. It looked natural and Haywood was wearing camo that matched the cover. I could just barely make out his outline, but then, I knew he was there, the moose wouldn't.

Satisfied, I walked back downstream to the cabin, and took my usual trail back in to the beaver meadow. I had told Haywood it would take me forty-five minutes to get back behind the pond and another fifteen or so to push the woods on that side of the meadow. I'd make plenty of noise coming through the bush and if the big bull was on his normal stomping grounds, he'd hear me coming and head for the river.

It was always advisable to make lots of noise when traveling through bear country anyway. Usually bears will do everything they can to avoid encounters with humans. If you make a lot of racket you will rarely see a bear. However, I didn't want to spook the bull while I was getting in position. So, at least for the first leg, I'd have to go quiet. I was wearing my live-oak pattern, soft fleece pants and parka, so I could move through the woods silently as long as I didn't fall over logs or snap dead limbs. The only leather I wore was my gun belt and the sling of my rifle, and neither creaked as I kept them supple with goose grease.

At the thought of the goose grease my mind, naturally, turned to Morgan. I thought of her long, lean body, taught and slick under my hands in the candlelight. She had been real; I knew it. Where had she gone? Why had she gone? I realized then that I had been looking for sign of her all morning. Even now I was sweeping the ground with my eyes for tracks. Not just moose or bear, but her tracks too. I was halfway to the pond when I crossed the big bear's trail. There was no doubt it was him. The size and depth were evidence enough, but the missing claws on the right forepaw removed any doubt. The tracks were very fresh. There was still some frost on the ground, but there was none in his footprints. He had been through here sometime that morning.

This presented a few problems. Not insurmountable, but problems nonetheless. First among them, of course, was the possibility that his mere presence would be enough to make the big bull move on. Bears didn't usually mess with a full-grown moose, but even a giant bull like this one would be uneasy with a bear around. He'd take his lady friends and leave. Another problem Trilogy presented was personal danger to myself. I didn't like sneaking through the woods when there was a chance I might surprise him in the bush. That could turn ugly.

I stayed there for a few minutes studying his tracks and weighing my options. I could, without shame, simply abort the drive, go back and collect Haywood and take him downstream to the slough where I'd seen the other bull. But, I wanted him to get the big one. Trilogy appeared to be heading in the general direction of the pond. I considered this for a moment, and decided to just continue on my own course. I was circling wide around the meadow, and not going directly to the pond, so odds were good I wouldn't bump into him. I checked the rifle to make sure I had a round in the chamber, and continued the way I had been going.

The day had warmed a good deal by the time I reached the point in the woods where I would begin my push. I set my rifle against a tree and unzipped my jacket. I already had my right arm out of the sleeve and was just beginning to remove the left when I heard him coming. A full grown grizzly crashes a lot of brush when he charges. I had just enough time to clear the .44 from its holster and bring it up as I turned – and he was on me. His head was enormous, and his mouth was open in a terrifying roar. I literally stuck the barrel in his mouth and squeezed the trigger as I fell backward. Then his monstrous weight hit me and we went down in a heap. He landed on top of me and crushed all the air from my lungs. I thought my ribcage would collapse and my heart would explode. Then he shifted slightly and rolled. I squirmed free and crawled toward my rifle, gasping for breath. The .44 was no longer in my hand, so I knew I had to reach the rifle. I never did. The effort was too great and I had no oxygen to sustain me. I blacked out.

I don't know how long I was unconscious. Certainly, not more than a few minutes. When I came around I was face down in the muskeg, my hand stretched out in the direction of my rifle. I lifted my head and looked to my left. The huge, dead bear lay not more than ten feet away. I knew he was dead. If he weren't, I would be; he would have torn me to ribbons. I struggled to my feet and some primal imperative drove me to get to that rifle. I had to hold it in my hands before I felt safe. I sagged against the tree, gripped its stock and slid to a sitting position facing the bear. He seemed even bigger dead than he had alive. From my new position, I could see the back of his gigantic head. I'd blown a sizable hole in it. I'd probably blown most of his brain out through it. There wasn't a lot of blood, but there was a lot of gore.

As I sat there gathering my wits and gulping air, I realized there was a burning pain in my left shoulder. I looked down. My shirt was torn and covered with blood. My jacket hung in tatters from my left arm. It too was blood soaked. It appeared he'd gotten his hooks into me. This complicated things. I didn't know how deep my wounds were but I knew I had to get back to The Varmitage before I passed out again from loss of blood. Haywood would be able to put me back together if I could just reach the cabin. It was almost too much, but I managed to get to my feet using the tree for support. I dropped the jacket off my left wrist and let the rifle slip from my grasp. Then I started off through the meadow.

I kept my feet moving, one ahead of the other. After what seemed an eternity I found myself at the beaver pond. I looked across it and knew it presented too great an obstacle to negotiate. I didn't have the strength to skirt it and I'd drown if I tried to cross. I sat down in the mud of the dike to rest. That's where Haywood said he found me.

When I came to, I was laying on my bed in the cabin. My left shoulder was bandaged and stiff, but wasn't giving me much pain.

Haywood had been sitting at the table and stood up when he noticed I was awake.

"Some people will go to great lengths to avoid helping butcher a moose."

"You got him then."

"I did. How are you feeling?"

"Stiff. Tired. How bad is it?"

"Nowhere near as bad as it might have been. Man, you were lucky. Three parallel lacerations about half an inch deep. You might have a couple of cracked ribs but nothing major is broken, as far as I can tell. No significant muscle damage. Lost a bit of blood, but not as much as you should have. I'm not too concerned about the injuries. I got them sterilized and stitched up. They'll heal. I was more worried about shock."

"What did you give me? I feel pretty groggy."

"Nothing special. An unpronounceable painkiller I keep in my bag. It'll wear off in a couple hours. Then you'll feel the pain. I'll give you another dose before you go to sleep."

"Did you see the bear?"

"Yeah. I heard your shot and then, a couple of minutes later the moose of all mooses came barreling out of the woods, right where you said he would. He came a little way out on the bar and stopped. I put one right through his motor box and he went down like a ton of shit. I started gutting him while I waited for you to come out after him. When you didn't show I went downstream and picked up your trail where you went into the woods. I suspected trouble as soon as I crossed the bear tracks. Then I found the bear. Amazing. Biggest fucking grizzly I've ever seen. Your pistol was still in his mouth and your rifle and your jacket were lying on the ground. The jacket was bloody and torn up so I knew you were hurt and probably making for the cabin. I found you on the beaver dike at the backside of the pond. Dragged and carried you're miserable ass back here. You gotta lose some weight, Pal."

The most I could manage was a weak smile.

"What about your moose?"

Haywood flashed his big grin.

"Well, now that you're out of danger and know the score, I'll go back up and bone him out as best I can. There are still a few hours of light left and I can get the hams and shoulders off the carcass and into the canoe. Might even be able to get the backstrap and tenderloin. I can leave the rest for morning. I'll cut off the antlers before we fly out."

"Fly out?" I was still a bit groggy. "You want to fly out tomorrow? How come?"

He laughed out loud. "You are a piece of work, indeed you are. Why do you think, for Christ's sake? I've got to get your sorry carcass back to a hospital. Then I've got to come back in here and skin out that bear. I know you don't go in for trophies but that bear's in the Boone & Crocket category. So is my moose for that matter. I've got to get those heads and hides to a taxidermist mo-ricky-tick."

He was talking a mile-a-minute.

"Mo...what?" I tried to make some sense of what he was saying, but it was no use. My brain was going slow motion, and he was super juiced – high on adrenaline.

He threw back his head and laughed again. "Mo-ricky-tick!" he barked. "Mo-ricky-fucking-tick! A-fucking-SAP!"

And, with that, he flew out the door with his skinning knife and bone saw. I dropped back on my pillow, and within minutes, was out cold again.

I remember waking up in considerable pain sometime in the night, and I remember Haywood giving me a shot of something and the pain draining quickly away. The next thing I remember, sunlight was streaming in the open doorway. Haywood came in and crammed his things into his black river bag, and hauled it outside. A chilly breeze was coming in the door, and I was cold and very thirsty. My ribs hurt. My shoulder hurt. My mouth tasted like the whole Chinese Army had camped in one side and shit in the other.

Haywood came bounding back into the cabin.

"Hah!" he bellowed. "You're alive! Had my doubts. How you feeling?"

"Awful," I answered truthfully.

"Splendid!" he chortled. "Always a good sign when the patient feels awful. A good sign if he feels anything at all. Indicative of superb doctoring."

"Would the superb doctor be so kind as to shut the fuck up and close the fucking door, and bring me a fucking cup of water?"

"Ah! Feistiness! Excellent. Excellent!" He kicked the door closed, and went to the sink and drew me a cup of water.

I started to prop myself up on an elbow, but my damaged shoulder wouldn't allow it.

"Shit!" I said. "That hurts."

"Perceptive to boot!" Haywood cried. "Mauled by a grizzly and still has the mental faculties to realize it hurts! He helped me sit up, and held the cup while I drank.

"Thanks," I said. Then, "Haywood – thanks for everything. I would have died out there."

"Nonsense," he objected. "Short nap on the beaver dike, a night in the mud and the freezing cold, you'd have been yourself in no time."

"Haywood..."

"Okay, okay," he got serious. "You're right. By all rights you should have died. You would have if you hadn't managed to get the barrel of that gun in his mouth. You only got off one shot you know. If he hadn't died instantly, well..." he trailed off.

"So," I asked, "what now? We out of here?"

"We're out of here," he said. "Soon as I get the rest of the meat loaded and figure a way to cart your ass up to the landing strip, we're gone."

I sagged back on the pillow. "I can probably walk if you help me. I just need to rest a bit first."

"You do that," he advised. "I moved all four quarters and the backstrap down to the landing strip last night. Two canoe loads. But, damn, those hams are heavy! I didn't bother boning them out, so there's way too much for one planeload. We'll take out a couple of quarters with us today and I'll come back tomorrow for the rest. By law, I'm supposed to tag the antlers and take them out with the meat but, since I've got a medical emergency, I don't think anyone will object. I'll get Hard Case to come back in with me tomorrow to help with the meat and the rack. Skinning your bear will be a two man job anyway. You want any of the meat?"

I had been trying to follow what he was saying, but was having trouble keeping awake.

"Meat?"

"Never mind," he said. "We'll bring out whatever we can carry. Get some rest. I'll be back in an hour."

I have no idea how long it actually was but, eventually, he came back and woke me up and gave me another cup of water.

"How you doing?" he asked. "Think you can walk a little, or am I going to have to carry you to the plane?"

"I'll walk. Just help me sit up and get my feet on the floor."

He did. When I was upright I was overcome with a wave of dizziness and nausea. I put my head between my knees and closed my eyes.

"Give me a minute, will ya?"

He patted my back and went outside. I heard him slamming the lid on the Coleman and banging and clanging pots and pans. He came back in and deposited my outdoor kitchen on the table.

"We'll clean up this mess tomorrow. You think you're ready to walk?"

I wasn't sure, but the dizziness and nausea had passed. There didn't seem much point in putting it off.

"I guess." I answered.

He took my field jacket off the peg, and brought it to the bed and draped it over my shoulders. Then he got an arm around me and helped me to my feet. A spear of pain shot through my right side. He looked at me with genuine concern. I tried to smile.

"Ribs," I said. "Maybe it's best if I just sort of lean on your arm."

He removed the arm he had clamped around me. The pain lessened but didn't go away altogether.

"That's better," I said. "Let's go."

It wasn't as bad as I'd anticipated. The fresh, cold air revived me somewhat and the activity got my blood pumping. By the time we were halfway to the landing strip I was actually beginning to believe I'd survive.

When we finally got to his airplane Haywood didn't waste any time. He helped me through the door and strapped me into my seat. I leaned my head back against the headrest and the next thing I recall was the roar of the engine and the gravitational forces pulling my back and butt against the seat as we lifted off the bar. I slept the whole way back.

I woke up briefly when we landed at Fairbanks. Then dozed

off again while he taxied into the little service area where he kept his plane. An ambulance met us and two paramedics helped me out of the plane and onto a litter. Before I could protest they had me into the back of the ambulance, and we were off to the hospital. Haywood promised to swing by as soon as he'd finished dealing with the meat and the plane.

Chapter 25

Doctor Scanlon was duly impressed with Haywood's field repairs. He gave me a good going over but could find nothing that needed redoing. He said the fishing line my friend had used for the stitches was a bit unorthodox, but it would do the trick; he hadn't bothered to replace it with proper suture material. He showed me the X-rays of my rib cage and pointed out that only one was cracked. Three others were bruised and would give me some pain, but they were not fractured. He handed me a small plastic bottle of pills and said they were for the pain and asked me when I had my last tetanus booster. I told him two years ago and he nodded and scribbled something on his clipboard. Then he prescribed a series of antibiotics, a few days of bed rest, and told me I could go home whenever Haywood came to collect me.

I thanked him and asked, "When did they bring me in?"

He was still making notes on his clipboard and didn't look up. "Yesterday afternoon."

"Well," I told him, "I think Haywood went back out to the Moose Jaw today. He probably won't be back until late tonight or tomorrow morning. Do you need the bed?"

He laughed. "Not really. You're welcome to stay overnight. Let's say, for observation. You can rest as well here as anywhere. I'll have them move you to another room if you don't mind. You don't really need to be in ICU."

"I.C.U.? Intensive care?"

He nodded. Just a precaution. Standard procedure with a bear attack. You came off surprisingly well, considering. The physical and psychological damage is usually much more severe. The bear didn't cause much trauma and your friend did the best field surgery I've ever seen. If the nightmares don't get you, you'll be fine."

"I don't think I'll have any nightmares," I answered. "It happened so fast I didn't get much material to base one on."

He laughed again. "So I understand. It's quite a story." He paused for a moment. "Speaking of which – the story is out. A reporter from our local T.V. channel wants an interview when you're up to it. I put her off for a while, but she'll be back. You'll need to be ready to talk about the experience. I'd recommend it, in fact. Talking about it can be therapeutic."

"Okay," I said. "Not just yet though. Let me get a few hours more sleep."

Doctor Scanlon agreed, made a few more notes on the clipboard, hung it on the end of my bed and left.

I nodded off for a bit, then the nurse came in with an orderly. They helped me out of the bed and into a wheelchair, then pushed me down the hall to an elevator. We went up or down a couple floors, the doors opened and they rolled me down another hall, around a corner and into a new room. It was a semi-private room but the other bed was vacant. The orderly waited while the nurse tucked me in. When they left, I nodded off again.

The phone woke me. It was Bernie Clive, a reporter for the Fairbanks Daily News-Miner. He wondered if he could have a few minutes of my time. Face to face would be best, but a short chat over the phone would be okay. I opted for the phone interview. He asked what had happened and I briefed him. He wanted to know about the bear – species, size, male-or-female, etc. I told him it was a grizzly, real big, and our relationship had been so brief I couldn't really attest to its sex. He liked that, and asked if he could quote me. Sure, why not.

Five minutes later the phone rang again. Karina Romanov, KXFX - Channel 7 News. Would I mind if she came to visit? Sure, why not? Could she bring her cameraman? Fine. Would later today be alright? I'd prefer tomorrow morning. Well, gee, if that was the earliest I could manage. It was. Okay then, she'd see me first thing in the morning.

By now I was fully awake and getting very hungry. The clock radio on the bedside stand seemed to think it was only three in the afternoon. My stomach insisted it was dinnertime. I pressed the "nurse call" button. A pert, well-starched nurse appeared in less than a minute. Good hospital. I asked her when dinner was served. She consulted her watch.

"Not for another couple of hours, I'm afraid. Getting hungry?"

I told her I was, and she was sympathetic but said I'd just have to wait. She could get me a drink if I liked. I told her no, it was alright, I'd manage. She smiled and left.

I picked up the bedside phone and dialed information.

A perky female voice answered. "Directory Assistance. What city please?"

"Fairbanks."

"What listing, please?"

"Domino's Pizza"

"Big Al's is better."

"I beg your pardon."

"Oh! Sorry – one minute, please, I'll get you the number for Domino's."

"No, no. Hang on. What did you say about Big Al's?"

"Big Al's is much better. I know I'm just supposed to tell you the number you asked for, but I'm also supposed to be "Information", right? My brother works at Big Al's. Their pizza's the best in town."

I loved this girl. "You've convinced me,"I told her, "Big Al's it is. What's the number?"

There was no "one minute, please", this time. She knew the number off the top of her head. She gave it to me. "I can connect you direct for an additional fifty cents if you like."

Why not? "Okay," I said," but before you do, what's your name?"

"We are not allowed to give out personal information," she said. "My name is Wendy. My brother's name is Phil. He's working today."

The line went dead and then I heard a series of tones beeping out the number for Big Al's. A man answered on the first ring.

I asked for Phil and there was a brief pause before he came on line. I told him Wendy had sent me and he laughed. Said she was their best salesperson. I ordered a large special and a giant coke. He asked for my name and address. I told him I was Gus O'Neill, and gave him the name of the hospital and room number. He was dubious. "Can we do that?"

"Sure, why not? I can have visitors. Send me a visitor with a pizza!"

"Okay," he said. "Give us half-an-hour.

I lay back on the fluffy pillow and used the remote to click on the T.V. Civilization did have its points.

***

Haywood showed up at eight the next morning. I was up, shaved, showered and ready to go. It didn't take long to check out. I think certain members of the staff were glad to be rid of me. There'd been a little fuss over the pizza when it arrived and then, at seven that morning, Karina Romanov and her Channel 7 News crew had come barging in insisting on an interview. The duty nurse had held them at bay as long as she could but, in the end, with my permission, she let them through. Karina was young and energetic, and knew what she was doing. She wasn't the super model cutie type reporter you see on the tube in the major markets; she was short and stocky and looked like a peasant out of a Chekhov novel. But she was good. It was over in five minutes. A few quick questions about the incident and a description of the bear was all the background she required.

"Could you please stay in bed and look a little more mangled? Yes, that's the idea. Freddie, let's try to get the shot from this angle so we can get all that equipment in frame. Great, it's in the can. Thank you. Should be on Evening News 7 at 7. Good-bye." And they were out the door. I guess news crews are the same everywhere.

***

When Haywood arrived the first thing I told him was that I was hungry. I'd missed breakfast due to the Channel 7 interview. The hospital was good, but a guy could starve if he spent much time there. Aside from hunger, I was feeling quite well. My stitches itched a little, and my shoulder was still sore, but my ribs didn't trouble me as long as I didn't breathe too deeply or, God forbid, cough. But, I could get in and out of bed unassisted, and I'd already taken a couple of short walks up the hall under my own power.

When the paperwork was completed and I was released, I tried to refuse the mandatory wheelchair escort but – it was mandatory. I think they just wanted to make damned sure I left the hospital. A male nurse wheeled me out the sliding glass doors, while Haywood walked alongside. He was unusually quiet this morning. Clearly, something was troubling him. I didn't press him. It would come out when the time was right.

He had parked his pick-up in one of the "Reserved for Doctor" slots. Well, after all, he was a doctor. When we were both strapped in, he drove out the Entrance Only and made an illegal left turn to get us heading back toward downtown.

We stopped at the North Slope Café, one of Haywood's favorite haunts, and had heaping platters of ham and eggs with home fried potatoes. Haywood filled me in on his return trip to the Moose Jaw as we ate.

He'd conscripted Hard Case to fly in with him to help with the skinning and butchering Haywood explained that they had arrived back at The Varmitage just after ten o'clock, yesterday morning. They had a little trouble with a young grizzly boar that had laid claim to Haywood's moose carcass, and had to fire shots to run him off before they could fetch the antlers. The hide and skull were so thick it had taken them nearly an hour of hard cutting and sawing bone to get them off. Then they hadn't been able to fit them into the plane. They measured sixty-eight inches across, and that was eight inches too long, no matter how they maneuvered them. Finally, they just strapped them across the struts of the landing gear. After lunch, they had gone back in to skin out my bear. Guess what? It was gone.

"Gone?" I was incredulous.

"Gone." Haywood said flatly. Now I knew what had been troubling him.

He went on. "We took the direct route back to the beaver pond. I showed Hard Case where I'd found you on the dike. Our tracks were still there in the mud. So were your guns. I'd taken them with me when I left the dead bear to go looking for you. Had to leave them on the dike so I could carry you back to the cabin. Then we followed my backtrail into the trees to the spot where the bear jumped you. No bear. We looked the place over good. Hard Case is one of the best crime scene detectives in Alaska. He went over everything inch-by-inch. Not only was there no bear – there was no sign a bear had ever been there."

He forked a large piece of ham into his mouth and chewed pensively.

"You sure you went back to the right place?"

He swallowed, took a sip of his coffee and nodded.

"I'm sure. Your jacket was still there, right where you dropped it. I hadn't bothered with it when I picked up your guns. It was ruined, so I left it. We brought it out with us yesterday. Hard Case wants to have the bloodstains checked out. Aside from the jacket, there was no evidence there had even been a struggle."

'Here we go again,' I thought. "No evidence?" I said. "What about bear tracks?"

He shook his head. "Lots of tracks, your tracks, my tracks, even a few new wolf tracks, but no bear tracks."

"Well," I said, trying to keep my voice down. "I know I didn't imagine the fucking bear. He was for real. These claw marks are for real, and my ribs are for real, and I sure as hell didn't tear up my own jacket."

He looked as agitated as I felt. "You don't have to convince me," he said. "I saw the son-of-a-bitch. Pulled your damned .44 out of his mouth. I even grabbed him by the ear to roll his head over so I could get a better look at the hole you blew in it. He was real alright – day before yesterday, at least."

"What did Hard Case make of it?"

He looked at me across the table for a long time, then forked another piece of ham into his mouth and chewed slowly.

"That's hard to say. He seemed to take it all in stride. He just sort of took off his friend hat and put on his cop hat, and started asking questions. In the end, I told him the whole thing; about the woman that was, and then wasn't; about the dead men and the lodge that were there one day, and gone the next. Hope you don't mind, but I had to tell him, there was no way around it."

I thought for a minute. "Did you tell him I shot one of them?"

He nodded. "Yeah. He put it all down in his little note pad. He wants to talk to you. Today, if you feel up to it. He said there's nothing to warrant him acting in an official capacity, but he's curious and would like to hear a few more details. This thing has got his interest up. He wants to hear your side. Will you talk to him?"

"Can't see what it will hurt," I said. "There's no physical evidence of a crime – nothing I could be arrested for."

Haywood signaled the waitress for the check. When she brought it, he dropped a twenty on the table and we left. I waved a ten at him as we went out the door into the parking lot but he held up a hand.

"On me," he said.

Haywood had taken a full week off for our planned moose

hunt, however, since the hunt had been cut short, he decided to spend the afternoon at the clinic. Although it was Saturday, his receptionist, Sally, and her teenage son were installing new computer hardware in the office. He wanted to see how they were getting along, and catch up on some paperwork. He said I could drop him off if I felt well enough to drive. I had declined, so he agreed to drive me back to his house, and then go in to work. He used his cell phone to call Hard Case en route. Hard Case said he'd come by a little after noon. He'd pick me up and treat me to lunch somewhere. When Haywood dropped me off at the house, I went in and stretched out on the couch. Bosworth joined me. I had planned on a little nap, but Bosworth's purring and biscuit-making on my sore ribs precluded that. After a while I gave it up, and went and sat at the table. Bosworth didn't seem to mind having the couch to himself.

I hadn't had a hot bath since June, so I took this opportunity to put that right. I filled the tub with hot water and even added some bubble bath I found under the bathroom sink. Then I stretched out in the tub and, keeping my shoulder above the water line, rested my head back on a folded towel, and soaked. It was the ultimate luxury, and having closed the door against the company of Bosworth, I was able to sneak in a little nap after all. I woke when the water cooled enough to get uncomfortable, drained out a few inches, then refilled it with pure hot. Ah, boy. I'd forgotten how decadent and wonderful a hot bath could be.

Chapter 26

Hard Case pulled up in front just a little past noon and tapped his horn. I grabbed my jacket, gave Bosworth a pat on the head and went out the door. As it was Saturday and he wasn't on official business, Hard Case had driven his personal vehicle, a two-year-old Ford Explorer. It was white and he didn't appreciate any comparisons with O.J.'s white Bronco. I opened the passenger door and climbed in. The interior was, as always, spotless.

We grinned at each other, and I delicately offered my right hand.

"Gently," I said. "Still mending."

Hard Case offered me a sympathetic smile, and took my hand. He gave it a squeeze, rather than a shake. He was large and gruff, but he wasn't inconsiderate.

"You're looking fit," I observed.

He patted his ample stomach. "Clean living," he said righteously.

It was a standing joke. Hard Case had the full compliment of vices. He drank to excess whenever the opportunity presented itself, and smoked non-filtered Camel cigarettes – at least a pack a day. He ate far too much, and enjoyed every mouthful. His doctor had opined that a bullet would be a quicker, although less certain way for Hard Case to kill himself. All this notwithstanding, I never saw him out of breath or lacking in strength, stamina or enthusiasm.

I nodded sagely. "Pure heart, clean mind, healthy body."

"That's me." He smiled, put the big SUV into reverse and backed out of the driveway.

We continued to make small talk as we drove out to Harley's Haven, a few miles west of town. It was on a dirt road and the access depended on the weather, but it seemed to do enough business to make ends meet. Hard Case liked it because it was quiet and out of the way, and they served gigantic hamburgers with huge slices of red onion, and made the best fries you could get anywhere. Always conscious of his diet.

When we had settled into a booth and ordered our burgers and beers, Hard Case lit a Camel and leaned across the table. His gaze was steady, but friendly.

So," he said, "tell me about it."

He was a good cop. Maybe even a great cop. He'd been with the Alaska State Troopers' Criminal Investigation Bureau since its inception, back in 1971. He had worked his way up from backcountry patrol to the top job. He wasn't a political animal by nature, but you didn't need to be political to succeed in Alaska, even in a government job. All you needed was the respect of your fellow Alaskans. Hard Case had earned that over his career and was now enjoying the fruits of his labor. Before his official retirement, he had spent the majority of his time managing office staff and trying to balance the budget for his department. Now, that was someone else's worry. The Troopers had brought him back under contract to do what he loved best – working crime scenes.

I told him my story. He listened without comment and took no notes. He just sat and smoked his Camel and sipped delicately at his beer from time to time. When I had finished, he stubbed out his cigarette in the ashtray and took out his notepad.

He said. "Mind if I make a few notes, Gus?"

I shook my head. I didn't mind.

"A few details," he began. "Let's start with the bear. Haywood said it was the biggest grizzly he'd ever seen. Had you seen it around your stretch of river before?"

I told him I'd seen his tracks several times but had only actually seen him once – the morning after I'd found the woman. After that, he spent a good deal of time around the cabin but I'd never seen him again, just his tracks.

He made a few notes. "Now Gus, I know you're good, but how did you know they were his tracks? There are a lot of bears around that section of the Moose Jaw, as I recall."

I told him about the missing claws on the front paw.

He nodded and thought for a minute. "Did he ever bother the cabin, or try to get at your cache?"

I said he hadn't.

"So, the first time you ever got close was when he attacked you."

I nodded again.

"And the attack was unprovoked. You weren't threatening him in any way?"

I said I wasn't as far as I knew. I didn't know what was going through the bear's mind. I had crossed his tracks and had gone out of my way to avoid going in his direction. I told him it looked as if the bear had circled and picked up my tracks. He'd followed me and attacked from behind. It was almost as if he'd been stalking me.

"Okay," he went on. "So, the bear charges you from behind, you hear him coming and get out your .44, turn, stick it in his mouth and pull the trigger. Is that pretty much the way it went down?"

"That's pretty much it. Although, I don't think I actually stuck it in his mouth. It was more like I was just bringing it up while I turned, and then the gun was in his mouth. I didn't actually stick it in, it just went in. Maybe he bit at it, I don't know. It all happened too fast."

Hard Case lit another Camel and took a deep drag while he thought.

Then he said, "Now, you pull the trigger, the gun goes off in his mouth, you blow his brain through the back of his skull and he dies instantly. His momentum brings him down on top of you, and in the process, you get a cracked rib and a raked shoulder. That it?"

"That's about it. I think he clawed me just as I squeezed the trigger. I seem to remember his right paw coming down on top of my left shoulder just as I fired."

Hard Case set the note pad aside and tapped an ash into the ashtray.

"After you kill the bear, you're out cold for a while, come to, and make your way to the beaver pond. Haywood finds you there, gets you to the cabin, sews you up, and in the morning you fly out."

I nodded once again. Nothing to add. He had it right.

"All sounds pretty straightforward up to that point. Now it starts to get funny. I go back in with Haywood and, as we professionals like to say, 'dare ain't no body'. Haywood's moose is there but your bear has vanished. I can certify that there was no bear. I looked the place over good. I would testify under oath, that there was no evidence, whatsoever, that there had ever been a bear. No tracks, no hair, no bone fragments, no brain tissue, no body.

There might be some blood; we won't know until we get the stains on the jacket tested. But, I'll bet it turns out that all the blood is yours."

Our burgers and fries arrived so he leaned back to allow the waitress to put them on the table. When she had gone he stubbed out his smoke and sampled a few fries. I waited.

"So, here's the rub. I know you and Haywood pretty well. You've both got your heads screwed on straight and, aside from being drunks and sexual deviates, you're fine upstanding citizens. You say a bear attacked you and you killed that bear. Haywood swears he saw the bear. He even touched it. So I have to believe there was a bear. But, I also have to believe what my own eyes saw the next day – no bear. This is where it comes apart. First, there was a bear, then there wasn't. If I accept both these statements as true, I must also accept as true that the bear vanished into thin air. I have trouble with that."

I nodded in sympathy. "Yeah. So do I."

He took a bite of his burger, chewed for a while and then swallowed.

"Let's put the bear aside for the moment." He sipped his beer. "Let's talk about the woman. It seems she also vanished. You said her name was Morgan?"

"That's what she told me."

"Morgan what?"

"Just Morgan. She didn't give me any other name. It was as if she didn't know, or couldn't remember."

"Physical description, age, unique scars or tattoos, you know." He picked up his pad and pen again.

I told him she was tall, close to six feet, slender and well sculpted. Not necessarily athletic, but well formed. She had red hair, green eyes, good teeth; age between thirty and thirty-five; no tattoos, three scars on her right shoulder blade made by bear claws.

Our eyes met and locked. He'd been chewing another bite of his burger. He stopped chewing.

"Three?" he said. "Not four, not five."

I took a swig of beer and swallowed. "Only three."

"Haywood said he had to stitch up three claw marks on your shoulder also."

"That's right," I confirmed.

"I'd like to have a look at them when we get back to Haywood's place, if you don't mind."

I said I didn't.

"Curious coincidence, don't you think?" He asked.

"Yeah," I said. "Same bear. But, it is curious."

We both focused on eating our burgers for a while. When he finished his he signaled the waitress for two more bottles of beer.

"Go on about the woman. Personality traits, accent, mannerisms, was she a genius, an airhead, did she come off as religious, politically active; or anything that struck you about her.

I told him she appeared cultured. She had a soft, quiet voice, good grammar and vocabulary, excellent table manners – probably a finishing school somewhere in her background. I told him what she'd said about working for a law firm in Seattle and about her being a fly-fisherman since she'd been a teenager, and about Jason, her missing fishing buddy.

Hard Case took it all down and then asked several questions about Jason. I told him what I knew and he wrote that down too. When he was finished he stared off into space for a while, absently sipping his beer with one hand and tapping his pen on the table with the other. I left him to ponder while I tucked into my fries.

Suddenly, he came out of his reverie, downed his beer in a long gulp, and signaled the waitress for the check. While she was bringing it, he jammed his note pad and pen back into his shirt pocket, and stood up. Lunch, clearly, was over.

I popped two fries in my mouth and took a final swallow of beer while he paid and left a generous tip.

Back in his Explorer, he said, "Something about all this rings a bell. I can't quite put my finger on it, but I want to do some checking. Won't be able to find out much today, it being the weekend. But, Monday I should be able to do some digging around.

He started the Explorer's big engine and drove out of the Haven's parking lot.

"You can tell me about this guy you offed on the way back to Haywood's."

I briefed him on my unsuccessful search for Jason, and the episode at the McCaslins' lodge. He wanted more detail regarding the shooting – weapon, load, range, how many shots I fired. Where did I hit him? Did I remove any physical evidence? Did I leave any behind?

I answered him as best I could. He didn't seem too upset that one of his best friends had, willingly, pulled the trigger on a fellow human being and then, with malice aforethought, given him another load in the face. But, he had been around long enough to earn the nickname Hard Case. He held few illusions regarding mankind's capacity for violence.

After I told him all I could about Roy, he wanted more detail regarding the second body I found inside. I described Larry as a giant, mean, ugly, homosexual rapist. I also offered my opinion that he was stupid as a post. Then I told Hard Case how I had last seen him at the fishing lodge.

Hard Case swung left onto Haywood's street.

"Think about what you saw when you looked into that room. There was the nude body of a big man on the floor. There was blood all over the place. The body was full of stab wounds and it was missing its genitals. Hold that picture in your mind."

I couldn't get it out of my mind.

"Now he said, let your mind walk back outside. Look at the guy you shot. He's also naked. He's got a knife in one hand and you said he had something else in the other. What was it?

I didn't have to think about it. I knew what it had been, I just hadn't elaborated on it when describing the shooting to Hard Case. Roy had been holding a wire in his left hand when he came out the door. I hadn't noticed it when I shot him but I saw it clearly enough when I inspected the body after killing him. Although my first load had mutilated his manhood, I could still see the wire wrapped and twisted around his genitalia. Even in death, he clutched it in his left hand. At the other end of the wire hung a gory mass of hacked and bloody meat, which I assumed to be his brother's missing parts.

I described this to Hard Case.

"So tell me, Gus," he said quietly, "What does all that suggest? What happened just before you arrived at the lodge? You must have thought about this before. Tell me what you think happened out there."

At this point he turned into Haywood's driveway, shifted into park and killed the engine. I told him what I thought had happened. He stared out the windshield, apparently lost in thought as his thick fingers drummed a gentle tattoo on the steering wheel.

"My, oh my," he said. It was almost a whisper. "My, oh my, oh my."

Then he turned to me and said, "Alright, Gus, that's enough for one day. Let me come in and have a look at those claw marks and then I'll get out of your hair."

We went inside and I took off my jacket and shirt and peeled back the dressing the nurse had applied in the hospital that morning. Hard Case had a close look. He clucked his tongue.

"Looks like Haywood put you back together pretty well. What did he use to stitch you up?"

"3X Tippet," I told him. "He liberated it from my fishing vest."

Hard Case chuckled and shook his head in admiration, waved good-bye, and headed out the door.

"Thanks for lunch!" I called out as it closed behind him.

His voice came muffled through the door. "Don't mention it."

Then I heard the heavy door of the Explorer slam and the big engine roar to life. His tires crunched in the gravel of the drive as he backed into the street, then he was gone. I saw that Bosworth had vacated the living room, so the couch was fair game. I quietly snooped around the house until I found him curled up and sound asleep on my bed in the guest room. I softly closed the door, locking him in, and went back upstairs to the living room and the vacant couch. It was only three o'clock but it had already been a long day. My ribs and shoulder were giving me a good deal of discomfort so I popped a couple of pills Dr. Scanlon had given me for pain and lay down on the couch for a little nap.

Chapter 27

My little nap took a bit longer than I had anticipated. I didn't wake up until I heard a car door slam shut out in the driveway. I opened my eyes to a dark room and switched on the table lamp next to the couch. My watch said it was just after eight. 'Wow,' I thought. 'Five hours!' I heard the front door open and close. A few seconds later Haywood came bounding up the stairs from the entry. I was just slipping on my shoes when he came into the living room.

He snapped on the overhead lights, deposited a load of mail on the kitchen table and proceeded directly to the refrigerator. He took out a bottle of Guinness Stout.

"How you doing?" He asked, popping off the bottle cap and flipping it into the garbage pail.

"Good, I guess," I said sleepily. "Doc Scanlon gave me some pain pills. I took two and zonked out for five hours."

He held out a hand and said, "Let's see 'em."

I fished the little plastic bottle out of the breast pocket of my shirt and tossed it across the room. Haywood snatched it out of the air with one of his oversized hands and read the label.

"No wonder," he said. "You're only supposed to take one at a time, as needed for pain. Not to exceed two in any twelve-hour period. He give you one this morning?"

"Yeah. The nurse did. My ribs were killing me when I woke up.

"Don't suppose you had any alcohol today?" he said, knowing I probably had.

"Couple of beers with Hard Case," I told him.

He shook his head sadly and tossed back the pill bottle. I started to bring up my hand to catch it, got a stab of pain in the ribs and aborted the effort. The pill bottle bounced off my chest and rolled under the coffee table.

"Allstate," Haywood said sarcastically. An old inside joke – "you're in good hands with Allstate".

He brought his beer into the living room and flopped down

into his overstuffed easy chair. He looked around.

"Where's Bosworth?"

"On my bed. I locked him in so I could have the couch to myself."

Haywood sipped his stout and nodded. "I better go feed him. He gives me fifteen minutes grace when I get home. Then he gets cranky."

I had to go to the bathroom anyway, so I volunteered to feed Bosworth while Haywood went through his mail.

After attending to Bosworth, and visiting the facilities, I went back to the living room. Haywood was just opening another stout for himself.

"I'd offer you one but, as a doctor, I can't encourage the mixing of drugs and alcohol."

I nodded my understanding.

"On the other hand," he went on, "I couldn't stop you if you overpowered me and had your way with my beverage supply. You know where the fridge is."

I thought about that for a minute, decided I was awfully thirsty, and went to see what he had in his "beverage supply". I took a bottle of stout over to the kitchen table and eased myself down into one of the old wooden captain's chairs.

Haywood discarded the last bit of mail onto a pile beside his chair and leaned back.

"How'd it go with Hard Case?"

I filled him in on our lunch. Then added, "He said he wanted to check a few things out and he'd get back in touch with me Monday. I think something I said stirred his memory."

I had just finished saying that when headlights swung into the driveway and heavy tires crunched on gravel outside the window. Haywood swiveled around and looked out.

"Speak of the devil," he said.

He got up and went to the front door and opened it. I heard the front steps groan under a heavy weight.

"Evening Case," I heard Haywood say, "Got time for a beer?"

"Why not?" Hard Case answered and came into the living room unbuttoning his topcoat.

He nodded to me. "Evening Gus. How you feeling?"

I told him I was good and thanked him. He sat down at the

table and Haywood brought over a bottle of Rolling Rock and another bottle of stout. He held them both up.

"What's your preference, Case?"

Hard Case inspected the choices, and pointed at the beer. "Can't handle that black stuff," he said. "Gives me the fantods."

Haywood slid the green bottle across to Case, who lifted it in a silent salute and took a long pull.

"Ahhh," he said, as if he hadn't had a beer in months, and clunked the bottle down on the wood surface of the table.

Haywood returned Hard Case's salute and took a long draft of his stout.

"To what do we owe the pleasure of your distinguished company this evening?"

Hard Case smiled over at me.

"Ah, Haywood," he said. "You are a caution."

A caution. I had to chuckle. I hadn't heard that expression since my childhood. I had no idea what it meant, but the sound of it always tickled me.

Hard Case went on. "You owe this after-hours visitation to our good friend, Gus, here," he said, tipping the neck of his bottle in my direction. "Something he said this afternoon put me in mind of an unsolved case I ran across when I was just starting with the Bureau. It's Saturday, and there's nobody working the File Room, but being the retired champ does carry a few privileges – I still got all the keys. I had to stop by the office on my way home anyway, so while I was there I went into the archives and dragged out the file. I took it home and reviewed it this afternoon." He sipped his beer and looked off into space.

"Strange, gentlemen, very strange indeed." He took another sip of beer and dug in his pocket for his cigarettes.

"Mind if I smoke, Haywood?" He already knew the answer. He was just being polite.

"Be my guest," Haywood said. "In fact, I think I'll join you."

He got up and went to the mantle and took one of his big Churchills out of the humidor.

I said to Hard Case, "Now look what you've done."

"Sorry," he said, "I just wasn't thinking."

Haywood ignored the aspersions being cast at his stogie. He struck a match and puffed away happily until the tip glowed to his satisfaction and the air around his head clouded with poisonous gases. Then he rejoined us at the table and sat back contentedly. He picked up where Hard Case had left off.

"What did you find so strange about the file, Case?"

Hard Case flicked the ash off his Camel. "I'll get to that in a minute, but first I'd like to get a couple more details from Gus." He looked over at me.

I shrugged. "Fire away."

His cigarette dangled from his lip and smoke curled up into his face. He closed one eye and stared at me with the other.

"Gus, when I asked you today about the loads you used on Roy, you said they were twelve gauge duck loads. Could you be a little more specific?"

"Sure," I said. "I guess they were actually goose loads. The last time I'd worn that field jacket I was hunting geese back in the beaver pond. I had the pockets full of twos. There might have been a few fours mixed in but I shot Roy with twos. I know, because I picked up the spent cases."

"Steel?"

I didn't have to think about that. I hate steel shot; it doesn't have the hitting power of lead, and it tears up your barrel, especially if you have a full choke.

"No," I told him. "Bismuth."

I'd starting using Bismuth back in the late eighties when it was still an experimental alternative to lead and steel. It fell in between the other two metals on the hardness scale and also on the density scale. It packed a little more wallop than steel and didn't pollute like lead. Its biggest drawback was that it was damned expensive. But, for shooting over water, it's all I'd used for several years.

Case made a steeple with his hands, fingertips pressed together at the top.

"Bismuth," he said pensively. He was quiet for a moment then continued, "You said you picked up the spent hulls. Did you pick up the wads too?"

"No, it didn't occur to me at the time. They must not have landed where I would have seen them or I would have remembered to pick them up. I didn't give them a thought until I was in the canoe, headed back downstream. Then it was too late."

Hard Case looked the perfect picture of the patient fisherman who has just seen his bobber dip for the first time.

"So," he said, looking me square in the eye, "it's fair to say you left behind a few pieces of physical evidence at the scene. Namely, two loads of number two bismuth shot, mostly contained in the body of the victim, and two plastic wads. I assume they were plastic; do you remember what brand you were shooting?"

"Remington," I told him. "The wads were plastic. They're probably the same ones I use when I reload Remington hulls. They're called Power Pistons.

Hard Case finished his beer and told Haywood, if he would be gracious enough to open him another, he'd explain what was so strange about the case file.

Haywood went to the refrigerator and brought back three beers. He announced that too much stout was bad for the bowels, then set a bottle down in front of me and slid one across to Hard Case. Case nodded his thanks, took a tentative sip, and began.

***

"I hired on with the Troopers back in '71, just as they were creating the Criminal Investigation Bureau. My first boss was Pokey Brewster. Name probably doesn't mean much to you boys, but he was a big man around here back then. Third generation white Alaskan. You don't find many of them, even today. He was a good cop. Anyway, every year or so, he'd have us break out the "Unsolved Cases File" and go through them to see if anything had come up over the past year that might tie back to one of the unsolveds. I can't remember that we ever had any luck but we did it anyway, every year, religiously. One of the cases went back to the late fifties. Pokey had worked it personally so he was able to give us a pretty good picture of what went down.

It seems that a group of doctors and dentists from St. Louis had all thrown some money in a kitty and bought a fishing lodge on Rainbow Creek. The creek got its name from the giant rainbow trout for which it was famous. I've seen some of the mounts that came out of that creek back then – they looked like footballs. Big and fat. Fishing was big business on all the Yukon tribs during the fifties. Trout, salmon, grayling – all big. There were five or six working lodges on the Moose Jaw alone and more on some of its feeder streams. Anyway, this consortium of doctors and dentists got together and bought themselves a fishing lodge. In retrospect, they were probably doing it as some sort of tax dodge, a Limited Partnership or some such thing. But, they were all outdoorsmen and liked their fishing so they bought the lodge. They didn't operate it as a commercial enterprise after they took over. They probably wanted to show a loss on their 1040s. There'd been an Athabascan family, mom and dad and two boys, working for the previous owner so the docs kept them on to help out around the place. They cooked and cleaned and kept the water tank filled and the woodpile stocked. The boys would skipper the boats and clean fish and wait table when there were guests.

The doctors would come in with their guests two, sometimes three times a year and have a big party. They were all from Missouri, and they imported a couple of Ozark boys to live at the lodge year round and look after the place for them. They were brothers. Roy and Larry McCarver, a.k.a. Roy and Larry McCaslin."

He looked at me, took a pull on his beer and said, "See what I mean about strange, Gus?"

I drank a few swallows of my beer and nodded my head. Indeed it was.

Hard Case continued, "Well, things went on just dandy for a few years. Looks like maybe Roy and Larry were running a little side business, opening the lodge to paying guests when the doctors weren't around. Set themselves up as guides, they did. Even got licensed and ran ads in the Seattle and San Francisco newspapers as the Rainbow River Lodge. They did a nice little business. Don't know if the doctors even knew it was going on, but if they did they didn't do anything about it.

Then, the first week of moose season in 1959, a couple of moose hunters came back to Fairbanks and reported they'd found a burned cabin and two dead men back up Rainbow Creek. Pokey flew out with a bush pilot and had a look. He wrote up the report that's still in the file. I tell you Gus, I don't know what to make of this, but I'm going to let you read that file and tell me what you think."

I told him I'd like to see it.

He said it was out in his car, but there were a few other things I should know before I read it. Then he went on.

"What Pokey found back in there was two mutilated corpses and a burned down fishing lodge – more specifically, the McCarver boys, and the Rainbow River Lodge. They found Roy in the main room, just inside the door. His body was badly charred but they were able to tell he'd been killed with a shotgun before he burned. You'll find the description of the wounds mighty interesting. They found his brother Larry in one of the sleeping rooms. He was a giant. He was also queer as a three-dollar bill. He'd done time in Missouri for the homosexual rape of one of his own cousins. While he was in prison he beat and sodomized every cellmate they put in with him. They finally had to put him in solitary confinement. I don't know how he got back on the street, but our justice system was as flaky then as it is now.

Anyway, like I said, they found him in a back room. He hadn't died as pleasantly as his brother; he'd had his cock and balls hacked off with a dull knife and he'd been stabbed in the chest, head, shoulders and back some thirty five times."

Case took a puff on his cigarette and had a sip of beer. Haywood and I sat quietly and waited for him to go on.

"Pokey wrote up his assessment of what had transpired. His report stated that it appeared the two victims had been overpowered or incapacitated by a third party-or-parties, long enough for the third party to strip them both and crimp-wire their nuts together through a heavy iron eye-bolt that was anchored deep in the log wall of one of the sleeping rooms. It further appeared that each had been given a dull hunting knife, and the third party had rigged a timed incendiary device to go off in the room with the brothers. The third party may or may not have explained the situation to them but, regardless, it was clear they understood. They had to extricate themselves from the snare wire or they would burn to death. It appeared to Pokey, that Larry tried to use his knife to cut the wire and dig at the eyebolt in the log wall. His brother didn't waste time on that approach. The evidence suggested that Roy stabbed Larry to death and then cut off his scrotal appendages, dragged them through the eyebolt, and escaped outside. He must have thought he was home free."

Case paused here long enough to have another swallow of beer.

"Here's where it really gets weird, Gus. The evidence also suggested he was met just outside the door by the third party, who shot him twice; once in the face and once in the balls. Then our mysterious third party dragged Roy's body back inside and let his little fire bomb do the rest. It was quite effective; the lodge burned to the ground. Nothing left standing but the stone chimney."

Haywood had gone absolutely white. I couldn't see my own face but I'm sure it was grim. Hard Case just sat, drumming his fingers on the tabletop. He looked over at me. "Like I said, Gus. It's all very strange."

I started to speak but Hard Case held up a hand. "There's more; let me finish. The Athabascan guy, the father, was the prime suspect. Pokey thought the whole thing looked like a vengeance killing, and the file on Roy and Larry indicated they were more than likely to incite a husband or father to commit such a crime. Fact is, there'd been rumors that Larry may have had a go at the youngest son. The authorities caught up with the father about a month later, over in the town of Circle. He and his family had been living around there for more than three months at the time, and he had a solid alibi for the entire week of the Rainbow River Lodge murders. They released him and continued the investigation. No other suspect was ever questioned."

I interrupted him. "Case, before you go on, why did you ask me about the loads and the wads."

"I'm coming to that," he said. "Pokey and the pilot sacked up the bodies in body bags and brought them back to Fairbanks. The medical examiner removed fourteen metal balls from Roy's head as well as a plastic wad from his throat. The wad matched one Pokey had found under the porch. He also removed eleven metal balls from Roy's lower abdomen, upper thighs and what was left of his nuts.

The odd thing about the metal balls was that they weren't lead. Some folks had been experimenting with steel shot even back in the fifties, so they ran tests on the metal. They weren't steel either. In fact, they ran every metallurgical test available at the time and they were finally able to determine the mystery metal to be an alloy of 97% bismuth and 3% tin."

At this point, Hard Case took his little note pad out of his shirt pocket and consulted it. "Bear with me," he said, as he flipped through the pages. "The report was pretty detailed, so I jotted down a few notes."

Haywood and I exchanged a glance while Hard Case looked for the data.

"Here you go," he said, tapping his note pad. "Bismuth is the element next to lead on the periodic table. Its atomic number is 83 and its atomic weight is 209. Nice to know, but the puzzling thing is that no manufacturer, at that time, was making shot out of bismuth. I checked that out on the Internet today."

Once again he referred to his notes. "Bismuth shot wasn't made commercially until 1994. It was also stated in the file that they had ruled out the possibility of an individual reloader having made the loads, because reloaders simply assemble shot shell components that are manufactured by companies in the munitions industry. This includes the shot. The point being, no manufacturers were making shot out of anything but lead in 1959."

He flipped his note pad closed, and returned it to his shirt pocket as he went on.

"While I was researching the bismuth on the Internet, I also ran a check on steel shot. I discovered they didn't even start making that commercially until Winchester came out with it in 1976. The U.S Department of Fish and Game didn't accept bismuth shot as legal for hunting waterfowl until 1997."

He finished his beer and clunked the bottle down on the tabletop.

"So, you see, they were able to identify the metal, it just didn't lead them anywhere. The plastic wads gave them a bit of a turn also. Plastic wads were being introduced around then, but nobody had ever seen one quite like the ones found at the scene. They ran comparison tests with every manufacturer's wads, and guess what? No matches."

Hard Case paused to light another Camel. I went to the cupboard and took out the Tullamore Dew. Beer just wasn't doing it. I held the bottle up toward the table. They both nodded, so I stacked three glasses and took them to the table with the bottle.

While I poured us each a generous dollop, Hard Case went on.

"Long about the same time, we had another unsolved case. Two missing persons. Funny thing was, they went missing while on a fishing trip on the Moose Jaw. Man and woman from Seattle. Disappeared in the bush, and were never seen or heard from again. Their names were Jason Thomas and Katherine Morgan."

A chill ran up my spine. Haywood downed his whiskey in one gulp and gestured for another. I poured, and Hard Case continued.

"Mr. Thomas was thirty-three years old, a rising star at Albright, Baker, Morrison & Kemp, Attorneys at Law. Miss Morgan was also thirty-three years of age, a tall redhead, and was employed as a legal secretary at the same firm. They were both reputed to be avid fly-fishermen. They were also reputed to be lovers. They had come to Alaska for a two week vacation, specifically to fish for salmon on the Moose Jaw, and trout on Rainbow Creek."

He paused for effect. "Oh, and by the way, in case you haven't already guessed, Rainbow Creek is no longer called Rainbow Creek. When the trout mysteriously vanished from its waters in 1960, somebody changed the name. Since then it's been called Deadman Creek in honor of the McCarver boys. That's the name on all the maps now."

We were all quiet for a long time after Hard Case had finished his dissertation. I opened the bottle and poured everyone another round. I left the cap off the bottle. The drugs and alcohol in my system were having their effect but Case's tale had come through loud and clear. I didn't know what to make of it, but I certainly saw the implications. They were just too far out to be considered seriously.

I studied the amber liquid in my glass. "Case, do you still have those metal balls in your evidence room?"

He shook his head sadly. "Nope. I looked around. Couldn't find the plastic wads either. Only thing we have is the sketch Pokey made of them. It's in the file. You can have a look."

I said that was good, if Pokey was a good enough artist, I could tell if his wad resembled a Remington Power Piston. I had no doubt that it would.

Once again, Haywood downed his drink in one gulp. He hadn't said anything for a long time. Now he stood up and leaned both palms on the tabletop. We both looked at his face. It was taut and ashen.

"Let's get something straight here," he said. "My father was a backwoods preacher, and I was raised in the good Christian tradition. I may not be much of a Christian anymore but I still hold some of my beliefs near and dear to my heart. What we're talking about here is pretty damned close to a ghost story. I don't believe in ghosts! I'm a man of medicine – a man of science."

The whiskey was getting to him and he momentarily lost his

train of thought.

Hard Case prompted him. "A man of science…"

Haywood picked up the thread. "That's right. I'm a man of science and I don't believe a word of this shit. There has to be a logical explanation for all of it."

"I agree," said Hard Case. "I just wish I knew what it was."

"Here, here," I added, and downed my whiskey in a single swallow.

"Well," said Hard Case, "now you've heard it. I'll bring in the file and leave it with you overnight. You can read it at your leisure, but I covered most of the high points."

He left his coat hanging on the back of the chair and went out the front door. I heard his Explorer's door open and then close again and, seconds later, Hard Case came back in carrying two large manila envelopes bulging with papers. He plopped them on the table.

"Here they arc," he said. "The fat one is the double homicide. The small one is the missing persons case. I'd like them back when you're done with them."

With that, he looked at his watch and said, "I better be getting home. Thanks for the whiskey."

He shrugged into his coat, waved good night and said, as he went out the door, "Enjoy your reading."

***

When Haywood and I were alone, he slid his glass across the table to me.

"Fill 'er up, Gus."

I could tell he was drunk, but so what? I filled his glass and gently slid it to him. I'd had enough whiskey so I opened another bottle of stout. Haywood waved his glass in the direction of my bottle.

"Don't drink too much of that stuff," he said. I knew he was about to deliver one of his infamous medical opinions. He didn't disappoint me.

"You'll be dropin' clankers in the morning. I don't want to be replacing my porcelain." He was, indeed, a caution.

We sat and quietly sipped our drinks for a good five minutes before Haywood looked at me and said, "What I said about this being a ghost story – it's something more than that, isn't it?"

I waited. He went on, "Closer to science fiction – time travel, that sort of shit. It's like you went back to 1959 and shot that fucker, then came back to now."

I sipped my stout. "Time warp?"

Haywood shrugged his shoulders. "Shit, I don't know. Nobody knows. It's all hocus pocus anyway; UFOs, shit like that." He tossed off his drink.

"Well," I said, "I'm not going to think about it any more tonight. I'm all in." I stood up, "See you in the morning Haywood."

He waved a hand over his head, "Night..." he said.

I went down to the guest room, rousted Bosworth from my bed, and turned in.

Chapter 28

Sunday morning, Haywood surprised me. He was frying bacon and eggs at the stove when I came up from the bedroom. It was six thirty in the morning. He looked refreshed and alert. That was hard to believe, considering the condition in which I'd left him last night. Even more amazing was the fact that the Dew bottle stood empty on the table. He'd killed it after I'd retired. No matter, I felt bad enough for both of us.

"Top of the Mornin' to ya, O'Neill!" He was in good voice.

"Umm," I answered.

He poured a cup of coffee and handed it to me. "Sorry. Forgot your morning persona. I'll give you a few minutes to rise from the dead before attacking."

He slid two eggs and a few slices of bacon out of the frying pan onto his plate. The toast popped out of the toaster right on cue and he added them to the bacon and eggs, picked up his coffee cup and disappeared into the den. I heard the computer's high-pitched whine and knew he'd be occupied for another half hour, at least. Thank God.

I took my coffee over to the table and eased myself into a chair. The table was a mess, cluttered with full ashtrays, empty bottles and glasses, and the two bulging file folders. I wasn't ready to tackle the file folders. My shoulder still ached but not as much as my ribs. My head hurt worse than either. The room still stunk horribly of Haywood's awful cigars and Case's pungent Camels and, I suppose, my pipe. The bacon smell couldn't hope to mask it.

I went over and opened the window. It was cold out but I had to have some fresh air. I'd just resettled into my chair and was sipping my coffee when the phone rang. Haywood had two lines; one for the computer and one for the phone and fax machine.

"Can you get that?" His voice echoed down the hall.

I walked over to the island and lifted the phone off the hook. "Hullo." I waited.

"Gus? That you?"

"Hello, Uncle Jack. It's me."

"Heard a bear ate you. You okay?"

"Yeah. I'll live. How'd you hear about it?" There was no doubt in my mind who had informed him. 'Haywood, you bastard.'

"Got an email from Haywood. Said you were in the hospital, and you'd be back at his place today. I forwarded it to Sylvia. Thought she should know. Seriously, are you okay? How bad did you get hurt?"

"A scratched shoulder and a cracked rib. The doctor said I didn't even need to stay overnight. Really, I'm fine, Uncle Jack."

"Thank God for that! When you coming home, son? We're all anxious to see you and hear about your adventure. Didn't give you much of a homecoming last time; we'll make up for that this time!"

'Oh, goodie,' I thought. Then I realized I had never really considered what I'd do at the end of the summer. I'd been so focused on getting away from it all I'd neglected to plan my return trip. In my heart I knew I didn't want to go back to it all. I wanted Morgan. But she was gone, and now I didn't know what I wanted. A gentle cough in the earpiece reminded me that Uncle Jack was waiting for an answer. I stalled for time.

"Ah...maybe in a couple of weeks. I want to let the rib stitch a bit and we've got a lot of moose meat down at the butcher shop. It won't be ready for another week, at least." That was all I could think of to say.

"Good," Uncle Jack answered. "I've always fancied moose meat. Make sure to bring me a few steaks when you come home."

I promised I would and tried to ring off, but Uncle Jack had more to say.

"By the way, "I've, ah, taken on some live-in help. Hope you don't mind."

"Live in help?" I asked. "As in a housekeeper?"

"No," he said, slowly. "More in the line of a personal assistant, doing research for my book and proof-reading my material – that sort of thing. But she does keep the place clean."

I could see where this was heading. "Uncle Jack," I asked, "have you found a suitable place to set up all your office equipment yet?"

"Actually, no. Afraid my whole publishing operation is still in the master suite."

"Including staff?"

"Uh…yes," he admitted sheepishly. "Staff included."

'So,' I thought, 'now it's Uncle Jack, his insufferable dog, his personal assistant, Casey, and his two girlfriends, and any of Uncle Jack's chums that happened by.'

My head was throbbing again. Five minutes talking to Uncle Jack could do that. I groaned aloud. Uncle Jack heard it over the line.

"Gus, are you sure you're okay? Haywood's message intimated you'd been under a lot of – stress – while you were back in there alone."

He left that hanging. So did I. I didn't know how much Haywood had told him, but I wasn't going to lead with my chin. If he had more to say, I'd give him a chance to say it.

"Gus? You still there?"

"I'm still here."

Uncle Jack realized he'd pushed it too far. He knew me well enough to know I wasn't talking. He withdrew.

"Well, glad to hear you're okay. The house is fine. Casey's fellow students moved out at the end of the summer. Another moved in; she's a redhead, and a real sweetheart. You'll like her."

'Redhead!' I came instantly awake. "Redhead? What's her name? How tall is she?"

"Tall? How the hell…? Wait a minute."

I heard Uncle Jack yelling something to Casey. Then he came back on the line.

"Her name is Kelly; she's about five foot two. But, Gus, are you sure you're okay?"

I let out a sigh of relief, and leaned my head against the wall. I realized I was sweating. I assured Uncle Jack I was really okay, and we hung up.

Great. All I needed, at this point, was Sylvia and Uncle Jack worrying about me. I had several things to work out in my mind and I didn't want any help from Europe or the Lower Forty-eight. I slammed my coffee cup down on the table. I'd kill that fucking Haywood.

I stood there a minute thinking about everything that had happened in the past three days. Then I sagged back into the chair.

Haywood wasn't the problem. I was. And Morgan was; and the McCaslins were; and that goddamned three toed bear. Haywood had jokingly observed that everything I put a bullet or a dick in seemed to disappear. It wasn't funny. That pretty much summed it up.

'What a mess,' I thought.

I heard Haywood shutting down the computer and knew I wasn't ready to talk yet. I got up and went downstairs to the guest bathroom and took a long, hot shower. It helped.

Back upstairs, showered, shaved and dressed in clean clothes, the world was a better place. Haywood had cleaned up the mess from the night before and had opened another window to help air the place out. He was loading the dishwasher when I came from my toilet.

"Well," he said, "you look like you might live, after all."

I managed a smile. "Yeah, I just needed to wash away the cobwebs."

There was still a little coffee in the pot. He split it between our two cups and handed me mine.

"Who was that on the phone?"

I sipped my coffee. "Uncle Jack," I said, glowering at him over the lip of my mug.

He looked sheepish. "Oh, yeah. Forgot to tell you. I sent him a message after I dropped you off at the hospital. That was before I knew how bad you were hurt."

I studied him. He was my best friend. Whatever he had done had been done with my welfare in mind. I smiled at him and his face relaxed into an apologetic grin.

I laughed a little, and shook my head. "Haywood, Case has you pegged. You are a caution. You knew the exact extent of my injuries; you put me back together. What, exactly, did you write to Uncle Jack?"

He looked a little shame faced. "You can read the message. It's in my Sent Folder."

"Just give me the gist."

He went over and sat down at the table.

"Basically, I told him a big ass bear jumped you in the bush, and that you blew his fat ass away. I also told him you were in the hospital and I expected you home today. I wanted to give you an extra day to heal before talking to him."

"Was there anything, between the lines, that might have suggested to him that I had gone a little crazy back there?"

He pursed his lips and considered that for a minute. "I suppose he might have read that between the lines. I think I may have listed cabin fever as one of your possible medical problems."

"Ah. Cabin fever...as in went stark raving mad due to loneliness?"

He frowned. I could see he was serious. He stared down at his big hands, laying flat on the table, each side of his coffee cup.

"Something like that. But I wrote that before Hard Case and I went back in; before I knew the bear had vanished. Up until then you were the only one who'd seen things that disappeared. Try to understand. The woman and the McCaslins – I never saw them. I thought they had been just, well, figments of your imagination. I really thought maybe you had gone round the bend."

I sat down across the table from him. "And now?"

He shook his head miserably. "Now, I just don't know. I saw the bear. I saw it and I touched it. It...was...real. It was there. I got its blood on my hands and its hairs stuck to the blood. They were not figments of my imagination. When Hard Case and I got back in there and found the bear gone, I couldn't believe it. I thought Hard Case was going to think we were both crazy. You know, mass hysteria, or something like that. But, I knew I wasn't crazy!"

He looked up at me, caught my mood, and let out a high-pitched, maniacal cackle. He pounded the table, crossed his eyes, and howled.

"I...AM...NOT...FUCKING...MAD!!!"

It was good to laugh. I was afraid we would go mad if we didn't maintain our sense of humor. It was one of those situations where you had to laugh to keep from crying.

Haywood sobered a little and went on. "Anyway, you get the idea. After the thing with the bear I started thinking maybe you hadn't gone off your nut. Maybe there was something weird going on back there. Then, last night, the story Hard Case told..."

He looked off into space for a while. I sat quietly sipping my coffee. At length, Haywood shook his head, and went on.

"I've been thinking all morning of what his story means. It

means the woman, and the bear, and the brothers were real – in 1959. You didn't imagine them. They were real, once upon a time. It's like something out of The Twilight Zone"

I waited for him to go on. He saw it the same way I did. I was hoping he'd have an answer. But, he didn't. Neither of us understood what, exactly, had happened, but it was comforting to know that he knew what I knew; the woman and the bear and the brothers had been, at one time, real flesh and blood. They were not figments of my imagination.

The room was getting cold and the stale air of the night before had, for the most part, freshened. I left Haywood sitting at the table while I went over and closed the windows. Then I wandered into the kitchen to make some toast for my breakfast. There were still four strips of bacon in the pan so I turned on the flame to warm them. I leaned against the counter top and waited for my toast to pop.

"So, how did Hard Case react? Out at The Varmitage, I mean."

Haywood pushed back from the table and stretched his legs out in front of him and folded his hands in his lap.

"That's the funny thing," he said. "I thought sure he would think I was nuts. But he didn't. He took it seriously and he told me, on the way back to Fairbanks, that the abnormal was quite normal out there. About every other case he'd ever worked in the bush had some – supernatural or paranormal – aspect to it. He said the Athabascans believed the spirit world existed side by side with the physical world and the two often merged. He told me that there were a hundred legends about a mystic bear spirit, and the indigenous tribes believed in them every bit as much as we believe in the death and resurrection of Jesus Christ. He wouldn't have even taken much interest in a disappearing bear if I hadn't told him about the woman, and you thinking you killed somebody. Then he became intrigued."

My toast popped, and I made myself a bacon sandwich and took it over to the table. I sat down and began eating.

"Well, considering the physical evidence from the scene of the crime, I did shoot somebody. I shot Roy. Don't ask me how it happened, but they were my bismuth shot pellets found in his dead body. They didn't even have bismuth shot in 1959."

He nodded his head slowly. "I know. It's hard to argue with

physical evidence."

He reached across the table, dragged the fat file folder to him and pulled off the rubber band that held it closed.

"Be interesting to see what that sketch of the wad looks like." He started leafing through the pages, talking as he did.

"Those three claw marks I stitched up in your hide are physical evidence too. So, now you have a tangible link tying you to the bear. You've also got the bismuth connecting you to the body of Roy McCarver. But, you've nothing to prove that Morgan was real. That's what's eating you isn't it?"

Haywood had hit the nail on the head. That was exactly what had been troubling me. I really didn't care if the bear was real, or the McCaslins brothers either. I wanted something solid – something tangible that proved, beyond any doubt, that Morgan had been real. But I had nothing but my memory of her.

"Right on, Haywood," I answered truthfully. "That's what's eating me."

***

Haywood had taken the truck and gone into the clinic that afternoon to see how Sally was progressing with the computer upgrade. I was still a bit stiff and sore, and had decided to stay at the house. I wanted to catch a little nap, and scan the files Case had left us. Haywood had already found the sketch of the wad and it took me only a glance to confirm it was, indeed, a Remington Power Piston. I hadn't expected anything else.

I spent some time reading over the missing persons case. I wanted to learn as much as I could about Katherine Morgan. There wasn't a lot of background on her, but there was more than I had known. The file described her as white female, fair complexion with freckling on face and forearms; height, 5'11", weight 125 lbs., naturally red hair, thirty-three years of age, DOB 11-17-36. Nothing new there except her birthday.

The personal history data disclosed that she had been born in Providence, Rhode Island. Her father was a diplomat and her mother was a music teacher. She had traveled extensively in Europe with her parents, and had lived two years in Brussels and two years in London. She had studied English Literature at Washington State University, but had not earned a degree. She had worked for a law firm in San Francisco for four years before moving to Seattle where she hired on with Albright, Baker, Morrison & Kemp. She was a legal secretary and worked primarily for two of the senior partners. She was known to be an avid sportswoman, enjoying skiing, sailing, hiking and fishing. She was considered to be an expert fly-fisherman, and was known to tie her own...

"Her own flies!" I shouted aloud. I jumped out of the chair and ran down the stairs and into the garage. The overhead door had no windows and it was dark. I found the wall switch and snapped it on. The fluorescent light blinked and sputtered to life as I dove into the stack of bags and boxes Haywood had brought back from The Varmitage. I rummaged through the river bags looking for my fly tying kit. No, no – he wouldn't have packed it in a bag. I started opening boxes. 'Shit! Nothing.' I took a deep breath and thought to myself, 'Calm down!'

I tried to imagine where he would have packed it. 'Did he pack it? Damn! He might have left it all at the cabin!'

I dashed back up the stairs and snatched the phone off its hook, dialed the number of Haywood's clinic, and then suffered, impatiently tapping my foot, through six interminable rings. Finally, Sally answered and began her canned greeting.

"Good Aft..."

I cut her off. "Sally! This is Gus. I need to talk to Haywood. It's urgent."

Sally dealt with emergencies on a daily basis; she was completely unflappable.

"Hi Gus. Welcome back, heard a bear got you. Hang on the line a minute; I'll see if I can find Dr. Jennings." I heard a mechanical click and then I was listening to soft, soothing, elevator music.

A minute went by and then Sally came back on the line. "Sorry Gus, Dr. Jennings left about ten minutes ago. Don't know where he was headed – maybe home."

'Where is that asshole?' I thought. I said, "Thanks Sally, I'll catch up with him later."

"If it's urgent, why don't you try his cell phone; he always has it with him."

'Of course!' I thought. To Sally, I said, "I'll try that. Thanks again, Sally. Bye."

I hung up and immediately dialed Haywood's cell number. He

answered on the first ring.

"Haywood!" I was breathless. "Where's my fly tying kit?"

"What?"

"My fly tying stuff – from the cabin! Where is it?"

He was silent for a moment. "It's still up at the cabin. I didn't bring it out with me. I remember seeing it over by the wall in one of those boxes. One of them was open and your vice and scissors and some feathers and shit were on top. I figured you'd want to keep it up there, so I left it."

"Did you see a little clear plastic box with one fly in it anywhere?" I was frantic and I'm sure he could hear it in my voice.

"Sorry, don't remember anything like that. What's this all about anyway?"

"Physical evidence." I quickly told him about Morgan's special flies.

"She tied one of her pubic hairs in a Caddis?" He was incredulous.

"Yes! Goddamnit! And there was still one left in the box. She tied three. I lost one and the other one…HOLY SHIT! Did you bring out my rod?"

"Of course! I'm not daft, you know. I brought out the guns and ammo too."

"Never mind them! My rod! It was still rigged with one of her Specials! Where is it?!"

"It's in its rod case, which is standing in the corner of the goddamned guest room where you slept last night! Where the hell do you think I'd put it?" He was clearly losing his patience with me.

"Sorry, Haywood, it's just… Ah, shit, you know. Sorry."

"It's okay, I know. Anyway, whatever you had on it is still there. I just broke down the rod, folded it in two and put it in your case, reel and all. I'm leaving the butcher shop as we speak. I'll be there in about fifteen minutes. I gotta hear more about these Specials."

We hung up and I bounded down the stairs to my bedroom, grabbed the rod case and took it back to the living room where the light was better. I knelt on the floor and unzipped the case. The Special was still there, secured to the hook keeper. Thank God! I remembered seeing a pair of fingernail clippers on the kitchen island, so I fetched them and snipped the line just above the fly. Then I took my prize over near the window and put on my glasses. I held it up to the light and examined it. My heart skipped a beat when I caught the flash of red within the deer hair body. It was still there. I'd had a moment of anxiety when I thought it may have broken off during the fight with the grayling, but luck was with me. I had her hair. She had, without question, been real. She had, without doubt, been with me in my cabin. She had, perhaps intentionally, left me this tiny memento of our time together. My heart was, literally, filled with the joy of knowing. It didn't matter that she may have – probably did – exist in a different dimension. Somehow our worlds had, for a little while, merged like the circles of feeding rings on the water.

My mind went back to that evening when I had waited in the canoe for darkness to fall and watched the fish jumping and the eerie, unworldly glow in the air as the mist rose off the water. The trout – the Rainbows – they were the key. Morgan hadn't come to my world; I had, somehow gone back to hers. I had gone back to 1959 and loved a woman and killed a man. It was the bear that puzzled me, old Trilogy. He had left his mark on Morgan, and some mystic bond had been formed between them. Together they had left a message in the hearth slab. Why? For whom? For me I supposed. I'd washed it and rubbed it like the genie's lamp, and they had come – or I had gone to them.

I thought about the morning after I'd found her, and Trilogy appeared across the stream. And he was always about the cabin. Was he guarding her? Is that why the McCaslins never came close after that one attempt? Was the bear protecting us from them? Yes. That was the way it looked. He'd even guided my steps home through the snow the night the wolves almost got me. Was he keeping me alive so I could complete my mission? Was it my destiny to kill Roy? Had Roy been just another pawn?

I remembered Morgan's kiss, and her parting words when we stood by the canoe before I left that afternoon, "…some things are preordained." Incredible. And her, there on the bank like a pagan goddess commanding the wind to carry me upstream to kill the man who had violated her.

But Trilogy hadn't attacked me in 1959. Haywood had not flown back to 1959. When he arrived Morgan and the McCaslins had vanished. That must have been the moment I returned to the present. But the bear had, somehow, followed me. He had followed me and put his mark on me, and now he and Morgan and I were all bonded together in some ancient, mystic way. And I had killed him – or had I? Perhaps I had merely sent him back. Perhaps he was back there keeping watch over Morgan right now.

Haywood's pickup turned into the driveway and rolled to a stop on the gravel. I was surprised to see it was snowing. Big, lazy flakes were drifting slowly out of the sky. There was already a little covering the blacktop of the road. I watched him climb out the driver's side and crunch across to the steps. He looked up through the falling snow and saw me at the window and waved.

I left the Morgan Special on the windowsill while I put my rod case back in the bedroom. When I came back to the living room Haywood was hanging his jacket on the hall tree in the entry.

He ran up the last five steps to the main level. "Did you find it? Where is it?"

I walked across the carpet to the window and lifted the fly into the light. He went to his desk and brought over a magnifying glass. I handed him the fly; he took it gingerly between his thumb and forefinger and brought it under the glass. He turned it this way and that, so it would catch the light.

He let out a low, appreciative whistle. "I'll be damned. You weren't kidding."

I realized I'd been holding my breath. I exhaled, relieved that he'd seen it.

"You going to show this to Hard Case? He might be able to run some DNA tests or something."

"And compare it against what?"

"Hmmm," he frowned. "I see what you mean."

He gave me back the fly and laid the magnifying glass on the table. "In any event," he said, "the hair proves she existed. She was real, and you didn't just make her up. That's something."

I nodded. "Yeah. I've been thinking about that. I told him what I'd been thinking.

He went over and sat at the table and began fiddling with the magnifying glass. Finally he looked me straight in the eye.

"Fergus," he said, then took a deep breath and continued. "You may be right. Maybe not. But if you ever told that to anybody but me they'd have you locked up. I think you better let it go. You don't really know what happened out there and neither do I. But if you dwell on it you definitely will go crazy. You went out there to get away from all the madness. At first I thought you may have taken a little back in there with you. I'm still not sure, maybe you did. When I brought you back and took you to the hospital I was pretty certain you'd gone off your rocker out there. After the thing with the bear, I just didn't know anymore. Then Hard Case drops this 1959 shit on us and you find a hair that proves your Morgan was real. I say, okay. You went through some weird shit out there, but you're not crazy – yet. Now, it's time to quit while you're ahead. Forget it happened and get on with your life."

It was a long speech for Haywood. I knew he'd been thinking about it all the way home. He was worried about me, for good reason. His advice was sound, but I knew I couldn't take it. I set the fly back on the windowsill and went over to the table.

"You're probably right, Haywood. You are right. It'll take me some time, but I'll put it behind me. Whatever happened out there, I'll leave it out there."

He studied me carefully for a while, then said. "Good. I hope you mean it, Gus."

I didn't, but I gave him my most reassuring smile.

"I do. You can relax."

He studied me for a few more moments and then slapped a palm down on the table. The wind from his hand ruffled the papers lying loose on top of the open folder. He jumped to his feet.

"Alright, then. First thing we gotta do is reintroduce you to the game of pocket billiards! Let's drive out to Skinny Dick's, have beer and burgers for dinner, and shoot a few games of pool! With your cracked rib, I ought to be able to kick your ass!"

I laughed. "Not on the best day of your life, Haywood. Let's make it best of five, and loser buys dinner."

He laughed too. "You're on! Let me feed Bosworth and we'll hit the road."

***

Skinny Dick's is a roadhouse twenty miles south of Fairbanks on the main highway to Anchorage. Even in the steadily falling snow, it only took a half hour to get there from Haywood's house. I'd been there a couple of times before. Anywhere else, it would have been nothing more than a biker dive, but here in Alaska it had a mixed clientele. On any given day you would see patrons ranging in age from toddlers to octogenarians, and in lifestyle from backwoods trappers to yuppie hairdressers. Dick welcomed all. He had the pictures on the wall to prove it. His walls were covered with photographs of Dick with every VIP in Alaska from 1966 to the present. He also had shots of himself with any female he could get to show her tits to the camera. He had quite an impressive collection of – shall we say, trophy racks. It was a relatively large place by Alaska standards. The open floor plan accommodated two pool tables, the mandatory video games, several eating booths, a dining island, and a full bar. Haywood and I liked the place because it served great burgers and fries, the beer was cold, and the pool tables were, more or less, level.

Despite the arrogance of my challenge, I wasn't as good as I had once been. I won the first game when Haywood sunk the eight ball a little early. He swept the next three games, so dinner was my treat. It was a fun evening and it served to take our minds off, what we had come to call, the Moose Jaw Mystery. Nevertheless, it did keep popping up in our conversation. We couldn't help it.

Halfway through the second game Haywood paused to chalk his stick and said, "Well, at least the goddamned moose was real. The butcher says it'll be ready next Tuesday. I didn't have a chance to check with you, but I assumed you wanted the same percent of cuts and sausage as usual."

I nodded. "Yep, that's perfect."

We both realized, at that point, it was going to be hard to avoid thinking about it.

Nevertheless, I knew now what I was going to do, and it was time to start laying the groundwork.

"I plan on flying home day after tomorrow. You can just have him ship my share of the meat to Morning Rock when it's ready, and bill me direct. I want to travel light anyway. I don't know how much I can carry with this rib."

He said that would be fine, and set about running the table.

***

It was still snowing when we left Skinny Dick's. There was already about four inches on the ground, and the snowplows were busy on the highway. On the way back to Fairbanks, Haywood said he'd see if he could get his Piper out of the maintenance hangar so he could fly me down to Anchorage Tuesday morning.

"Don't bother," I said. "Alaska Airlines has a flight every two hours, and they're dirt cheap. I'll just take one of them."

"We'll see how it goes." He wasn't usually evasive in his answers. When he was, you knew he'd rejected your suggestion. If his airplane was ready, he'd insist on flying me down. I didn't pursue the issue.

After a short silence he said, "By the way, you want those moose antlers? I dropped the head off at a taxidermist's. I asked him to mount it European style. Something about those enormous antlers sticking out of a naked skull appeals to me. Trouble is, I don't have anywhere to hang it.

"Sure. I'll have the whole thing made into a hat. When Sylvia and Gaspard come to visit, I can meet them at the airport wearing it. They'd appreciate the irony of the gesture."

Haywood chuckled. "At least you can joke about it. I don't think I could be as gracious as you've been about that whole situation." Then he laughed and shook his head. "Ah, boy – sorry. I just had a vision of you standing in the arrival hall down at DIA wearing a sixty-eight inch rack of moose antlers; you'd cause quite a stir."

He laughed again and then went on, "Seriously though. I'd like you to have them. You could hang them over the big stone fireplace in the main room. You'd have something to remind you... Oh, shit. I'm sorry. I keep stepping in it."

"It's okay. I haven't really stopped thinking about it either. It'll take some time. Anyway, yes, go ahead and have it sent down to Morning Rock when it's mounted. I'll store it for you, over the big fireplace, until you get a house with higher ceilings."

"Fair enough," he said. "Thanks."

It was only eight thirty when we rolled into his driveway. He had an invitation to spend the night at Donna's house, so he dropped me off out front, pressed the button on his automatic garage door opener and said he'd see me sometime tomorrow. I got out and waded through the new snow to the garage. I had worn my low top ducks and I got a shoe-full on the way. I kicked them off, stepped over and around all the boxes and bags scattered on the garage floor, pushed the button to lower the door and went upstairs.

I logged onto Haywood's computer and checked my email. There were several in the Bulk Mail Folder, which I promptly blew away, and only two in the Inbox. One was from Uncle Jack reminding me to let him know when I'd be arriving, the other was from my old boss in England, asking me how things were going. I answered both of them. I told Uncle Jack I couldn't give him a return date yet, but not to worry, I'd check in with him when I could. I also answered my old boss and told him everything was fine.

***

I was well and deep asleep when the phone rang. The bedside clock said it was almost midnight. I groaned and padded up the stairs to the kitchen. It was still ringing when I got there, so I answered it.

"Hello," I said, trying to keep the irritation out of my voice.

There was a slight delay, common in Alaska, since virtually all long distance telephone calls are transmitted via satellite.

"Fergus! Is that you darling?" It was Sylvia. The last person on earth I wanted to talk to. The last I had heard, she was somewhere in Holland. I wondered what time it was there. I did some mental calculation and decided it was about ten o'clock in the morning.

"Hello, Sylvia. How are you?"

"Oh, Fergus!" Some things never changed; she still began most of her sentences with Oh, Fergus! "How am I? Good God, dear – HOW ARE YOU is more the question, isn't it? I got an email from your uncle saying you'd been mauled by a bear! Tell me that it's not true!"

"Okay," I told her, yawning, "It's not true."

"Liar! I know it's true! How badly were you hurt? You haven't lost any limbs I hope. Please tell me it didn't scratch your face. I always loved your face. Of course, facial scars can give a man a certain rough charm. Look at all those fencers from that awful university in Heidelberg. Some of them..."

I hated to disappoint her. "Sylvia, take a breath. He didn't claw my face. I came out relatively unscathed; three scratches on my shoulder and one cracked rib."

"My God, Fergus! How could you have been so foolish as to

get that close to a bear?"

What could I say? "Just wasn't thinking, I guess. How are things in Holland? How's our dear friend, Gaspard?" I asked. To myself, I thought, 'Sneaky little prick.'

There was another hesitation on the line. Then, "Yes, well, things are fine here. Gaspard and I have stopped seeing one another. The relationship seemed to have lost its naughtiness after you left. Ruined everything. I'm moving to Brussels in two weeks. I have a friend down there. And Brussels is so much more – cultured – than Holland, don't you think?"

"Why not go all the way? Move to Paris – the Left Bank?"

"Oh, Fergus, don't be gauche." She tittered a little at her double entendre.

Before she could dwell on her cleverness, I said, "Is your new boyfriend French?"

"Oh Fergus! You're being intentionally gauche. Actually, it isn't a BOY-friend. I'm exploring another facet of my sexuality."

When I realized she was serious, I said, "For Christ's sake, Sylvia! You're not a lesbian! What the hell are you doing? Have you gone completely mad?"

"That's unkind, Fergus. It's unlike you. I think your going to Alaska was a mistake. You're becoming so American, fighting with bears and then calling me mad! I don't think I know you anymore."

"I'm sorry, Sylvia. Perhaps you're right. Go to Brussels and explore your new sexuality with my blessing. I hope you find happiness. Really, I do."

"Aren't you the least bit jealous?" She sounded disappointed.

I decided to humor her. "Only if she's French."

"Oh, Fergus, you don't care anymore. I hear it in your voice. You just don't care."

She was right. It came as a surprise to me too, but I really didn't care. Her dabbling in homosexuality shocked me a bit, but I had to admit, didn't upset me in the least. She could sleep with anyone she pleased. It no longer concerned me.

Nevertheless, I couldn't be cruel. "Of course I care, Sylvia. It's just that..."

She didn't let me finish. "Oh...my...God...Fergus," she said. "There's another woman."

I didn't know if she was looking out the window at a pretty

Dutch girl walking by, or accusing me of having my own affair.

"What?"

"I said, you've found another woman! Admit it! That's it, isn't it! YOU'VE FOUND ANOTHER WOMAN!"

I thought of Morgan. Sylvia was right. I had found another woman, sort of. How could I explain? I tried. "Well, actually..."

"BASTARD!" she screamed. "OH, YOU ROTTEN BASTARD. HOW COULD YOU?!!"

The phone went dead. I took it away from my ear and looked at it with wonder.

'How could I?' She was completely mad. I shook my head, hung up the phone, went back down to my room and crawled back into bed.

***

I woke at seven the next morning. Bosworth had hopped up on my bed to remind me that he hadn't had his breakfast. I stroked his head, got out from under the warm covers and followed his erect and swaying tail up the stairs to the kitchen. He rubbed against my legs while I got out his food and filled his bowl. I carried it over to his corner and put it on the floor. Bosworth dismissed me and settled in to eat. I went to the window overlooking the driveway and was somewhat amazed to see the heavy, white blanket that had accumulated overnight. It looked to be close to a foot, and the snow was still falling.

I didn't expect Haywood any time soon, so I put on a pot of coffee and got out the yellow pages. By the time I had found and written down all the numbers I wanted the coffee was done brewing, so I went out to the kitchen, poured a cup and fried two eggs with bacon. When I sat down to eat my breakfast, Bosworth hopped up on the table to see if I might be willing to share. I broke off a piece of bacon and tossed it toward his bowl. He eased himself from the tabletop down onto a chair seat, and from there to the floor, where he proceeded toward his bowl at a majestic pace. One mustn't display undue excitement over a mere scrap of bacon.

I spent the rest of the morning down in the garage, sorting through the things Haywood had brought back from the cabin. I took both shotguns, my .444 Marlin and the .44 Blackhawk out of their cases, stripped them down and gave them a good cleaning and oiling. Then I set aside everything I'd be taking with me when I left.

With a little sorting and culling I was able to get it all into one river bag. That done, I set about putting the garage into some semblance of order. I repacked several of the boxes and labeled them to identify their contents. Then I found places, or made room for them on the shelves or under the workbench. It took me the better part of two hours, but in the end you could see the floor again. Haywood would actually be able to park his truck inside during the winter months. When I had finished, I went upstairs and used the phone to make my travel arrangements.

***

Haywood pulled up and parked in front of the garage just before noon. He came in stomping his feet on the entry hall floor and brushing snow out of his hair. He took off his jacket and shook it out before hanging it on the hall tree.

"Can you believe it?" He yelled up the stairwell, "It's still coming down! Forecast says we'll be getting close to two feet!"

He bounded up the stairs. "Any coffee left?" He was obviously in high spirits.

"Yup!" I tried to match his enthusiasm, "Half a pot – you can pour me one too."

He kicked off his boots at the top of the stairs and went into the kitchen.

"How's the rib?" He asked, pouring the coffee.

"Still a little sore. I've backed off on the pipe some. Coughing hurts."

He nodded. "I know. I've cracked a few over the years. Just breathing hurts."

He brought our mugs to the table and settled into a chair. "I've been thinking about those stitches. That 3X tippet I used won't dissolve, you know. You'll need to have them taken out when the wounds mend. Keep the skin soft with Vaseline and they'll come out a lot easier."

I nodded. "What do you do, just cut them and pull them out?"

"That's about it. Feels a little weird, but they slip right out. Casey or your uncle can do it if they're not squeamish about such things."

We sat quietly sipping our coffee for a while and then he said, "Had lunch yet?"

"No. I've been packing and making my flight arrangements.

And, by the way, I knew you'd insist on flying me down to Anchorage tomorrow, but the weather is the shits, so I booked an Alaska Airlines connector out of Fairbanks at three-thirty. Non-refundable ticket, so don't object.

He grinned across the table at me. "Got me all figured out, don't you?"

I grinned back at him. "Read you like a book."

"Fair enough. I'll drive you out to the airport tomorrow afternoon. What about all your gear?"

"I'll take just one bag. If it's okay with you, I'll leave the rest here."

"No problem. Plenty of room in the garage. Leave it all if you like."

I shook my head. "No, there are a few things I'll need to take. Besides, I'm not leaving my fly rod here with you. I've seen you lusting after it."

He laughed. "It is pretty."

"Speaking of the garage…" I stood up and told him to follow me. When I showed him what I'd done, I couldn't tell if his face was registering astonishment or horror. Some things are very personal – like a bachelor's messy garage. Whatever was going through his mind, he had the good grace to thank me. He could always mess it up again after I'd gone.

***

Haywood made a couple of his famous sandwiches for lunch – salmon salad and capers on sourdough toast, with, of course, a slab of red onion. I opened us each a bottle of beer while he labored over his creations. We ate them standing at the kitchen counter and he told me Hard Case had called him on his cell phone and asked if we were done with the folders. He wanted to return them to the file room before someone noticed they were missing.

I shrugged my shoulders. "I've no more use for them. He can have them back whenever he wants."

"Good," he said, around a mouthful of sandwich. "I'll call him after lunch and tell him. He can swing by tonight after he gets off work and pick them up. Give us a chance to have a farewell drink before you go."

"I think we need to make a liquor store run. I didn't come across any in the boxes you brought back from the cabin, and we killed the only bottle you had when Hard Case was here last night. I know there's no more in your liquor cabinet; I checked.

"Shit, that's right. I left four full bottles up at the cabin. Well, I'd planned on putting a few hours in at the clinic today anyway. I have to get up to speed on the new computer. I'll swing by the liquor store on the way home."

I thought for a minute. "How about I drop you off at the clinic. I've got a few things to pick up in town – presents and such. When I'm done, I'll buy the booze, then pick you up at the clinic."

"That'll work," he said, as he washed up at the sink.

Before we left for town, Haywood checked our beer situation and discovered there were only two bottles left. He got them out of the refrigerator and popped them open.

"May as well make a clean sweep," he said.

We sat at the table and drank the beers while Haywood made out his shopping list and I, mentally, made out my own. It didn't do me much good to write down my shopping lists, as I usually left them lying on the table anyway. Over the years, I'd just started keeping it all in my head.

When we had finished the beers, we donned our winter coats and boots and trudged through the snow to his truck.

I mentioned he could start parking in the garage now and avoid wading through the snow. He answered with a non-committal grunt, so I assumed I had, indeed, crossed the line in organizing his shelves and clearing his floor.

It had been just over an hour since Haywood had come home, but even in that short time, the cab had become quite cold. I was driving, so I cranked the heater up full. It was just beginning to get comfortable when I dropped Haywood off at the clinic.

He climbed out and looked at his watch. "Take your time. Come back and get me when you're done. I can take care of everything here in a couple of hours."

I told him it might be closer to three hours. He said that was fine, slammed the door and waved. I pulled out of the clinic's parking lot and drove straight to Wal-Mart, where I knew I could get half the things I needed to buy. I spent an hour shopping there. When I came out it was still snowing, and the truck had gotten cold again. I made four other stops, then drove out to the airport and stored all my purchases in a luggage locker inside the terminal.

Then I drove back into town and visited the liquor store before going to pick up Haywood. It was almost five o'clock when I pulled into the clinic's parking lot. I rolled to a stop directly in front of the office and hit the horn a couple of times. A female head appeared in the window and then disappeared back into the office. After a few minutes Haywood came out, waded through deep snow, and climbed in the passenger side.

"Get all your shopping done?"

I told him I had.

"I called Hard Case just after I got here. He'll swing by my place at six. You already stop at the liquor store?"

"Yup. I bought three bottles of Dew and a case each of Rolling Rock and Alaska Ale."

"Perfect," he pronounced. "That'll get us through the night."

When we pulled into his driveway Haywood reached up and hit the button on the automatic door-opener.

"Go ahead and drive in; I know you're dying to."

A good sign. He was weakening.

***

Hard Case arrived an hour later. He said he couldn't stay long because the snow was still piling up and he wanted to get home while he was relatively sober. He said it wouldn't do for a man in his position to be found drunk in a snow bank.

Haywood acknowledged the wisdom of this and asked, "What'll it be?"

Hard Case didn't hesitate. "Whiskey." Then, by way of explanation, "It's damned cold out there."

Haywood laughed and poured three glasses of Dew, and we sat in the soft chairs in the living room around the fire.

Case raised his glass. "Good seeing you again, Gus. Safe trip home."

Haywood said, "Here, here."

I raised my glass and thanked them. It was good, sitting there with my best friends. I had been alone most of the summer. Now the summer was over, and as Hard Case had said, it was time to go home.

Hard Case asked if I'd gone over the files and wanted to know my take on them. I told him I thought it was all, as he had said earlier, very strange, but I'd decided to let the dead rest and try to forget the whole damned thing.

"You really think you can do that, Gus?" he asked. He knew I couldn't.

"Probably not," I answered truthfully. "But, I don't have a lot of options, do I, Case?"

"No," he said. "You went through some weird shit out there, Gus. As I told you back in June, crazy things happen in the bush. But, I must admit, your killing a guy forty years ago ranks right up there with the strangest cases I've ever come across. If you can put it all behind you, you're a better man than I am. That said, you've got to try."

I nodded. "No choice," I said. "I'll try."

He said that was best. Then he complimented me on The Varmitage, and said he'd like an invite to do a little fishing up there next summer. I told him he and Haywood didn't need an invite.

"Knowing what we know about the place, it belongs to all three of us," I told them. I said they could use it anytime they wanted, as long as they took their own whiskey.

Hard Case laughed politely, and thanked me. Then we all had one more drink and talked about the size of Haywood's moose. I offered Hard Case a half share of my meat for his help packing it out. He accepted gladly. When it was clear we had run out of things to say, he set his glass on the coffee table and got to his feet.

"Well," he said, " Time I got home."

He thanked us for the drinks and bid me another farewell, while Haywood brought the files from the table and gave them back to him. He tucked them under his arm and buttoned up his coat. At the top of the stairs he turned back to look at me.

"By the way Gus, I'm going to recommend they close both these cases. It's been over forty years, and they should have been closed long before this. I see no point in adding anything to the files before I do. It would serve no purpose and might excite the interest of the tabloids. Just thought you'd like to know."

I nodded to indicate I understood. "Thanks, Case," I said. "I appreciate that."

He winked an eye, turned and went down the stairs. Haywood went down with him and let him out the door.

Chapter 29

The next day was clear and the sun came up over a beautiful white world. I looked out the window and the glare off the shining snow hurt my eyes. At least my head didn't hurt. Haywood and I had taken it easy after Hard Case left. We'd been punishing our livers a little more than necessary, and it was good to rest them now and then. Haywood was in the shower when I came up from the downstairs toilet. He'd already brewed a pot of coffee. It was full, so I assumed he'd put it on to drip while he showered, meaning he hadn't been up long. That was unusual since it was nearly seven o'clock.

I poured a cup for myself and sat in the easy chair where I could look out the window at the lovely, white landscape. Bosworth hopped up in my lap and made himself comfortable. I wished him a good morning and then did my best to keep his tail out of my coffee.

Haywood came down the hall with a towel wrapped around his waist and his hair sticking out in all directions.

"Morning Gus! Don't feed that damned cat; he's already had his breakfast." He went straight to the coffee pot.

"Morning Haywood. You slept in this morning – must be getting old."

"Horseshit! I just didn't get much sleep the night before. Had to catch up."

He took his coffee back up the hall to finish his toilet. I just sat and luxuriated in the big soft chair and marveled at how blue the sky could be up here and how white the fresh snow. I also thought about how bitter cold it would be in about one month. The Chamber of Commerce propaganda admits to an occasional thirty-below-zero day in Fairbanks. In truth, it often hits thirty below for three or four days running in the winter. It sometimes drops to fifty below. I thought about winter on the Moose Jaw. It would probably be even colder up there.

When Haywood came back down the hall he was dressed and ready to face the day.

He poured himself another cup of coffee and held up the pot inquiringly. I shook my head, and he put it back on the heat and came over to look out the window.

"Pretty, isn't it," he said.

"Yeah," I said, "I've been sitting here thinking the same thing. Look at those mountains off in the distance, they're actually glowing."

He sipped his coffee. "You'll be flying out of here when it's still light. If the day stays clear you'll get a great view of Denali. It'll be amazing today after that storm we had."

"I'll try to remember to put my camera in my carry-on."

Haywood snapped his fingers. "That's what I've been meaning to ask you. Did you take any pictures this summer? I didn't find any film lying around, but I did find your camera, so I packed it and brought it out."

I nodded. "Shot a few rolls. Kept the exposed film in a box on the shelf. Most of them are of the cabin going up. There are some of the bears fishing and a few from the burn. Nothing really exciting."

"What's on the film in the camera right now?"

I thought for a moment and then shook my head sadly. "I get your drift, but I didn't take any shots after I found Morgan. She isn't in any of the pictures. Considering what we know, chances are pretty good she wouldn't have shown up anyway."

He nodded his head. "Well, it was just a thought."

He sat his empty cup on the table. "I've got another thought too. This one's a keeper. Let's drive down to the North Slope and have breakfast. I'm tired of cooking and I feel like one of their four egg omelets. What do you say?"

"Sounds good. I'm getting tired of your cooking too." I deposited my cup on the table next to Haywood's and went down to the bedroom to put on my boots.

***

Haywood ordered, as he had announced he would, a four-egg omelet. I opted for the poached eggs on corned beef hash. We both went with the sourdough toast. There's nothing better than the sourdough you get in Alaska. I'd bought a newspaper out of the vending machine on the way in. This was a luxury, since Haywood didn't subscribe to one at home; he read his on the Internet. I dealt him a couple of sections and kept the Business Section for myself. We were halfway through the news when our food arrived. We put the newspaper aside and dug into the steaming platters.

It was Tuesday, and all the stores were open. When we left the North Slope, Haywood said he had to pick up a birthday present for one of the female technicians at the clinic. He asked me what I'd recommend for a forty-something old maid who had set her hat for him and he was trying to keep at arms length. He always seemed to attract stray cats.

I thought for a minute and suggested a scarf and matching gloves.

He considered this, then rejected it. "Touches body parts – too intimate."

"A scarf and gloves? You must be kidding."

He looked serious. "No. You got to be careful with these old spinsters. They read hidden meaning into every little gesture." He was actually uncomfortable.

Even the pain of a cracked rib could not prevent me from enjoying the best belly laugh I'd had all summer. What a wonderful predicament to find him in. I resolved to do whatever I could to lead him into the trap of a suggestive present. He rejected them all; the wine, the tickets to the opera, the flowers. Finally he'd had enough.

"Goddamnit Gus! You're not taking this seriously. If you're not going to help then – don't help."

'Wow,' I thought. 'He's really sweating this one.'

"Okay, Haywood," I gave in. "If you want to give a special gift that doesn't suggest any intimacy or desire to become intimate, you give her a nice crystal vase. It hints of flowers. It suggests that she should have flowers – but it's not flowers. And no woman can have too many vases."

His face was transformed by an enormous smile. "Gus! By God, that's perfect."

Forty-five minutes later we walked out of an upscale home furnishings store with a very nice crystal vase, already gift-wrapped. Haywood was relieved. He was pleased that the store's wrapping paper was recognizable, and she'd know he wasn't a cheapskate.

When we were back in the truck he said, "Gus, you're a genius.

The vase is just right. Now, we still got a few hours to kill before I take you to the airport. What shall we do."

I thought about that for a minute. Haywood's quest for a birthday present had reminded me I still had another stop to make. Let's drive out to that gift shop we passed on the way to Skinny Dick's the other night. I still have a few presents to pick up for the folks back home."

"Soaring Eagle Gift Shop," he said. "I know the place." He put the truck in gear and we shot out into the traffic.

We spent an hour at the gift shop. I bought a pair of moose hide moccasins and a few baubles and bangles. On our way out the door I noticed a rack of True Grit flannel shirts I hadn't seen before. One was deep green with large black bears as the pattern. We both admired it.

"Who's it for?" Haywood asked, noting I had selected a "Men's Medium".

"Casey," I told him. I never went home to Colorado without taking something for my son. Haywood waited while I went back to the counter and paid for it. The clerk asked if I wanted it boxed. I said no, I had to pack it in my luggage.

It was eleven o'clock by the time we finished our shopping. Since we were halfway down the road to Skinny Dick's, I suggested a rematch for lunch and Haywood agreed.

The lunch crowd hadn't arrived yet and we had the place to ourselves. The bartender recognized us from the other night and greeted us as regulars when we came in the front door. We ordered beers and burgers without consulting the menu. The bartender got our beers and told us the burgers would take about thirty minutes as they were just firing up the grill. We told him that was fine, we'd shoot a few games of pool while we waited. He opened the cash register and slid six quarters across the bar.

"Pool's on me," he said. "For the wait. I'll bring your burgers over when they're ready."

Haywood thanked him as he scooped the quarters off the bar, and we went over to the pool table.

By the time the burgers arrived Haywood had already beaten me two games. It was clear my shooting hadn't improved any over the past few days. I was glad to take a break and eat before facing the inevitable. We ordered two more beers and sat down to an early lunch. We ate quietly. We'd said just about all there was to say, and we were just killing the clock until it was time to head to the airport. We still had to go back to Haywood's house to collect my bags, but I was all packed and ready, so that would take no more than a few minutes.

"When you figure on coming back up for a visit?" Haywood asked.

"Depends on whether or not I take another job. If I do, I probably won't be able to stay for more than a few weeks. I'd try to come in July in that case, for the salmon run. It also depends on your schedule."

His mouth was full of burger so he just nodded.

"You going to Hawaii again this winter?" I asked.

He swallowed his mouthful. "Yep. It's already booked. Two weeks. Assuming Donna hasn't found someone better by then, she'll be going with me."

When we finished our burgers we took our beer back over to the pool table and drank them while Haywood ran the table from the break. I picked up the bill and started for the bar. Haywood snatched it out of my hand.

"You bought all the whiskey and beer yesterday, I'll get this one."

I objected. "A bet's a bet."

"Yeah," he said. "But playing you for money is a mean thing to do. I oughta be shot. Let me pick up this tab to ease my conscience."

I laughed and agreed, for his conscience's sake.

He took the tab to the bar and laid some bills on top of it. The place had filled up with lunch customers, and the bartender was busy serving two new arrivals. He looked up and waved. We waved back and went out to the truck. We drove directly to Haywood's, loaded my two bags in the bed of the truck, and then drove out to the airport. I told Haywood I would have just enough time to check in and go to the gate, so there was no point in his paying for parking and coming in. He dropped me at the curb and got out to help me with the bags. He lifted out the heavy river bag and set it on the curb. I took the carry-on and my rod case.

We stood for an awkward moment – men never know quite how to say good-bye to a friend. Suddenly he swept me up in a bear hug, then, just as suddenly, released me.

"Shit! Forgot about the ribs!"

I laughed and told him it hadn't hurt. Actually, it had hurt a good deal.

"You going to be able to manage those bags?" He was still worried about my ribs.

"No problem. I'm checking the big yellow one and the carry-on's not heavy."

There wasn't anything left to say except good-bye. I stuck out my hand and it disappeared into one of his.

"Take care," he said.

I said, "Don't let the bears eat you."

He smiled, climbed back in the truck and drove away. I stood on the curb and watched until his pick-up merged with the other cars heading for the airport exit. Then I dragged my bags over to a bench, sat down and lit my pipe. I would miss Haywood.

Chapter 30

I spent the night at the Comfort Inn-Fairbanks and had a taxi pick me up at eight. I asked the driver to wait while I collected two pair of state-of-the-art snowshoes and a box of leg traps from Polar Express Outfitters. Then we continued out to the airfield from which Bush League Pilots, Inc. operated their Air Taxi service. The pilot helped me transfer the bags from the cab to a Helio-Courier, which is an old Porter design modified for steep take-offs and landings. It didn't take long. There was just the yellow river bag, the gear I had retrieved from the airport locker, plus the crate of leg traps, the snowshoes, and my rod case. When it was all aboard we went into the office where I paid my fare, and waited while they recorded my flight data and made out my receipt. That done, we went back out to the tarmac, climbed into the airplane and strapped ourselves in. I was, once again, bound for the Moose Jaw.

The pilot warned me that there had been significant snowfall in the Interior over the past few days, and he may not be able to land on the bar I had indicated. I told him that was okay. He was to put me down as close as he could get. He went on to say there was more snow in the forecast for later today, so he wanted to get in and out as quickly as possible. I understood.

After we were airborne the pilot said, "Trapper?" The box of traps had served its purpose.

I said, "Yup." Trappers are typically taciturn, so I felt safe assuming the "man-of-few-words" role.

After a long silence, the pilot said, "See you're packing in a fly rod. Planning to stay 'til spring?"

"Yup."

That "Yup" must have done it. He didn't try to communicate with me for the rest of the flight. When the cabin came into sight I was a little disappointed to see there was no smoke coming out of the chimney. I don't know what I had expected, but my spirits sank a bit.

The pilot said, "That your cabin?"

"Yup." It had worked well so far; why mess with a good thing?

He did a low-level flyover. "That the bar you want to put down on?"

I looked down. "Uh-huh."

He made two more passes and said, "Okay. The snow doesn't look too deep. I think the tires will handle it. But, if we go down and it's deeper than it looks, you're going to have to help me clear it for take-off. You good with that?" Obviously, he knew enough by now to stick to yes-or-no questions.

He was looking at me, so I decided not to waste a precious word. I simply nodded.

The pilot must have considered it a contract because he banked back downstream in a sweeping arc and then put the nose into the wind. As we dropped earthward, I watched the snow covered landing strip grow larger and larger in the windscreen. His two bounce touch-down was almost a perfect replication of Haywood's first landing on that bar, except he managed to keep us out of the water. As soon as we had come to a complete stop, he revved the engines, swung around and taxied back to the downstream end of the bar. I looked at the tire tracks we had made during the rollout. I was relieved to see the snow was only about five inches deep, and I hoped that meant I wouldn't have to shovel. Judging by the progress of the plane during taxi, I assumed it could handle this depth with no problem.

When he reached the end of the bar he swung the nose into the wind again and killed the engine. We got out, and he helped me unload. When we had the bags laid out in the snow, he looked at the sky anxiously. It was overcast and growing darker by the minute.

"Let me see if I got this straight," he said.

I waited; he expected nothing less. I was, after all, a man of few words.

"You want us to do a fly-over one month from today. If there's a fire burning out in front of the cabin, we land and pick you up – if not, we don't."

"That's it." I said.

He nodded. "Okay, then. See you in a month, maybe." He climbed back into the cockpit, cranked up the engine, gave me a classic RAF salute, and off he went. I watched him until his plane cleared the trees of the bend up by the burn. The plane quickly disappeared into the low cloud ceiling and, just as it did, there was a splash in the still open water in the middle of the creek. I looked in that direction. There was nothing to see but the ice along the edge of the bank and the ripples spreading outward from the center of the ring. Then there was another splash farther upstream, and I watched the ripples moving, inexorably closer. I understood.

I didn't wait for the rings to merge on the water; I knew they would. I shouldered the yellow river bag, and picked up my rod case in the other hand. That was all I could manage on the first trip; I'd come back for the rest later. I struck inland. It was dark in the woods. The only illumination was the soft glow of the snow-shrouded ground. In the dim light I could see old Trilogy's tracks in the fresh snow of the trail, leading up and over the rise toward the cabin. I was neither startled nor surprised. His huge, mangled paw had guided me home before. I'd killed him, of course. But that shot was yet to be heard.

I continued down the path, dropped the river bag on the front porch and leaned my rod case against the log wall. I stood there in the cold, my hands deep in my pockets, looking at the front door I had built so very long ago. What lay beyond? Was I, indeed, mad – or simply a fool? A slight breeze stirred the treetops and snowflakes appeared against the black backdrop of the lowering sky.

I took a deep breath, opened the door and stepped through. It was cold and dark inside. The windows were shuttered, and no light filtered through. I stood quietly inside the door, waiting for my eyes to adjust to the gloom.

Her voice came out of the darkness.

"You'd better go kill some geese before they all fly south. It's going to be a long winter."

A warmth came over me, and I felt the pain in my ribs and shoulder drain away into the stillness.

It was, indeed, a magic place.

THE END

Made in the USA
Charleston, SC
30 March 2016